AN UNLIKELY OUTLAW

Brody crossed the room in two vicious steps, wrapped a hand around her upper arm, and yanked her to her feet.

Her eyes, distilled by the confrontation to palest blue, glinted with rebellion.

"You wanted freedom, Jasmine?" he asked.

She met his stare directly. "Yes."

"Enough to trick a man into marriage?"

"Yes."

"Well, you won't have it." His hazel gaze bore into her. The line of his jaw firmed with savage intent. "You don't deserve it after what you've done to me. I'm going to see to it that you never in your life taste freedom again."

It was war.

Other **AVON ROMANCES**

COURTING CLAIRE *by Linda O'Brien*
HIGHLAND LAIRDS TRILOGY: THE MACLEAN GROOM
by Kathleen Harrington
A KNIGHT'S VOW *by Gayle Callen*
MY LORD DESTINY *by Eve Byron*
THE PERFECT GIFT *by Christina Skye*
SCOUNDREL FOR HIRE *by Adrienne deWolfe*
THE SEDUCER *by Margaret Evans Porter*

Coming Soon

HIGHLAND BRIDES: HIGHLAND HAWK *by Lois Greiman*
MAIL-ORDER BRIDE *by Maureen McKade*

And Don't Miss These
ROMANTIC TREASURES
from Avon Books

THE BRIDE OF JOHNNY MCALLISTER *by Lori Copeland*
HAPPILY EVER AFTER *by Tanya Anne Crosby*
THE WEDDING BARGAIN *by Victoria Alexander*

REBECCA WADE

An Unlikely Outlaw

AVON BOOKS NEW YORK

AVON BOOKS, INC.
1350 Avenue of the Americas
New York, New York 10019

Copyright © 1999 by Rebecca Wade
Inside cover author photo by Nic Nicosia
Published by arrangement with the author
Library of Congress Catalog Card Number: 99-94463
ISBN: 0-380-81021-2
www.avonbooks.com/romance

First Avon Books Printing: December 1999

AVON TRADEMARK REG. U.S. PAT. OFF. AND IN OTHER COUNTRIES, MARCA REGISTRADA, HECHO EN U.S.A.

Printed in the U.S.A.

WCD   10 9 8 7 6 5 4 3 2 1

For Chris.
My own personal hero,
my best friend, my husband.
I will be eternally grateful for your belief.

I love you.

Prologue

Tyler, Texas
April 10, 1875

"**T**his girl is a menace."

Jasmine scowled at the man. "I am not! I'm simply—"

Her father's grip tightened on her elbow, a voiceless command that warned her not to speak further. She clamped her lips shut and latched them with her teeth. *I'm simply . . . braver, quicker and smarter than you are.*

"Thank you for bringing her home, Sheriff," her father said to the man. "I appreciate your help."

"You're welcome, Lee. You know I've always liked you, been a supporter of yours all these years." The sheriff pushed back the brim of his Stetson, revealing lank straw-colored hair and a face pinched with frustration. "But I can't be spending all my time chasing your daughter halfway across the country whenever she pulls a damn fool prank."

"I know," Lee replied. "I'll speak to her."

"If you don't mind my saying so, marrying her off might be more what's called for."

Jasmine's lips sprang open, but her father silenced her retort before it began by digging his fingernails all the way to her elbow bone. She winced.

1

"She needs a husband to steady her," the sheriff continued. "Someone to guide and direct her. To tame her down."

"Thank you, Sheriff, I'll consider that."

Sheriff Hutton looked back and forth between father and daughter. His lips twisted into a sideways grimace before he tugged the brim of his hat back into place and turned away.

Jasmine watched him cross the yard and mount his horse. Silently, she heaped evil curses on the man's head. Sheriff had really done her in this time. That bit about marrying her off was guaranteed to send her father hurtling over the edge of sanity.

Both father and daughter waited without moving or speaking until the sheriff disappeared around the bend in the road that led away from the Double J ranch. Then Lee released her with a low growl and stalked across the porch to the wooden veranda table. Savagely, he ground out the cigar he'd left smoking in a beaten silver tray. "What did you do this time?" he asked, his words tight with suppressed anger.

Beyond the shade of their porch the sky stirred in a sunset tapestry of orange and gray. A longing to escape this conversation and ride hell-bent for the horizon shifted through her. "Well . . . "

"Well, what?"

Reluctantly, she returned her gaze to him. The spring breeze, scented lightly with the smell of smoke, passed between them. Dark brown hair lifted off his broad, handsome features. He stood a whole head taller than she and half a body size wider. At his sides, his fingers twitched, a reaction left over from decades of drawing guns from hip holsters.

"Jasmine?" he asked sharply.

"I was just walking down Broadway this afternoon, that's all. And I happened to notice Sheriff sitting outside the Blue Horseshoe, kind of leaning back in his chair and napping.''

A bulging vein snaked down her father's throat.

"He had his badge just sitting there, pinned to his shirt. It occurred to me that it might be fun to . . . borrow . . . his badge for a few minutes and ride around town wearing it. You know, issuing orders, spinning my six-gun, galloping after suspected outlaws.'' She grinned, her genuine pleasure in her misdeed momentarily overstepping her caution.

"You think that's funny?'' Lee asked.

"Don't you?''

"No,'' he snapped. "I think it's reckless and I think it's childish. Damn it, Jasmine, I should be able to expect better of you! That's the third time this year the sheriff has had to escort you home. You're lucky he didn't throw you in jail this time.''

"Oh, Daddy, he overstated things. It really wasn't that serious—''

"It's serious to me.'' A chill slid past her father's blue eyes, deadening the affection for her that usually resided there. She hated it when his eyes cooled like that. It made her feel overly daring and precarious, as if she'd climbed out too far on a ledge that had no footholds.

"Do you have any idea what it felt like to stand there and listen to him tell me that I need to marry off my own daughter?'' he asked, his cheekbones standing out starkly.

"I imagine it felt—''

"Pretty damn bad, since I've been trying to do just that for the past five years, without success. That man is mostly a fool, Jasmine, and it galls me to admit that he was right. But he was. It's way past time you marry.''

Jasmine's heart sank to her stomach and lodged there. "Daddy, let's not have this discussion again—''

"No, let's *do* have it. This is the last time Sheriff Goddamned Hutton is going to come dragging you back here!''

"Daddy, I—''

"No!" His blunt hand sliced through the air in a gesture that reduced her arguments to nothing. "I don't want to hear it. No excuses this time."

Her toes clinched inside her boots, causing the wooden planks below her to creak.

"I've brought more men into this house than I can count, hoping that you'd find *just one* that you wanted to marry so I could see you settled and safe." His eyebrows converged. "Well, I'm sick of trying. You've got one month left."

"One month for what?"

"To find a husband."

Her gaze raked over his face. "What?"

"You heard me."

She whipped a strand of auburn hair behind her ear and tried to tame the sudden fear coiling like a rattler in her belly. "And—and if I don't find a husband in a month's time?"

"You can damn well move off my land."

Her ribs squeezed her breath. Oh, God, this couldn't be happening. Her Daddy wouldn't—

"There are plenty of those women's schools back east. They'd probably jump at the chance to dress you up in a corset and teach you some manners."

Surely he was joking. He wouldn't stick to such a ludicrous proposition. He couldn't!

She read determination in his expression. And bleakness. *He could.*

Her fingers curled into her palms. She'd only ever had one dream for herself. And while it included guns and horses and sleeping beneath the stars, it had never, not *ever*, included a husband. She pushed down a swallow. "I'm not going to marry anyone, Daddy."

"You're twenty-four years old, Jasmine. The way you're headed you're going to die a spinster. Is that what you want?"

"Hell yes, it's what I want!"

"Then pack your bags."

Horror engulfed her. Not a single reply or cussword or plea occurred to her. She began to sputter.

He stared at her, eyes narrowed. "I'm not relenting this time. You've got one month."

On a strangled scream, she turned, pounded down the porch steps, and hurried past the forlorn little kitchen garden he'd ordered her to plant. Only the stupid black-eyed peas, potatoes, and okra had survived.

She threw aside the rawhide thong and shoved the corral gate open. Even as she called to Diamond, her horse, she wished that she could overrule her instincts, wished she could confront her daddy calmly and rationally. But the frustration roiling inside her screamed for outlet. She *needed* to run.

Diamond trotted to her and Jasmine grabbed a handful of mane, mounting bareback. As she galloped past the porch, she risked a glance at her father. His jaw was granite, his eyes cold and glittery.

She bit her lip and looked away, her last hope plummeting.

Diamond gained speed until they sprinted along the dirt road away from home.

Jasmine felt like crying. Like shaking her fist at the sky and sobbing. Any weaker woman would, she told herself. Any marrying kind of woman would.

But she wasn't the marrying kind. How her daddy, of all people on earth, expected her to be was a mystery. He'd raised her himself, single-handedly. *He* was the one who had given her a taste of true freedom. And yet now, despite his own past, he had the audacity to demand that she exchange her beloved independence for the poor bargain of matrimony, respectability, and a lifetime of dishwashing. She'd strangle under the crushing weight of such a life.

She couldn't marry. But nor could she part from her father forever. He was her only family and she'd idolized him since the day he'd taught her to walk.

She squinted into the coming gloom of evening. Her hands fisted in her horse's mane. Cool air stung her cheeks.

She needed a plan.

Chapter 1

May 4, 1875

J asmine sat on her heels in the corner of the dark, empty shack. She tapped her fingers against her lips in a wild staccato beat. And waited.

If I'm unfortunate enough to become pregnant from this encounter, at least he'll give me a pretty baby. She comforted herself with that wry thought every time she grew so nervous that she feared she'd dissolve into a mass of quivers. It wasn't helping enormously, but she kept right on trying. *If I'm unfortunate enough to become pregnant from this encounter, at least he'll give me a pretty baby.*

The plan should work. She'd gone over every facet of it in detail, searching for gaps or areas of weakness.

There were none. Well, there was one.

Whether or not he would come.

Brody McClintock. The handsome father of her potentially pretty baby.

She'd spotted him for the first time three weeks ago in town. Even now, she could see him as clearly as she had on that overly warm, dusty afternoon.

From one block away and across the street, she had stumbled to a halt at the sight of him. He stood leaning against the front of the saloon, talking to Lisbeth Morisette. Instantly, Jasmine categorized him as a stranger.

He was so tall of stature and broad of shoulder that he shrank Lisbeth to the rank of curvaceous midget. His hat rode low over his forehead, but even the shadow cast by its brim couldn't mask the piercing intensity of his eyes. They fairly glowed across the distance.

Jasmine neared the couple cautiously, gauging the stranger all the while. When she drew alongside them on the opposite side of the street, she hid herself in the dim doorway of Simpkin's General Store. From there, she could make out the clean, rugged lines of the man's face. He was wildly handsome with his tanned cheeks and his shirt opened at the neck and his well-used boots. But it wasn't just his handsomeness that appealed to her. It was his presence. He seemed wondrously, dangerously idle.

She lingered in the doorway watching him until he strode from the saloon's porch and escorted Lisbeth down the street. As soon as they'd walked half a block, Jasmine dashed headlong across the road and straight into the mouth of the Blue Horseshoe saloon.

Stella, who worked there, was her most trusted informant and one of the town's foremost gossips. Jasmine found her in the smokiest corner of the establishment, winning the weekly tithe away from two Baptist deacons.

When Jasmine asked about the good-looking stranger, Stella's ruby grin spread wide. "His name's Brody Mc-Clintock and he's a drifter." Her eyes sparkled. "He's said to be a man of shady character. Good with a gun, evidently. An outlaw."

Right then and there, even as goosebumps puckered her skin, Jasmine had known that she'd finally found her plan. And her fiancé.

Since that day, over the past three weeks, she'd watched from a distance as Brody's flirtation with Lisbeth had progressed. She herself had never even spoken to the man. Their only significant interaction had been a prolonged moment of eye contact a week ago in front of the livery shop. As it happened, their lack of communication suited her perfectly. She was content to leave the seduction to Lisbeth, who, as the town's most available widow, knew the art of romance far better than she.

Tonight she'd stood across the floor from the couple at Sue Ellen Granger's dance and watched Lisbeth bat her lashes and stare adoringly into Brody's eyes. It was then that she'd finally decided to set her plan into motion.

She'd intercepted Lisbeth over the punchbowl and informed her that one of her other boyfriends had been seen entering Annie Willard's house at well past ten o'clock. Lisbeth had abandoned the dance in a froth of anger. Shortly after, Jasmine had sent a note to Brody. Ostensibly, it was a sensual invitation from Lisbeth, asking Brody to meet her here, in this shack. At midnight.

Jasmine's frantic lip tapping ceased. She pressed down hard with her fingertips, flattening her mouth and cheeks. What in the hell had she been thinking? This plan was never going to work.

On the night of her father's ultimatum, she'd fashioned this and several other harebrained schemes out of sheerest mad desperation. Both the option of marrying one of Tyler's not-so-eligible bachelors and of being carted off to a boarding school had horrified her. So much so, that she'd dreamt up the idea of wedding herself to an irresponsible ingrate who could be counted upon for nothing except to abandon his newfound wife at the earliest possible moment.

Fate had handed her the ideal candidate in the person of Brody McClintock. He was a drifter. A man of shady character. An outlaw.

He was perfect.

Several times during the past weeks, in her rational daylight moments, Jasmine had doubted the wisdom of this strategy. If her father had shown even the slightest relenting, she would have been happy to discard it. But ever since their fight, her relationship with him had been strained to the point of tearing. He didn't laugh with her anymore. Or tell her jokes, or even sit with her over coffee in the evenings after the cowboys had retired to the bunkhouse. He communicated with her in clipped monosyllables, except when he took the time to remind her that he wasn't backing down from the deadline.

She tilted her head into the shack's corner and stared upward at the ceiling. Moonlight shimmered through the lines between the splintery boards.

Outside, crickets sang in the tall grass. Beyond the gaping hole where a door should have been, she could see the ambling outline of a longhorn making its way to the stream. All around her whistled the smell of the crisp night wind, accompanied by the spice of musty wood. She shivered.

After leaving the dance, she'd taken a quick detour by home for supplies, then ridden directly here. She knew this hut well. It stood on the boundary line between their ranch and the Grangers'. It had been abandoned for years and she'd played here often as a youngster.

When she'd arrived, she'd spread three blankets in a soft mass of folds, positioning the makeshift bed in the darkest corner. Then she'd hidden her lamp under a barrel out back. Last of all, she'd pulled the pins from her hair and repositioned it in a replica of the tower of curls Lisbeth favored. She'd also worn a snug-fitting gown that resembled the gown Lisbeth had had on and dabbed Lisbeth's rosewater scent on her pulse points.

Oh God. It had to be near midnight by now. She hadn't budgeted a lot of waiting time into her schedule and she'd swear that she'd been waiting for at least fifteen minutes. Where was he?

Brody McClintock leaned against the Grangers' barn and threw back the last swallow of whiskey in his cup. He rarely touched alcohol. But on occasions like these, he wished the stuff could make him drunk. Instead it only served to make him more sober.

He scowled at the cup's empty bottom, then set it aside.

The boisterous crowd milled and hummed in the chaos between dances. Not for the first time, Brody noticed that the men cut him a wide berth. The women showed more interest.

He locked gazes with a particularly brazen girl who couldn't have been a day over sixteen. She smiled beguilingly at him, her yellow ringlets bobbing.

He nodded at her.

She blinked, spun, and rushed away. The hem of her pink dress disappeared around the corner of the house.

No doubt, she'd gone to search out her friends and tell them how close she'd dared come to the renegade.

What a damned joke.

Brody reached into his pocket and fished out the note he'd been handed earlier in the evening. He flipped it open with his thumb and reread the contents.

Lisbeth wanted to meet him tonight. There was no mistaking the invitation inherent in the note. And no mistaking exactly what her invitation meant.

The fiddler plunged into a fresh tune and the fast, piquant notes of his instrument flavored the air. Brody squinted into the kaleidoscope of dancing bodies. Lisbeth had dogged his steps since he'd come to Tyler. She was pretty enough. Personable enough. But he'd encouraged her for an entirely different reason. He'd encouraged her because of the information she supplied him.

There was a woman like her in every town he'd ever visited. A lifetime resident of the place, eager to talk. Lisbeth knew the history of each person who lived in Tyler. And day after day, she'd filled his ear with their stories. Up until now, it had been an agreeable relationship.

But lovemaking—lovemaking was a different matter. He ground his boot heel into the stubbly grass and refolded the note. It had been a long time since he'd had a woman. But he'd gone longer before.

The girl with the blond ringlets returned with two friends in tow. All three giggled nervously.

This sort of scrutiny was the worst part about being his brand of Texas Ranger. He'd always preferred to let a town think the worst of him until he'd gotten an honest feel for the situation. Hell, he *wanted* them to mistake his identity. It was how he operated. But lately, the days of enduring their stares and their speculation weighed heavily on the reward of seeing justice done in the end. Too heavily.

God, he was tired.

The last thing he'd needed tonight was for Lisbeth Morisette to get ideas. But then, he sure as hell didn't need her mad at him, either. Her acid tongue could end his job here before it had begun.

He jammed the note back into his pocket and pushed away from the wall. It had been a long night. He'd watched as much as he could stand. Done his duty. Learned faces and caught the currents that went unspoken.

He passed the trio of girls without a glance.

The dancers' boots pounded the earth with a rumbling rhythm, warming the chilling air with waves of sound. Brody skirted past them, wondering briefly what it would feel like to be as carefree as they. It had been so long since he'd felt that way, he'd forgotten.

He pulled the brim of his hat even lower and turned up the collar of his coat. The familiar darkness swept in on him as he strode toward the corral and his horse.

He was late. Maybe he wasn't coming. Muscles tensed along Jasmine's rib cage and across the back of her neck and shoulders.

Surely he was coming. Any normal, red-blooded male would accept a proposition from the beautiful Lisbeth. Wouldn't he? She strained her ears to listen.

The answering clop of horses' hooves began as a soft beat, seeming to reverberate from the very earth. Gradually, the sound translated itself into a deeper pulsing, until it burst through the mystical valleys of her intuition and became reality.

Jasmine couldn't breathe. She held herself completely rigid. He was actually coming. She could hear the grinding of stone and foliage that signaled the approach of a horse.

The moisture in her mouth rolled down her throat leaving a parched tongue and dry cheeks. Whatever had she been thinking of when she had formulated this idiotic plan? She could boast of absolutely no experience, physically, with men. And yet she'd cast herself in the role of a lusty widow.

Oh, hell.

The tread of the horse stopped abruptly. She listened as the stranger dismounted.

He was here. *Hell*.

Jasmine dived across the shack, landing on the mound of blankets. She edged as close as she could to the shadowed wall, then leaned on her elbows and threw back her head in what she hoped was a tantalizing pose. Her cold fingers felt like they belonged to someone else when she balanced on one arm, reached up, and hurriedly opened the top several buttons on her gown.

The crunch of his footfalls stopped on the threshold.

Suddenly, he filled the portal, silhouetted by a tapestry of moonlit sky. Her gaze skittered up the outline of his form, from splayed boots to the hem of his ankle-length coat and over the expanse of his chest. The darkness hid his face from her, but his stillness and his sheer size spoke volumes. He was so powerfully built that his shoulders brushed the sides of the doorway.

She made an attempt to lick her lips, but an arid tongue met parched skin. This was really happening. Anxiousness clattered over her nerves, threatening to send her entire body into violent convulsions.

If I'm unfortunate enough to become pregnant—master your fear, she scolded herself. *Stick to the strategy. You are in control. He is merely a handsome, overgrown puppet.*

Brazenly, she shifted toward him and purred.

"Lisbeth?" His voice was low and calm.

"Mmmm," she answered, praying that Lisbeth would make these kind of asinine noises when seducing a man.

Brody took two steps into the shack and stopped.

She waited for him to cross the remaining distance. When he didn't, indecision froze her. Her instincts split between trying to reach out and draw him to her and risking another ridiculous noise.

He moved neither forward nor back.

Worried that a stray beam of starlight might accidentally find her face, Jasmine decided to take action. Serious action.

She reached for her already gaping neckline. With false languor she flicked open three more buttons. One edge of the fabric fell to the side, exposing a swath of white lace. She attempted a seductive moan, which came out sounding to her like the whine of a heifer in labor.

He still didn't move.

Why would he? Her impeccable imitation of a pregnant cow had probably repulsed him.

Her chest rose on a breath once, then twice. *Come,* she pleaded silently. *Take the bait.*

He shrugged out of his coat. The heavy cloth fell in a heap behind him. With barely a whisper of sound, he knelt beside her, unbuckled his gun belt, and set it within arm's reach. His big body moved with deceptive smoothness.

She could barely believe that he'd actually come to her. Oh God. *If I'm unfortunate enough to get pregnant from this encounter, at least. . . .* Careful to angle her face away from him, Jasmine arched her spine and presented him with an expanse of chest and neck. Her modesty flared so strongly that she had to battle back the urge to shrink from him and clutch at her gown.

This was never going to work. He would know that she wasn't Lisbeth. She couldn't pass herself off as something she wasn't. He wouldn't want her—

Rough fingers slid along the pulsing veins at the juncture of her throat.

Jasmine almost screamed with surprise, with the lightning of his fingers meeting her sensitized flesh, with victory.

His touch brushed down the center of her chest, resting at the point where the fabric of her gown parted. He flattened his palm and her bottled scream melted into a softened sigh.

His hand moved quickly and expertly, pressing beneath her chemise and capturing a breast.

Despite herself, she gasped. Her nipple puckered into his palm, spilling sensation from that one tight bud to every corner of her body.

I'm in control, she assured herself, as her brain scrambled to shrug off its stunned paralysis. *I'm in control. This is what I'm allowing him to do. This is the plan. I can handle him. He's my puppet—*

He leaned down and covered her lips with a kiss. Sensually, he tasted her.

Jasmine's elbow quaked. No sooner had she registered the tremor, than his free hand slid behind her back, lifting her weight onto his forearm. Cradling her with his strength, he lowered her onto the blankets, then followed her down, fitting his chest and hips intimately along her side. The heaviness of his body against hers felt wondrously, perfectly male.

For a brief moment Jasmine blinked at the ceiling, hardly able to believe that it was the same ceiling she'd gazed at just minutes before. And yet so different. Now the lines of moonlight twinkled downward with fresh delight because a man lay beside her, resting his body along hers. A man who still held her breast in his palm. A man incredibly real and alive. A man who smelled of pine trees.

He gripped the back of her head, turned her face more fully to his and kissed her again. This time his lips parted. She could sense the smooth rush of his breath against her lower lip, feel his nose rub against her cheek. She didn't know what he expected of her, so she simply relaxed her mouth, surrendering it to him completely.

His tongue entered her in a silken thrust.

She gasped at the unexpected rush of feeling.

At first he kissed her languorously, testing her. Then he delved more deeply, demanding a response. Tentatively, she allowed her tongue to mingle with his, to taste him in return. He answered her with a ragged groan.

Her eyelids sank closed. She should be managing this exchange. Monitoring the time and the developments. Oh, but the way he was kissing her. . . .

He hadn't moved the hand that cupped her breast or changed its pressure at all. And yet she felt it so intensely— his touch that was bond and brand at once. Instinctively she lifted toward it, deepening the contact.

Her emotions met and swirled with the sensations. Together they raced around the inside of her stomach, twisting like a hurricane up her chest and reaching golden fingers around the column of her neck.

He kissed her passionately, commanding her truest response. And to her amazement, she gave it to him. Her body forgot the game. The reply she offered him was as full-blown as a rose straining toward the sun.

Her newly discovered arousal made her brave. She sought out the last remaining buttons of her gown. Struggling mindlessly, she freed them from the tangle of cloth. The constriction around her chest loosened like a sigh, allowing her breasts to press free.

So artfully did he disengage his hand from her hair that

she didn't notice its absence until he used it to push her gown off a shoulder. Cool air twisted around her upper arm and snaked across her collarbones. The hand that held her breast stroked away. He used it to guide the other side of her gown over her shoulder.

Alarm clanged between her ears. Never had she shown a man so much of herself. She shouldn't be doing this. But this was the plan. Risk all.

Pretty baby. If I'm unfortunate enough to . . . from this encounter—

The rugged edge of his jaw rasped against the delicate skin at the curve of her neck.

She shimmied, helping him push the dress down to her waist. The top half of her body lay naked before him. Naked with the pillowy cool of the blanket caressing her back. She tried to look up at him, suddenly needing to be reassured by the shadow of his face. But he was too close to see.

He pressed a long, upward caress from her belly button to just beneath the skin of her breasts. Involuntarily, she sucked in air. Her muscles tightened against the onslaught of pleasure she'd already come to expect from his touch.

But he didn't touch her breasts. He made her wait, primed and hardened for the feel of him. Then he bent to kiss her.

Their lips met and opened in the same instant. She moaned without intending to and the sound of it seemed to come from another woman. A woman with a lush body and feverish skin whom she didn't recognize.

She ran her palms over the crisp, roughly textured front of his shirt. Her fingers sought their way to his neck, raking once through the hair at his nape before pulling on the neckline of his shirt. She needed him to be as naked as she.

He followed her unspoken demand by leaning back onto his knees. He pulled open the top buttons of his shirt, then stripped the garment over his head. She thought she saw the sparkle of a silver necklace cushioned in the muscle of his chest.

He hesitated, looking down at her.

Don't let him recognize me, she prayed. *Return to me. Don't make me wait for you.*

Inwardly, her body writhed.

He lowered on top of her. Skin gloried against skin. With a choked cry, she pulled his head to hers and took his tongue into her mouth. Her nipples thrilled at the miracle of his flesh pressing against them, rubbing.

Just as he was parting her legs with his knee, the sound of voices drifted through the open doorway.

Men. Calling to one another. Shouting orders. Horses clawing the earth, eating the distance.

What . . . what was happening? Jasmine fought for some remnant of sanity. It came to her in a quick, cold flash.

Her father.

When Brody rolled onto his side, he took all of Jasmine's heat with him. Nothing remained inside her but remorse and icy logic.

When she began to sit up, he stilled her with a subtle gesture. Feeling devoid of feeling or heart, she watched his profile tense.

"Stay," he whispered.

The single word caused longing to throb in her throat. Her body remembered.

He retrieved his gun belt and fastened it around his hips. "They must just be passing by."

She stared at the gaping portal. Beyond, she could make out the figure of two riders. They looked like dark archangels, riding out of hell against a backdrop of ebony. They charged directly toward the shack.

She'd done it. For the first time Jasmine truly realized that she'd sealed her fate. No turning back.

Belatedly, Brody must have guessed that the men were actually going to find them, because he pulled hard on one of the blankets, throwing it over her. Then he reached for his shirt.

Too late, she thought, as she glanced at him. *It's too late for you.*

She thrust her arms into her dress and managed to button it halfway. Beyond the walls, she heard the riders pull their horses to a halt and jump to the ground. In a span of seconds, a man's bulk filled the doorway. The coarse sound of a match scraping wood whispered through the room. A flame rushed to life.

In the consuming darkness, the single glimmer of light illuminated the face and form of Lee Jamison. Shadows fell beneath his eyes and nose, starkening the wildness in his expression.

Lee thrust the match toward the wick of the lantern he carried. It caught, and the fire leapt and clawed within its glass enclosure. Jasmine squinted up at her father through the wash of golden color. He looked like a madman. His clothes had been tossed on. His hair tousled over his scalp. Stubble darkened his jaw.

Her confidence teetered. It hurt far more than she'd expected to do this to him. But he'd left her no choice. She clung to that truth. He'd left her no choice.

Behind her father, John Sims, the Double J foreman, stood with arms hanging limply at his sides, eyes round with shock.

Her attention returned to her father. "Daddy," she said carefully, "don't do anything rash."

Brody, who'd been watching the intruders, whipped his chin toward her.

She met his gaze.

For a long moment they simply stared at each other. Her heart thumped loudly as she watched his vision scan over her face. Up to her hairline and down to lips which still burned with sensitivity from his kisses. His eyes creased

with confusion and she knew that her soon to be husband
had just realized his mistake.

"Jasmine," Lee hissed.

Both of the apprehended lovers looked toward the immediate threat.

"Who—who is this man?" His words raised in volume,
each cutting across the space with the force of a whip.

"His name is Brody." A tumult of conflicting emotions
surged through her: the melancholy burn of guilt, the stab
of pain over hurting her father, the recoiling instinct that
feared Lee's wrath. Last of all, slowly pushing to the surface, came a nudge of wild excitement, the kind that quaked
giddily in the face of danger. She'd done it.

"God damn it!" Lee yelled. "Get up. Both of you."

Her triumph faded. Neither she nor Brody moved.

Lee reached for his holster and slid out his gun. Without
hesitation he cocked the weapon and aimed it at Brody. "I
said, get up."

"Now, Lee," John said from the doorway, "let's think
this thing through—"

"Think it through?" Lee snapped. "I already have."
The point of the gun flicked upward. "Get up!"

Very slowly, Brody straightened to his full height. Jasmine rose beside him.

Earlier in the evening, she'd been certain of her father's
reactions. Now she wasn't so sure. "Daddy," she said,
"don't you dare kill him."

"I should, for what he's done to you."

"Done to me? He hasn't done anything I didn't let him
do. Look at me."

"I don't need to look at you." Lee's finger moved restlessly over the trigger. "Button up that goddamned dress."

She clutched at her gaping neckline and shot a look past
her father to John. She scowled at the foreman pointedly,
inciting him to action.

"Ahh . . . Lee," John said. "Maybe you should lower that firearm a little—"

"If you value your job or your life, John, then you'd best not say one more word."

The foreman shook his head and walked from the shack.

So much for assistance from John. The responsibility of getting them all through this situation alive fell upon her alone. Jasmine presented the men with her back, hurriedly finished buttoning up the front of her dress and turned to face them.

"I hope you don't think that you can disgrace my daughter in this way and walk free of it," her father said.

"No." Brody's lips barely moved as he gave the terse reply.

"Because this," Lee gestured with the gun toward the pile of blankets, "this is too grave to overlook." Alarmingly high color seeped into her father's face. Angry red patches stained his cheeks and forehead.

"Daddy." She stretched a hand out to him.

He responded by grabbing her wrist and yanking her behind him. "By God, get out of the way, Jasmine. I'll kill him for this!"

"No!"

"I will."

She scurried around until she faced her father head on. With both hands, she gripped his biceps. "No. No one is going to be killed."

Lee pushed her aside without taking his attention or his aim off the younger man. "What do you have to say for yourself?"

"That I'll accept whatever consequences you see fit."

Jasmine turned to Brody. It surprised her that he didn't try to voice the truth, to point out that she was a complete stranger and that she'd tricked him into this entire encounter. Instead, he stood with silent pride, his gaze resting solemnly on her father.

Brody's face, which had always been cased in darkness or distance, was now illuminated by lantern light. His tanned skin made his watchful hazel eyes seem all the brighter. He had lean cheeks, firm lips, and a small cleft centered in his chin. Short chestnut brown hair, some strands streaked lighter than others by the sun, stood out in tracks made by fingertips. Her fingertips, she realized with a start.

His shirt hung untucked and fell open in a wide vee over his chest. Chiseled pectoral muscles leapt under her perusal.

"Damn right, you'll accept my consequences," Lee hissed.

"We're both equally guilty, Daddy," she said, looking to her father. "Decide what you think we should do and let's be done with it." She knew her father so well, loved him despite the fact that his stubbornness had driven her to this. *Say it*, she thought. *Go ahead.*

"I'm taking you both to Reverend White's," Lee said. "We're going to have us a wedding."

Jasmine didn't react at all. Her best poker face disguised the kick of joy, the rush of accomplishment. Sweet Daddy, she thought, of course we're going to have a wedding.

Brody didn't scowl or speak or even sigh. He simply took his gaze off Lee and moved it to Jasmine, his eyes glinting with dangerous finality.

Chapter 2

Brody stood on the front porch of the reverend's house with the complete stranger who was to become his father-in-law on one side and the intimate stranger who was to become his wife on the other.

Ever since the lantern had been lit within the shack and he'd looked at the woman next to him and discovered an unknown pair of aqua eyes looking back, he'd been struggling to tame his confusion and fury.

The girl with the messy auburn hair had tricked him. That much was clear. Even so, he'd been trying to convince himself that she couldn't have wanted this outcome. Surely, she'd not purposely involved her father. Hell, she'd never even met him. She couldn't *want* to marry him.

But the more he tried to convince himself, the more his gut instinct told him otherwise. And he'd been on the trail too long not to trust his gut.

The reverend's wife answered Lee's knock wearing a voluminous cream-colored dressing gown over her night dress. Her hair hung in two thin gray braids, and the flush of very recent sleep colored her skin. She thrust her lantern toward them and squinted. "Lee?"

"Yes, Mrs. White, it's Lee Jamison. Is the reverend awake?"

She eyed the threesome with startled wonder. "Ah . . .

no, Lee. Mr. White is sleeping at the moment."

"I'm sorry for the inconvenience, ma'am, but we'll be needing his services tonight."

Her free hand fluttered over the end of a braid. "Oh?"

"Yes." Lee cleared his throat, obviously uncomfortable. "My daughter is getting married."

"Oh!" Mrs. White tried unsuccessfully to mask her amazement. She gaped at Jasmine, then peered at Brody.

Brody gritted his teeth and forced himself to nod.

"Well . . ." she licked her lips. "Do come in, all of you. That's it. Come on in. Make yourselves comfortable." She ushered the rumpled pack of visitors into her home.

The dimensions of the front parlor were already small. But when Brody entered the space, the walls seemed to shrink inward on him. The reverend's wife had covered her furniture in watery pink fabric and strangled the windows with lace and swags of floral curtains. He felt like a bobcat trapped in a satin cage.

Mrs. White set the lantern on the coffee table with a thump so loud, she jumped at the sound of it. "Oh! I'll just . . . just go and get Mr. White. He's—"

"I'm up, Dear."

Brody turned to see a portly old gentleman walk into the room, pulling his suspenders over his shoulders as he approached. The reverend first shook hands with Lee, then extended his hand to Brody. Brody took it and returned the greeting.

"Jasmine," the reverend said, nodding to the girl.

"Hello, Reverend," she answered softly.

The girl had been acting like this ever since they'd left the shack. Overly quiet and calm. She'd accepted her father's decree that they should marry without hysterics or tears.

The reverend folded both hands over the topmost platform of his sizable belly and regarded them. "Here for a wedding, are we?"

Either the minister had overheard Lee or he'd noted the disheveled appearance of him and the girl. Brody wondered a little wildly just how frequently fathers escorted daughters to the reverend's house for these middle-of-the-night visits.

"Yes, we're here for a wedding," Lee answered.

"Indeed. A wedding." Mrs. White attempted a bright, enthusiastic smile, which ended up wobbling badly. "If you'll excuse me . . . I'll go and whip up a batch of biscuits. I'm certain we could all use a biscuit right now." Her voice trilled at a cheerful note that grated against Brody's ears as she disappeared through the hall door.

The reverend picked up a Bible from a tiny round table with a doily on it. The skin around his eyes and lips settled into serious lines. "Are you certain that you're willing to go through with this wedding?" he asked the girl.

"Yes, she's going—"

"Lee." The minister extended his palm towards the rancher, subduing his speech. "I'm asking Jasmine."

"Yes," the girl said clearly. "I'm going through with it."

Brody gazed down at her. Brown hair shot with cinnamon highlights spilled over her shoulders and halfway down her back in a mass of curls. A few of the tendrils remained captured by pins, but the majority had fought their way free.

She was only of medium height, but seemed taller because of her almost tangible confidence. The tight, wrinkled blue gown she wore accentuated perfectly proportioned feminine curves. She must have missed a button when fastening the dress, because the fabric bagged at a point below her bosom and met unevenly at the top. Her chunky riding boots looked glaringly out of place coupled with the frilly hem of her gown and the lilac stretch of carpet that framed them.

"May I have your name, Sir?" the reverend asked.

Brody looked up abruptly.

The reverend gazed at him, his bald forehead reflecting a round patch of light. Bushy brows rose expectantly. "Your name?"

"Brody McClintock."

"Brody, I asked Jasmine, and now I'll ask you. Do you intend to go through with this?"

He paused. Out of the corner of his eye he watched for a reaction from the girl, something that would give away her motives. But she waited for him to answer with what appeared to be supreme indifference.

"Yes," he said. "I'm going through with it."

There had never been any doubt. Not from the moment they'd been discovered by her father. He'd been caught making love to the girl. If he didn't stand up and take responsibility for what he'd done, he'd have no honor. And honor was the only thing he had left to live for.

In his memory, he saw two wooden crosses, side by side, silent and unforgiving. Shade fell over them, darkening the freshly turned earth they guarded.

He'd made a vow before those graves to live the rest of his life alone. It had been his penance to suffer, never to love again, and never to marry. Over all the years, he'd understood that so strongly. And now the very honor that had bid him make his vow was bidding him to break it.

By marrying a stranger.

Bile rose up his throat. What a goddamned waste this was. A *goddamned* waste. The stupidity of how he'd trapped himself into this and the wrongness, the *utter* wrongness, of breaking his vow to wed a woman he didn't know maddened him.

He wanted to turn away and deny the reality of what was happening. But this wasn't the kind of mistake a man turned away from.

"Come stand over here," the reverend said. He motioned the couple forward to take positions in front of him, facing each other. "Lee, move up. You can stand behind them."

The girl's father took his place near Brody. His expression was taut with fury, his big hands twitching at his sides.

"Yes, that's fine," the reverend said. "Just fine."

The girl gazed up at Brody through unblinking almond-shaped eyes. Their color was amazing, the palest blue he'd ever seen, like the hue of a baby's dress or a store-bought mint stick. A light smattering of freckles dusted her nose. Her features were dainty. Unmistakably beautiful.

Could this woman, with her thick work boots, her mis-buttoned dress, and her tangled hair, have planned for this to happen? What kind of woman must she be if she had? Not one he could respect. Not a woman he wanted to shackle himself to for the remainder of his life.

Outwardly, he held himself very still. Inwardly, powerlessness lashed at him like tongues of fire twisting up from hell and flogging what was left of his soul.

He would find out if she'd purposely trapped him. Heaven help her if she had, because all the beauty in the world wouldn't be enough to save her.

"Let us pray," the reverend said, resting one hand on Brody's shoulder and clasping his Bible tighter with his other. He lowered his head and began by asking the Lord for guidance.

Brody continued to stare at the girl and she returned his gaze. Two sentences of the prayer rambled by before she ducked her head, presenting him with a view of riotous curls.

"Biscuits are ready!" Mrs. White held open the kitchen door with the toe of her slipper.

Jasmine glanced at her father. She severely doubted that he'd be able to stomach either small talk or biscuits.

Lee stuffed his hands in his pockets. "If you'll excuse me, ma'am, I won't be staying."

The eagerness written across Mrs. White's face melted into a mixture of disappointment and concern. "No?"

"I've—I've got chores to attend to back at the ranch."

The lady was too kind to ask what sort of chores he did smack in the middle of the night. Instead, she gifted him with a smile. "Yes. Why, of course. I understand."

Lee walked to the front door and paused, resting his hand on the knob. "Thank you for your assistance, Reverend. I apologize for inconveniencing you at this hour."

"It's all right, Lee. Apology accepted."

"We'll be seeing you around town," Mrs. White chirped.

A bubble of panic lodged in Jasmine's throat. Her father was leaving her.

He didn't spare her a glance. Looking as if time and heartache had ravaged him from a robust man to a shrunken shadow in a single hour, he let himself out.

She stared at the door for a long moment after he'd gone, ridiculously hoping that he might return for her.

But the knob didn't budge. The hinges didn't squeak.

Of course he wasn't coming back. This feeling of desolation made no sense. She had always anticipated his leaving at this point in the plan. Her father couldn't know that she'd married herself to a drifter, a man with so little character and responsibility that he probably wouldn't even stick around long enough to ask her if she took butter on her biscuits.

"Time for a snack, everyone! Come on in here."

Her limbs feeling heavy and numb, Jasmine walked into the kitchen. The room fairly glowed with golden light, as if elated over the cozy secret it was about to witness. Passing the stove, which emanated heat and the crackling sound of kindling, she took a seat at the functional wooden table alongside the reverend. Her husband remained standing.

Her husband. The rugged stranger with the magnetic hazel eyes. The man whose demeanor and posture whispered to her of danger. For an instant their gazes met and she vividly recalled the taste of him. The erotic fire of his hand cupping her breast. The cool air caressing her naked ribs.

"Thank you for your hospitality," Brody said to Mr. and Mrs. White.

"Well, yes," Mrs. White replied. "You're welcome. Please, have a seat." She lifted a napkin-covered bowl from the stove top.

"I have to be going, ma'am."

He was leaving her already? Jasmine furrowed her brow against the irrational sense of loss that swamped her. She wanted him to leave, of course. Just not—not quite so soon. And not in public.

"Oh, what a shame," Mrs. White said. "Didn't you hear? I've made biscuits."

He nodded.

"I'm sure he'll come back for biscuits another time, Dear," the reverend said.

Brody's lips thinned. Seconds crawled past. "I hate to impose upon you further, but would it be acceptable for . . . her . . . to stay here tonight?"

Mrs. White's brows sailed upward.

"If that would be of assistance to you, Brody," the reverend answered, obviously choosing his words carefully, "it would be our pleasure."

Brody dipped his chin, then turned toward the door—and freedom.

He was most definitely leaving her! Jasmine leapt to her feet. The legs of her chair wailed across the floor.

His progress stopped.

"Where are you going?" she asked, her voice sounding loud and edgy in the silence.

"Into town. To secure a place for us to live." He glanced over one broad shoulder, the searing light in his eyes daring her to challenge him. "Is that acceptable to you, wife?"

This was it. The end. Her one and only marriage was over. "Perfectly acceptable," she answered.

He shoved the door open and strode from the room.

Jasmine stared at the second silent door frame she'd been presented with in a span of minutes. Why did she feel so lousy? She should have been ecstatic. She'd caught this particular man specifically because she'd known his nature. From the first moment she'd laid eyes on Brody Mc-Clintock and learned his profession, she'd known. And that's why she'd married him. She'd trapped a husband who wouldn't stay caught.

Jasmine faced her hosts. The reverend clutched his napkin to his lips like a shield. Mrs. White's bottom lip sagged downward.

With all the dignity she could muster, Jasmine pulled her chair beneath her. She hoped that the smile she pasted on her lips spoke volumes about her tolerance and sense of humor. In truth, she felt little of either. "Please pass the biscuits," she said.

The reverend's napkin took a somersaulting dive for his lap. Mrs. White's lip snapped up. They handed her the bowl, then stared at her as she set about polishing off four biscuits in quick succession.

But despite her grand show of indifference, she couldn't shake the feeling that no one at the table had been fooled.

The only two men in her life had just abandoned her. And if she couldn't make her father forgive her, there would be no one left to love her.

Chapter 3

꧁꧂

Jasmine urged Diamond to quicken the pace through the misty morning toward home.

She desperately needed to patch things up with her father. Usually when they fought, she outlasted him, waiting until he broke and offered his apology, which she would then graciously accept. But this time was different. She hadn't been able to sleep except in snatches because she kept remembering how crestfallen her father had looked when he'd walked out on her last night.

Brody hadn't been sad like that when he'd left. He'd been strong and cold and untouchable. He—

She shoved a lock of hair to the side and with it the remembrance. There wasn't a thing to be done about Brody. He'd gone for good, and she needed to quit thinking about him. Her relationship with her father was what mattered now.

This morning she'd return to her daddy as a married lady, free from any law but that of her own devising. At this hour, her father would be eating breakfast with the cowboys. She'd slide into her chair, give him her best smile, and apologize privately after they ate. Then she'd resume her role in his household with one stipulation: she'd no longer be expected to wash dishes.

Despite the fact that she'd begged her father to let her

31

work the ranch like the cowboys did, and despite the fact that he had enough wealth to hire ten dishwashers, he'd long ago assigned the chore to her. He'd said the duty would help her learn to manage household tasks. But the only thing dishwashing had taught her was how much she hated to be given orders and how hugely she detested household tasks.

She also detested tight-fitting gowns. The *instant* she got home, she'd change out of this deplorable dress. When she shed it, she'd also be shedding the last evidence of Brody's scent and touch and breath. Somehow it was important that she do that immediately.

Diamond rounded the last bend before the ranch. The cluster of buildings that composed the Double J spread into view. Her boxy two-story frame house with the wide front porch dominated the scene. The pathetic little kitchen garden squatted next to it. Stupid okra. What good were vegetables anyway, she wanted to know, when they lived on beef and bacon?

Two towering live oak trees stretched their shade across the lawn and over the glistening little stream which meandered along a cleft in the earth. The prairie, covered in a collage of wildflowers, folded outward in every direction.

She panned the landscape again. Inexplicably, the unease she'd been experiencing since last night intensified, knotting at the bottom of her belly. Something was wrong. Something. . . .

There. Right at the front entrance of the ranch. Right beside the metal placard that proclaimed the ranch to be the Double J, sat a cart piled with trunks. Her vision narrowed and locked on the sight. With little more than a change of posture, she sent Diamond into a full-blown gallop.

The closer she drew to the ominous grouping of trunks, the sicker she felt. By the time Diamond stopped beside them, nausea heaved through Jasmine's stomach.

She dismounted in a jumble of skirts and approached the stack. Six trunks had been loaded onto a cart. The empty harness attached to it waited only for a horse to pull it away.

With an awful vacuum of noise rushing through her ears, she lifted the top on the nearest trunk. Within rested her childhood toys. A wooden horse her daddy had whittled for her. An assortment of toy guns they'd used when her daddy had played chase with her as a child. A pair of small boots her daddy had given her the day he'd told her she was a real cowboy.

She slammed down the lid. Moisture rushed to her eyes, spilling a few hot droplets over the barrier of her lashes. Furiously, she pushed the tears away.

These were her things. Her father had banished her things from his house. He'd banished *her*.

She kicked the post that held the "Double J Ranch" sign. Pain sliced through her foot and up her shin. For goodness' sake, he'd named this ranch after her! Jasmine Jamison! He couldn't exile her from a ranch that was her very namesake.

She glared toward the house. At the office window, a curtain twitched. He was watching her. But he wasn't coming to argue or to apologize or to greet.

Grinding her teeth against the hurt, she stomped across the yard, past the corral, and up the porch steps. She pushed on the front door as she had pushed on it ten times a day for the past fourteen years. But instead of swinging open, as it had on each of those occasions, the door came up against the wooden bar that served as its lock.

She stared at the smooth wood in shock, uncomprehending for a moment.

Then she hissed with outrage. Her father had locked her out. By God, he couldn't do this to her! She raised her fists and pummeled the door. "Daddy!" she screamed, not daring to stop and listen for an answer. "Daddy!"

Panic swirled dangerously high within her and she knew her fear pushed too close to the surface. But she had to make him listen and understand.

Just when she'd decided to kick the door down, she caught the sound of footfalls approaching. Her bruising fists fell to her sides. She drew herself up and tried to gather her composure.

The creak of the bar being lifted sounded in the moment before the portal pulled inward. Her father filled the narrow opening. As usual, he wore a vest. Today he had on the one with the navy blue checks. That small familiarity soothed her, until she lifted her eyes. The bitterness and accusation in his expression stole her words. Never before had he looked upon her so coldly.

"I packed your things for you," he said, his voice dull. "There's no reason you need set foot inside this house."

This house? It was their house together! His and hers. She scrambled to remember the things she had prepared to say to him. Weakly, she cleared her throat. "Daddy, I'm not moving."

"Yes, you are."

"No. No, I'm not."

"You're a married woman now, Jasmine. This is no longer your home."

She cringed. Time to squash her pride and beg forgiveness. "Daddy, he left me."

His eyebrows lowered. "What?"

"He rode away from the reverend's after you left."

"He rode away?"

She nodded. "He's a drifter." It wasn't hard to let her anxiety show. She bit her trembling bottom lip. "I'm so sorry," she whispered and meant it. "Please forgive me."

For a prolonged moment, his gaze probed hers. She could hear the clank of the cowboys' forks as they consumed their breakfast in the dining room beyond. The aroma of coffee wafted down the hall, beckoning her inside.

Her Daddy would have compassion on her now; she was certain of it. He loved her. He'd let her come home. In minutes, she'd be sitting where she belonged and sharing food with the others.

"No," he said.

The muscles in her face slackened. "No?"

"You chose your path, Jasmine. Now you're going to have to live with it."

Her heart fluttered. "But I don't have anywhere to go!"

"I guess you'll have to find that husband of yours and complain to him about that."

"Daddy, he abandoned me—"

"I guess you'll have to complain to him about that, too."

"I don't know where he went—"

"More to complain about."

She gaped at him, terrified that she might not be able to hold back the tears that burned her throat. *"Please, Daddy."*

Pain carved brackets beside his lips. "I've loved you all your life, Jasmine. Still do. But this is a lesson I believe you need to learn. My answer's no." Bowing his head, he stepped back and shut the door. The ultimate insult of the bar being dropped into place struck her like a slap in the face.

Oh God. Tears seeped from the corners of her eyes. She groaned in mute frustration and wiped at the wetness with her forearm. The blue calico fabric she'd come to loathe absorbed her heartache.

She'd pushed him too far. But she'd been so sure. Sure that he'd forgive her, that he'd take her back when her husband abandoned her.

Her father was the one person in the world she counted on. From her earliest memory her Daddy had spoken of his limitless love for her, demonstrated it to her in countless ways. How awful to suddenly discover that his love *did* have limits. Limits drawn by the rigid structure of his will for her life. Limits marked by the boundary of this ranch, separating his dreams from hers.

She set her jaw against a rising stem of heartbreak and disillusionment. She'd wounded him badly, she knew. But nothing, nothing should have justified this.

She stumbled off the porch and back to the cart piled with her trunks.

"Diamond." The word came out as little more than a rasp. "Diamond," she said again, more forcefully.

Her horse trotted over to her, looking splendid in the morning light. The mare's coat glowed red-brown except for a perfect white diamond emblazoned on her forehead.

Numbly, Jasmine went through the motions of attaching the harness to Diamond's back. Then she climbed into the driver's seat and shot another look toward the ranch and her father's window. No movement from within answered her.

The next time, he'd be the one asking forgiveness. She wouldn't come to him again. Not after this.

She took an aching breath and flicked the reins. "Go, girl."

Diamond pointed her nose toward home.

"No." She guided Diamond's head in the opposite direction. "We're not going home."

Jasmine didn't have to think about where to turn for help. There was only one option. She went directly to Emma.

Emma Larkin owned the property that ran against the Jamison ranch on the western side. At forty, never having been married, Emma managed a sizable herd of cattle and resided in the sprawling house her father had once built for her mother.

Jasmine pulled the cart to a rumbling stop in front of Emma's place. The old whitewashed building had suffered through numerous refurbishments. But somehow, despite its strange angles, its unusual floor plan and its disjointed additions, the house had always charmed her. Perhaps because Emma had lovingly stuffed the windowboxes with flowers and painted the house's trim a bold, clear peach.

At this particular moment, Jasmine badly needed the comfort the flower boxes and the peach trim heralded. The ride had steadied her fragile emotions, but only slightly. Only enough to put on a brave veneer and not shame herself completely in front of her dearest friend.

After unharnessing Diamond and releasing her into the corral, Jasmine bounded through the front door, praying that Emma would be home. "Emma!"

"In here."

Relief melted through her. She crossed the foyer and burst into the parlor.

Emma sat in front of the room's side window, at her little half-circle table. A jug of bluebonnets stood on the center of the surface, next to a neat stack of correspondence.

A palette of yellows, ranging from the frothy cream of the curtains to the deep buttercup of the sofa pillows, welcomed Jasmine with a sunny embrace. The braided rug that warmed the floor swirled all the yellows together, mixing in a dash of blue with one sure stroke.

Like the rest of the house, this was a space to live in. To put your feet up in. To fill with laughter. A house that had been made for a family and children to enjoy. A place where Emma lived alone.

Immediately upon seeing her, Emma set aside the letter she'd been reading. "What's happened?"

"Something awful."

"What?"

"It's my father."

Emma's features paled with alarm. "What about your father?"

"It's nothing life threatening."

"No?"

She shook her head.

Emma pulled her dainty spectacles off her nose and held them suspended in air, halfway to the table. "You had a fight?"

"Yes. How'd you guess?"

Setting her glasses atop the pile of papers and carefully folding the ear pieces inward, Emma sighed. "A fight with your father is usually what gives you this haunted look, Jasmine."

"I look haunted?"

"Decidedly haunted."

Jasmine crossed to the table and swiveled a chair out to face her friend. They sat so close, their knees touched.

Emma regarded her with a level look of concern. Gray hair the color of a thundering sky hung to her chin in a soft bob. Its texture was so delicate that it seemed to bounce and sway of its own accord. Today the sunlight highlighted the charcoal strands with shades of lavender.

"Are you going to tell me what's happened?" Emma asked.

"You won't believe it."

"Try me." The elegant bow of Emma's smile accentuated high cheekbones. Unmarred, almost translucent ivory skin and the feminine sweep of her brows set off the warmest pair of silver eyes Jasmine had ever encountered.

She loved Emma's face. And for the thousandth time, Jasmine thought how beautiful her friend was. In the quietest, most accessible and least intimidating way, Emma Larkin was a beauty.

Jasmine took a deep breath. "I got married last night."

Quiet drifted between them. The smell of bluebonnets teased her nose. Somewhere in the room, a cat bounded after a fly.

"You mean it, Jasmine?"

"Yes. I'm afraid I do."

Emma knew about the ultimatum her father had given her, but Jasmine had kept secret her plan to seduce Brody. She told the whole of it now, from how she'd first spotted him in town, to last night in the shack. When Emma asked how her father had managed to catch them at such an inopportune moment, she explained that her father had never been able to sleep until she was safely under his roof. If she wasn't home by midnight, he always checked her bedroom. Sitting atop her dresser, she'd left a note forged to look like it had come from Brody, detailing the time and place of their clandestine meeting.

Emma listened to the entire story without so much as a murmur. But when Jasmine told her how her father had packed her things and turned her out of her home, Emma's eyes filled with sympathy. "I'm so sorry, Jasmine." She pressed to her feet and held open her arms.

Jasmine rose and eagerly accepted the hug. Emma's embrace was soft and firm at the same time. Her scent of crisp, flowering herbs surrounded Jasmine as soothingly as did Emma's arms. Jasmine pulled away only when she sensed that her emotions teetered on the verge of overriding her defenses. She refused to dissolve in a flood of tears.

The two women walked, holding hands, to the sofa. Each took an end, hugged a pillow to her stomach, and lifted her feet onto the coffee table.

The lilting calm of the house enfolded them. Emma's cat raced down the hallway, its claws clicking against the wooden floor.

"Your father will come around," Emma said.

Jasmine noticed the way her friend's expression softened at the mention of Lee. For quite some time, she'd known of Emma's affection for her father. In fact, adoration of the man was an emotion they'd always had in common. Up until today.

"Lee's got a soft heart underneath all that temper, especially for you." Emma smiled reassuringly. "He'll come around."

Jasmine wasn't so sure. She bit her tongue, leaned her cheek against the cushiony back of the sofa and gazed steadily at Emma.

"This husband of yours," Emma said. "Any idea where he might have gone?"

"None, and that's just the way I want it. An absent husband is a perfect husband."

"Uh-hmm." She didn't look convinced. "What happened just before he walked out?"

"We exchanged vows and then he left. He didn't even take time to eat a biscuit."

"A biscuit?"

"Yep. Believe me, he's gone."

Emma's forehead wrinkled. "If he were going to flee, why would he have gone through with the ceremony?"

"To avoid one of Daddy's bullets to the heart."

"But he could have tried to bolt on the way to the reverend's."

"I know. I kept waiting for him to try. Just as I kept waiting for him to insist that he'd never laid eyes on me before." She shrugged. "He didn't attempt either."

Emma picked at the embroidery on the pillow she clasped. "He sounds almost . . . honorable."

"No. He's perfectly dishonorable. And he's gone. He's miles from here by now. Miles and miles. Maybe all the way to—"

The unmistakable tread of boots pounding across the wooden porch severed the tranquility of the house. Emma and Jasmine both sat bolt upright and stared at each other.

The heavy approach ended in a musical jangle of spurs. A moment of ominous silence followed. Then came a distinct knock.

"Your father?" Emma mouthed. Unconsciously, she pressed a hand through her hair to tame it.

Jasmine's stomach clenched. She wasn't ready to forgive him yet. Violently, she shook her head. "I'm not here," she whispered.

Rising to her feet, Emma smoothed the front of her dress and walked from the parlor.

Jasmine hugged the pillow to her belly. She heard the door swing open.

"Hello. Is there something I can do for you?" Emma asked.

"Yes," came a chillingly familiar voice. "My name is Brody McClintock and I'm here to collect my wife."

Chapter 4

❧❧

"Ah . . . yes, Mr. McClintock," the slim woman with the remarkable gray hair answered him. "I'm Emma Larkin."

"Pleased to meet you."

"Won't you come in?" she asked.

Brody nodded and followed her through the foyer into a yellow parlor. Upon entering, his hostess came to a swift halt. She scanned the room with what looked like confusion. "Have a seat," she murmured, waving him toward a chair.

He sat. The lady walked slowly to the sofa, then perched on the edge of it.

Where in the hell was the girl? His mood had been shredded by a sleepless night. He didn't have near enough patience to play hide-and-seek with his wife. He'd already been to the Double J, where they'd tersely informed him that she'd likely come here.

"New in town?" Emma asked.

"I've been here about three weeks."

"Really?" She laid one hand over the other on her lap, then quickly shifted, burying her hands in the folds of her split skirt. "Where are you staying?"

"At the Horseshoe."

"Oh, yes, I know it well." Her smile looked pained. "Have you found it acceptable?"

"Yes."

She struggled through a thick swallow. "The Bledsoes are fine people. They run the Horseshoe very—"

A floorboard wailed from the region behind the sofa, cutting off Emma's words. Brody watched a fiery blush illuminate the woman's throat and climb into her cheeks.

His brows elevated. "Large cat you got back there."

Emma peeked behind the sofa and then stared at him dumbly. Her face stained the vivid shade of rhubarb. "As I was saying . . . those Bledsoes," her voice emerged as little more than a squeak. "They sure do run a fine establishment. . . ."

The noise of an invisible throat being cleared sounded through the room.

From behind the sofa, a thatch of curls, then a face, then the upper body of his wife appeared. Brody couldn't help but grin as she straightened to her full height. Never had he seen such wild hair. And that damned blue dress.

He would have been even more gratified, had she been embarrassed at being caught. But instead, she looked directly at him with those aqua eyes and frowned. He couldn't detect a thread of self-consciousness in her, only annoyance.

"Hello, Jasmine," he said.

Emma twisted in her seat and feigned surprise. "Oh, hello!" she said, making a dire attempt to finish out the charade. "Did you find m-my pendant back there?"

Jasmine pursed her lips. "Sure." She handed Emma a fur ball.

Emma took the offering and squashed it between her palms. Clearly mortified, she stared at her knees.

What manner of woman was this that he'd married? A woman who hid behind sofas and passed fur balls for pendants.

He felt a stab of pity for Emma, who had obviously been drawn into his wife's deceptions, despite her better judgment. He couldn't bear to stand around and watch the woman's blush continue to darken while she worked to avoid his gaze. "We had best be going," he said to Jasmine.

"Where?"

"Back to town."

For the first time in their acquaintance, he saw a spark of anxiety flash across her features.

"Where are you going to be staying?" Emma asked her kneecaps.

"In a house I rented for us in town."

Jasmine's eyes widened with dread.

"I've just thought of something," Emma said, glancing up. "I've a house here on the property that's vacant. My brother built it before he left to fight in the war. When he didn't return, my parents and I hadn't the heart to tear it down. I'd be delighted for you to stay there."

No one spoke.

"I could certainly use the company," Emma added.

Brody watched Jasmine. Ultimately, he wanted her calm so that he could get close enough to garner some answers. If moving into the house of a friend would encourage her to let her guard down, so be it. "Thank you for the offer," he said to Emma. "We'll accept."

"Excellent." Emma sprang to her feet. "Just let me get some linens for you and enough food."

"I don't want to trouble you," Brody said.

"It's no trouble, I assure you."

"I'll have to insist on compensating you."

"No, truly," Emma replied. "It's the least I can do."

"Nevertheless, I insist."

She eyed him for a long moment. "Very well. If you'll excuse me. . . ." She glanced back and forth between them, then retreated into the hallway.

Brody pushed up from the chair and faced his wife across the room. It was the first time they'd been alone since their passionate moments together under the beams of moonlight.

Too well he remembered how she had responded to him in the darkness. Like a woman starved for his touch. Both brazen and shy, frantically needy under a thin shell of reserve. His loins stirred at the memory. Disgusted by his physical reaction to her, he made himself recall the way she'd looked at him once they'd been discovered by her father. Coolly, assessingly. As if she didn't recall the way they'd burned together.

Without a word, he stalked from the house and went to wait for her beside the wagon.

Jasmine dropped the stack of blankets Emma had sent with them onto the living room table. In answer, a thick cloud of dust rose from the surface. "Just a trifle dirty," she mumbled.

The frame house stood on a hill a half mile from Emma's place. The shutters were tightly locked, the furniture covered in trailing white fabric. Dust coated every surface. She could feel, pressing close around her, the darkness and ghostly quiet that had been the house's only residents for more than a decade.

The front door creaked open.

Brody. Oh *God.* Ever since the moment he'd come to claim her, her brain had been spinning. All the possible retributions he might want to inflict had occurred to her, along with suspicions regarding his motives and doubts about his mental health. The man was a hazard. If he wouldn't leave her alone of his own accord, then she'd have to find a way to force him out.

She walked across the living area and into the kitchen, which seemed even murkier than the main room. Brody followed her and lowered twin boxes of supplies onto the counter top. More swirls of fine, gray dust launched into the air.

Brody flicked open the latch on the back door. He twisted the knob and pushed, but the door didn't budge. Propping one booted toe and a brawny shoulder against the door, he tried again. This time, a scraping sound tore through the room in the instant before the door gave way and burst open. Fresh sunlight poured in, touching forgotten objects.

Jasmine watched as Brody proceeded to tug open the room's two windows and throw aside the shutters. The kitchen seemed almost human again. Already, she could feel the day's warmth pervading it by degrees. Without the layer of grime, it might even be livable.

Brody leaned against the edge of the chopping block and slapped his palms against his thighs, clearing his hands of dust.

Jasmine couldn't take her eyes off him.

She'd chosen wrongly, she realized. This man was too desirable. His pants pulled snug across his hips when he leaned like that, emphasizing strong thighs. Muscular shoulders worked beneath the dark gray cloth of his shirt. He wore the garment parted at the neck and rolled up over his forearms, revealing the white undershirt beneath.

Brody's hands stilled. Slowly, his gaze traveled up the length of her and their eyes met. She could almost sense the swish of his breath as she recalled how he'd leaned down to take her tongue into his mouth.

Though they now stood in a barren, timeworn house in the middle of the day, she felt as she'd felt when he'd filled the doorway of the shack. Attracted, entranced, undecided. And something else . . . a feeling she was altogether unfamiliar with and knew at once that she hated—insecurity.

What in all the world was she to do with this oversized man who wore his pants so well?

"How'd you get your name?"

"What?" she asked, dazed.

"Your name." He crossed his arms over the expanse of his chest. "It's unusual."

"My father named me." It hurt to speak of her father out loud. She watched Brody's lips tighten and assumed the reference gave him no pleasure, either.

"Evidently, I was conceived in a field of jasmine," she said. "My father swears that he can smell it still. He named me after it as a reminder. Over the years he's been fond of saying that I grew up—" *As wild and beautiful as the flower itself.* She bit her bottom lip.

"That you grew up what?"

"It's nothing."

He gazed at her steadily. "I didn't see your mother at the wedding last night."

"I've never had a mother."

He didn't reply, just kept staring at her with those bright hazel eyes.

"She ran off when I was a baby. My father and I haven't seen her since."

"Do you miss her?"

"No." She pressed her fingers against the bridge of her nose, leaving a wide, dusty smudge. "I never had much use for a mother who'd abandon my father. He was always plenty for me."

She hated this conversation. Every reminder of her father was like a delicate bloodless incision into her heart. "What of your parents?" she asked, hoping to end the line of questioning. It was an unwritten code in the West that you didn't ask a stranger about his past.

His bearing tensed. "What of them?"

"Where do they live?"

He turned away and busied himself unloading the contents of the boxes. "We'd better clean this place and unpack."

He'd reacted precisely as she'd expected. Good. At least she'd not entirely lost her knack for controlling men.

After finding a broom in the hallway closet, she set to work on the living room. Her long sweeps began halfheartedly, but gradually became feverish in pace and intensity.

Examine the situation, she urged herself.

For some unknown reason Brody had returned and claimed her as his wife. How ludicrous, that the two of them should move into this house together. How ludicrous that he should even *think* it. And yet as far as she could tell, he planned to stay here with her indefinitely.

She simply could not allow it to happen that way.

Why had he come back?

Think like a criminal would, Jasmine.

He's come back to rob me.

That would be unfortunate for him. He can't have any of my things.

He's come back to have his revenge.

Let him try. I've got a gun.

He's come back to exert his power over me as a husband to a wife.

The rough tip of the broom stilled in the corner it had been attacking. That was it. He intended to exert his power over her as a husband to a wife.

Her grip on the broom tightened to a stranglehold. She couldn't let anyone have power over her. Especially not when she'd just purchased her independence with the most precious thing in the world to her—her relationship with her father.

The broom took up its rhythm again, swiping across the wooden floor, leaving tracks in the graying dust. Moisture rose on her forehead and slid down her cheeks.

She *had* to make Brody leave.

But how could she accomplish it?

Jasmine pushed open the front door with her rear end, then propped it with the toe of her boot. Three vicious strokes saw the pile of dirt deposited on the front porch.

He'd leave if she disgusted him or angered him. But how

could she offend him deeply enough to drive him away? Thieves were not easily offended. It would have to be something good.

She paced to the far corner of the room and resumed her sweeping. What would offend a thief?

She'd swept her newest pile of dirt all the way to the door when the answer occurred to her. It was so blindingly clear that she almost laughed.

A thief would be offended by the same thing that offended all other men: being outsmarted by a woman. No trick she could ever play on Brody would be as devious as the one she'd already accomplished. She let go of the broom. It fell to the floor with a loud *clack*.

She'd simply tell him the truth. She'd explain how she'd trapped him.

Grinning, she walked toward the kitchen. But near the doorway, her steps slowed.

The living room chairs were sturdy and well crafted, she noticed. Round, pale-colored stones made up the sweep of the fireplace. She particularly liked those round stones. With a bit of fabric at the windows and a rug under the table. . . . Maybe a bookshelf and a plant or two. . . .

As of this morning, she was in need of a home. Where better for her to live than here, on the property of her best friend?

Quietly, she crept back into the heart of the living room, knelt, and plucked up the handle of the broom. She'd wait until later to hit Brody with the news of his entrapment. First, she'd let him donate a little free labor to the cleaning of her new house.

Brody leaned against the fireplace, watching as Jasmine polished off the last of Emma's cookies. Throughout the day, she'd exhibited an appetite that surpassed merely healthy and bordered on astonishing.

Jasmine licked her fingers with relish, then sat back into

one of the room's cavernous chairs, her feet tucked beneath her. Lips as soft and tender as ripe cherries curled into a satisfied smile.

God, she was beautiful. But there was something more about her than mere beauty. A sort of vibrancy that beckoned to the core of him. She was unbearably alive. And so damned assured. She had a way of making him long to bury himself in her and draw some of that lifeblood into himself.

His gaze scanned her small features, the ivory skin, the brown smudge marring her nose and cheek. He looked for clues to the answers he sought. And though he found none in the angles of her face, the foreboding that twined through his belly was almost answer enough.

"The house looks lovely, doesn't it?" she asked.

He shot a cursory look at their surroundings. The interior of the house fairly shone. "Yes."

They'd been cleaning and unpacking all day, pausing only for dinner, again for supper, and briefly at sundown to light the three lanterns he'd brought.

To her credit, Jasmine had worked like a demon, never resting until they'd scoured the farthest corner of the second bedroom. Only then had she set aside her tools and looked up at him with a blazing smile.

That smile, like the one she was bestowing on him now, had had more than a justifiable amount of triumph in it.

His unease shifted. "Jasmine."

"Hmm?" She practically purred. Her eyes glowed with dangerous secrets.

An ugly instinct reared within him, the same instinct he'd had about her in the reverend's house. *She'd expected this outcome.*

"We need to discuss what happened last night," he said.

"I agree."

Her immediate response surprised him. So did the eagerness that seemed to light her expression from the inside.

"Perhaps you could explain to me how it was that I received an invitation from Lisbeth last night, but encountered you in her place."

"Certainly."

He braced himself.

"It's simple, really," she said. "I sent you the note and signed Lisbeth's name."

He took in a breath. Pumped it out. Told himself to keep calm. But her blithe declaration had shattered the dam of his emotions. He felt his temper swell. "Why me?" he asked, the words raw against his throat.

"You saw me in front of the livery shop once, remember?"

He did remember. A lovely girl in a Stetson and britches, standing at the far edge of the store front. He recalled the way she'd nodded when he'd seen her, before vanishing around the corner.

"That doesn't explain why you chose me."

"I thought that would be obvious. You must realize that you're handsome. I knew that if I got pregnant you'd give me a pretty baby." She smiled.

He pressed his hands against his thighs in an effort to catch and restrain the plunging fury that threatened to sweep him away. He wasn't a man to be moved by passion. Not for many years.

"But your handsomeness was not my only criterion," she continued. "I was also informed of your . . . profession. And it suited me."

"Did it?" he rasped.

She tilted her head. A spiraling lock of hair swept against her shoulder. "It did."

"So you arranged a meeting with me."

"Yes."

"You wanted your father to find us."

"Yes."

All noise ceased for Brody. Nothing, nothing penetrated

to his brain, save the face of the auburn-haired girl and her gentle shrug. With that shrug, she condemned him to a life of matrimony, she broke his vow, she branded herself to be the devious witch he'd suspected her to be.

"Why?" he managed.

"Because I needed to get married. My father issued me an ultimatum." Her lips pulled into a frown. "I had to wed or he was going to send me off to a girl's school. As much as I dislike the idea of being married, I *hate* the idea of a girl's school."

"So you selected me as your husband because of my appearance and my occupation?"

She contemplated that for a moment. "Not the occupation in itself, but more what that occupation would guarantee me. Namely, your absence."

He saw her plan then with perfect clarity. All his questions fell together, answered, like a puzzle completed.

This was the truth.

He'd wanted it and she had happily handed it to him.

He crossed the room in two vicious steps, wrapped a hand around her upper arm, and yanked her to her feet.

She gasped in indignation.

Brody glowered down at her. "Do you have any idea what you've done?"

Into the tense silence, he heard the ominous click of a gun's hammer being pulled back. A barrel pressed unyieldingly against his belly.

"Yes," she answered. "I'm very clear about it." Her brows drew together. "Now let go of me."

He read the fearlessness in her expression and it infuriated him. His hand slashed upward, sending the gun sailing out of her grasp. It careened into the wall and thudded to the floor.

Her lips parted in shock.

"You insult me," Brody growled.

Her eyes, distilled by the confrontation to palest blue, glinted with rebellion.

He released her with a curse. She stumbled backward. Before she'd even caught her balance, he retrieved her gun. He spun out the cartridge of the pearl-handled six-shooter and let the ammunition fall into his palm. Then he set the weapon on the table and slid it toward her. "You point that at me again and I'll use it on you."

Jasmine, who'd so recently smelled the sweet scent of freedom, needed to realize that her predator had instincts equally as sharp as her own.

Let her be afraid, he thought.

He turned on his heel and stalked from the house.

Jasmine waited for one full minute, then let herself out the back door. Not so much as a murmur of noise accompanied her as she skirted along the outer walls of the house. When she reached the side of the porch, she huddled into a crouch. Here, shadow fell on her thickly, disguising her from his sight.

She squinted into the darkness, impatient for her eyes to adjust. Gradually, shapes emerged. The sweep of the land, the stark outline of the corral. And Brody.

Her pulse tripped.

He stood beneath the towering oak that dominated the yard. Above him, the mighty tree jutted into the sky with pining fingers, as if petitioning God for answers. Beyond, the land fell into a gentle valley.

Jasmine held her hands outstretched before her and peered at the slim fingers illuminated by moonlight. They quivered. She demanded them to steady.

They quivered some more.

Disgusted, she pulled her knees in front of her and wrapped her arms around them, firmly locking her hands together. Brody had gotten to her. More than she wanted to admit.

She watched him survey the dark void of Emma's property, his hands shoved in his pockets.

Her chin settled onto her knees. *Leave,* she urged him. *Go away.*

He only stood.

When she'd told him the truth of how she'd tricked him, he'd been utterly and obviously horrified. Though she'd humiliated herself with the gun incident, she couldn't have hoped to succeed more completely in her original goal. She'd offended him.

Now he had little choice but to saddle his horse and ride into the night and leave her to her dreams. He *had* to.

Brody began to pace. She studied the way he held his spine, straight and tall. She studied his gait. He had the stride of one accustomed to walking the plains and riding the wide barren stretches. She studied his body. The broad shoulders she'd come to recognize cut into the night.

The man wore physical power like a cloak. She could see it swirling around him even now, a mantle of writhing spirits.

An outlaw.

Yes, that was right. He had the keenness of a thief, the quickness and strength. And a way of making you feel at peril in his presence.

An outlaw. His profession was her birthright.

Her father had been at outlaw once. At the age of twenty, Lee Jamison had joined a thieving alliance with three other men. Together, they'd stolen from banks up and down the East Coast for sixteen years. Though the arm of the law had tried to apprehend them, the men were too careful to be caught and too cunning to be killed. Their robberies had been brilliantly planned and executed affairs, and for the most part bloodless.

After each hit they split up and bided their time, sometimes for as long as a year. Because of that, the only reliable hallmark of their lives had been the ceaseless travel.

Her father had told her once that it had been exactly that, the travel, which her mother had been unable to stand. He didn't talk of Kathryn much and Jasmine never asked. But from what she could gather, her father had been between robberies, cooling his heels and his trail, in some tiny town in Pennsylvania when he'd met her. They'd fallen in love.

That was the part that rankled Jasmine. How her intelligent father could ever have fallen in love with such a mealy-mouthed woman was beyond her. But he had. And after only a small taste of the life Lee lived, Kathryn had chosen to leave her husband and her infant daughter and return to her small hometown and the boring existence she'd enjoyed before marriage.

Jasmine had often told her daddy it was an outcome which suited her fine. And it was.

With her mother gone, her father had simply taken her with him, inducting her into the only life he knew. They'd lived a nomadic existence together, surrounded by tough men, in difficult climates and in unending cities.

Whenever he'd had to part from her to do a job, he'd hired some grandmotherly person to keep an eye on her. Not really trusting grandmotherly types, Jasmine would wait in silence with her fingers crossed until he came galloping back. Then she'd hug him tight, and they'd pick up stakes and move yet again. From the time when she'd been old enough to sit her own horse, she'd striven to ride as fast and shoot a gun as well as he did so that she'd never slow him down.

Her father had given her a heady taste of freedom during the first ten years of her life. A taste that still lingered in her mouth.

Then one night, she'd slipped from her pallet way past her bedtime and pulled herself bareback onto her horse. With the intention of showing her daddy how good she'd learned to shoot from the saddle at a dead run, she'd charged past the men huddled around the fire. She'd spun her gun on her finger, then shot at her tin can target. Her bullet had launched it sky.high into the air.

All the others had congratulated her. Except her daddy. He'd looked stricken. He'd pulled her off her horse, taken her gun away, and tucked her back into bed. That night he'd said that she deserved better than he'd given her.

By dawn, they were gone. Two months later, they'd come across Tyler. Her Daddy had loved it from the start. With his stolen money, he'd bought land and cattle and started a new life.

At first, he'd continued to feed her dream with stories of his adventures. But over the years, his stories had grown fewer as his crusade to gain respectability had become more fervent.

Lee had reformed himself completely. He'd not dabbled in anything even remotely suspect in all the years they'd lived in Tyler. It was a truth which suffocated her. Maybe he'd irrevocably erased his past life from the slate of his mind. But not her. She remembered. And the dream of returning to it had sustained her through the boredom of lonely evenings and the drudgery of dishwashing.

Excitement. Wildness. Power. Danger.

She wanted them all. If her father could rob banks and live on the range with his friends, then so could she.

A vision slipped into her mind. She was riding behind her father, gripping hard around his waist. Scenery flashed by as her derrière thumped rhythmically against the saddle. They raced along a ridge and she leaned way over, so that she could see the wink of the silvery river that snaked through the canyon. The wind lifted her hair and twined through the strands. She laughed. Her father laughed, too, a song of pure, sweet joy.

That had been the best day of her life. The best time of her life. No matter what it cost her, she intended to have that life again.

She watched Brody pace across the stretch of ground

he'd weathered with his strides. Then he turned sharply and walked to the ramshackle corral where the horses rested.

That's it. Go.

He stopped, one boot propped on a fallen cross piece. A warm, silky tug drew at her abdomen. The heat disconcerted her. It was longing and pleasure at once, a feeling she didn't understand, but instinctively savored.

Brody's horse came to him. She watched as Brody slipped something from his pocket into the animal's mouth. She could faintly see Brody's lips moving. She strained to hear his words, but nothing except the rustle of wind carried to her.

Leave. Her internal plea had grown less angry and more desperate. *Let me have my dream.*

Brody lifted his head as if he'd heard.

She held her breath.

He slipped one more morsel to his horse and walked toward the house. His long strides jangled with purpose.

Her heart spiraling toward her tummy, Jasmine shifted her weight onto her feet. Half crawling, half running, she sped back to the rear entrance, slipped through the door, and scooted into the main bedroom.

His footfalls echoed across the living room and hallway, so loud they rattled her brain. He stopped at her doorway, his powerful body framed with rays of lantern fire. In the light he was every bit as foreboding as he had been in darkness.

She resisted the urge to fidget or look away.

He positioned his hands against the top of the doorway and leaned on them gently, cocking his hip back. The casual posture didn't come close to fooling her.

"You wanted freedom, Jasmine?" he asked.

Dread shuddered down her spine, but she met his stare directly. "Yes."

"Enough to trick a man into marriage?"

"Yes."

"Well, you won't have it." His hazel gaze bored into her. The line of his jaw firmed with savage intent. "You don't deserve it after what you've done to me. I'm going to see to it that you never in your life taste freedom again."

It was war.

She locked her teeth together, violently resenting the erratic pounding of her heart.

He released his hands from their position. "And take off that damned blue dress. If I see you wearing it in the morning, that'll be reason enough to chain you to the porch post." He turned away.

Her fingers quivered. She sat on them.

Brody walked the length of the house and back. Fleetingly, he shot past her view as he strode into the opposite bedroom, holding a handful of linens and a pillow. He shut the door behind him with controlled finality.

She'd have been encouraged if he'd slammed the portal. But that awful, quiet click sent her last bastion of hope plunging.

Chapter 5

Emma's heart jumped into her throat and lodged there. Lee was waiting for her. She could see his horse standing in front of her porch, its reins draped over the edge of the corral. The strong, almost arrogant-looking animal suited its owner perfectly, to her way of thinking.

She cantered across the last stretch of land toward home. She'd risen early this morning. After assigning duties to her staff and eating a quick breakfast, she'd decided to take a jaunt over to her brother's house to check on Jasmine. Jasmine's horse, and Brody's, had been nibbling the overgrown grass inside the corral. Other than that, there hadn't been a single sign that anyone resided within. No movement. No smoke rising from the chimney. She could only assume they were sleeping late. Though it would probably be more logical to assume they'd murdered each other.

Willing her muscles to steady, she dismounted. As she made her way up the front steps, she fought to regulate her breathing. Its rhythm had turned fluttery and shallow.

Whatever was the matter with her? Lee was just a man, after all. A man she'd known for years.

She let herself in and walked directly to the yellow parlor where she knew she'd find him.

He looked up when she entered and quickly stood. "Hello, Emma."

Not just a man, after all. But a man she had loved for what seemed the entirety of her adult life. Her lungs squeezed the slight bit of oxygen she'd managed to capture, making her breath feel more like liquid lead. "Lee."

They stood facing one another across the swirly golden rug. She hoped like crazy that her emotions didn't show too plaintively in her expression. "How are you?"

"Not well." His midnight blue eyes communicated his anguish. "I guess you know why I'm here."

"I guess I do."

He held his hat in his hands. Weathered fingers moved restlessly around the brim, causing the Stetson to twitch and turn. Emma beat back an almost overwhelming desire to still those fingers with her own. Instead, she eased onto the couch. He folded into his chair.

Looking at him, she remembered just how much she adored the way his clothes fit him. The familiar dark vest, the work shirt beneath, and the perfectly tailored pants. She wondered briefly, wildly, if this was an appropriate time to congratulate him on his good taste.

"Jasmine did come here, didn't she?" he asked.

Emma pushed her thoughts to the topic at hand. "Yes, she came here. Directly after she picked up her trunks at the Double J."

"Where is she now?"

"Well, Brody had rented a house for them in town. But I could tell that the prospect of moving there with him horrified Jasmine. So I suggested they live in Colin's old house."

His hands stilled.

"They left yesterday around midday. I sent them over with some linens and food."

He nodded, his chiseled features serious.

"Just now I rode over to check on them," she continued, "but from the yard I couldn't see any evidence of activity from within."

"Their horses?"

"Outside."

Visibly, he relaxed. "She hasn't bolted, then."

"No, she hasn't bolted."

He set his hat on the coffee table and raked his fingers through his thick, dark hair. "Do you know who he is, Emma? This McClintock?"

She wished to God that she did. For Lee's sake and for Jasmine's. "No. I met him yesterday when he came for her. But only briefly."

"Where the hell did he come from?"

"I don't know. I can tell you, though, that Jasmine didn't intend for him to stay around very long."

"No?" He searched her face. She allowed him time, knowing he'd come to the correct conclusion when he was ready.

"I thought as much." He swore under his breath. "That man is just a prop. She wanted me to find them so that she could outmaneuver the deadline I'd given her."

Lee's love for his child blazed across his features, blatantly obvious. It had always been thus. A bond so strong between father and daughter that Emma despaired of ever finding any room for herself in a heart where Jasmine reigned supreme.

Lee Jamison loved only one woman. And though it twisted her insides to face that truth for the hundredth time, she couldn't find any fault with Lee. His adoration of his daughter was the quality she valued most about him.

Long ago, she'd given up any realistic hope of ever having a romantic relationship with Lee. And yet . . . every time she saw him, even after fourteen years of fruitless infatuation, her heart still forgot itself. "Why did you give her a marriage deadline?" she asked softly.

"I gave her the deadline in the heat of anger. But I decided to enforce it afterward, when I was rational." He roughly massaged his forehead with his fingers. "Something had to give. She couldn't go on like she was forever.''

"But why? She could have remained unmarried and lived at the ranch with you indefinitely.''

"No. That's not good enough for her.''

She wondered if he realized that he'd just insulted her. A spinster's life on the ranch had clearly been good enough for Emma Larkin. "In whose estimation?''

"Mine. Besides, Jasmine wouldn't have been happy living with me for much longer. Over the years she's dreamed of something more. And I'm afraid I know what that something is.'' He looked at her beseechingly. "I had to do whatever I could to stop her from that. It's my fault that she's romanticized it.''

She didn't have a clue what he was talking about. Clearly, some form of paternal guilt had ravaged his judgment.

"I had to try and keep her . . . keep her on a steadier course,'' he said.

Emma smiled sadly. "No one, not even you, Lee, can keep another human being.''

He glanced out the window. When Kathryn, Jasmine's mother and his wife, had run away from them, he'd determined never to let his daughter slip though his fingers as his wife had. He'd always believed that he could hold onto Jasmine, so long as he held her tightly enough.

Lee returned his attention to Emma. His gaze drifted over the calming line of her nose, the quieting curve of her lower lip. "I'm sorry.'' He rested his head against the chair back. "I haven't had much sleep the last two nights.''

"I know. It's been a tough couple of days.''

God, how he appreciated Emma. Her even-tempered, logical personality made up for many of the deficiencies in communication between him and his volatile daughter. "Do you think you could mediate things between Jasmine and me?''

"I don't know if that would be such a good idea.''

"Why? I respect you. Jasmine respects you. Who else is going to mess with the two of us?"

Unexpectedly, she grinned, revealing a line of pearly teeth. "Maybe I can talk to her for you. Then I'll have to talk to you for her. Will you listen to reason?"

"Yes. Do you think she'll eventually come around and forgive me?"

"Have you forgiven her?"

"The minute she drove off yesterday with that damn cart full of trunks, I forgave her. Do you know, she didn't look back once?"

"Didn't she?"

He shook his head. "Jasmine can be stubborn when she wants to be."

"How surprising, considering the gentle disposition of her father."

His brows shot up.

Emma winked.

Jasmine considered wearing the blue dress again just to spite Brody. But she couldn't quite bear to put the hideous thing on again. Instead, she ran down to the creek and doused herself in frigid river water. Then she donned her usual attire of a man's white shirt, a pair of riding pants, and boots.

Throughout the morning after her bath, she shut herself in her room and focused on the job of unpacking her trunks. She only dealt with the cases that contained clothing and household items. The childhood memories, along with all the expensive trinkets her father had purchased for her over the years, remained untouched.

Just as she was shoving the last of her undergarments onto a shelf in the armoire, a knock sounded at her door. Half the pairs of stockings she'd been holding drifted toward the floor.

She decided not to reply to Brody's summons. Let him rot.

"Jasmine," he said, his voice muffled by the wooden barrier.

She leaned down and quickly tried to scoop the renegade stockings into her arms.

He turned the knob.

She shoved her feminine cargo toward its shelf.

Brody stepped into her room, bringing a brace of fresh air with him. He wore a clean, pressed shirt and a pair of worn leather chaps over his trousers. His hair was slightly mussed, as if he'd just taken off his hat. She liked the color of his hair. It wasn't flat brown. It was lighter than that and gilded by sun.

"Are you hard of hearing?" he asked.

"No."

His jaw firmed with displeasure. "Then answer my knock the next time."

She tunneled all her defiance into a single withering glare.

"I'm leaving," he stated. "But don't get your hopes up. I'll be back by sunset."

"Where are you going?"

"To attend to the profession you find so attractive."

Outlaw work. Despite his sarcasm, excitement pulsed through her. Her mind filled with an array of spellbinding possibilities. "Do you need an—an assistant or partner or something?" It humbled her to ask, but the potential reward was worth the cost.

"No." His lips pursed. "But if I did, I'd prefer to employ assistants who wear their undergarments *beneath* their clothing."

She glanced down. One black stocking had caught a snag on her shoulder. It fluttered all the way to her waist, the toe pointing toward the floor in a graceful sweep. Snatching up the offending bit of silk, she fisted it into a ball and threw it in the direction of her armoire. "Am I suitable now?"

"Perfectly." He stalked from the room.

She blinked. Had he really said she was suitable? Surprised, but thrilled by his unexpected acquiescence, she grabbed her hat and bandana and followed him into the kitchen.

He waited beside the table for her. "You're more than suitably dressed to manage the dishes." He flicked his chin toward the pile of plates and bowls left over from his breakfast.

"Dishes?" she asked, horrified.

"Yes, dishes. Welcome to your new life, Jasmine."

She stood, frozen, staring at the dismaying assortment.

"I don't want you leaving the property today," he said. "Is that clear?"

Her paralyzed vocal chords could not respond.

Vaguely, she heard his footfalls cross the house and the front door close behind him. Then the echo of hooves as he rode from their home.

Dishes.

She'd offered him her sizable services as an outlaw, and he'd replied with an order to do dishes. Dishes! They'd become the scourge of her life.

At present, her fate teetered on a very precarious base. There were many things she wasn't sure of. But she *was* sure that she hadn't ruined her relationship with her father for this. Not in a million years would she have traded her Daddy's yoke and her Daddy's dishes for Brody's. Her husband would see her in hell before she'd stick her hands in his dishwater.

Very deliberately, she picked up a weighty ironstone plate. Bits of egg and ham stuck to the bottom. With a grim smile she dropped it directly onto the floor, where it spun on its side and flipped over. A mixing bowl followed. Then a cup and saucer and frying pan. Last came the fork, knife, and spoon. For good measure, she even sprinkled salt and pepper on top.

She returned to her room and dug through the trunk closest to the end of her bed. Inside, she found her stash of bullets. She grabbed out a handful, fed six to her gun, and pocketed the rest.

"Jasmine, you mean to tell me that you *wanted* to marry him?"

"Of course I did, Stella. You've seen him, so you must know why I'd want to be his wife." Jasmine discarded a two of hearts and a six of spades.

"Oh, sure. He was staying here, you know. Every time he'd stroll out the front door, all us girls would rush to the window for a parting glimpse."

"And?"

"He's heaven in motion. That man has some nice kind of build, and his . . . assets appear more than generous."

The two men at their poker table took their turns.

Stella dimpled her cheeks and looked generally confused when it came to her turn. Her act went unappreciated. They were all residents here. They all knew that Stella could turn as many tricks at the poker table as she could above stairs in the private rooms.

Jasmine came to the Blue Horseshoe Saloon only rarely these days. The girls who worked here were her friends, and their tendency to age at twice the normal rate disturbed her. Still, the saloon remained one of the best places in town to hear and tell information. She'd already hit the general store and Mrs. Hudson's bake house. This was the last stop in her day's work of stifling rumors.

As she'd expected, the story of how she'd come to be married had spread through the small town like a brush fire. Naturally, everyone depended on her to counter the gossip. It was only right.

Stella played her hand. "Last I knew, it was Lisbeth who had an interest in Mr. Brody McClintock."

Jasmine regarded her cards. "How could she not find him attractive? I don't blame her for that. In fact, I'm grateful to her. She was the one who indirectly introduced us."

"That so?" Stella asked, her blue eyes round.

Jasmine nodded, then placed a bet.

"I never figured you for the marrying kind, Jasmine. Not after all these years your daddy's been trying to get you down the aisle." Stella eyed their fellow players. "How 'bout you boys?"

"Never figured it."

"Nope."

Jasmine bestowed a serene smile on the three of them. "I've been reformed."

Stella's laughter started out as a giggle, then quickly gulped its way into a loud guffaw.

"I'm out," Jasmine said, when it came around to her. She scooped up the healthy pile of coins she'd won during the past two hours and stashed them in her pocket. "Stella, I realize that I've likely broken a lot of hearts with my marriage." Her eyes danced. "I'm counting on you to let my suitors down gently."

The woman's red lips widened with delight. "Speaking of broken hearts, here comes one now."

Jasmine looked up to see Hank Bledsoe walk into the saloon. She groaned. Hank had been her father's most recent candidate for the position of her husband. And despite the fact that everyone else in Tyler found him likable, she'd never been able to stomach the man. When he wasn't trying to corner her with cloying conversation, he was attempting to sit too close. She excused herself from the poker playing circle and headed for the door, hoping to sneak past him unnoticed.

"Jasmine?"

He spotted her before she'd even finished tying her pink

bandana. Reluctantly, she halted her withdrawal. "Hank."

He stopped mere inches from her, fully infringing on her personal space. He had a wiry body that mismatched his overly boyish facial features. Blond hair. Smelled nice. Good teeth.

No, she still couldn't abide him. Something about the size of his pores.

"I—I heard that you'd been married." His weight shifted from one boot to the other. "Is that true?"

"It's true."

His bottom lip protruded and his eyes filled with puppylike disappointment. "You married McClintock?"

"Yes."

"But why? You barely know him."

"Oh, Hank. Don't tell me that you haven't heard the story of how we came to be married."

"I have, but I didn't accept it."

"Well, you should have." She shrugged. "It's absolutely factual."

"Jasmine, are you out of your mind?" He reached out and gripped her upper arm. "What about the man's profession?"

"What about it? So he'll be gone much of the time. I don't mind." She longed to wrench her arm out of his grasp and give him a tongue lashing, but reminded herself to have a little mercy. The man was emotionally distraught.

"It's a dangerous occupation," he hissed.

"Yes, but I've always believed a little danger to be a career asset—"

"Jasmine." Brody's voice cut though the smoky air and lazy conversations of the saloon. The single word drew the attention of every individual within. Chairs squeaked as the spectators jostled for a better view.

Brody wore his hat pulled low, a line of shade masking his expression. As he approached, she noted the dusty streaks on his chaps and the way his holster hugged his hips.

The silky tug from last night returned. Softly and sweetly, it pulled at her belly.

With so many people watching, she tried to appear as normal as possible. If only Brody didn't have such presence. God, you either swooned in front of him, feared him, or loathed him. She doubted anyone could be indifferent.

Hank reacted to Brody like a child caught in a forbidden activity. He stood mute, without even the foresight to remove his hand from her arm. *What a ninny.* How could her father ever have thought to associate her with such a man?

Brody reached them and very deliberately peeled Hank's fingers from her arm. "Thank you kindly for unhanding my wife."

Hank licked his lips. "It wasn't—"

"I think you'd be better off not to speak," Brody said.

Hank pressed his lips together and rolled them inward.

For the benefit of the patrons, Jasmine smiled at her husband. He didn't return the gesture, just took her hand and led her from the premises. She waved at Stella and the boys as she passed.

Brody pulled her onto the street and then sidestepped into the alley between buildings, drawing her in after him. His hand gripped hers for a prolonged moment. Despite herself, Jasmine noticed the stark strength of his hold, carefully controlled so as not to cause her pain. Awareness streaked up from her fingertips, escalating the rhythm of her heart.

His eyes glowed darker at the centers and glimmering hazel around the outside. She hoped he'd hold her hand just a little bit longer.

He scowled and dropped her hand. "Don't ever tell a man that you expect your husband to be gone most of the time," he said, his tone cutting. "It's as good as an invitation into your bed."

"It is not!"

"It is. I'll have to kill him over a thing like that the next time."

"What? Brody, I was simply—"

"Who was that kid?" The muscles in the hollows of his cheeks hardened.

"His name is Hank Bledsoe. His father owns the saloon. As of two days ago he was my daddy's choice of a husband for me."

"God help him."

"I beg your pardon!"

Brody regarded her with a sharp edge of mistrust. For some unholy reason, it hurt her to recognize it. She was well accustomed to bearing the brunt of a man's frustration. But always before, her daddy had doled it out to her along with generous portions of love. In Brody she saw absolutely no affection. Just bitterness and cold, clear dislike.

"Have a care for people, Jasmine," he said. "You're far too reckless with the lives of others."

"I was only trying to—"

"Tell me. Tell me what in the *hell* you were trying to do here in town, when I told you to stay home today."

A rush of heat roared across her cheeks. "What right do you have to tell me—"

"I'm your husband. I have every right."

"But—"

"*Enough.*" He swiveled toward the mouth of the alley.

Her hands fisted at her sides as she watched him disappear around the corner. His habit of interrupting her explanations more than maddened her.

She ran after him, her boots pounding across the packed dirt. By the time she reached him, Brody was well into the street. He turned as if fully expecting her. In one swift motion, he clasped her around the waist and set her onto Diamond's back.

Jasmine landed on the saddle with a thump. Her hair tumbled across her face and her thoughts reeled. All she could feel, all she knew or recognized was the scorching awareness of where his hands still touched her hips.

Their gazes locked and she read surprise in his eyes.

In the next instant, his hands streaked away from her. He muttered an oath and turned away.

Her heartbeat frantic, she watched him mount his horse, then wheel the animal in the direction that led out of town. Her body flushed with heat. Did he remember the breathless moments they'd shared when no dictates but those of their bodies existed?

His horse burst into a gallop, leaving her dazed and alone atop her mount on the center of Broadway.

No. He didn't remember. It had been another's woman's body he'd hungered for. His ardor had belonged to Lisbeth, and she'd stolen it. He'd never desire her in that way. She'd never even thought of *herself* in that way, until his kisses and his touch had aroused this hateful yearning in her.

Jasmine squashed on her hat and urged her horse after Brody. Loving a good race, Diamond immediately lengthened her strides, stretching and pulling her way across the earth. The small collection of buildings that formed the town of Tyler streaked past.

Jasmine banished all thoughts but one: to catch and surpass Brody. Suddenly it meant a great deal, to win over him. Even in something as basic as a horse race. Focusing solely on his form, Jasmine whistled at Diamond and allowed her more rein.

The horse flew.

In the wide expanse of field just beyond town, Jasmine pulled alongside Brody, then sailed past. Exhilaration made her light-headed. She laughed with victory.

She's lost her mind, Brody thought. He'd hoped to put a little distance between himself and Jasmine so that his brain could cool. Otherwise, he'd not have pushed his horse to this bruising pace. That she would attempt and achieve this speed stupefied him.

Jasmine, her lips parted on a grin, rode just ahead of him. Those damned pants of hers clasped snugly to her legs and bottom. Wind flattened her shirt across her chest, clearly defining the swell of her breasts. A few tendrils of russet hair skated on the wind, outlined by the blinding blue of the sky.

He stared, surrendering control of their flight to his mount while he drank in the sight of her. She was elemental. Ungodly beautiful like this, all brazen instincts and straining wildness.

Jasmine was as far from the kind of woman he admired as stars from the sun. And yet more alluring than he could believe. Stunning in her uniqueness.

A savage bolt of lust fisted in his gut.

Furious with himself, he tore his vision away. He couldn't allow himself to credit the desire he felt for her. He checked his horse's pace.

If her goal had been to beat him, then it appeared she wasn't satisfied with her accomplishment. He watched her race onward, heedless of his slowed speed. Woman and horse dashed across the scooping contour of the land, then disappeared from sight.

He'd have to take that horse from her if she couldn't treat it with more care.

God damn it! Brody sent the ends of his reins sailing through the air. They connected with the animal's hindquarters. Instantly, his horse resumed the chase.

Jasmine slowed Diamond very gradually. By the time they passed Emma's, she rode at a gentle trot. Briefly, she considered stopping in to see her friend, but decided that an early arrival back at Colin House, as she'd come to think of it, would be more advisable.

With a glance over her shoulder, she confirmed what

she'd been confirming for two miles. No Brody.

A giggle escaped her. With the quicker shortcut she'd taken across a wide swath of Double J land, he was probably fifteen full minutes behind her.

She'd already angered Brody once today. No, twice, what with their race. Just how much goading could a man like him take before he'd finally relent and abandon her? And when he reached his limit, would he simply leave, or try to beat her with his belt? She hadn't any idea. Her grip choked the reins. If Brody *ever* tried to beat her, he'd have one hell of a fight on his hands.

Diamond was walking up the last stretch of hill to Colin House when the sound of galloping hooves rumbled across the valley.

Jasmine turned in the saddle and gasped at the sight of Brody charging across the field. His arms pumped, his legs hugged his straining animal. He looked as ominous and as angry as the sky before a tornado.

Diamond's steps minced with alarm. "Shhh," Jasmine soothed.

But before the murmur could have the desired effect, he was upon them. Brody caught the cross piece of Diamond's bridle and launched himself from the saddle.

For the second time that day, Jasmine felt herself being lifted. This time he pulled her from her seat and set her onto the ground. Again her hair cascaded in front of her eyes. And again she felt the reverberations of his touch ripple through her body.

Brody held the leads of both animals in one hand and wrapped his other hand around her elbow. Grimly, he tugged her toward the house.

"What are you doing?" she demanded, stretching her steps to keep up with him. "Never scare my horse like that!"

He didn't even glance at her. "*Now* you show compassion for your animal. A little late, wouldn't you say, after the way you pushed her?"

"Pushed her? My horse is perfectly fine. Look at her! It's yours that is panting for breath."

The statement was true enough. Diamond had been given ample time to cool down and recover, while Brody's horse had been ridden hard all the way from town. His mount's coat seeped with sweat.

"You say one more word," Brody gritted out, "and I'll make good on my threat to tie you to the porch post."

She clamped her lips together. This probably wasn't a very good time to tell him about the dishes she'd piled onto the floor. Moments ago, she'd wondered what would happen when he truly lost his temper. She chewed on the inside of her cheek. Suddenly, she wasn't so eager to find out.

Brody released the horses in the yard, stormed into the house, and escorted her toward the kitchen.

God have mercy, Jasmine prayed. She shut her eyes.

Her captor ground to a halt.

She squeezed her lids harder.

Then soft, like a melody repeating itself along the corridors of the mind, came the smell of potatoes. Of beef and onions.

Cautiously, she cracked open her eyes.

A cowboy, slight of frame and long in years, stood beside the oven. He wore a stain-spattered apron tied smartly around his waist. Dark eyes sparkled from beds of sun-woven wrinkles. His peppery hair displayed the evidence of a recently discarded hat.

"By God, Brody," the cowboy said with a smile, "unhand that girl!"

Jasmine dared to peek at the floor. Every last morsel of her dish tantrum had been erased.

God *had* had mercy on her. He'd sent her a savior in the form of a small, bright-eyed stranger who, by the smell of it, had a way with cooking.

Chapter 6

The makeshift handcuff was an enormous annoyance. Jasmine sat on the porch, her boots dangling over the edge of the planks. Brody had shackled her wrist securely, if delicately, to the post. The instrument of restraint was her own black stocking, one and the same as had disgraced her earlier in the day with its tendency to cling.

She kicked viciously at a nearby pebble and sent it careening toward the corral. Brody had warned her that he'd tie her here if she so much as uttered another word. In her opinion, a simple greeting to the kindly stranger in their kitchen hardly qualified.

Brody had disagreed.

For the last several minutes, he'd been cooling his horse by walking the animal in wide circles around the property. Whenever he passed by her end of the homestead, she glared mightily at him.

He hadn't yet had the decency to notice.

From behind where she sat, hinges squeaked. Jasmine angled her head and watched her savior emerge from the house. He carried a tray laden with a meal and a steaming cup of coffee.

In true savior fashion, he laid the food on the porch next to her.

"Name's Tom," he said.

She moved to extend her right hand in greeting. It came up hard against its bond. With a frown of irritation, she lifted her left. "Mine's Jasmine."

He clasped it warmly. "Hello, Jasmine."

"Hello."

He disappeared back into the house. Moments later he reemerged, this time bringing his own dinner and a chair. With faultless balance, he arranged his tray across his knees.

Jasmine watched him with interest. "Are you a friend of Brody's?"

"I am. Are you?"

"Oh, no. I'm his wife."

The coffee cup he'd lifted halfway to his lips froze in midair. He slanted his head forward and studied her with quizzical brown eyes. "Truly?"

"Yep."

"Well, I'll be." A trace of a smile played across his lips as he set his cup on the tray. "That's something I never thought to see."

"I can understand why. Brody's extremely difficult."

His lips quirked up. "It's not that so much. There've been plenty of women over the years who've been ready and willing to marry him."

"Then how come they didn't?"

Brody stifled Tom's answer by choosing that moment to walk up the steps and into the house. Jasmine shot an ugly grimace at his back, then selected a forkful of potato. In the sullen silence, she allowed her gaze to travel over the vista of Texas land that spread out from Colin House. She loved this time of day, when the sun gilded earth, air and people to gold. In the distance, a small grouping of cattle who had drunk their fill walked lazily toward shade. Birds swooped across the sky in hushed circles.

"Do you often eat outside, Tom?" she asked.

She heard his fork settle onto his plate. "Yes. I'm forever on the trail, it seems."

"And when you're at home?"

"As a rule I only eat on the porch when lovely young women are handcuffed there."

She looked up at him and laughed.

He smiled, sending grooves into the skin of his cheeks.

The front door swung open. Brody walked out carrying his dinner in one hand and a chair in the other. He settled next to Tom.

Jasmine glanced away. She hated the man. Didn't want to see the sun turn his eyes the color of burnished emeralds. Didn't want to see his hair lift and ruffle on the breeze.

She took a bite of steak. Her darling Tom had already cut it into pieces for her. She sampled another bite. And another.

"Glad you made it here," Brody said to Tom.

"It took me a little while. I swear the trek home and back takes longer every year."

"Your sister well?"

"Very well."

"Good."

Several minutes passed quietly, every person concentrating on his dinner. Jasmine had to squelch several flares of self-consciousness. It wasn't every night that she ate one-handed before an audience.

The sun's last blaze had begun to fade when the men set aside their trays and relaxed into their chairs.

"Good meal," Brody said.

"Thank you. Your, ah . . . method of storing dishes and such made the job easy."

Cautiously, Jasmine turned her position so that she could observe Tom. His eyes sparkled with her secret, a secret she could see he intended to keep. Her affection for him deepened.

Both men reclined, their legs stretched out in front of them, boots crossed at the ankles.

"Brody?" Tom asked.

"Hmmm?"

"Your wife here doesn't seem to me to be threatening enough to merit a leash."

Brody focused his attention directly on her. A long, lazy grin dawned across his face. The cleft in his chin deepened.

Jasmine felt as if the sun had resurrected itself. Humor changed his features, stripping away years and regrets. She blinked at him, dazzled.

"You wouldn't say that," Brody replied, "if you knew her."

Her dreamy appreciation of him shattered.

"Aw, let her go," Tom said. "I'll take my chances."

Brody laced his fingers together over his flat belly. "I'd grant you many favors, Tom. But that one is just too costly."

"You can't leave me here all night," Jasmine pointed out.

One of his brows arched up. "Can't I?"

"No!"

He shrugged. With one hand, he tipped his hat down over his eyes. He settled back against his chair and sighed.

She looked from him to Tom, down at her shackle, and back at Brody.

By the time the moon sat directly overhead, Jasmine no longer thought Brody had been kidding. He really was going to leave her out here all night.

He'd fastened her stocking to the post with a strange labyrinth of knots and twists.

At first, when the men had retired inside, she'd worked ceaselessly at untying it. After what seemed like an eternity, she'd come to the conclusion that she'd not be released from her silken chain unless she could cut through it. At

that point, she'd searched for a loose nail. The pads of her
fingers had swelled tender and red from trying to tug one
free.

No luck.

No hope.

She leaned against the post, resting the back of her head
on the smooth wood.

Brody was likely hoping that she'd repent of her evil
ways and beg forgiveness after this. If so, he was sadly
mistaken. She wouldn't crack. Not after one measly night
in the cold. Still, during the hours of quiet, she'd begun to
worry just how much longer he intended to perpetuate the
charade of their marriage. The kind of man who would tie
a woman to a post and leave her there overnight was going
to be a difficult man to reckon with.

*I'm going to see to it that you never in your life taste
freedom again.*

Never. That was a long time. Surely he hadn't meant
that.

She tugged at her right wrist. The sensitive skin flashed
with pain.

Maybe he *had* meant it.

The stars glowed steadily, patiently. The stillness consumed her, huddling like a heavy black quilt over the prairie.

Her spirits teetered on the edge of equilibrium and then
took a steep plunge. She missed her father. Not a subtle,
sentimental miss, but a gnawing ache. A void that yawned
and grew and pained her like a mortal wound. Her throat
convulsed. Behind her eyes, heartache burned.

He hadn't come to check on her. Her instincts kept expecting him to storm through the door of Colin House or
intercept her in the fields. He hadn't. And it was entirely
unlike him not to. Maybe she'd made him so mad this time
that he didn't love her anymore.

Her life stretched before her, barren and flat. Without her

father, there'd be no one to care about her. No other man would ever compliment her as he did, or laugh with her, or find beauty in her features.

Freedom, she reminded herself.

Freedom. The word wailed through her like an eagle's keening cry. But for the first time, the echo of her dearest, deepest dream had a hollow ring to it that she couldn't quite ignore.

She told herself not to be silly. Her independence was the ultimate goal—the best life had to offer her. She simply needed to reevaluate and learn from her mistakes. Setbacks could be overcome and her ambitions met. They had to be. She'd practiced all her life, she'd learned her lessons well, she'd excelled at the skills needed to become a profitable outlaw. Success *must* result from that kind of dedication.

Tomorrow she'd practice her shooting. If Brody gave her more orders, she'd break them. He couldn't tie her to the porch post every night.

She made a mental reminder to slip her knife into her boot tomorrow morning. It would be a pleasure to slash this ridiculous silk stocking to ribbons if he attempted to tie her here again.

She would outlast or outsmart Brody. Whatever it took to force him to leave.

Her eyelids sagged downward. She'd not sleep. How could she, in this hideous position? But maybe if she just relaxed. . . .

Brody finally abandoned his bed and the farce others called sleeping. Without bothering to don a shirt, he collected his knife and lantern.

He hated the fact that he couldn't rest for thinking of Jasmine on the porch.

He padded across the living room and let himself out the front door. Jasmine's head was propped against the post. Those maddening lips lay parted in slumber. Her hands had relaxed, slim fingers curling. Her work boots dangled off the edge of the porch.

Jasmine, with her wild hair, the ridiculous pink bandana, and a thick, rusty smudge across her forehead. She must have tried to pry free a nail, then brushed her temple.

He shook his head, stealing himself against the tenderness that welled unbidden within him. Any man fool enough to fall in love with her would be doomed to a life of heartbreak. Her exterior, so shiny with promise and life, disguised a faithless heart.

Two wooden crosses, side by side, rose in his mind's eye. Those crosses would never move from their airless little hilltop. Forever they'd stay planted in the earth above the bodies they protected. A reminder, lest he forget.

Timeless guilt bore down on him, crushing his insides, twisting and breaking his life's hope.

He'd made a vow all those years ago, under the shadow of those graves. To live the remainder of his life alone. Jasmine, this dangerously sweet-faced woman, had forced him to shatter that vow. He'd do well to remember that.

An insect buzzed around his lantern. It bumped into the glass, paused, and returned to its quest.

Without his knowing it, he'd taken hold of the ring that hung on a chain around his neck. The band's edges bit into his palm. He looked down and saw that the necklace cut a glistening trail all the way to the middle of his ribs. Determinedly, he released the plain, silver ring. It fell against his skin. Warm and comforting.

He walked to the door. He'd leave Jasmine here to fidget the night away in discomfort. The hungry insects could eat her alive, for all he cared.

He'd pulled the door less than halfway open when she moaned, so softly that the sound died upon reaching his ears.

Reluctantly, his gaze returned to her. Her lips mumbled something incoherent, then pursed into a scowl.

The nights could get chilly in the spring. The dew would torment her. She'd shiver—

He crossed the porch and knelt beside her. Unsheathing the knife he'd brought for specifically this purpose, he cut clean through the makeshift cuff.

She didn't stir.

Pressing an arm beneath her knees and another behind her back, he lifted her into his arms.

Her eyes flashed open. The lantern light drew bright reflections in the hazy blue depths. Blue like the cleanest sea in God's creation. Blue like the fancy colored glass some women displayed in cabinets.

"Am I free?" she asked, her voice hoarse.

"Yes." He couldn't bear to look at her, so he stooped to pick up the lantern, then carried her indoors. A fire breathed red in the hearth. Ashy embers curved and turned in welcome.

Jasmine didn't fight him. She simply let herself be carried.

He could smell her hair. Its scent was fresh and clean like snow. An elusive smell, wholly indefinable.

He felt himself harden for her. Hell, he wanted to be buried inside her so bad. To claim her hard and deep. To teach her a lesson by the spilling of seed.

Unceremoniously, he dumped her onto her bed.

Jasmine levered her weight onto her elbows and gaped at him.

He could almost feel the tight sheath of her. The forceful strokes. The thrusting, searching ecstasy.

Angrily, he turned toward his room and the meager solace it offered him.

Chapter 7

Emma pulled her horse to a halt a goodly distance from Jasmine. She'd ridden all the way out here to Jasmine's shooting gallery on the off chance of locating her friend. Yet now that she'd found her, the job she'd come to do, that of restoring the relationship between Jasmine and Lee, daunted her. She felt like a spy trying to serve two masters.

From beneath the brim of her felt hat, she silently regarded her friend's activities. Jasmine opened her satchel and pulled out an assortment of glass jars and tin cans. Emma squinted. The glass containers still appeared to be full. As usual, Jasmine positioned her impromptu enemies using boulders, tree branches, and dirt mounds as bases. Once finished, she swung into the saddle and cantered about two hundred yards up the field. Turning Diamond in a tight circle, she faced her targets, then exploded with speed.

Emma watched, enthralled. At the very last instant, Jasmine whipped her six-shooter from the holster around her hips and aimed it. Three shots rang out in quick succession. Jam splattered from the first target. Peaches from the second. And what looked like beans from the third.

She didn't stop to taste. Once she'd cantered two hundred yards in the opposite direction, she swiveled and made another pass. The remaining trio of tin cans launched into the air.

Jasmine hopped off her horse and spun her revolver twice on her finger before sliding it into its holster. Then she went to work lining up new adversaries.

Emma shook her head. Her friend's unswerving determination never failed to amaze her, even after all this time. She directed her horse forward. "How are you shooting?" she called, when she was near enough.

Jasmine set a beaten tin can on its stump and turned. "Hi, Em." She groaned as she straightened and placed both hands on her lower back. Her fingers kneaded a couple of times. "I'm shooting about the same as always."

"That's good, then."

"It's decent."

"Looked awfully good to me."

Jasmine swung onto Diamond's back and maneuvered the horse next to Emma's. The women extended their hands and laced their fingers together. The horses started forward at a walk.

Comfort, so much a part of their friendship, pulsed between them. "How have things been up at the house?" Emma asked.

The look Jasmine slid her out of the corners of her eyes spoke volumes. "Frustrating."

"Haven't been able to bend that husband of yours to your will yet?"

"Not quite yet."

"I take it he won't be picking up stakes and moving anytime soon?"

"Believe me, if he doesn't, it's not from lack of trying on my part."

Emma chuckled. Releasing hands, they accelerated into a side-by-side trot. "Mind if I join you?"

"Not at all. The usual?"

"The usual."

They rode away from the targets, deep into the prairie, then faced the display on horseback. Whenever she visited Jasmine here, it was their habit to practice distance shooting, Emma's specialty.

She didn't have to ask who'd shoot first. Emma always received the first turn, likely in deference to her age. She smiled as she slid her rifle from its position in her saddle.

Extending her arm, she peered down the length of the weapon, carefully aligning the sights. As always, her muscles strictly obeyed the commands of her will. Her fingers didn't shake. The rifle didn't twitch.

On a soft exhale, she hugged the trigger. Even as the first can toppled, she moved to the next. Calm control eased through her veins into her arms. She fired again. Total absorption. Faultless concentration. Her third bullet met its mark.

She took one cleansing breath and handed her rifle to Jasmine.

After five shots, Jasmine managed to unseat the three remaining cans.

Jasmine handed the rifle back with a grumble. "I'm still nowhere near your level."

"You are too! I can't shoot at all from a run. I have to be stationary."

"But that aim! I can barely even see the cans from here." Jasmine scowled in the direction of her ramshackle targets.

Emma's aim had been bred of necessity. When Colin had gone off to fight in the war, she'd been the only one left at home to defend her aging parents. Shooting a rifle had become an imperative skill, a skill she'd been forced to learn quickly. Comanches were a constant threat in those days. As were bandits and horse thieves.

As the years of the Civil War dragged, one overlapping with the next, children and women had come to live in the Larkin home. She'd accepted anyone who'd asked, until both Colin House and her own were filled with a gradually rotating sea of faces.

The ponderous responsibility of keeping so many defenseless people safe had honed her shooting skill.

Six times during the war they'd been threatened. And each time her aim had saved their lives. In the years since, she'd been grateful for the ability she'd acquired to protect herself. A woman alone in this part of the country was considered by some to be easy prey.

It amused her that her prowess with a rifle should have become such widespread knowledge across two counties. A couple times a year some young man or another would challenge her to a shooting match. Each time, she declined. Not only because she preferred not to publicly humiliate the gentlemen, but because she fancied keeping her small legend alive.

Emma looked to her friend. The shade of Jasmine's hat fell across her face, ending in a bright line of sun bisecting her throat. Her skin shone with exertion's moisture and the open neck of her shirt stuck to her chest in damp patches. As she watched, Jasmine pulled the brim of her hat even lower, causing the circle of shade to jostle down to her shoulders.

This was as good a time as any to broach the subject of Lee. Still, the words clogged her throat and she had to goad herself to speak them. "Your father came to see me."

Jasmine twisted in the saddle to regard her. "Did he?"

"Yes. He's . . . upset about the way things have been left between you."

"And he wants you to smooth it over."

Emma tucked a tendril of pale charcoal hair under her hat. "He wants me to be a mediator between you."

"And you told him you would?"

Brackets of displeasure curved into the skin on either side of her lips. "Yes."

Jasmine's chest rose and fell on a deep sigh. "I don't

know if a mediator will be good enough this time, Emma. Do you realize that he hasn't come to check on me? Not once.''

''He's probably not sure he'd be welcomed.''

''He packed my things—all of my things—into a cart! He kicked me out of my home.''

''His temper can be ferocious—''

''Perhaps it's time Daddy learned to control his temper.'' Jasmine's expression hardened as she shifted her attention to the windblown fields of grass surrounding them.

Emma's horse shuffled beneath her, transferring weight from hoof to hoof. She stilled him with a subtle movement of her wrist. ''You're bitter,'' she said carefully, ''and you're angry at him right now. And I'm sure he's bitter and angry with you, too. But I don't think, not for one moment, Jasmine, that this is the end between you.''

She saw her friend wince and knew, as well as she knew this stretch of Double J land, how badly Jasmine missed Lee. ''Stubbornness has its place,'' Emma said. ''But not in this. Not when it's hurting you both so much. Take some time, Jasmine, to forgive him. But don't wait so long that you risk your relationship.'' Sadness for the family she'd lost trembled within Emma. ''Believe me when I say that there is nothing on this earth as precious as family.''

Tears scorched her throat. Her memories of her mother, her father, her brother rose up like elusive ghosts, intertwining, then disappearing on the breeze like threads of mist. ''You haven't any idea how lucky you are to have him.''

Jasmine bowed her head. When she looked up, her eyes were filled with remorse. ''I'm sorry that you've been put in this position, Em. When I'm ready, I promise you that I'll let you know.''

Emma nodded. How precious Jasmine was to her. A fierce flame to her own coolness. Passion opposing calm. Wildness meeting reason.

Jasmine breathed fervor and tumultuous emotion into her days. Without her for a friend, she feared the bleakness of her routine would squeeze all color from her life.

Jasmine gestured in the direction of Colin House. "Come on. Let's race."

Emma laughed. Jasmine persisted in challenging her to races, even though she never proved a worthy opponent. "You go."

Jasmine grinned and launched herself toward the targets she needed to collect before heading home. Emma watched her go, wondering if Brody had noticed yet just how lovely his wife was.

Jasmine burst into the kitchen. Swiftly, she upended her satchel on the surface of the table and began to sort out the collection of bent, bullet-ridden tins.

The door swung open and she glanced up in time to see Tom walk in.

"Came to investigate all the noise...." His gaze halted on the merchandise. "So that's where all my cans went."

She tested a smile on him.

Leathery hands planted on narrow hips. Lines of mirth grooved the skin around his eyes. "What about the peaches and the jam and all the other goods that lined these shelves this morning?"

"Tom," Jasmine said, trying to keep her lips from twitching, "in every war there are casualties."

"Young lady, I don't know what you were doing, shooting at the peaches Brody bought. And I'm not going to ask. But the next time you decide to wage war on defenseless fruit and vegetables, you'll have me to reckon with."

She laughed, grateful for his humor and his understanding. "I suppose Brody will just have to buy more. What a shame." With a shrug, she hoisted the cans into her arms, turned, and opened a low cupboard with the toe of her boot.

"No, you don't," Tom said. "Put those out back. You

can save them for your next destructive urge."

She nodded, walked out the back door, and set the pile an arm's reach beyond the step. Then she settled herself into a chair at the kitchen table.

Tom rumbled around the room, setting water to boil, measuring out coffee grounds. Jasmine studied his lean frame and efficient movements. By some fortunate twist of luck, it appeared that she'd managed to catch Tom here alone. There were so many questions about Brody that she needed answered. Questions lining up all the way along her tongue and down her throat.

She'd no doubt that information was the key to controlling Brody. And thus the key to grabbing her own destiny.

Tom leaned against the wall next to the stove while he waited for the water to heat. She was encouraged by the indulgent expression he leveled on her.

"Have you been friends with Brody long?" she asked.

"Oh, ten or eleven years, I guess."

"You ride with him?"

"Pretty much everywhere he goes."

She'd already come to this conclusion. Every bandit benefited from an accomplice. Clearly, Brody was the leader—the active, dangerous participant. Tom likely researched the mark, gathered information, masterminded the job.

"How did you two meet up?"

He tilted his head to the side, remembering. "The war had just finished. We met on the road home."

"Brody was in the war?"

"Sure. So was his little brother, Clay."

A flurry of questions swirled through her head, so many that she worried she'd forget one. "He has a brother?"

He stuffed his hands in his pockets and bent to check the status of the water. "Is that so surprising?"

"It is to me. Is Clay still alive?"

"Very much so. In fact, he's to be married in a week's

time. We'll be making the trip to the family's ranch for the services."

Excitement bubbled through her, scattering all the carefully crafted questions in the wake of her anticipation. When they left for the wedding she'd be alone for days. Maybe weeks! A little time was exactly what she needed to rework her plans.

Freedom.

". . . property is down near Nacogdoches."

She tried to remember what he'd been talking about. "Whose property is that?"

"The McClintocks'," he replied, raising his brows.

"Yes, of course. The McClintocks."

He guffawed and lifted the kettle from the stove using a well-worn rag to protect his fingers.

She watched as he coasted through the familiar dance of serving coffee. The cowboys drank it like water, as basic to their survival as air. After filling two mugs, Tom set one in front of her and took the chair across the table.

He moved with such ease and grace. For a man of his advancing age, his litheness surprised her. Even now, sitting with his shoulder blades propped against the top rung of the chair and a boot crossed over the opposing knee, he seemed almost elegant.

Tom sipped his coffee, letting his eyelids drift down as the brew ran along his throat and into his belly.

She tasted her own coffee. Steaming hot and strong enough to make you flinch. Just how she liked it. "Tom, last night you were saying that there'd been several women willing to marry Brody over the years." She attempted to appear only mildly interested in the question.

"Was I?"

"I don't know. I think so."

"Hmmm," he murmured. "I don't recall."

"Tom! I distinctly remember you saying that there had been plenty of willing women!"

"Oh, that's right," he said. "*Now* I recall." Eyes the color of molasses glinted mischievously. He tapped his temple in a gesture that blamed a feeble brain for its forgetfulness.

There was nothing feeble about him. Especially not his brain.

"When Brody walked up, you were about to tell me why he never married any of the other women," she muttered.

"Was I?"

"Tom!"

He beamed at her exasperation, then gently set his mug down. By degrees the warmth and laughter in his face changed. The contours of cheek and chin grew serious, almost solemn. He turned the mug round and round with his fingertips, watching its leisurely spin. "For almost as long as I've known Brody he's not been interested in marriage."

"Why?"

He frowned softly. "I don't rightly know. Never asked. But I have a theory."

"Which is?"

"That he's never married because of a woman. A woman he loved."

Hurt slashed through her chest like lightning, shocking her with its force. That's not what she'd hoped to hear, she realized. A wandering life would have been a better answer. Or best of all, freedom, the basis of her own anti-marriage sentiment. But not love. Not for Brody with the stern visage and grim personality. "He seems too harsh to love a woman."

"Harsh?" Tom sucked down a mouthful of coffee and pondered that. "Maybe he is harsh in some ways. But that wasn't always the case. When I first knew him he was just a kid. Delighted to be coming home. Full of ideas and brimming with hope."

"What happened?"

"He discovered that he'd lost Elena."

Jasmine stared at him, mildly horrified by this truth that she hadn't really wanted to know. She felt sick. "Elena? That was her name?"

"That was her name."

Tom continued to turn his mug. Round and round the handle went, a soft clunking accompanying the movement.

Jasmine fidgeted. Her boot nudged a forgotten tin, causing it to skitter across the floor. She reached down to retrieve it. "I guess Brody took losing her pretty hard."

"Yep. I didn't believe that he ever intended to marry . . . after her."

"How long has it been since then?"

He chewed the edge of his lip. "Almost eleven years."

"And you two have been together all that time?"

"Yep."

She gulped down a quick sip of coffee. Still hot enough to burn the skin off the top of her mouth. "What kind of duties are you responsible for in the partnership?" she asked, eager to change the topic.

"Oh, just about whatever Brody needs doing. I used to ride in on the raids and such. But I'm getting a little old for that now, so I mostly work from the camp, planning or organizing supplies."

She'd guessed Tom's position correctly. Jasmine silently congratulated herself on her insight into the criminal dynamic. All the years in Tyler hadn't completely leached the knowledge from her.

She could tell that her precious Tom was really warming to her now. Maybe if she asked nicely, he'd let her in on their illegal activities. She ran her fingertips over the mangled tin can. "What kind of a job are you working on now?

He tilted his cup to his lips. "Brody is concentrating his efforts on the Hanson/Williams feud."

She frowned. The two local families had been feuding for years. Of late the battle had heated to the point where lives had been lost on both sides. But neither family owned much worth stealing. Unless Brody and Tom wanted the Hanson herd. Their cattle had multiplied well over the last two round-ups. "I suppose he hopes to intensify the fighting," she speculated, "and then, while the families are distracted, move in and nick off the herd."

Tom looked at her in surprise. After a moment, he released a burst of chuckles, low and sweet.

She didn't so much as smile.

When he noticed that she wasn't joining in his humor, his laughter fell off.

"It wasn't a completely ludicrous assumption," she said. "It's a common enough tactic. Divert and then spring into action." She gestured with her hands.

His peppery brows dropped over his eyes. "Jasmine, I don't know what you're talking about."

"Oh, Tom, you can trust me. I won't tell a soul."

"Trust you?"

"Sure. With your plans. I got it, didn't I? Divert with more fighting, which would leave the cattle unattended. No one to ride the lines if everyone is involved in protecting the family."

He allowed her words to fully penetrate. "We don't want their cattle, Jasmine," he said slowly.

Her lips pursed. Foreboding trickled down the back of her neck. "Then why? Why bother with the feud?"

"Why bother?"

"Why bother if there's nothing in it for you?"

"Because that's our job. Peacekeeping is our job."

She clenched her tin. Hard. The rough, scratchy surfaces pressed into her palm.

His cup stopped turning.

"Peace," she rasped. "You want peace?"

"Why, yes, Jasmine." He leaned forward and rested his elbows on the table. "Brody is a Texas Ranger."

Chapter 8

A Texas Ranger. The words battered against her ears and were rejected by her brain. "A what?" she breathed.

"A Ranger. You know of the Rangers, Jasmine. Hell, in these parts, children are raised on Ranger legends." Concern softened his eyes, melting the molasses into a thick stream. "Didn't you know about Brody's profession?"

Jasmine tried to swallow, but the moisture in her mouth condensed, lodging in her throat. "I was told. . . ." The muscles in her neck worked convulsively. "They told me he was an outlaw."

Tom's eyes rounded. He fell against the back of the chair, clearly stunned. "Well, I know Brody has been lying low, keeping to himself until he can figure what's been happening between the families. Maybe the local folk mistook his appearance, his proficiency with a gun. I can't imagine . . . whoever started that rumor was completely mistaken." He spread weathered brown hands. "Couldn't have been more mistaken."

Couldn't have been more mistaken.

Jasmine's heart beat her blood through her veins in erratic waves. Her breath panted. Too shallow. She pulled at the neck of her shirt, needing space. But the collar already hung wide.

A Texas Ranger.

Dear Lord above, he couldn't be. A sharp edge of metal bit into her finger. Blindly, she looked at the can she still held. It bent as if in agony, flaps of flesh pulled back where the ammunition had riddled it. Ruined.

She felt like that bullet-eaten tin.

"Darlin', you going to faint?"

Through furry vision, she watched Tom rise from his chair and hover next to her.

"Suddenly you don't look so good," he said. "Can I get you something? Water?"

"No." Nothing could fix this.

"How 'bout going to lie down?"

Grimly, she nodded. She needed to be alone. Didn't want an audience watching her gruesome demise. Still holding her mangled tin, she staggered to her feet.

Tom placed a firm hand on her lower back and escorted her down the hall to her room. "I know it must have been a shock," he said gently. "But better to discover him a Ranger, don't you think? Better a Ranger than a bandit."

She couldn't reply. Numbly, she shuffled to her bed and stretched out across the quilt.

"Just call," Tom said, "if you need anything." Worry dug fresh groves into his forehead. The door clicked closed after him.

Better a Ranger than a bandit.

The dear man had no idea how wrong he was.

The implications of this new revelation swirled around the room like phantoms. Each one pressed against her thoughts momentarily, then sailed away.

Her dream of freedom, just days ago so close and clear, began to waver and fade from view. All the traits she'd believed Brody to possess now came into question. When she'd chosen him as her temporary husband, she'd depended on his dishonor. A healthy disrespect of sworn vows had been important. A man who'd run from authorities had figured into her plan.

But instead, she'd married a Ranger. Brody likely had enough honor for two lifetimes and loyalty in spades. He'd never run from the authorities. He *was* the authority.

She released her tin. It rolled off the edge of the bed and landed with a sharp clang. She covered her face with her hands. Fingertips pressed against her forehead and temples. What had she done? *God.*

Her father was still a wanted man in the East. Were Brody to discover the secret of her father's former career, he'd jump at the chance to apprehend him. They'd confine her father like an animal: caged, lonely, shamed. Then they'd probably hang him, to make an example of what happened to outlaws who ran.

Fear shuddered through her. It couldn't happen that way. She couldn't *let* it happen.

She had to escape. There weren't any other options now. She could no longer afford to wait for Brody to leave. She needed to run, as far and as fast as Diamond could carry her. In response, Brody would either mount a fruitless search for her, or he would simply give up and move on. Either way, he'd leave Tyler and her father's secret would be safe.

Time. She needed time to plan. A quantity of money to accumulate supplies. And a traveling companion. It was out of the question to travel across country alone—insanely dangerous. There had to be some band she could join up with. Or a trail drive. Anyone.

Tom had said that he and Brody would be leaving soon for Clay's wedding. If she couldn't sneak away before then, their absence would give her the perfect opportunity to disappear.

"Jasmine?"

Brody's voice jostled her from her dark thoughts. With

effort, she pushed herself to sitting and dropped her feet over the side of the bed. Needle shards of pain assaulted her brain. The longer she'd thought of her plight, the more ferocious her headache had grown.

"Jasmine."

The room lay in shadows. Without her noticing, afternoon had converged with evening. Gingerly, she stood.

"Open the door," Brody said. "Don't make me—"

She pulled back the door. "What? Don't make you what? Were you going to storm in here and spank me?"

They stood mere inches apart. Lantern light from the hall illuminated him lovingly, but only reached tentative fingers toward her.

Brody frowned. The meager light was sufficient for him to make out the dark circles that ran beneath her eyes and the chalky pallor of her skin. What in the hell was wrong with her? He hadn't expected her to answer the door looking so forlorn. Despite himself, his compassion stirred. "Are you sick?"

"Just a headache." He saw defiance and pride in the way she held herself. Eyes so light, they seemed devoid of color except for the gray rings around the outside of her pupils. A dirt stain scored her chin.

"Looks like you and I both need a bath," he said.

With one hand, she belatedly tried to soothe the torrent of waves that composed her hair. With the other, she pulled together the neck of her white shirt. "No. I'm fine."

"I disagree."

"I said that I'm fine." She shot a look toward the kitchen. "Is dinner ready?"

"Almost."

"Then I'll just change into something. . . ."

His gaze caught hers. A yearning, born last night of her scent and her touch, drifted through him like a curl of smoke trapped in a bottle. "Come with me," he said.

She shivered and crossed her arms over her chest. "No.

I'm perfectly capable of choosing my own bath times." She nudged the door toward the jam.

He caught it before it closed. No way was he going to let her boss him around. The water and the washing would do her good.

In a single fluid movement, he lifted her into his arms. He carried her down the hall and through the living room. "I'm getting damned tired of your difficult nature, Jasmine."

His cargo struggled and hissed like a wildcat.

"Brody!" Tom called from the kitchen. "Where on earth are you going with her?"

"To the stream."

Tom rushed forward, wiping his hands on his apron. "Promise me you won't drown her."

"No such promise given."

Brody kicked the front door open and stalked across the lawn. A few of her well-placed punches came dangerously close to his head, so he clasped her even tighter against him, trapping her flailing limbs. "Stop it," he ordered.

She stilled.

"Thank you."

Venomously, she bit his shoulder.

Fitting, he thought. Perfectly fitting.

He reached the narrow river and lifted her into midair.

"I don't want a bath!" she shrieked.

He dropped her into the water.

With a loud, unladylike splash, she disappeared beneath the current. Arms and legs thrashing, she finally righted herself, then came up sputtering. Quicksilver water swirled all the way to her waist. Masses of hair dripped around her shoulders, shedding ribbons of water down a shirt that glowed soft white in the waning light. Her features glistened. Perilously beautiful.

Brody looked away, hating his attraction to her. He took

the bar of soap from his back pocket and set it on a flat rock near the stream. Then he stripped off his shirt.

Jasmine watched him from her watery position. Muscles played across his naked chest when he leaned down to pull off his boots. Subtly, she licked her lips. Her own boots shifted restlessly in the squishy mud they'd sunk into. The moon picked out the slender, glowing line of the necklace he wore, showcasing the small ring that hung at its lowest point.

Wearing nothing but his trousers, Brody waded into the river. When he reached the deepest part, he ducked under.

Jasmine's teeth chattered. She bent her knees, lowering herself into the tide up to her shoulders. Cool water flowed across her body. Pressing against her chest and abdomen. Swirling around and between her legs.

In an explosion of droplets, Brody surfaced. He slicked back his hair with his hands and stared at her. "You cold?"

"Not at all." She ground her teeth together to keep them from another treacherous clack.

Funnels of water slid over the rounded power of his shoulders. One adventurous rivulet coasted down the center of his chest, gaining speed over his belly and finally finding its way home near his hips. What incredible hips. They looked to Jasmine to have been formed by a master sculptor: lean and muscled. She wanted to press her palms against his belly and then circle behind to test the defined sinew of his lower back.

He reached toward shore. "Give me your hand."

She jerked her attention to his face.

A dimple carved into a chin shadowed with stubble. "Your hand," he prompted.

Anticipation tightened her nerves. She envisioned him placing her hand on his stomach, just as she'd been imagining. His own palm would cover hers, adding pressure, sliding her fingers along the expanse of his warm, sleek skin.

Eagerly, she extended her hand toward him, palm up.

He dropped the cake of soap into it. "Wash."

Jasmine blinked at the soap.

"Be careful not to drop it," he added. "It might be a little hard to retrieve in this current."

He really *had* dragged her all the way out here and thrown her into the stream so that she could wash herself. He must find her truly filthy.

Angrily, she lathered the soap between her palms. What a fool she was. What an idiot, to have been standing here mooning at him.

She washed her hands, then rubbed the suds over her neck and face. Her sodden shirt hindered any further ministrations, so she finished by rinsing the soap away. "That's as much as I can wash in these clothes," she said.

"Then take them off."

She froze. Her fingernails dug crescents into the soap.

Brody's eyes glittered, even across the dimness. She watched his bare chest expand with his breath. He moved silently through the water until he stood before her.

He skimmed the pad of his thumb across the soap and reached up to her chin. Gently, he rubbed the suds into flesh that had been cold. Skin that now rushed with heat from his touch, from his breath.

"You missed a spot," he said.

She watched him, stunned by the tumultuous crashing of sensation inside herself.

His fingers stroked up the side of her face, holding her cheek with exquisite gentleness. Testing the feel and texture of her skin, his thumb moved over her nose. He closed her eyelids and outlined her brows. Then he traced the gentle slope of her earlobe.

Her lips parted. She opened heavy eyes to watch him.

His hands found the first button of her shirt. Almost before she could assimilate what was happening, he'd slipped the button from its hole. Breeze met pebbled skin. Another button slipped free.

What was he doing? This wasn't like the first time when they'd been caught together under slashes of moonlight. That time they'd been strangers, whose unexpected attraction had met the demands of plans and trickeries. This time she knew how much he disliked her. And she freely acknowledged the depth of her dislike for him.

He lightly caressed the valley between her breasts. Her nipples hardened, pressing against soaked cloth. Heaven, but she wanted him.

She felt a gentle tug as he lifted her shirt free of her pants. The last button opened and the two halves pulled away, exposing her undershirt.

Jasmine didn't have to look to know that the dainty garment would be transparent and sticking to her skin.

His gaze traveled to her breasts. Drops coasted from his chin, a chin that had been chiseled by nature and bravery.

She straightened her shoulders. A core, feminine part of her reveled in his regard. To be looked at with desire was a heady kind of ecstasy. For so long, she'd lived in a world where no man had aroused this part of herself, this needy, burning center. Now Brody had awakened it. And she wanted to weep with both joy and frustration.

She could never have Brody.

But in this moment, that truth was secondary. In this dark moment of water that reflected the stars, the man was all that mattered. Tall and laced with cords of strength, he stole her breath.

Brody bent toward her.

She searched his gaze as he neared, her pulse hammering her ears.

Their lips touched and the sound of her bliss was like a thousand shooting stars. He pulled her against his chest and snaked his arms behind her back. Supporting her neck with one hand, he slanted his head to the side and deepened the kiss.

Lust pulled and surged through her body. Too much. The feel of his skin upon hers. The pressure of his lips. The hand that slid along her spine and arched her breasts against him. They were the movements of a man who knew exactly what he was doing. It had become a game to him. Of domination.

She forced her head to the side, breaking the kiss.

For a prolonged moment he continued to hold her. Her mind, dulled with desire, staggered to regain balance. Frantically, she wondered what she would do if he didn't release her.

But he did release her. His arms withdrew from their snug hold, disappearing into the stream.

Brody's heart ached almost as badly as his pride. Jasmine didn't want him. He stepped away, the water curving low around his hips.

"Why-why did you do that?" she asked.

He inhaled, his breath hitching slightly. He had no reason he could give her. He knew only that he'd needed, just for one moment, to capture some of her fire. To taste it. To subdue it. To show her that he could control her as completely as she'd controlled him.

He'd been a fool. Whatever victory he'd garnered had been shallow. His body hurt for her now, speaking to him more of defeat than of triumph.

"You wanted to punish me," she accused. Her nipples thrust against the sodden fabric of her shirt.

His desire for her leapt, fueled by anger. It was his *right* to have her, if he so chose. He didn't have to answer for his actions to her or anyone. "You are my wife, Jasmine. If I wanted, I could lay you on the bank and punish you until Monday and no one could stop me."

Her nostrils flared. "You wouldn't dare take me forcefully."

"Wouldn't I? Be careful what you suppose about me."

She pulled back her fist and hurled the soap onto the rocky stretch of ground beside the stream. Using her arms for leverage, she fought her way out of water.

"There are duties that a wife owes to her husband," he said coldly. His own words sickened him.

She bolted up the bank, tall splashes kicking from her boots.

He had to make her pay for what she'd done when she'd tricked him into marriage. He needed to see remorse in her, or fear. Anything that proved he'd broken the shell of her arrogance. "I'll come to you when I want, Jasmine, and claim the one allowance this relationship affords me."

She stopped dead at his words. Eyes glinting a pale, diluted fury, she turned. "You mistake me, sir, if you think my name is Elena. I'll never surrender to you what she might have freely given."

White-hot talons of rage seared through his chest. He leapt from the stream and pounded toward her. Jasmine tried to flee too late. He caught her arm.

The fear he'd needed to see moments before flared in her eyes.

It brought him nothing. No relief. Only more self-hatred. "Don't say her name," he growled. Air panted from his chest. The talons sunk deeper, graphically reminding him of what his love of Elena had cost him. "Don't ever say her name to me again." Unshed tears burned behind his eyes. The frustration was unspeakable, the anger so intense it shook the earth.

Jasmine tried to twist out of his grip. "Let me go!"

"Never again," he insisted, holding her firm. "Never speak of her again."

She glared at him, rebellion pouring from her in waves. "Never," she bit out, "again."

His fingers released her haltingly, the muscles rigid.

Once freed, Jasmine tore into the darkness toward the

beacon of golden light radiating from their cabin.

Brody lowered himself to the ground and sat with his legs bent before him, his elbows resting on his knees. He laid his forehead on the bridge of his wrists.

It had been too much. To hear Jasmine, with her witchy hair and her unholy bravado, speak Elena's name. His past was as private as the most secret coils of his heart. No one breached that sacred ground. Especially not Jasmine.

Still, that was no excuse for his actions.

He'd threatened to make love to her against her will, for God's sake. Never in his life had he raised a hand against a woman. He'd always hated men who used their physical strength as a weapon. He'd tracked such men. Arrested them. Thought them bullies and idiots. What a hypocrite he'd been, to have believed himself above them. Now he was the bully. The idiot.

Jasmine made him crazy. She lit fire to his emotions and stirred his body and irritated the hell out of his mind.

Over the last decade, up until now, his physical desires had never compromised him. He'd appeased himself, when necessary, with whichever woman presented herself. But it had always been a loveless contract, in no way involving his emotions or his brain.

His body had deceived him the night he'd answered Jasmine's forged summons. And his body, heart, and mind had conspired to betray him again tonight. Even after what Jasmine had done to him, even with all the things he knew about her. . . .

He was starving for her.

Chapter 9

Lee sat on his front porch in a rough-hewn wooden chair, one hand resting across his stomach, the other cradling a cigar. He watched Emma dismount, neatly secure her horse's reins to the post, and cross the lawn toward him. She looked fresh, like the first stirrings of fall after the drought of a Texas summer.

He stood to greet her.

Emma reached the steps and set a boot on the first level. Her split skirt parted slightly. "Hello, Lee."

"Hello, Emma."

She swept off her hat and ran a hand through her hair a few times. "Jasmine's not quite ready to see you yet."

It was precisely what he'd expected, and exactly what he hadn't wanted to hear. He lowered his cigar and regarded the view of his ranch. He'd always enjoyed a quiet smoke out on the porch after dinner. Since Jasmine had left him, he valued this solitary time alone with nature even more. It gave him time to try and make sense of what had become of his life. "That's what I was afraid of," he said. The dashing of whatever small hope he'd been carrying cut worse than he'd thought it would.

Emma sighed. "She promised that she'll tell me as soon as she feels up to seeing you."

He nodded. "You want to go for a walk?"

"Right now?"

"Right now."

"Well. . . ." She fanned herself once with her hat, then smiled. "Yes."

The steps wheezed when he descended from the porch. Together he and Emma walked past the cowboy's bunk house. Then took the dirt-packed path that led to the open fields beyond.

Once again, Emma combed a hand through her hair. Sterling gray strands curled lovingly around her fingers.

The woman had some kind of wonderful hair. And he liked the way she wore it. No fussy knots or buns. Just a simple fall, cut beneath her chin.

She lifted her hat.

"Would you do me a favor?" he asked.

The hat paused in mid air. "What would that be?"

"Leave it off. I was just now enjoying your hair."

Her features softened with surprise. She missed a step and had to take two rapid ones to catch up. "My hair?"

He dragged on his cigar, then released a coil of smoke into the air. "I like your hair."

Her usually serene face illuminated with rosy pleasure.

Emma was beautiful. The thought occurred to him in a subtle flash of realization. It was something he'd never even considered before. Emma, his neighbor and longtime acquaintance, was beautiful. The idea bemused him. It was like waking up one morning, eating a forkful of the eggs you always ate for breakfast, and realizing that they tasted utterly delicious.

He studied her as they strolled down the path, their shoes crunching pebbles. "Why is it that you never married, Emma?"

She missed two steps this time.

He supposed he should feel ashamed for asking her such a personal question, but he didn't. Not after he'd spilled so much of his heart to her regarding Jasmine. "I hope you don't mind my asking."

"No. . . ."

"We're friends, after all. I assume we can be honest."

"Of course."

They reached the top of a rise. From here, land fell out before them in a tumbling blanket of green. Wildflowers, blue and fuchsia and yellow, sprang from the earth in wide swirls. Lee stopped and puffed thoughtfully on his cigar.

Emma halted next to him. She could hardly believe that she and Lee were out on a walk together. Less, could she imagine that he'd complimented her hair and asked about her marital status.

"So tell me," he said, without looking at her.

His profile was perfectly, gorgeously masculine. Tanned skin and strong features. A Jamison man surrounded by Jamison land. Emma struggled to control the weightless twirling inside her belly. "I never married because the opportunity never presented itself."

He shifted his full attention to her. "I find that hard to believe."

"It's true. There was a window of time, before the war, when I suppose I should have married. But no one ever made me an offer I wanted to accept." She tried to look uncaring. "Besides, my parents needed a great deal of help on the ranch. They didn't say so outright, but I understood that they wanted me to stay with them. They never encouraged me to wed."

"Didn't they?" Dark blue eyes observed her so completely that she felt stripped of clothing and secrecy.

"No." She knew they were both thinking of how he had strongly encouraged his child in the opposite way, with heart-wrenching results.

"Do you wish now that they had advocated a marriage?"

"Sometimes. It's easy to blame them for my lack of children, for the absence of a family. But the truth is that the right man never found me." She pushed a section of hair behind her ear. "Somewhere along the way I made a choice to be alone, rather than link myself to a man who didn't move me."

She didn't tell him that her body had been restless and hungry once, when she'd been young. Didn't tell him that she'd had needs before the demands and strictures of duty had intervened. The sad truth was that time and the constant denial of those needs had withered them. Only this one man, full of power and bluster, so cleanly, gloriously male, could still make her body yearn.

She loved him for that.

"What of you?" she asked. "Why did you choose to marry?"

His brows shot up and he chuckled. "Me? I've no idea."

"I don't believe you," she said with a persuasive smile. "You must remember."

He squinted toward the hills that somersaulted into the distance. It had been a boy's heart beating in his body back then. He struggled to recall what had been true for that long-changed heart. "I remember that Kathryn was beautiful. And I remember that she possessed a trait that strongly attracted me, a trait I was completely unfamiliar with."

"Which was?"

"Respectability." He brought his cigar to his lips. "I hadn't grown up with it. I'd never practiced it. I hadn't even known anyone respectable until her."

"How did you meet?"

The scent of his cigar drifted around them, capturing them in a fragrant bubble. He breathed deeply, enjoying its smell. "I literally walked into her. On a street in a little Pennsylvania town called Whitemarsh. She was the mayor's daughter, a girl who'd never even set foot outside the city limits. And I was a young man who did nothing but ride. I think to her, I represented danger and excitement." He gave Emma a wry look. "At the least, it was an ill-advised match."

He talked of it so seldom. Of Kathryn. It surprised him that the words came with such ease, that the memories no longer pained him.

They shouldn't hurt, he reminded himself. It had been too many years and his wife had given him too priceless a gift. He felt little for Kathryn now except appreciation for having borne him his daughter.

"How long were you together?" Emma asked.

"A year. Looking back, I suppose we were lucky to last that long."

"Why? What happened?" Her expression held such deep curiosity that he smiled.

"That's a highly personal question, isn't it, Miss Larkin?"

She didn't even blink. "We're friends, after all. I assume we can be honest."

Lee tilted back his head and laughed at the heavens. "Indeed, we are friends."

"Then tell me."

He rolled the cigar between thumb and finger. "Kathryn couldn't take the life. Her dream of me and my romantic existence didn't match up with the reality, or even come close. The days of riding were hard on her. The heat in the summer bothered her, as did the cold in the winter. Plus, she missed her family." He stuffed his free hand in his pocket. "Kathryn was feminine and dainty. She didn't belong with me."

"But then Jasmine was born. How could your wife have left her child?"

"I'm not sure." He sighed. "I know she loved Jasmine in her own way."

Emma's brows drew down skeptically over eyes the color of stormy weather.

He felt a strange urge to defend Kathryn. Mostly because

he knew he'd not given his wife the choice to keep their daughter. "I think Kathryn understood that while I might let her go, I'd never allow her to take Jasmine away from me. In the end, she realized she'd have to choose. Either a life with Jasmine and me on the range, or a life without her child, back home with her family." He shrugged. "She chose the latter. She ran away in the middle of the night with a horse and enough gold to see her home."

"And she's lived ever since in her little Pennsylvania town?"

Lee slipped the cigar between his lips. On a slow exhale, a curl of smoke snaked upward. "I suppose so. I've never heard from her since."

"She's never tried to contact you?"

"Even if she'd tried, she'd not have been able to find me."

"I don't understand. When did the marriage end?"

"End?" He regarded her through eyes that had seen every sorrow and every joy a life can offer. "As far as I know, I'm still married to her."

Tom set a plate of scrambled eggs, ham, and biscuits in front of Jasmine.

"You're a dream," she said to him.

"Why thank you, ma'am," he replied, tipping an imaginary hat to her. He returned to the stove and started filling his own plate. "What are your plans for the day?"

"The usual."

"And that is. . . . ?"

"You sure can cook, Tom." Jasmine sidestepped his question and attacked her breakfast with a vengeance.

Two days had passed since the unfortunate scene with Brody by the stream. Since then, they'd established a tentative truce. Brody hadn't suggested any more baths. And she hadn't taken his beloved Elena's name in vain. Even Tom had pitched in by covering for her whenever Brody gave her an order she couldn't stomach. Like doing dishes.

It was Monday and Brody and Tom would be leaving for Nacogdoches on Wednesday. She simply *had* to keep the truce alive until then so that she could escape this den of Rangers. Hourly, she reminded herself to behave. Her worst fear was that if she angered Brody, he'd tie her wrists to Diamond's saddle horn and take her with him. If that happened . . . worry tightened her throat. If that happened she didn't know when or if she'd have another opportunity to run.

Tom ate across from her in companionable silence, broken by the occasional rattle of a fork against a plate or the thump of a mug meeting table.

When the door squeaked open behind Jasmine, the temperature of the room instantly changed. She didn't have to look. Even without a visual image, she was unbearably aware of Brody. His scent wafted to her, mingling with the pungent aroma of coffee. The sharply clean woodsy fragrance haunted her. Every time she'd smelled it over the past two days, images of stars and a quicksilver stream had risen in her mind. His fingers massaging suds into her chin.

That's as much as I can wash in these clothes.

Then take them off.

She stared hard at her eggs. Her appetite waned.

"Morning," Tom said.

"Morning," Brody replied.

She heard his boots move to the stove and knew that he was filling his plate. Out of the corner of her eye, she snuck a peek. He wore a clean dark brown shirt. She hadn't seen that shirt before. Her forehead wrinkled. Just how many items of clothing did the man have to torment her with—

"Have you packed?" Brody asked.

Jasmine glanced at Tom, awaiting his reply. Tom stared back at her, raising his brows in question. Warily, she pushed her gaze to Brody. He turned with a plateful of food and looked at her.

The silence stretched. Surely he hadn't been speaking to her.

"Do you have everything ready for the trip, Jasmine?" Brody asked.

Oh, heaven. He *had* been speaking to her. "The trip?"

"The trip to Nacogdoches, for my brother's wedding."

She gaped at him. Then at her plate. Then back at him. She hadn't done one thing! She'd been sitting here eating her eggs. Eating her eggs *quietly*. He had no justification to punish her. "I'm not going on the trip," she answered, trying to keep her voice calm.

Brody's expression didn't change. Except for his eyes, which chilled to chips of ice. "Of course you are." He pulled out the chair at the head of the table and lowered into it. "I thought Tom had told you."

She knew the shock and horror showed on her face, but couldn't help it. "He told me three days ago that the two of you were going."

Tom cleared his throat.

Jasmine turned her attention to her friend. When she noticed the discomfort settling around his lips, her stomach began to churn. He was going to side with Brody.

"I'm sorry, Jasmine," Tom said. "It's my fault. I mentioned that we'd be going to Nacogdoches, thinking that you knew you'd be included in that 'we.' "

She pressed her lips together. Think! She absolutely *could not* go with them on their trek across Texas. "I can't go," she said to Brody. "I'm afraid the trip would be too exhausting for me."

He gazed at her solemnly for the space of three heartbeats. Then his lips curved into a lopsided grin. "Try another, Jasmine. I wouldn't believe that one in a thousand years."

"It *will* exhaust me!"

"Exhaust a woman who spends all day riding hell bent around this territory on her oversized horse? I doubt it."

Her hands clasped beneath the table, so tightly that her nails stung flesh. "Not only would it be exhausting, but it would interfere with my plans."

Brody took a swallow of coffee. "What plans?"

"Emma and I"—she wildly searched her brain for an explanation he'd find plausible and acceptable—"will be volunteering our time to Dr. Tifkin as he tends to the town's sick children."

"This weekend?"

"Yes."

He propped his elbows on the table. "Do you often help the doctor with the sick children?"

"I do what I can."

A chuckle rumbled through his chest. "You're an angel of mercy, Jasmine."

"Now, Brody, I'm sure Jasmine does those children a whole lot of good," Tom chided.

How mortifying. Brody laughing at her. Tom loyally trying to defend her lies. And her freedom once again lying like shattered glass at her feet. "Brody."

He took another swig of coffee. "Yes?"

"Please go without me," she said gravely. "I'd much prefer to stay here at Colin House."

All traces of humor drained from his face. "I'm not leaving you. There's no telling what brand of trouble you'd get yourself into if I did. Tom won't be around to make up stories for you. No one will be here to fetch you from the saloon or make sure you don't break your neck on that damned horse."

"I don't need a protector! I can stay here alone for a week without causing trouble."

"Sorry." He opened his biscuits with his fork. "I'm not leaving you." His knife sunk into the ham, carving it into neat squares. "We leave day after tomorrow."

Jasmine waited for him to look up at her. She formulated

more arguments and considered more pleas. But Brody fully ignored her.

Her hands clenched tighter. Nails dug deeper.

A day and a half.

If he refused to heed reason, then she'd simply have to escape before then.

Diamond's front legs strained forward. Her mane arched skyward and her tail streaked behind her like a banner. Her coat, the color of sun-struck cinnamon, glistened in the morning light.

Jasmine hunched over her horse and let the air pound against her face. The earth sailed beneath them in a dizzying swarm of beige and deep brown, speckled with gray.

The speed usually helped. Freedom almost always gave her a rush of exhilaration.

But not today. Her spirits lagged so low that not even Diamond, who was trying so hard, could lift them. That fact depressed her even more.

He's beaten you. Give up. The ugly refrain dogged her thoughts, tugging her deeper into despair.

He's beaten you.

Her self-confidence, so carefully cultivated by her father over all the years of her childhood, wavered. How could she hope to compete against Brody? He was smarter than she. Quicker. And fueled by a cold core of vengeance she didn't fully understand.

She'd made a horrible, *horrible* mistake when she'd married him. That error had jeopardized her father's safety and risked her only dream.

When Diamond coasted over a fallen tree, Jasmine lifted smoothly in the stirrups, executing the jump by instinct. The horse landed in a thunder of hooves and careened forward.

She forced herself to contemplate surrendering to a life alongside Brody. But she couldn't even imagine herself scurrying around the house, doing his bidding, cooking meals, cleaning, and washing dishes. *Dishes*.

She grimaced as she glanced toward the horizon to check the weather. Her attention caught on a circle of burned ground marring the earth beside her. Quickly, she checked Diamond's speed and directed the horse toward the fire ring at a trot.

Jasmine stared at it from her perch atop Diamond. The camp had been well positioned. A lake dipped into the ground just yards from the site and trees surrounded it on three sides, providing privacy.

Whoever had stayed here had chosen a spot far from town. She herself had only ridden across this remote land because it figured into one of her circuitous secret shortcuts.

She swung a leg over Diamond's neck and dropped to the ground. Her excitement nudged upward as she walked to the edge of the lake. A web of hoof prints scored the earth. Concentrating, she began to pick out distinguishing marks of size, shape, and horseshoe design. Four different horses had refreshed themselves here.

She strode back to the camp.

Diamond followed her, the tips of her reins dragging and bumping across the earth.

Jasmine knelt beside the remains of the fire and again studied the markings in the dirt. The ground was harder here, and she couldn't decipher much. She searched the grass around the circle. When she spotted a wet patch, she parted the strands and discovered a smattering of coffee grounds beneath. She dipped a fingertip into the blackened grit and found it to be moist.

Adrenaline began to pump. Her heart pulled in blood hungrily, then sent it surging through her limbs.

She stepped toward the fire.

Diamond followed, standing sentinel at her right shoulder.

Jasmine kicked at the coals with the toe of her boot. A

fine cloud of smoky ash rustled into the air, revealing a light pink heart.

Still warm. *Still warm.*

Jasmine gasped with laughter and joy. Still warm! Brody hadn't beaten her. Of course he hadn't. How could she have thought such a thing? Especially when he wasn't as smart as she, or as quick.

In one agile motion, she mounted up. "Come, Diamond, we're going home to fetch my things."

The horse responded by tossing her head and trotting in the direction of Colin House.

Jasmine could picture the thick brown saddle bag she'd readied in preparation for this occasion. It sat beneath her bed, quietly containing all the munitions she'd need for a long trip. She'd retrieve it, then race to catch up with the group of travelers. It mattered not who they were nor where they were going. Anything was better than her present situation.

She laughed and thumped Diamond's neck with her palm.

Today was the day she'd ensure her father's safety and in doing so finally get the better of Brody McClintock.

Chapter 10

Brody returned to Colin house later than usual, near sunset. Tom's horse was in the corral, lapping at the water trough. But there was no sign of Diamond. Which meant Jasmine wasn't home yet.

"Damn it." She'd disregarded yet another of his orders.

He frowned as he tended to his horse. Since when had he cared like this about the comings and goings of another person? Since never. He'd always kept to himself and afforded others the same courtesy.

But he couldn't bring himself to do that with Jasmine. He did care where she was, and when. And he couldn't make himself not care, no matter how hard he tried to control his emotions.

Control. He grunted derisively.

Lately, he had no control at all where she was concerned. He couldn't even manage to untangle her from his thoughts. All day long, she was in his mind. When he should have been mulling over the feud he'd been sent to squelch, he was thinking about her. Whenever he saw a jackrabbit sprinting like hell toward freedom, he thought of her. Whenever he looked at his hands, he remembered touching her.

He tugged the saddle off his horse. As he carried it toward the lean-to that held the tack, his gaze scoured the landscape for a girl riding her horse too fast.

Nothing. Only peaceful darkening vistas. Overly quiet.

He returned to his horse, led him into the corral, and latched the gate. As he walked to the house he stripped off his gloves, wryly thinking he might be able to make good use of them against Jasmine's backside when she finally arrived home.

Indoors, the smell of bacon and potatoes spiced the air. Lanterns lit the interior and the stove shed comfortable warmth. The atmosphere should have been welcoming. Instead it felt flat and empty without Jasmine. He stopped at the door to the kitchen. Tom glanced up from the stove.

"Have you seen Jasmine?"

"Jasmine?" Tom patted his hands dry on his apron. "No. I thought she was with you."

"She wasn't."

The worry that creased Tom's face sent anxiety uncurling inside Brody. "When did you last see her?"

"This morning."

"This morning?" He worked to keep himself still, to not panic. "Is that usual for her? To be gone so long?"

Tom's lips pursed. "She's gone most of the day, usually. But always before she's come home by now."

"Where do you think she might have gone?"

"Don't know. She likes to ride into town. And I know she practices shooting some, but she wouldn't be practicing now, what with darkness coming."

There was another possibility. One that suddenly seemed so blatantly obvious Brody couldn't believe he'd not considered it sooner. "Do you think—" God, the words came hard. He swallowed. "Do you think she left me?"

Tom sighed, his dark eyes troubled. "Let's not jump to conclusions. She may very well be over visiting Emma, or riding home even as we speak."

As much as Brody wanted to believe him, he found no solace in his words. "I'll check her room."

Tom frowned and continued wiping his spotless hands over his apron.

Jasmine's presence lingered almost tangibly in her room. He could smell her clean scent with every breath. See her belongings resting on the dresser, the bedside table, the windowsill. He lit the lamp on her dresser, feeling like the worst kind of intruder.

Everything looked exactly as it had the other times he'd been inside her room. He checked a couple of the drawers and the armoire. If she'd left, she'd taken very few things with her.

He extinguished the lamp and walked down the hall.

Tom waited in the doorway to the kitchen. "Did she take all her things?"

"No. But if she's not home in two hours," Brody said, "I'm riding to Emma's."

"Fair enough." Tom gestured over his shoulder. "Do you want to eat?"

"After she's home."

"I'll just set this aside for later."

Brody passed through the front door and came to a halt on the porch, his vision probing the encroaching shadows for sign of her. He leaned against the post. Straightened. Jammed his hands into his pockets. Raked his fingers through his hair. Cursed her. And himself.

Then he started to pace.

Four men. Two with long, dark hair falling down their backs. One wearing a white Stetson. One riding a fine chocolate-colored horse. These men were the travelers Jasmine tracked. Her new family.

They rode as if they'd been riding together for years, traveling in a long-accustomed formation. The man with the nice-looking horse led the pack and set a grueling pace.

The one in the Stetson came next, followed by the two with black hair riding side by side.

Jasmine could tell from the way they sat their horses that this particular pack of men wouldn't appreciate being spied upon. So she'd been scrupulously careful. For most of the day she'd followed their hoof prints, far removed from the group. Only twice before had she ventured near enough to catch sight of them.

This was her third sighting. Dusk had fallen and the leader had just chosen to make camp on the bank of a river.

From behind a grove of oak trees, she watched as the men lit a fire and began the chore of cooking dinner. She wouldn't approach them yet. It would be safest to wait until she'd observed the group long enough to categorize them.

Satisfied that they'd be stationary for the next several hours at least, she walked Diamond along the river in the opposite direction and found a secluded place to let her drink. The terrain dipped gently here, spiced with trees that stretched sinuous arms heavenward.

Nightfall didn't feel the same here as it did at home. In Tyler, she knew the land by heart. Every sound was as familiar to her as breathing. In this place . . . she cocked her head and attuned herself to the noises of the night. In this place, unfamiliar critters scuttled through the rushes. Shadows slid across the surface of the river in eerie designs. And the air teemed with unaccustomed scents.

She crossed her arms over her chest and reminded herself that freedom was going to take a little getting used to at first.

When Diamond had drunk her fill, Jasmine guided her back in the direction of the men's camp. By now it was fully dark and she could see the firelight burning in the distance, licking toward the shy stars. The network of trees between herself and the flames painted an elaborate black pattern over the blazing red.

She staked her own solitary camp a considerable distance

up the slope from the men. Trees and foliage stood between her site and theirs, protecting her from view. The men were also too distant to hear her, which meant that she could go about her business without being hampered by the constraints of sound.

After caring for Diamond, she unfastened her pack and peered inside. All her traveling items lay neatly within. She flicked open her bed roll, aired it, and then positioned it across a level stretch of ground. Her dinner consisted of a chunk of bread and a slab of the dried meat she'd purchased in town yesterday for just this purpose. She washed the food down with water from her jug.

Cold air slid beneath the covering of her shirt, pebbling her skin. Funny, she thought, as she yanked a coat from the pack, the night never seemed this cool at home. Nor this black. It made her uncomfortable, sitting in the darkness without light to warm her or brighten her surroundings.

She rose and walked toward the line of trees, until she could see the men's camp below. They all sat facing the fire, their backs propped up on their saddles. It looked like they'd finished dinner and cleared away the remnants.

Now, she decided. Now was the time to acquaint herself with her new friends. She glanced over her shoulder and confirmed that Diamond was sufficiently occupied with a snack of grass. The last thing she needed was for her giant of a horse to come trotting after her and alert the men.

Jasmine started down the hill. She chose her steps carefully, trying to set her feet on patches of ground that didn't skitter with falling rocks or crack with broken branches. The nearer she drew to the men, the more cautious she became.

When she was almost within hearing distance, she dropped onto her stomach and crawled as close as she dared. She waited, muscles tensed, to hear their voices fall into focus.

But only intonations arrived at her ears. Only meaningless syllables.

She slithered across another few feet of grass. The foliage grew lush here. She prayed that it disguised her well.

Again, she waited and listened. This time the dialogue was clearer, but still inaudible. She frowned and tried not to breathe. Aiming her face in the direction of the men, she pulled the sides of her ears forward slightly, creating a cup to catch sound in.

"I say we leave the coach alone, Carl," the one wearing the Stetson said to the leader.

"Leave the coach alone? What kind of a damn fool idiot are you, Mason? We've done the coaches a hundred times before," the leader replied.

"Yeah, but it's too soon."

"What's too soon?"

"Another job." The one called Mason rubbed the back of his hand across his upper lip. "I say we ease off for a while, you know, put some distance between us and the Rangers who's looking for us."

Jasmine wanted to hoot and dance in excited circles. Instead she was trapped immobile and her delirium forced to jangle impatiently through her body. These men were outlaws! She could feel the foolish grin as it snuck across her lips. Oh, bless the sun and moon and stars and grass and the sharp rock digging into her hipbone, even. She'd found herself a band of outlaws who were running from Rangers just like she was. Her luck had well and truly turned.

"How many times do I have to tell you that there aren't any Rangers onto us?" Carl, the leader, asked.

"I heard word—"

"No. You heard gossip." Carl's brown hair protruded from the back of his neck in a short ponytail. His wide forehead contrasted with small, deep-set eyes. "It's not the same thing as the truth."

Mason parted his lips to speak, then appeared to think better of it.

Jasmine eyed the other two men who sat silently within the circle. They'd shed their hats, allowing black hair to hang in a scraggly mass around their shoulders. Both were dark-skinned with eyes like chips of ebony. Mexicans.

All four men were dressed in showy fashion, with expensive made-to-order boots, finely woven shirts, and gleaming cartridge belts with silver buckles.

"Let's just continue on to Wichita, like we planned," Mason said hopefully. "We'll get us some of that whiskey at the—"

"Are you so rich that you don't need more money? Is that it, Mason? You so wealthy a man that you can pass up an easy score?" Carl asked.

"C'mon, Carl. You know I don't got no more than any of the rest of you."

Carl eyed Mason contemptuously. "Well, what if I'm not satisfied with what I got so far?"

Mason fidgeted. "But we done this exact hit before. They might be onto us, expecting us by now."

"Yeah, and horses might talk one day. Human bein's might fly. I can't be concerned about what might happen. We're doing the job. That's all there is to it."

Talk ceased.

Jasmine watched avidly from her grassy position. She tried to ignore the itch crawling along the bottom of her arm.

"We intercept the stage in the morning," Carl said, "down at the valley road. It should be there around midday. We'll take our positions after breakfast and wait it out. Everybody clear?"

"Clear," Mason answered glumly.

The Mexicans nodded.

Jasmine chewed eagerly on her upper lip. In the years when she'd ridden with her father's gang, she'd been taught that outlaws were like family to one another. Their lives depended on mutual trust, secrecy, and loyalty. Once she joined up with these men, she would become a part of that trust, that security. She'd be accepted into their inner ring. They'd protect her from Brody.

The topic of conversation quickly turned to Wichita and remembrances of the bawdy pleasures the men had shared there in the past. Easing backward, Jasmine retraced her creeping, crawling path. She made her way up the rise by hiking in a half-crouch and shooting looks over her shoulder periodically to ensure that the men hadn't spotted her.

Once back at her camp, she sat cross-legged on her bed roll and stared at the glow of the faraway fire. Unwarranted, a picture of Brody rose before her. A mystical cowboy with his dusty trousers and his hat situated so low that the only part of his face she could see were those gold-green eyes. They glowed. They asked her why she'd run away. They promised her that she'd never find the freedom she sought.

With a single shaky exhale, she thrust the vision away.

Wichita. It was as good a destination as any. When her band of thieves set out to rob the stagecoach in the morning, they'd discover that they'd gained a fifth and unexpected member.

She slid her pearl-handled Colt from its place at her side. Her fingers ran over it, finding comfort in the gun's cool contours.

This was it. The opportunity she'd been training for all her life. The chance to become an outlaw.

She rode behind her father, grasping hard around his waist and watching the scenery flash by as her derrière thumped against the saddle. They raced along a ridge and she leaned over, so that she could see the wink of the silvery river that snaked through the canyon. The wind lifted and twined through her hair. She laughed. Her father laughed, too, a song of pure, sweet joy.

Jasmine spun the gun on her index finger, then stashed it in its holster with lightning speed.

Emma bolted upright on the sofa the moment the first footfall hit the porch stair. By the time the knock sounded, she'd set aside her book. By the second knock, she'd snatched a shawl off the peg in the hallway and was hurrying toward the door.

She swung the portal open and found Brody standing on the other side. His eyes were dark and turbulent. His grim expression framed by the collar of his duster.

Emma rested a hand over her pounding heart. "It's Jasmine," she guessed. "What's happened?"

"She's gone."

"Oh, Lord." She pulled the door wide and stepped back so that he could enter. "Where?"

Brody doffed his hat and walked into the foyer, his movements spare. "Don't know. That's why I came here."

She closed the door and leaned against it. Brody was staring at her with such intensity that she had to glance away and take a respite before looking at him.

"Did she mention anything to you?" he asked.

"No, nothing." Despite his intimidating presence and the worry crowding in on her, she made herself think. "It's—it's not like her to run without telling me. She knows how much her father and I would worry."

"Could she have left you a note?"

"Maybe."

His jaw worked. "Do you want me to help you look?" Urgency radiated from his body like heat from a brand.

"No, I know where to look. I'll do it." While she scoured the downstairs rooms, Brody stood unmoving in her foyer. Her nerves jumped every time his hat slapped rhythmically against his thigh.

When she'd searched the first floor, she rushed past him

up the stairs and stood in the center of her bedroom. Where would Jasmine hide a note? Someplace where she'd be sure to find it. She checked the drawer where she kept her undergarments, her mirror, the top of her dresser. Her breath pumped. She tossed back the quilt on her bed, then ran her palm beneath her pillow—where it crinkled against a sheet of paper.

She yanked the small sheet into view. A note.

Jasmine had scrawled words across the page in bold penmanship, words that confirmed Brody's fears.

For a moment Emma stood immobile, hearing the slap of hat against thigh, trying to decide what to do. Jasmine's spirit belonged to the wind, too capricious and willful to catch. For years, she'd watched Lee try to pin her down, without success. Emma knew Jasmine wouldn't take any more kindly to Brody's interference.

And yet . . . Emma understood her friend well enough to know that Jasmine's fearlessness was her strength as well as her weakness. Because of it, she had a habit of rushing into situations that threatened her safety.

Emma combed unsteady fingers through her hair and descended the stairs toward Brody.

His gaze latched onto her. He cared about Jasmine. It was as clear to Emma as sunshine in July. She could trust him to protect her dearest friend.

Without a word, she extended the note to him.

Brody took it, fear and anger churning inside him. How in the hell could Jasmine and her unruly ways affect him so strongly?

Em, I've gone. I came across a group of travelers this morning and I've decided to ride out with them. Please tell Daddy that I'm safe and that I've gone of my own accord. I'll be back in a few months for a visit, so miss me just a little while I'm gone. If Brody comes around asking for me, please tell him that I'm never coming back. You might need to be firm on that point.

> *All my love,*
> *Jasmine*

I came across a group of travelers this morning and I've decided to ride out with them.

"Jesus." He'd driven her away. The realization hit him like a punch to the gut. He braced against it. "Any idea which travelers she's referring to?" he asked, searching Emma's eyes.

"None. What are you going to do?"

"Go into town and question anyone who might have come into contact with them."

She toyed with the trailing ends of her shawl and nodded.

He turned to go. Her fingers wrapped around his elbow before he'd taken a single step. "You'll find her, won't you?" She looked up at him imploringly.

"Yes." He loathed the worry constricting his throat. "I give you my word that I will."

"I'll tell her father what's happened," she murmured, releasing him.

Brody donned his hat and strode from the house. He knew he should only care about finding Jasmine because he'd vowed to steal away her freedom. But at the moment he didn't give a damn about his vow. He'd driven her away, for chrissake. If anything happened to her it would be his fault. Even knowing how much she detested their marriage, he'd left her alone. She'd jeopardized herself because he'd not watched her carefully enough.

He mounted his horse and the beast whirled toward the darkness into which Jasmine had disappeared. He'd not rest until he found her.

Jasmine shifted in the saddle, cracked two knuckles, and yawned. This waiting was tiresome. She'd hidden her horse and herself in this spot three and a half hours ago. Three hours and fifteen minutes ago, she'd become restless.

Diamond threw her head twice in quick succession, reflecting her owner's anxious state of mind.

"I know, girl." She squinted down the road toward where the coach would be appearing. "We just need to have patience."

This morning her brain had come fully awake well before the outlaws even stirred. As she'd watched dawn streak over the horizon, she'd pulled her coat around her and hunched over another meat sandwich.

She glanced at the rumpled state of her shirt. Wrinkles creased the fabric at the inside of her elbows and all the way up the front. It felt dank against her skin. Almost oppressive. She didn't like the way her clothes hung against her body when they'd been slept in. A bath was in order and a fresh shirt. One of Tom's meals wouldn't go astray—

She cut off her train of thought before it could go any further. How soft she'd become over the years! Ridiculously soft. Foolishly so. She snorted. How ludicrous for a woman outlaw to concern herself with such trivialities as baths and clothing and meals. Once she'd begun riding across the plains with her gang, she'd go for weeks without a bath. She'd forever be eating beans and biscuits.

She toyed with the reins. Fleetingly, she wondered how long she'd be content with a dirty body and beans for supper.

The sound of an approaching coach tripped across the wind. Her vision sliced toward the bend in the road. The sound grew louder.

The stage was coming. At any second it would round the corner into the shallow valley. She could make out the whine and creak of its wheels over the din of the horses' hooves.

This was it. The real thing.

Her stomach jumbled into a web of knots, but her brain

issued its commands clearly. She pulled her pink bandana over her face. An exhale collided with the cloth, feathering breath over her cheeks and lips. She rose up on the stirrups, checking their length and sturdiness for the thousandth time. Her hand flexed over the reins as she gathered them.

The coach jostled around the corner and into view.

Jasmine eyed the driver, noted the fitness of the horses, estimated its load, and calculated its speed. She verified that her second gun waited securely in its position over her left hip. Then she slid her six shooter from its holster.

Six bullets. To be used wisely.

One gulping breath.

Go. Go, she ordered herself.

She spurred Diamond into action. They sailed from the cover of trees and galloped toward the oncoming coach. *Position yourself wisely. Anticipate. Reply with accuracy.* The memorized instructions filled her brain, overran her senses.

The driver of the coach spotted her within seconds. He reached for his gun.

She moved first, aiming and firing before his weapon had even cleared its pouch. Her bullet sank into the wood mere inches from his shoulder. She envisioned a tin can flying into the air, spinning end over end.

Perfect.

The driver's shooting hand hesitated, then found his gun. He stretched it toward her. Jasmine veered Diamond to the side and ducked. The shot cracked across the air.

No pain seared her body. Diamond didn't falter.

He'd missed.

She goaded Diamond into a ferocious sprint.

The driver slapped the reins against the buckboard, yelling frantically at the horses. Within the stage, she could see the pale faces of the passengers turning to peer at her. She raised her weapon. They ducked.

She sent another two bullets whizzing into the driver's

seat. The distance to the coach diminished, until, in a blur of color and noise, it passed her. She spun Diamond around and galloped behind the careening vehicle.

Her gaze raked the valley. Where were the men? She'd positioned herself before them, knowing that if she were to gain their trust she'd have to make the first attack. As planned, she'd driven the coach forward, so that they could stop the team. Now she needed them.

Her heart raced so fast it ached. Where were they?

Like ghosts materializing from mist, four figures simultaneously emerged from the valley walls. Guns blasting, they converged on the stagecoach.

Her shoulders slumped with released tension.

The coach's driver unloaded a round of defensive fire. She watched the outlaws weave and dodge, daring their foe to have superhuman aim. He didn't. Soon the driver exhausted his ammunition. The Mexicans swept alongside the team, grabbing the churning mass of bridle and reins, slowing the horses.

Jasmine allowed herself a tight smile. For her first attempt at robbing a stage, she'd had a relatively easy time of it.

Just then, the unmistakable sound of metal rending the air droned past her ear. A bullet. She swung in the saddle.

Another coach raced toward her from behind, the driver standing on his perch, the horses pounding the ground with their hooves.

Two carriages. In the same motion, Jasmine lifted her gun and turned her horse. Using an identical tactic as with the first, she rode toward the vehicle nearly head on. The point of the driver's gun followed her.

She shot once at his seat cushion. The pillow twirled, feathers flew. In her mind, another tin can shot high into the air.

But this driver had cooler hands than the last, deadlier instincts. In the instant before he pulled the trigger, she pressed herself flat against Diamond's neck. His bullet whistled close, burying itself in the barrier of rock over her shoulder.

The coach drew nearer. She rode hard for it. How soon could she dart behind its cover? How soon would his aim find its mark between her ribs? Diamond charged ahead, muscles bunching and straining.

Again, the man leveled his weapon.

Jasmine raised her own. She shot once. Missed too high.

The driver tensed.

She narrowed her vision, seeing nothing but the can of peaches, placed on the farthest branch, testing her heart and her skill. She fired. This time the man's weapon flew from his hands. He bellowed with surprise and fear. Jasmine watched the peaches explode, the syrup arcing deep into the sky.

That had been her last bullet.

She and Diamond roared past the stage toward safety. As they flashed by, a gun protruded from the passenger window. Shots erupted around her.

Jasmine directed her horse behind the speeding coach, holstered her spent gun, and pulled free her second.

The massive carriage slowed with a jerky lurch. Then another. Jasmine kept her gun at the ready. She could hear shouts from the front, but didn't risk a look at her partners, not while a gunman had a clean shot at her from the coach's side.

Finally, the whole procession rumbled to an ominous halt. Women inside the coach were screaming, men whispering orders at one another.

Jasmine leapt from Diamond, stashed her gun in its holster, and crawled under the stage. Ever so carefully, she peeked up the side. The gunman's weapon no longer rested beyond the window's edge.

"Just wait," she heard a man murmur from within, "I'll

shoot him once he's nearer. Just a little nearer. . . ." A gray steel tip nudged over the side.

She spared a look in the direction of the outlaws. One of the Mexicans approached the coach, both guns trained on the driver, unaware of the imminent threat.

Without daring the slightest sound, Jasmine slid out from beneath the coach. She tucked her boots under her and balanced on the balls of her feet.

The gun pressed out two more inches. When the hammer clicked back, Jasmine sprang up. She wrapped her fingers around the barrel and heaved downward with all her might. The gun flipped out of the man's hands, spraying a bullet into the earth in front of her, then landing in her lap. She scooted beneath the carriage before the man could so much as catch a glimpse of her.

A stream of curses polluted the air.

Crouching in the shade of the carriage's underbelly, she listened as her cohorts robbed the coaches and their passengers of money and belongings. The smell of gunpowder swirled on the breeze. She should go and assist the others, she knew. But she needed a moment to collect herself.

Her limbs began to shake. She held the passenger's gun across her palms. A Colt .45, single-action Army revolver, 1873 model. The peacemaker.

She tried to control her breath, pushing it in and out of lungs that burned with tightness. It had been every bit as exhilarating and challenging as she'd dreamed all her life. But where was the rush of accomplishment she'd counted on?

The women in the coach were whimpering now, choking back hysterics. *She* had done that to them. She was responsible for the loss they would suffer today and she hated the pall that fact cast on her success.

Frowning, she stuck the weapon into the waistline of her trousers and crawled toward the familiar forelegs of her horse.

Diamond stood perfectly still where she'd been left behind the coach. Her eyes were wide and alert. Jasmine ran her hands over Diamond's nose and along both sides of her neck, assuring herself that her horse hadn't sustained any injury.

The Mexicans consolidated the stolen goods into two canvas bags and remounted their horses. Jasmine checked her bandana to make sure it still covered her face, then trotted Diamond out from behind the coach and joined the throng of outlaws. The leader cut two quick glances in her direction. With a flick of his fingers he motioned for the Mexicans to ride ahead. The two men broke into an easy gallop, taking the lead. The rest of them fell into stride behind them.

The leader turned to watch the coaches as they slid from view, twice firing in warning at them. Mason also emptied a few chambers in their direction. Following their example, Jasmine took out her spare six-shooter and released three bullets into the region of sky above the coaches.

Their victims slipped from sight.

Though the leader sent her another hard look, he didn't stop to question. He simply rode to the front of the pack and set a blistering pace into the wilderness.

Chapter 11

C arl, the leader, had slowed their pace over the last few miles. Jasmine watched with a mixture of anticipation and curiosity as he finally pulled his stallion to a complete stop. It was the first time they'd rested since robbing the coaches almost four hours ago.

An alcove of trees surrounded them, growing dense and close, choking off much of the sun.

Carl dismounted and stormed directly toward Jasmine. He jerked his hat from his head and held it in one meaty fist. "Who are you?"

She didn't move from her position in the saddle. Neither did the other three members of the gang.

He grabbed the side piece of Diamond's bridle. The horse shifted nervously.

"I asked you who you are," he growled. Before she could even formulate a response, he jerked her pink bandana downward, exposing her face.

He grimaced and leaned in for a closer look.

Jasmine watched his expression smooth with amazement. His eyes grew sharp and bright. "Take off the hat."

On a sigh, Jasmine swept off her Stetson. Curly hair, the shade of chocolate mixed with a glaze of strawberries, tumbled around her shoulders.

Carl blinked at her.

The gang sat their horses, speechless.

Jasmine kept her gaze fastened on Carl. To do otherwise would have shown weakness and she was intensely aware of how important this initial exchange would be to her future. She *had* to make them accept her into their circle. No other options remained for her.

Carl staggered backward a few steps and placed one hand across his abdomen. Then he began to laugh. Deep belly laughs that reverberated off the circle of trees. "It's a woman!" he howled.

She glanced uneasily at the others. They sat atop their mounts like statues, their attention firmly fixed on her. They seemed to be undecided between suspicion and mirth.

Carl swiped at his eyes, finally winning control over his humor. "C'mon down here, girl," he said. "Let's have a look at you."

She arced a leg over the saddle and landed in front of him.

"What's your name?" he asked.

"Lily."

"Lily what?"

"Of the Valley."

Again, a moment of tense silence that could have fallen toward anger or amusement. Again, it fell toward amusement.

Carl guffawed, then grinned, displaying a set of uneven, discolored teeth. "Well, Miss . . . Lily of the Valley. Or should I say Miss Valley?" Another bark of laughter. "Maybe you ought to tell us what you think you were doing back there, when you charged that coach."

"I was robbing the thing."

"Single-handedly?"

"Of course."

"You mean to tell me that you didn't know we were waiting for the same coach, just up the road?"

Her brows elevated. "How could I? You'd concealed yourselves."

"Then it was just a coincidence that we were all robbing those same vehicles?"

"What else? Had I known you were nearby, I wouldn't have ridden in alone, now would I? I'd have waited for your assistance."

He rubbed his knuckles through the hairy skin beneath his chin. "Forgive me there, Lily, but I find it hard to believe that you . . . that a woman would ride in alone."

Her eyes sparked with platinum fire, challenging him. "I'm a good shot."

"How good?"

"Good enough to shoot the second driver's gun out of his hands."

His lips parted in derision. "No way in hell—"

"It's true," said a voice behind her.

Jasmine's attention leapt to the man who'd spoken. The Mexican in the black vest, the same one whose life she'd protected.

"I saw her do it," he said.

"Couldn't have," Carl replied.

The man nodded, slow and deliberately. "She also stripped a passenger of his gun."

For a heavy moment, no one spoke. Carl eyed her with stark mistrust. "What are you? Some kind of rodeo star, or something?"

"No. Just a rancher's daughter."

He ambled back to his horse and laid a hand on the stallion's neck. "What's a rancher's daughter doing robbing stagecoaches?"

She shrugged. "Same as you. I'm in it for the money."

"What you need money for?"

"I have expensive tastes." Her lips curled into what she hoped was an irreverent smirk.

It wasn't true, any of it, about the money. Dollar bills

and shiny coins had no part in her dream. But these men would never be able to understand that. Money was their language.

Evidently her answers satisfied Carl, because he transferred his attention to his saddle and began freeing the cinch strap. "We camp here for the night."

His decision surprised her. They'd wait a whole night for the law and their victims to catch up with them? It seemed smarter to rest for a short stint, then continue the ride. "You don't think it would be best to stay on the move?" she asked.

Carl paused in his work. His wide brow furrowed. "I said we'd stay."

"But—"

"I said we'd stay." The look he gave her brooked no argument. "That's it."

The boys on horseback still hadn't made a move. "That's it," Carl said forcefully to them.

All three dismounted and began to talk quietly among themselves as they stripped their horses.

Carl hoisted the saddle off his horse and set it on a bare patch of land. Instead of walking directly back to his mount, he detoured toward Jasmine.

"From now on I'd be keeping my opinions to myself if I were you," he said. "None of us boys is going to be taking orders from a woman. Even a woman who wears pants." He leered at her, an expression he probably supposed would pass for a smile.

"Understood," she replied, though she had to clench her teeth to get the word out. She'd clearly offended his authority. If she wasn't careful, she'd alienate her gang before she'd even passed a day in their company. And she couldn't risk that.

"Where you men headed?" she asked.

He scratched under his chin again and she wondered if there was such a thing as beard lice.

"Up Wichita way," he said. "That where you going?"

"I might be."

"Well, I might be inclined to let you travel with us."
His hair lay mashed against his forehead, slick with sweat.
"I like you, Lily. But I'm gonna have to like you a whole
lot more to share a cut of our money with you." He pointed
his index finger upward and held it against his lips in the
universal sign of silence. "That means no more back talk."

A stale, mildly bitter odor drifted from him when he
leaned close. Struggling to mask her revulsion, Jasmine
mimicked his gesture. She laid her finger over her lips. And
nodded.

Jasmine sat to the side of the group of bandits, observing
them.

The campfire snapped and crackled. Overhead, the trees
rustled and stars speckled the distant heavens.

Shortly after their dinner of bread, flour gravy, and dried
meat, the men had pulled out their flasks of liquor. They'd
been drinking steadily for an hour and had grown louder
and more boisterous with every passing minute.

She hunkered lower against her saddle and pulled up the
collar of her coat. The chilling night wind brushed past her
earlobes.

When she looked up again, she caught Carl staring at
her.

He wiped the back of his hand across his shiny lips and
nodded.

She nodded back.

When Mason finished telling a particularly dirty joke,
Carl and the others laughed uproariously.

Jasmine frowned.

At first they'd spoken politely to one another, as if
acutely aware of the woman in their midst. But their stories
and jokes had become more and more lewd with every
drink. They glanced at her often now, with stark appraisal.

She told herself she was imagining things, being overly cautious and sensitive. But caution and sensitivity weren't in her nature. Which meant that if she felt threatened, she probably was threatened.

Flasks glinted in the firelight as all four men raised them to their mouths in unison.

Her fingers flexed over her gun. She'd taken it from its holster several minutes ago. Now it sat on her lap, safely concealed by her coat.

They were drunk. If they tried anything, she could easily handle their slow-moving bodies and sluggish intelligence.

She wiped her runny nose with her handkerchief. If only she weren't so bone-tired. Her limbs weighed heavily with exhaustion. Too little sleep had dulled her brain.

She blinked a couple times, then stared hard at the men. She'd simply have to stay awake.

Barely opening her eyes, Jasmine shifted the angle of her neck and turned onto her side. A soft moan escaped her lips. Not quite yet morning. Time left to sleep.

Even beneath the cover of her blankets, she was cold. Chill rose through the hard earth, penetrating the shields of cloth and clothing. Her joints were unbearably stiff and her back ached.

On the flush of an outward breath she forced her mind to blank and shut out the discomfort. Her fists balled the covers beneath her chin.

The quiet of dawn had almost lulled her back to sleep when her blanket lifted. Frigid air flushed over her calves and licked up her legs. Something pressed against her ankle.

In an instant, she came wide awake. She jerked onto her elbows.

Carl sat at the end of her bedroll. He winked at her as he stroked his hand over her knee.

Jasmine scrambled backward, out of his reach. Every one

of her senses honed to almost unbearable sharpness. She could see him too clearly. A patchy, uneven beard covered his chin. Swollen lips pulled into a lecherous smile.

Fear coiled in the center of her chest, its grip immediately choking.

He chortled at her—but the sound held no happiness. "What's the matter, not in the mood?"

"No." Shoving a thick curl away from her face, she forced her brain to turn, to plan her defense. "No, I'm not in the mood."

"Well, we can fix that soon enough." Carl scooted toward her. His eyes were red and puffy, his skin ashen. His gaze moved over her body, measuring her.

Had he slept? Probably a little. From the looks of it, he'd awakened recently and eased his suffering with even more alcohol.

The queasiness she'd felt the night before roiled in her stomach. Her mouth grew pasty. Where was her gun? She must have fallen asleep holding it. But she couldn't see it now, didn't feel the familiar bulk of it in its holster. "You're suffering the aftereffects of too much whiskey," she said, striving for a light tone.

"I know. I could use a little release this morning."

"Release?"

One edge of his lips tweaked up. "A little something sweet to clear the mind." He grabbed for her ankle.

Alarm spiked through her like a knife driving to the center of her heart. She jerked her foot out of the way. "Try some coffee."

"Had coffee."

"Try some more."

"I'd rather try you."

Jasmine jumped to her feet. But her legs tangled in the blanket and her balance teetered. She fell, her rump smacking against the dirt and her shoulder thudding painfully against a tree stump.

Carl captured her left foot. With a forceful tug, he pulled her across the ground toward him.

Her panic shot higher. This couldn't be happening to her. He wasn't really saying these things to her, grabbing her ankle. But he was. Her father would kill him. Her father wasn't here. No one was here. God, what was she doing alone with these men? Where was her gun? She couldn't fight them off without it. Yes, she could. *Bite back your fear. Think.*

She bent her right leg and thrust her hand into the interior of her boot. The knife she carried there felt solid and strong, reassuring against her fingers. Heaving it into the air, she pointed it at Carl, just inches from his face. "Let me go."

He arched away from the knife's point, but kept a firm hold on her ankle. She saw his vision focus on the weapon, sensed the dangerous change in his demeanor.

In one motion, he released her ankle and sent both hands streaking toward the handle of her knife.

Jasmine pulled the dagger away before he could grab it. Keeping the weapon aimed at him, she said, "Let's just go on with the day, Carl. Forget about this. Eat our breakfast—"

He lunged for the knife.

She whipped it in a circle and nicked a slice of skin off his forearm.

He didn't howl or grunt as she'd expected. Instead, he quietly examined the cut as it filled with a line of blood. Then he looked up at her, his eyes black with violence. "Bitch."

She gripped her knife even harder.

"Mason! Get up." Carl's order stirred the other man from sleep. Mason raised his head and stared at them.

"Hold her arms," Carl said.

Groggily, Mason pushed to his feet and took a couple steps in their direction. "Damn, Carl, I—"

"I said do it, you half-brain. Now!"

Resigned, Mason approached. She saw his lips purse and soften as he collected bitter moisture in his mouth, then swallowed. His gaze roamed over her, seemingly searching for weaknesses.

Like two hunters, she thought wildly. They've cornered their prey. Now they're circling, gauging the best time to pounce. Alarm closed in on her. She tried to think, tried to reason—"Come closer and I'll cut you," she warned Mason. She struggled to divide her attention equally between both men, her gaze darting back and forth.

Carl lurched toward her. She swung her knife at him. He pulled back. A fake.

Mason leapt in from the other direction and grabbed her wrists. He pushed back on them, burying her hands in the dirt over her head. She kicked upward in defense, connecting with the sensitive area between Mason's legs. He screamed. The pressure on her wrists slackened, but didn't lift enough to free her. Mason bent double on top of her arms. His cry of pain choked into a throaty growl.

Carl wrestled down her thrashing legs, trapping them against the ground.

Jasmine gasped. She tried to kick free. Couldn't. Carl's fingertips bit into her skin.

I can't move, she thought. *I can't move.* Terror hovered at the edge of her consciousness, waiting to plunge her into a black void.

The knife. It was all she had left. She twisted the blade toward the fleshy part of Mason's hand, which still shackled her wrist. Channeling all her might, she yanked downward. The weapon met muscle, cutting deep.

Another wrenching scream.

Mason's hold on her slackened.

With a vicious grunt she stabbed the knife at Carl.

He intercepted her arm and pinned it back against the earth. This time her hand slammed into a jagged rock. Pain carved into her flesh. She lost hold of the knife as it skittered beyond reach.

"Whore!" Mason yelled. He cupped his bloody hand to his chest.

Carl climbed on top of her, subduing her with the superior weight of his body. His sour scent filled her nostrils. She'd never seen eyes so terrifying.

She couldn't move. Fear. Bald, crazed fear leapt inside her like a caged animal, snarling and seeking escape. No escape. She twisted her head to the side, avoiding Carl's face as it neared her own. His smell made her gag.

"What's a matter? Still not in the mood?"

A sob broke on her lips. She thrust her head to the other side. Colors of trees, of dirt. Faces she didn't want to see, sneering lips.

"You know, I just don't care, Miss Lily. Don't care if you're not in the mood." She felt Carl's hand fumbling between their bodies. "It just doesn't matter to me."

The deafening explosion of a gunshot drowned out his laughter.

"It matters to me." The words were as harsh as the crack of a whip. Recognition penetrated to the center of Jasmine's frenzied brain. She knew that voice.

Carl twisted toward the newcomer, lifting much of his weight off her. She saw him reach for his gun and jerk it upward.

Another explosion. Carl's body absorbed the force of the bullet with a prolonged shiver. Then he toppled to the side, freeing her. Her range of vision cleared.

Brody stood before her. He held the Mexicans immobile, one under the barrel of his gun, the other's neck under the pressure of his boot. His second gun trained on Mason.

Brody.

Sweetest relief. It coursed up to her eyes, clogged her

throat. His figure cut a tall, unyielding line into the hazy hues of the surrounding forest.

"Should I kill him, too?" Brody asked, his gaze aimed at Mason.

Jasmine sucked in a mouthful of breath. "No. Let the judge do it."

"Fine." The tip of his gun nudged upward a fraction. "Get up," he ordered.

Mason staggered to his feet, still cradling his injured hand.

"Can you stand?" Brody flicked a look at her and then back to Mason.

She sat up so fast that dizziness muddled her vision. Sheer determination to prove her courage to him persuaded her legs to bend. Unsteadily, she rose to her feet. Her limbs felt stiff and dull. Nausea pooled in her stomach.

Brody nodded toward Mason. "Tie him up."

Jasmine glanced at the campsite and spotted a coil of rope fastened to a nearby saddle. She released it and approached Mason from behind.

Brody's unceasing aim encouraged the man to offer her both hands. His blood dripped onto the dirt near her feet as she bound his wrists behind his back. She strung the rope round and round, then between his wrists, not caring that it bit his flesh. Near the end of the length she knotted it off and stepped away.

"Now tie his feet to his hands," Brody said.

She pushed Mason to his knees and forward onto his stomach.

Jasmine bent his legs back and looped the rope around his ankles.

When she'd completed her task, Brody shifted his gun to the Mexican prostrate beneath him and lifted his boot from the man's neck. His victim wheezed into the dirt, but had sense enough not to attempt retaliation.

"More rope," Brody said.

Jasmine scurried to two more saddles and freed two more lengths of rope. They performed the same ministrations on each Mexican. Daintily, Jasmine dusted off her palms on her pant legs and watched as Brody stripped the men of their weapons.

When the task had been completed he strode up to her. Without meeting her eyes, he captured her elbow and led her toward the line of trees.

"What about them?" she asked, jerking a chin toward their captives.

"They're not going anywhere."

He delved several paces into the lush tangle of foliage, drawing her after him. The sun peeked over the edge of the horizon, dappling them both in the day's first warmth.

Brody stopped and gently turned her to him. Eyes of shadowy hazel gazed at her with such profound pain and worry that tears sprang to her own eyes. His powerful fingers coasted along her arms, bringing warmth and circulation to limbs long ago seeped of feeling.

Under his care, the queasiness that had plagued her since waking smoothed away. Cramped muscles relaxed.

He cupped her face in his hands. His features were fierce and stark. "Are you hurt?"

Her heart thumped. She raised her hand and showed him the gash where the rock had sliced through skin. "Only a flesh wound."

He took her injured hand in both of his, holding it with exquisite gentleness. Then he laid it carefully on his forearm. "Damn it to hell," he breathed, as he studied her injury.

"It'll heal," she assured him, her heart melting.

His gaze sought hers. "Was that the first time they'd tried . . . ? Or had they already. . . ."

She frowned. "If they had, I wouldn't have told you to wait for the judge."

An exhale broke from his lips. He shook his head.

Slowly, like the turning from night into day, a crooked smile spread over his mouth. "My God." Using the arm that wasn't cradling her bleeding hand, he hugged her hard against his chest. His fingers pressed her head into his shoulder. "I don't know whether to kill you myself or laugh out loud because those savages didn't do the job for me."

Jasmine released a hysterical giggle. His unexpected kindness, so undeserved and yet so badly needed, undid her. Within the security of his embrace, she began to tremble.

She felt the tears that had been brimming since he'd rescued her overrun her lashes and make tracks down her dusty cheeks. The fear those men had put her though had been terrible. Bitterly, she forced her mind to confront it. The black rush of horror when Carl had mounted her. The mind-numbing realization that she couldn't escape. The vanishing of her hope.

That moment of dawning realization and dying hope had been the bleakest moment of her entire life.

The strong support of Brody's arm tightened around her. Her safety was real. As real as this tall Texas Ranger with eyes that cast spells. How magnificent he'd been. How magnificent, with his gun and his commands and his unflinching control.

He'd killed Carl for her. The memory made her feel both grim and grateful. She buried her face in his chest.

"Let's go wash your hand," he whispered against her hair.

She rubbed her face on the cloth of his shirt, drying the tears. Despite her reluctance to leave his embrace, she made herself edge away in the direction of the stream. Before she completed a single step, he bent and lifted her into his arms.

Her puffy-eyed gaze shot up to his.

He looked down at her and grinned. "Damsels in distress receive some advantages."

His smile was so infectious, so stunningly handsome, that an unbidden laugh escaped her. The welling of joy ironed away the lingering blotches of darkness. "I'm no longer in distress."

He reached the stream. The hand beneath her legs slid away and her feet swung to the ground. "Then I guess you no longer receive the advantages," he said, his eyes twinkling like emeralds on beds of moss.

With a gallant inclination of his head, he turned toward camp. Just as abruptly, he swung around again. "Oh, and while you're washing out that gash, you might want to toss a little water here," he laid a finger on her forehead, "and here," he touched her nose, "and here," her cheek, "and here, here, and here."

Jasmine grimaced. "That dirty, huh?"

He tipped his hat to her. "Filthy."

She watched him stride into the trees, a string of soft chuckles floating on the breeze behind him.

Feeling her spirits lift, Jasmine gently cleaned her cut and then splashed water over her face and neck and arms. The droplets stood on her skin, making her shiver in the morning air.

Never had she been so glad to see her unwanted husband. The man could be churlish and overbearing at times, but heaven, he had a fantastic sense of timing. He also had a heart. He'd proved it by giving her his compassion when she needed it most.

She returned to the camp as Brody was releasing the last captive's feet. He'd left all three men's hands bound, so it cost him extra effort to hoist the Mexicans onto their horses. Mason stood at the edge of the ring, awaiting his turn.

Brody shot her a glance. "In my pack, I've got bandages."

She knelt beside her own pack. Her uninjured hand burrowed deep within. "So do I."

Brody lifted Mason's saddle onto his horse and began fastening the straps. Jasmine located the white gauze and wrapped it around her hand.

The sound of twigs mashing broke the peace of the tiny clearing. She looked up in time to see Mason sprint from view, his thick boots throwing pebbles.

"Stupid," Brody breathed. He abandoned his chore and ran after Mason, his strides gobbling the distance.

Jasmine snapped shut her jaw and ran after him. A long white string of bandage trailed behind her, bouncing and unfurling with every step. She watched Brody launch himself at Mason and tackle him from behind.

Both men landed hard on the ground. Brody climbed to his feet first, yanking Mason up after him. Mason struggled wildly as Brody pushed him back up the trail.

"Please," she heard Brody hiss to Mason. "Give me one more reason to shoot you. Just one more. I'm aching for it." Gone was the man who'd comforted her so tenderly. Returned was the deeply angry avenger.

She stepped out of the way as the men swept past.

Mason twisted his head to glare at her. "She's the criminal! She robbed the coaches down on the valley road yesterday!"

Brody stopped.

Jasmine stared at his back, watching the muscles of his shoulder blades flex.

He would find out about her role in the robbery now. Her breath jumbled into a knot halfway up her throat as she realized how much she wanted to keep it a secret from him. For the first time ever, he'd shown her a little affection. It was still so new and frail. And though it surprised her to admit it, she wanted to hold onto it just a little longer. She wasn't ready to see loathing in his eyes again when he looked at her.

Slowly, Brody turned, forcing Mason to turn and face her also. "And how would you know who robbed the coaches unless you were there?'' he asked his prisoner, his voice deceptively calm.

Mason's face crumpled with despair. ''She—she rode in first! She charged the carriages!''

''You expect me to believe,'' Brody said, ''that this lovely, fragile young woman of proper breeding is a bandit?''

Fragile? Jasmine thought. Her lips bowed into a frown. Fragile! Lovely she'd accept. Proper breeding, maybe. But even if the man was being fully sarcastic, he didn't have to attach a vile word like ''fragile'' to a description of her.

Mason sputtered. Frustration tinted his face red. ''Yes! That's exactly what you should believe! She shot the driver's gun right out of his hand. She—''

''Let me be sure that I understand,'' Brody said. ''You expect me to believe that this woman is a bandit. Furthermore, you expect me to believe that she shot a man's gun right from his hand.'' Momentarily, he paused. Then a bark of laughter filled the air, startling Jasmine.

''But she did!'' Mason cried. ''I—''

''Enough. I found the stolen property in your satchels, not hers. Keep talking and I might add kidnapping of this little woman to the list of your transgressions.''

Little woman! No. Now, that was almost too much to forgive.

Mason snapped his gaze toward the sky and moaned.

Brody didn't look again at Jasmine. He finished preparing Mason's horse, then pushed the man into the saddle.

She chewed the inside of her cheek. When Mason had begun telling Brody about her brush with banditry, she'd been sure that Brody would believe him. Instead, he'd painted Mason to be a raving fool and her to be a delicate belle. Though his tactics rankled, she'd not had to utter a word in her own defense.

Counting her blessings, she bit the edge of her bandage, tore it off, and secured it. Then she saddled Diamond.

The only horse standing unattended in the thicket of trees belonged to Carl. Very consciously, Jasmine had avoided looking at the man's dead body. But even without trying to, she knew that he slumped on his side. That his eyes were open. That a dark, wine-red stain marred the earth beneath him. A corner of her heart quailed. A corner of her heart was gravely satisfied. "What do we do with. . . ."

Brody looked at her. She gestured in Carl's direction.

"We're going to take these men to the sheriff in Sulphur Springs. I'll notify him of the body, and he'll send his men out to see to it."

She nodded and went to fetch Carl's horse. The stallion's perfect bone structure and sleekly honed muscles combined to make him a breathtakingly beautiful animal. As she approached, he stared at her with deep, dark eyes. His coat, the color of liquid chocolate, shone richly.

Jasmine raised her fingers toward him. He sniffed, then blew a warm breath over her palm.

She smiled and walked the animal back to the others. As Brody secured his saddle, Jasmine asked, "What's going to happen to this horse?"

He ran a hand along the stallion's neck. She knew he was examining the animal's worth, as she had.

"Whatever you want," he answered. He took the reins out of her grasp, lifted her into the air, and set her atop Diamond's back. Then he handed her the stallion's reins.

A thrill slid through her. "What do you mean?"

He swung into his own saddle and gathered the leads of the three horses with handcuffed riders. "I mean that the horse is yours."

"This horse?" she gasped, pointing to the chocolate stallion.

"That horse."

"Does the law allow me to keep him?"

He nudged his mount into a walk. The procession started

forward. He turned in the saddle and pinned her with his gaze. "I am the law."

She wanted to throw her arms around Brody and kiss him. If she'd been close enough to reach him, she just might have tried.

"I'm certain that horse is stolen property," he said. "Since we'll never be able to track down its rightful owners, you can have him. You deserve him after what the bastard did to you."

She glanced at the lovely stallion. He belonged to her! As she followed Brody and the others from the clearing, awe settled over her like a mantle. She'd just gotten Diamond a brother.

"Who is that woman?" Mason asked Brody in a low whisper. His eyebrows pitched together and he regarded her with extreme suspicion.

"You boys have just experienced the pleasure of knowing Jasmine Jamison McClintock," he said. "My wife."

All three of the men whipped their gazes toward their female ally-turned-enemy. Her hair fell in an outrageous tangle around her shoulders. Her grimy pink bandana still encased her neck and her features shone with dreamy euphoria.

"Your wife?" Mason hissed.

Brody sighed, blowing out a heavy breath. "My wife."

Chapter 12

Jasmine watched Brody's back.

It was a good back. Strong. Wide shoulders. The promise of finely sculpted muscle running along the sides of his spine.

Above them the clouds hung low in the sky, wide and flat, lined with gray. The late afternoon sun hid behind their covering, tipping the wind with chill.

Under her careful scrutiny, Brody tugged on the double sets of strings at the rear of his saddle. He released his rolled duster, unfurled it and shoved his arms into it. The garment fell long, parting at the saddle and draping down to his stirrups. The weighty brown fabric of the coat concealed his back from her.

Her posture wilted. So much for the one amusement that had sustained her over the last several miles.

All day long, since depositing the criminals in Sulphur Springs this morning, they'd been making steady progress southward toward Tyler. Brody had rarely spoken to her. Nor had she attempted conversation with him. In all truth, she didn't know what to say. Brody had deeply surprised her this morning.

He'd been concerned about her. There could be no mistaking it. He'd actually taken her in his arms and comforted

152

her. He'd held her bleeding hand as if it were a priceless diamond. He'd carried her to the stream.

Brody had done that. The same man who sat so straight on his mount in front of her.

She felt a wash of affection for him. That she didn't want to feel affection for him, and that she knew he didn't want to receive her affection, could not be helped. She could, however, ignore the attraction traveling between them. Brody was still a Texas Ranger. She'd no doubt that he would still hang her father if given the opportunity.

As soon as she arrived home, she'd get word to her daddy. Through Emma, probably. If she sent him a note through Emma warning him about Brody, he'd run. There wasn't much more she could do for him at the moment. She hated that it had come to this. The cost of her mistake would take an enormous toll on her father.

She ground her teeth, furious with herself. With Carl. With that fool Mason. How had she gotten into such a perilous predicament? She'd gotten into it by trusting the men to treat her as the men in her father's gang had treated each other, that's how.

According to what she'd learned as a child, no outlaw should ever turn on a member of his gang as Carl had turned on her this morning. The only reason she could credit for why'd he'd have done such a thing was that Carl had not seen her as one of them. He'd not accepted her as an equal and a partner, as she had intuitively done for him.

He'd only been able to see her as a woman. A diversion.

Jasmine fidgeted with the reins, twining them through and around her gloved fingers. She'd never given much thought to her gender. In her world, it hardly qualified. Her father had taught her everything he'd taught his cowboys. Nothing had been beyond her capabilities just because she was a woman. In fact, her father had led her to believe that she could accomplish anything she set her mind to. But with Carl and the others, her gender had presented an un-anticipated hurdle.

Next time, she'd not be so gullible.

There *would* be a next time. But she knew that she needed to do some serious thinking before she dashed for freedom again.

Inarguably, she was relieved to be heading home. Without a doubt, she hadn't felt the joyous exhilaration she'd expected to feel when she'd confronted those carriages. And there was no disputing that she'd made a terrible judgment call when she'd chosen her band of outlaws. These facts were true. And their truth puzzled her.

Freedom. Her heart's cry sounded distant. Weak.

With a start, she realized that tonight she didn't want freedom. She only wanted a bath and a change of clothes and for Brody to cook her a meal that didn't include a dried meat sandwich.

Brody wasn't going to cook her dinner, Jasmine realized. As yet, he'd made absolutely no move to unpack his pots and supplies. And by the look on his face, if he did see fit to feed her, he'd probably crush a bread roll under his boot heel, then kick it to her.

She'd watched him grow more remote with every creek they crossed and every meadow that passed beneath their horse's hooves. Since he'd chosen this spot to camp for the night, his seclusion had intensified. He'd withdrawn into himself.

Jasmine hadn't the faintest idea how to get his kindness back. Nor did she know if she had a right to ask for it. Or if she really wanted it back at all. Perhaps it was safer for them both to keep their distance. She knew how to act around him when he was angry. She knew nothing about how to handle a husband who got friendly.

His coat pooled around him as he hunched over the fledgling fire and fed a few more sticks to the blaze. Amber firelight brushed his shoulders and stroked over his face. She could see the faint lines around his eyes, the hollows of his cheeks, and the soft spot on his temple where his hair brushed back. It was a powerful face. Unyielding, yet heartbreakingly human.

Jasmine shot to her feet and averted her gaze. She didn't want to sit here ogling him. Anything but ogle.

Her attention panned the darkened sky. Purposely, she'd waited to take her bath, not wanting to parade nude around him in daylight. Now that night had fallen, the trees and the dimness would combine to offer her privacy. She should go. She should bathe.

She cleared her throat.

Brody kept his gaze on the fire.

"I—I'm going to take a bath."

He continued to stare moodily into the flames.

She waited.

He ignored her.

Jasmine cleared her throat again, this time more strenuously.

His eyes lifted to hers with deliberate insolence. "You didn't ask me for permission when you vanished with a gang of thieves. I can't imagine that you'd ask my permission for a bath."

Her nostrils flared. "I didn't ask your permission for a bath!"

"Didn't you?"

"No!" Unreasonable anger quivered through her. She knelt beside her pack and furiously yanked clothing from its confines. Her arms brimming, she stormed toward the river. With every step, the light diminished, cloaking her more deeply in the ring of darkness that surrounded Brody's precious little inferno.

At the water's edge, she set down her bundle and began stripping off her clothes. After each item she flung off, she shot a furtive glance at Brody.

He remained totally indifferent.

Wind swept past, singing like a living spirit as it drove the water downstream. Her teeth began to chatter. She tugged off her boots, stripped her socks from her feet, and then unfastened her pants.

Only anger warmed her. What an obnoxious man Brody was. How could she have given him any credit? Any at all?

Another look over her shoulder. He still hadn't so much as peeked in her direction.

Cad.

It had never been Jasmine's style to ease into a river. She had no patience for the indulgence of toe dipping or elaborate shivers. Holding her nose, she simply jumped in.

Frigid water absorbed her into itself. She stood up and sucked in a breath.

Quickly, she reached for the cake of soap. With firm strokes she pressed it over her limbs. When she massaged the suds into her neck she recalled Brody, in another river, on another night. Water swishing low around his hips. Droplets coasting over chiseled muscles.

She shook her head to scatter the recollection. Her fingers scrubbed behind her ears, then worked the soap through the thick mass of her hair.

The current pressed at her from behind. Purposely, knowingly, she turned, so that the river could flow against her chest and hips and thighs. It was erotic—that swirling pressure. Her body responded to it with heightening awareness.

She remembered Brody moving soundlessly through the water. Hands that mingled, stroked, disappeared.

With a choked groan, she struggled to get a hold of herself. Cease these disturbing imaginings of Brody. Just finish the bath!

Ducking her head back, she rinsed the soap from her hair. The sodden curls weighed heavily on her neck when she pulled herself upright. As she fought through the water toward the bank, she confirmed that Brody still sat beside the fire, unmoved.

Cad.

She mounted the grass and stood shivering in the darkness as she searched for her fresh clothes. Her questing grasp kept coming up with one sock and a clean bandana. She needed underwear! Another sock. The bandana again. The sock again. Her movements grew frantic. At last, her fingers swept against soft fabric. She grasped at it and thrust it skyward. The moonlight confirmed it to be her underwear. Jasmine donned both pieces, then pulled on her pants. Her shirt was in a tangle. She hissed and wrestled it onto her arms, only to realize when she attempted to fasten the buttons that she had it wrong side out. Frustration mauling her, she yanked it off, then aimed one of her standard glances in Brody's direction.

And froze.

The fire burned heartily. Two pots had been placed over the flames. Cheery light radiated in a golden halo from the blaze. But no man sat beside the fire's warmth.

She chewed the inside of her cheek. Her vision swept over the immediate area, making two quick scans. Nothing. Her blood quickened, then raced along her veins. She felt like a sinner being stalked by hell's invisible demons. Again, she scanned the scene. This time, her gaze stumbled over a black shadow leaning against a tree at the river's bank.

She squinted hard.

"Are you going to put that shirt on or are you waiting for sunrise?" he drawled.

Jasmine jumped at the sound of his voice. Her shirt! She was holding her shirt in her hands, standing on the edge of moonlight in her trousers and a body-hugging French camisole top. She scrambled with her shirt. It had been difficult to don before. The task of donning it became impossible now.

Brody began to chuckle. His amusement grew in direct proportion to her mortification.

"I'm pleased that my predicament entertains you," she said scathingly.

He responded with a sharp crack of laughter.

Her embarrassment washed away under the superior force of her ire. Snatching up the rest of her things, she strode to the fire and dropped the pile on her pallet. Here, there was light. Here, she could unweave all the twists and knots she'd inflicted on her shirt. She no longer cared if Brody saw. No modesty was worth humiliation.

With satisfaction, she noticed that Brody was no longer laughing.

In truth, Brody felt far, far from laughing at that moment. She had been arousing by the river as she'd attempted to dress, the outline of her naked form dark, against a palette of even greater darkness. She had also been humorous. But in the firelight she surpassed humor and was more than arousing. She was painfully, brutally close to irresistible.

He continued to lean against the tree, merely turning the angle of his shoulders so he could watch her. The feminine confection of lace she wore had been made to seduce a man's senses. It revealed the supple curve of her breasts and the dusky hue of her nipples.

Brody shifted, genuinely uncomfortable. He knew he ought to look away. But didn't.

Jasmine untangled her plain white shirt and smoothed her arms into the sleeves. Without bothering to turn around, she fastened a few of the buttons, then pulled at the band of her trousers and tucked in her shirt. Next came a thick pair of socks, her boots and a leathery black coat that must have belonged to her father.

Once her ensemble was complete, she plopped onto her pallet and sat cross-legged. Efficiently, she folded the dirty clothes she'd abandoned and stashed them in a compartment of her bag.

Now that she had nothing left to do with her hands, she appeared to be experiencing a minor crisis. She squirmed. Interlaced her fingers. Squirmed again, then cut a look at him.

She had eyes like silver. At night, they were never blue as they were during the day. In darkness they became gray like a flashing sword. The fine arch of her cheekbones displayed exquisite ivory skin. Her expressive lips were washed with a rich shade of pink.

She jerked her gaze away from him and looked around with what appeared to be mild terror for something to occupy herself. Her attention settled on the twin pots that rode above the fire. She stretched her fingers toward the nearest handle.

"Don't," he said.

Her hand paused.

"Have you had much cooking experience, Jasmine?"

She glared at him. "No."

"Well, if you had, you'd have learned not to touch hot metal pots with your bare fingers."

Her hand slithered back to her side. "I have very . . . hardy . . . skin."

Her words coaxed a smile to his lips. God, she amused him. What sort of woman rode the range in undergarments too fine for a nobleman's mistress? Or took baths in icy streams after nightfall? Or dared to raise her chin and aim those glacial eyes at him? Jasmine could be maddening, but she could also be damned endearing.

He pushed off the tree, crossed to their makeshift camp, and lowered himself onto the fallen log behind Jasmine. He leaned forward and propped his elbows on his knees.

"What are you cooking?" she asked.

"Tom packed some vegetables for us. I'm warming those and making bread."

"Almost ready?"

Snatching a rag from the ground, he arched forward and

slid one of the pots off the flame. "The vegetables are. The bread isn't."

Jasmine nodded, then leaned back so that her shoulders rested against his log. He watched her gaze turn to the stars.

The warmth of the fire burnished his skin, heated the backs of his hands, sank into his face. Their horses meandered through the grass behind them and a bird squawked as it coasted down river.

Brody lost himself in the delicate line of Jasmine's exposed throat. He could see the lacy top of the camisole at the vee of her shirt. It moved with the rise and fall of her breath.

His fingers twitched. He wanted to touch it, to pull the lace away from her peachy skin and taste her. She tasted like she smelled, he knew, like sunshine.

Her auburn hair glistened with the sheen of water. He would bury his face into the silk of it before crushing his lips to hers. Then he would unfasten her trousers and—

"We seem to be taking a lot of baths in each other's company lately," Jasmine said.

"Yes." His voice sounded overly deep. "I'd noticed."

"I don't recall inviting you to participate in mine this evening." She turned to stare at him, a wicked light of teasing in her eyes.

She's flirting with me, he thought, mildly amazed. "No, and I don't recall needing a license to watch my wife dress."

"But indeed you do! Said wife would be the issuer of such a license."

"Would she?"

"Most definitely."

He couldn't stifle a grin. "In that case, I suppose I'll need to apply for a license."

Her expression melted into lines of delight. "For which occasion?"

"All occasions."

"Certainly not."

"But you must. The spectacle of you dressing tonight was so graceful, so flawless, so feminine—"

"Enough!" Jasmine giggled. "Don't remind me. I've never in my life had such difficulty putting on a shirt." She smiled at him and he caught a flash of white teeth.

He held her stare.

Gradually her smile faded. Understanding passed between them, a pulsing acknowledgment of mutual desire.

"You are going to watch me bathe whenever you please, aren't you?" she asked in a breathy whisper.

He watched her lips move as she spoke, read the hesitant invitation in them. His gut ached for her. "Hell, yes."

They were so close, leaning toward one another. His need of her strained, blotting out logical thought. Only Jasmine existed. Jasmine with the smile that made his heart turn over.

He bent his head and touched his lips to hers. Little more than a graze. He heard her response in the gasp of her breath. Heat coursed through his body.

He pulled her onto his lap and kissed her again. This time her lips parted for him. She knew what was coming. The realization throbbed through his brain in the instant before his tongue plunged deep.

In the cocoon of his embrace, Jasmine writhed. The sensations were thickening, spinning through her, daring her to abandon herself completely.

Almost roughly, he parted the heavy obstacle of her father's coat. His hands lifted and caressed her breasts, then pressed down her sides. He was measuring the swell of her hips, molding her buttocks against his thighs. She could feel the hard evidence of his arousal. She loved the feel of him. Everything about him.

She put her soul into the kiss, holding nothing back. They tasted each other so fully that her hunger for him became a whirring void. No self-consciousness left.

Jasmine twined her arms behind his neck and pulled him nearer, wanting him inside her very being. Her breasts arched into his chest. The tight buds of her nipples pined against the restraining lace of her camisole. Her fingers buried into his hair, then pressed along both sides of his face.

Brody.

She pulled back a little, breathing harshly. For a prolonged moment, she didn't open her eyes. She simply gloried in the closeness. His nose against hers. Lips a hair's breadth apart. Foreheads touching. Sweet, seeking longing.

She needed to see the fire in his eyes. Her fire. For a moment, she embraced the anticipation. Then, cupping his face, she opened her eyes. She saw cheeks tinged with color. Eyes so crushingly beautiful that she wanted to kiss them and weep over them at the same time.

Brody regarded her with utter stillness, smoky desire clouding his features.

This man. This man of power and stark beauty. He kissed her with achingly sweet passion. He wanted her. He shared her pounding, yearning need.

A desperate sob clogged her throat. She stroked her palms down his chest, over the stiff knit of his man's shirt. And lower. Over his hips and along his thighs.

His eyelids drifted closed. She shut off her own vision and leaned into him again. Her lips sought and found his. Soft and warm. She kissed him. Opened her mouth. Ran her tongue hesitantly over his bottom lip.

He didn't kiss her back.

She moaned gently, hating him for this game. Reveling in the intensifying knot of lust in her core.

He turned his head to the side.

She laid her temple against his cheek. What was he doing? Her foggy brain had lost its reason in the pounding of her blood.

Brody's muscles turned rigid beneath her.

Still, she waited, longing for his caress. At any moment

his fingers would find her, she knew. Her whole body waited for that touch, nerves strung so tight they burned.

Nothing.

Worry whispered through her. Something was wrong.

She sat back so that she could look at him. He stared blankly into the woods, his profile clean. Wanting to soothe away whatever demons troubled him, she lifted her hand to his cheek with a feather-soft stroke.

He flinched.

His reaction cut to the center of her heart. She dropped her hand.

He didn't speak. He didn't need to.

The reality of what she'd done to him when she'd trapped him into marriage wove through the air between them. Elusive and yet so real Jasmine could almost feel the lethal edge of it as it whispered past her.

She couldn't reach Brody now. He was lost to her.

Tears of misery stung her eyes. Her gaze moved over him, seeing him as what he was. A man she couldn't touch. He didn't belong to her. Could never. To him, she would always be the cruel child who had forced him into a marriage he didn't want.

She scrambled off him and crawled over the narrow space to her pallet. Her knees drew up against her chest and she wrapped her arms around them. Resting her chin on her knees, she fixed her gaze on the fire.

Alone. Completely. No touching or looking at him. Cold. This was how she wanted it, to be separate. Wed to a man who hated her. This was the fate she'd chosen. She huddled into herself, coveting her agony, letting it hack deep gashes into her fragile hope.

This uninvited attraction she harbored for Brody had started off subtle. But now, tonight, it churned within her, terrifyingly strong, a force she could no longer ignore. Tonight it had compromised her power.

Clearly, Brody experienced no such struggle. He manipulated whatever desire he felt toward her, toying with it when it suited him. Cutting it off when it became the least bit intrusive.

Her quest for independence had just taken on a new aspect. No longer was it only about freeing herself from the bonds of an overprotective father and a repressive little town. Now she needed freedom with fresh desperation. For the sake of her own sanity, she had to rid herself of this husband who beckoned to her and pushed her away in the same sweet second.

She heard him stirring. He walked into her line of vision and lifted the remaining pot from the flames.

She couldn't bear looking at him, so she kept her gaze trained on the fire. Sightlessly, she stared into the golden ribbons of heat. Her silence was total. Inside and out.

Vaguely, she was aware of him shifting pots, filling plates. When he leaned forward and set her food in front of her, she smelled his sharp, woodsy smell. Like evergreen. It was a smell she'd inhaled into herself. A smell she'd breathed when his tongue was claiming hers.

Brody retreated and his scent curled away. He carried his plate to the other side of the fire and sat on a tall, flat rock. He placed one boot against the rock's front, so that his knee supported his plate.

Jasmine tried to ignore him. At the same time, she couldn't help being overwhelmingly aware of him. She heard his fork scrape his plate, then settle onto its rim.

His gaze weighed on her like a physical thing. "You better eat something," he said. "I don't want you to be hungry."

She almost laughed at his audacity. He'd rejected her entirely, cut her to pieces, and then proclaimed to worry over something as minor as her hunger. Bitterness forced her attention from the fire to the man. She resented everything about him. His refusal to release her, his highhanded tactics, his handsomeness. She found herself regretting that he'd come after her and begrudging him the fact that he'd been able to track her down. No mortal man should have been able to locate her so quickly. "How did you find me?" she asked, her lips tight.

He looked reluctant to answer.

"How did you find me this morning?" she repeated.

"Is that really what you want to ask me, Jasmine?"

"Yes, it really is."

He frowned and set his plate on the ground. When he straightened, he crossed his arms, the fingers of one hand looping over the opposite bicep. Her gaze fixed on those fingers. Fingers that had stroked her breasts, run along her hips, cupped her buttocks.

"I talked to Mr. Simpkins at the general store the night you left," he said.

She pushed her stare from his hands to his face.

"I figured any band of travelers who'd come through Tyler would have taken the opportunity to restock their supplies."

"How did you know that I was with a band of travelers?"

"Emma showed me the note, Jasmine."

Emma? She'd left that note for her dearest friend, trusting her not to show Brody. In fact, she remembered specifically asking Emma to tell Brody that she wasn't coming back. Betrayal swirled though her, sharpening her aloneness. "Why would she do such a thing?"

"Probably so that I could save you from a fate like the one you were on the verge of this morning."

She hated the reminder of her weakness. Worse, she couldn't argue with his logic. "Someone in the gang had spoken with Mr. Simpkins?" she asked, needing to stay on the subject.

"Yes. Simpkins talked with Mason. Evidently, Mason was hungry for conversation, because he chattered for a long time, even informed Simpkins they were headed to Wichita.''

"That doesn't begin to explain how you found us. There's a lot of territory between Tyler and Wichita.''

Brody shrugged. "Only one widely used trail. I took it, assuming that if you'd joined up with a respectable group they'd have chosen it.''

"They didn't.''

"No. They weren't respectable.''

Everything he said slighted her pride and brought a sour taste to her mouth. She was acutely aware of how much this whole debacle brought into question her judgment and her ability to fend for herself.

"I stopped in Quitman and met with the sheriff,'' Brody said. "He told me they'd just had a stagecoach robbery a few miles up the road. I guessed then that I'd found the gang I sought. And you.''

"But even from the point of the robbery,'' she argued, "we rode a long way—''

"Not long enough.''

She clamped her lips together. "That's what I told them.''

His brows drew down with displeasure. "Near the site of the robbery, I came across your tracks. Predictably, they headed north toward Wichita. By dawn I'd caught up with you.''

"I commend you on your timing.''

His arms unlocked from their clasped position. His hands fisted. "It's nothing to joke about. What you did was defiant and thoughtless and incredibly dangerous.''

There, she thought, he's chastised me directly. Somehow, that gratified her. "I didn't ask you to come after me.''

His body grew incredibly still. The only indication of the anger within him was his eyes. They raged at her like red-hot coals. "There seems to be something that you don't understand yet, Jasmine. We are married. I am the husband you chose."

Her jaw clenched.

"And you're going to have to live with the consequences of your choice. I promised you that I'd never allow you to taste freedom. I meant it."

She rocked onto her toes and pressed up to standing. "What does my freedom matter to you?" she demanded. "Let me go! With my freedom comes yours."

He slapped the back on his hand into the opposite palm. "I gave a vow when I married you. And if you think it means nothing to me, then you're a greater fool than I thought you were."

"I am no fool, Brody McClintock!"

"No? Then you're a spoiled, arrogant brat."

She rushed at him. Her arm pulled back. The violence of her emotions carried her away and she slapped him across the face with furious force.

Brody let her hit him. He didn't shield himself or catch her hand. The stinging slap of her palm snapped his face to the side.

He held himself motionless long after she'd dropped her hand. While he glared into the darkness, she listened to the whoosh of his breath and the dense thud of her own heart.

God, what had she just done?

By degrees, Brody turned his chin toward her.

She didn't flinch or look away, even though ire and indecision swam through her brain.

"I'll never let you go," he said. "If you run away from me again, I'll track you down. Do you understand me?"

She held her tongue, mistrusting it.

"Don't try to escape from me again."

She sensed that his anger trembled on the precipice. She wanted him to loose control, as she had. To disgrace himself in front of her. "I can make no such guarantee."

"If you test me again you'll regret it."

"Will I?"

"Yes."

"What are you going to do, Brody? Whip me?"

His gaze raked her face. "You'd like me to. Because then you'd have cause to hate me." He swung on his heel and strode from the campsite. His boots pounded against the earth before he vanished into a mantle of night.

"I already have cause to hate you," she whispered.

Chapter 13

Jasmine banged in the front door of Colin House, jolting Tom awake from his mid-afternoon nap.

"Jasmine!" he sputtered.

She smiled an apology at him and strode across the living room. In the kitchen, she began rifling through the cupboards for a snack. Four days of ceaseless riding had made her hungry.

Tom followed her, stalling in the kitchen doorway, his sleepy expression a jumble of wonder and relief. "Jasmine!"

"Hello, Tom." She slid aside two glass jars of plum jelly and located the cookie tin. Inside, she found the crumbling remains of one and a half sugar cookies.

"How've you been?" he asked.

"Oh, fine."

Tom grinned and shook his head in amazement. "What have you done with Brody?"

"I slayed him. It took a little doing, but I managed it." She tilted her head back and popped a handful of crumbs into her mouth.

"Slayed him, did you?"

"Yep."

Tom chuckled, then walked fully into the room and picked up the kettle. "Care for some coffee with that?"

"Yes, please."

The front door whooshed open and closed.

Tom looked over his shoulder at her, his brows elevated.

She frowned and shrugged. "Troublesome man." Her fingers scooped more cookie. "Wouldn't stay dead."

The moment Brody strode into the kitchen, all pleasantness fled. In its place came the arctic gale she'd been enduring since he'd stalked into the forest last night.

Jasmine amended her position, leaning her hip on the cupboard and facing her beloved Tom. At least one of her housemates was a kind, loving, handsome man. Shame it couldn't have been her husband.

"Welcome back," Tom said to Brody.

A belligerent grunt was the only response.

Tom slid a questioning look at her. She wrinkled her nose to indicate Brody's temper.

"Are you hungry?" Tom asked.

"Yes," Brody replied.

"Well, Jasmine has some . . ."

Both men's attention fell upon her. Lifting one delicate brow, she tilted the tin in Brody's direction. Three minuscule crumbs littered the bottom.

"Jasmine *had* some cookies," Tom said.

Deliberately, she licked her fingers.

"Do you want me to fix you up some bread or something?" Tom asked.

"No, coffee will do until dinner." When Brody pulled out the chair, its legs scored across the flooring.

"So . . . what happened out there?" Tom asked.

Jasmine knew Brody was staring at her, waiting for her to explain, but she refused to bow to his silent pressure. If he wanted to tell his friend the gory details, then he was on his own.

"I caught up with them near Sulphur Springs," Brody finally answered. "Our Jasmine here was robbing stagecoaches with a gang of outlaws."

Her attention sliced to him.

He smiled. A slow, knowing grin that taunted her. Casually, he stretched out his legs and crossed muddy boots at the ankles.

She thought he hadn't believed the story Mason fed to him about her! Why, he'd laughed at Mason! Called her lovely and fragile and a woman of proper breeding.

She could now see in his cool hazel eyes that he believed her to be none of those things. Not one.

Tom, wearing a troubled expression, carried the pot to the table and filled three mugs. "Robbing coaches?" he asked.

"Not only robbing coaches, but leading the charge, it seems, riding into fire head on."

Dazedly, Tom plunked the kettle back onto the stove. He gaped at her, those wrinkles she loved knitting worried lines into his bronzed skin.

Heat rolled up her neck, gaining speed and force when it reached her chin, exploding into a ball of fire along her cheeks.

"And not only leading the charge," Brody continued, "but shooting the driver's gun right out of his hand."

Tom let out a low whistle.

The fireball of her cheeks set ablaze her forehead and scalp.

"I had a talk with the boys on their way to jail. Seems they didn't even know she was a woman until hours after the fact."

Jasmine knew that within her boots, her toes were blushing.

Brody picked up his cup, sniffed at the brew appreciatively, then took a sip. "I'd no idea that she was such a good shot. For our own safety, Tom, I guess we'll have to limit her target practice in the future. Hate to have my wife riding around, shooting my gun out of my hand."

"Might be a little embarrassing," Tom agreed. He gave

Jasmine a teasing smile as he lowered himself into a chair.

She hated Brody. He and his traitorous sidekick could both rot. Her instincts tore between storming from the room and waiting long enough to take the sip of coffee she dearly needed in order to wash down the wad of sugar cookie lodged beside her windpipe.

"We're behind schedule for our trip to Nacogdoches," Tom said. "You intend for us to leave tonight?"

"Is everything ready?"

"Yes."

"Then an hour should be long enough to eat and rest."

The ghastly news hit Jasmine like a hammer between the eyes. "We—we're still going?"

"My brother's getting married," Brody said. "Yes, we're still going."

The dreaded trip. Leaving in an hour. She couldn't imagine meeting Brody's family, shaking hands with them and sharing small talk, pretending to be civil to a husband she'd flee from at the soonest opportunity. "But—"

"We're all aware of your disregard for marriage, Jasmine," Brody said. "But I'm guessing that marriage is still a fairly important institution to Clay. I'm going to be there for him and so are you. We leave in an hour."

Very carefully, she turned and set the cookie tin in its place. She could feel the blood that had so recently lit her cheeks seeping from her face.

"And bring a dress," Brody said.

Grinding her teeth, she scooped her cup from the table and stalked toward the door and freedom.

"Oh, and Lily . . ."

She halted so suddenly that coffee swished over the rim of her cup and scalded her thigh.

"Miss Valley. . . ."

Her neck muscles throbbed as she faced Brody.

He looked devilishly handsome with that ridiculous cleft in his chin and his sandy brown hair a short, riotous mess.

Eyes of glinting green-gold mocked her. "You have a crumb," he pointed to the edge of his chin, "right here."

With a disgusted hiss, she threw the kitchen door aside and stormed through. The living room and hall sailed past in a collage of color. She turned into her room. After kicking the door shut with her heel, she leaned against it.

Her sanctuary. She tried to ease her temper by focusing instead on the calm of her surroundings. This room had belonged to her such a short time, but already it welcomed her, offering comfort and empathy. Her own quilt covered the bed. Her monogrammed silver hairbrush and mirror sat atop the dresser next to a stack of books she'd had since she was a child.

Dismally, she brushed the crumb from her chin, then raised the cup to her lips and swallowed several sips of the pungent liquid. It slid into her belly, renewing her.

She simply couldn't go to Nacogdoches. If she did, she feared that she'd never be able to fight free of Brody.

Her gaze scanned the collection of furniture that filled the space. Mentally, she measured each item, wondering how long she could withstand an offensive from behind a barricade of furniture.

Not long. Physical objects would be no match for Brody, especially considering that she'd also have to repel his forces from the two windows.

She needed something that was beyond physical manipulation. In desperation, she set down her cup and threw open the doors to her armoire. The first garment she spotted was the voluminous white nightie that Emma had given her last Christmas. She'd worn it all four days last winter when she'd had the flu. . . .

Her lips slowly elevated into a smile.

She started unfastening the row of buttons down the front of her shirt. She wedged her boots from her feet and sent them on a circling flight into the corner. Her first experimental cough rumbled through her chest.

Flu! Stifling a victorious giggle, she tossed her shirt onto the floor. Brody and his high-handed control already made her ill. A touch of flu wouldn't even be hard to feign.

Jasmine's cough was guttural and racking. She prolonged it to such an anguishing degree, that Brody was amazed.

He stood outside her door, his boot heel grinding into the floor boards. With equal measures of irritation and impatience, he wondered what in the hell to do with her.

She was faking this sickness, of course. That she would attempt such a stunt on the cusp of their departure only solidified his opinion of her. His beautiful wife was headstrong to the point of self-destructiveness.

Not for one instant during their exchange of the past night had Jasmine crumbled. Instead she'd confronted him, baited him, yelled at him. She'd made him furious. But despite himself, she'd also impressed him. With her pride and fervor and wild courage. No woman of his acquaintance had ever shown him such heart. He'd not even known such a brazen brand of woman existed until the lantern had been lit in the darkened shack and he'd turned to see Jasmine blinking up at him.

She was the witch who had tricked him into marriage, shattered his most solemn lifelong vow, and plunged him into a world that no longer had clear edges of black and white. He wanted to hate her because of it, to punish her. But he also wanted to make slow, sweet love to her so that he could watch her unforgettable aquamarine eyes explode with wonder.

She'd sat on his lap by the fire last night and touched his cheek with heartbreaking tenderness. Never had he wanted to hurt her less. Never had it been more important to withstand her.

So he'd withstood her. His gut had tightened beyond bearing and he'd finally had to stalk away so that he could rein in the dangerous mixture of anger and lust she inspired in him.

All day today, as he'd ridden before her, he'd wondered who he'd hurt more. Her or himself. Because the embarrassment he'd caused her could be no worse than the regret that dogged him, filling him with longing and guilt. His love could never belong to Jasmine. The breaking of his vow hadn't changed that fact, not in his heart where it mattered. That he wanted her so badly anyway, knowing that he couldn't love her, shamed him.

For a decade he'd held himself apart, guarding his loyalty and his love, refusing to risk the ultimate cost ever again. If he bargained away those years of repentance to couple with a woman whom he couldn't even trust, he'd devalue his vow. And there'd be no honor left in him.

Jasmine had no humanity. Nor gentleness nor softness. Only for a fleeting moment, when she'd touched her lips to his, had he thought maybe—

A violent cough sounded from within the room, so forceful that it threatened to shake the panes in their windows. With a wince, Brody turned the knob and walked in. No need to knock, when he already knew the occupant within wouldn't grant him permission to enter.

Jasmine lay in bed wearing a vast white night dress. The stiff cotton scooped low around her neck, allowing him a generous view of her skin. Monstrously wide sleeves ballooned to her wrists, and thick pleats formed lines below her breasts to where the gown disappeared beneath the quilt.

Surprisingly, her face actually looked pale. Her eyes were unfocused, her hair tousled. In both hands she clutched handkerchiefs.

He walked to the foot of her bed. "Do you honestly expect me to believe that you are sick?"

She brought a fist to her lips and turned her head to the side as she coughed. "I know the timing is suspicious . . ."

"I'd say."

"But this has been coming on since the first night on the range. I slept on my pallet without a fire and the cold must have made me ill. Didn't you hear me coughing today on the ride home?"

"No."

"If you'd turned around occasionally, you might have noticed." She pressed one of the handkerchiefs to her forehead and dabbed dramatically.

Laughter welled in his chest. He fought to subdue it. The scene in the kitchen had already humiliated her enough for one day. Calmly, he crossed to her armoire and opened the twin doors.

"What are you—"

"Packing." He pressed all the gowns that hung within to the side, then quickly scanned each one before thrusting it to the opposite end of the rail. The dresses were lovely. Sumptuous fabrics sewn into swags and flounces, with tiny waists and graceful trains.

He pushed an apricot and two yellows to the side, before stopping at a burgundy gown. Clearly, it had been made for evening, with a plunging neckline and tiny sleeves. He slid a glance at Jasmine. She was sitting bolt upright and watching him avidly, her weight crushing the two handkerchiefs under her palms.

When she noticed his perusal she sank back on her pillows and attempted an indifferent wheeze.

He gestured toward the dress in question.

"My father takes—used to take me to New Orleans once a year," she said faintly. "Made me buy all manner of hampering clothing."

His lips curled into a smile as he lifted the burgundy gown from the closet and hung it on the door. The continuation of his search unearthed a gray gown and a navy gown that he knew intuitively would suit her to perfection.

He slipped all three over his arm. "Are you going to do your packing from here?"

Her previously dull eyes glittered. "I'm sick!"

"Very well." Kneeling, he picked up her saddle bag and upended it near her feet. All kinds of survival gear and rations fell onto the quilt.

"What are you doing?" she shrieked, scrambling to cover her treasures from his gaze.

"Best lay back, Jasmine. Wouldn't want you to over-exert yourself in your delicate condition."

A gorgeously plump bottom lip plopped downward. She fell onto the pillows with a soundless thump.

Ever so gently, Brody folded her gowns and placed them within the leather bag. Then he crossed to her dresser and opened the first drawer. Underwear lay within. He bit back a groan and buried a hand into the heavenly confection of fabric. He came up with an overflowing handful and promptly deposited it in her satchel.

The next drawer revealed neatly folded work shirts. He took two. Then a pair of breeches, some clean socks, a few pair of stockings, and from the bottom of the armoire, a pair of lace-up, high-heeled shoes. They looked as if they'd never been worn.

He glanced at Jasmine.

"I prefer to wear boots with my gowns," she said dryly.

He stashed the rest of her clothing in her bag. "It appears that you're ready."

"Ready?"

He hoisted the satchel and swung it onto his shoulder. "For our trip to Nacogdoches."

The cough that had been conspicuously absent during his flurry of packing reemerged. She covered her face with a wrinkly hanky and blew her nose with gusto.

When she came up for air, he smiled and tried to entice her with charm. "Come with me, Jasmine."

"No."

Charm fled. "Come with me walking, or come with me over my shoulder. Your choice."

"Brody, I'm not feeling well—"

"I don't believe you. Walking, or over my shoulder?"

Her glare could have silenced a pack of howling wolves. "You're going to be sorry for this."

"Undoubtedly. Almost everything about our relationship so far has made me sorry."

She hurled both handkerchiefs toward the wall. They took twin dives into the air, then promptly fell into her lap. Viciously swatting at the dainty squares, Jasmine eased herself from bed as if the task were painful. "May I have some privacy?" she asked, her tone scathing.

"Not on your life."

Her bare feet met wood. She walked past him, her gown billowing. Off the dresser top, she grabbed her brush, a mirror, and a handful of hair pins. Careful not to look at him, she reached for a pocket of her satchel and stuffed the items inside.

He gazed at the top of her auburn curls and grinned.

Still ignoring him, she strode into the corner and abruptly sat on her bottom.

Brody's grin dissolved. He was about to bodily hoist her into the air and cart her from the room, when she reached for a clean pair of breeches. After tugging them on under the cover of her tent-like nightie, she flipped out a pair of socks and donned them. Her beloved boots came last.

Thus attired, she rose to her feet and passed by him as if he were little more than a boorish statue.

He followed her at five paces. In the living room, she swept her hat and bandana into her arms. By the time he caught up with her, halfway to the corral, her hat sat atop her head and her pink bandana was jauntily tied.

Tom stood in the yard holding the horses. His amused gaze scanned Jasmine as they approached. "Dressed for bed?"

"I'm sick," she answered.

Beneath the line of his hat, Tom's face creased with worry. "Sick?"

"Of behaving herself," Brody finished. He turned to Jasmine. "I wouldn't manipulate Tom's sympathy if I were you. One night he may be the only thing between you and strangulation at my hands. Better to save his sympathy till then."

Tom chortled.

Jasmine pretended she hadn't heard. "Why isn't Diamond saddled?" she asked Tom.

Brody tipped her chin to the side and up, until her face angled toward him. He waited while she gradually slid her gaze to meet his. "Because Diamond has a limp," he said. "She's strained a muscle in her foreleg."

"No!"

"Take a look." He released her.

Jasmine whistled to Diamond. Her horse, barebacked and surrounded by the bonds of the corral, trotted over to her. Brody's eye confirmed the presence of the slight limp he'd noticed earlier. He could tell by Jasmine's tight expression that she, too, saw the injury.

"I think it would be best to ride your new horse this trip and give Diamond a rest," he said.

She nodded and approached Diamond. Laying a slim hand on the horse's nose, she pressed a kiss into her forelock.

Warmth melted down Brody's insides. The words of endearment she murmured to the animal drifted to him on the cool breeze of a dying afternoon.

He swallowed.

She walked to the chocolate stallion, briskly patted his neck and swung into the saddle. The white cotton gown bagged around her waist, rippling in the wind.

My God, she was actually going to wear that gown over her trousers and boots. She'd even accessorized it with her bandana. Numbly, he began strapping her bulging satchel to the back of her saddle.

"What's your horse's name?" Tom asked her as he handed her the reins.

Brody fastened the last leather tie and joined Tom, both of them tilting back their heads to gaze up at her.

A frown flashed across her lips. A gaze of purest blue bored into his heart. "Vengeance."

He blinked at her. This time, despite his intentions, he let laughter run from his chest and temporarily ease the pressure of the burdens he carried.

"I'm serious," Jasmine said.

"I know." And that made it all the more funny. He appreciated the humor in her. God, he did. He wondered if she had any idea how little he'd laughed over the past decade.

Jasmine grimaced. "I see you've not even the decency to restrain yourself from laughing in my face."

"I'm sorry, Jasmine." He coerced his lips into a straight line.

"Well." She repositioned her hat. "I may be inclined to overlook your bad taste if you'll agree to swing by Emma's on our way out."

Looking up at her, with the sky an immense patchwork of blue behind her, he found he couldn't refuse. Likely couldn't have refused her anything in that moment. "As you wish," he said with a wry smile.

Her nose scrunched and he thought he heard her mumble something about her dearest wish and a stake up his rear end.

Jasmine rode ahead of them to Emma's, asked them to wait for her outside, then dashed up the steps and into the hallway. "Em?"

Her friend's face poked out the kitchen door. "Jasmine?"

Jasmine experienced a bewildering mix of emotions at seeing Emma. A good portion of joy and love ran through the resentment and hurt over the way Emma had tattled to Brody. "Em, we're about to leave—"

Emma scurried down the hallway and crushed her in a shockingly powerful hug. "Please don't go running off like that again," she whispered into Jasmine's hair. "I worried about you."

"Is that why you showed Brody my note?"

Emma pulled back enough to look her in the eye. "You're angry about that."

"Some. I specifically asked you not to tell him."

"I know." Emma stepped away, her expression bereft.

Jasmine's irritation eased a little.

"Forgive me," Emma said. "I broke your trust."

"Yes."

"I prayed it was for your greater good."

Emma didn't need to say more. Jasmine knew her well enough to know that's precisely why she'd done what she'd done. Emma was her best friend. In fact, Emma was her only friend. And she could ill afford to hold a grudge against her *only* friend. "You told Daddy?"

She nodded. "I thought your father was going to shoot his way across Texas, looking for you."

"Oh, no."

"Oh, yes."

Jasmine sighed. "That's the last thing I wanted."

"Are you ready to forgive him yet?"

She weighed her heart. More than anything, it felt weary. "I think I am, when I get back."

"Where are you off to?"

"Nacogdoches, for Brody's brother's wedding. That's why I came by. I need for you to tell Daddy something for me."

"Anything."

"Tell him—" She gnawed the tender inside of her

cheek, trying to think how best to phrase it. "Tell Daddy that Brody is a Texas Ranger."

Emma's eyes rounded.

"Tell him that I'm doing the best I can, but that he needs to help me out some." Surely that would get the message across. Once he knew that Brody was a lawman, he'd understand that he had to leave Tyler and head for safety. Her father knew better than anyone the danger of his past and the necessity of when to run.

"I don't understand," Emma said.

"I know." Jasmine reached for her hand and squeezed. "I don't understand anything in my life lately, either. But if you just tell him that for me, that'll be enough."

"You know I will."

Jasmine kissed her on the cheek and strode to the door.

"When will you be back?"

"I don't know." Jasmine tried to contemplate the coming string of days in Brody's presence and couldn't quite manage it. "Soon, I hope." She reached for the door knob.

"Oh, and Jasmine?"

She paused.

"Why in the world are you wearing that night dress?"

As soon as Emma topped the hill and saw the group of cowboys standing below, she knew which man was Lee. Of course she did. She'd have known him blindfolded at a hundred paces.

The men were in the fields three miles south of the Double J ranch house. From what she could tell, Lee and his foreman were overseeing the treatment of an injured bull.

She rode toward the throng of men. When Lee turned and spotted her she smiled, for once allowing her excitement to stream unchecked.

He began to walk in her direction and then run, leaving his men staring after him.

She laughed. This was joy defined, to bring him the news

of Jasmine's safety. To be so gladly welcomed.

Her mount trotted across the last few yards to him. Lee reached up and grabbed hold of the animal's bridle with one hand. With the other he nudged up the brim of his hat. "Jasmine's back?" he asked.

"Yes." She grinned. "Jasmine is back."

"Unhurt?"

"Unhurt."

With a barrage of laughter, he reached up and swept her from the saddle.

Emma's toes groped for but never found the ground. The hem of her divided skirt flung outward as he twirled her in circles. His throaty whoop of delight flavored the air.

She wrapped her arms around his neck and held on tight. When he came to a stop he continued to hold her. The rest of the world wobbled dizzily behind Lee. But his face . . . his face was as clear and detailed as in her dreams.

Lee gazed at her with startled wonder.

She licked her bottom lip and tested a smile on him. She knew how desperately he'd been praying for Jasmine's safe return.

Behind him, John Sims, the Double J foreman, cupped hands to lips and called, "Has Jasmine been found?"

Lee jumped slightly at the question. After setting Emma down, he turned toward the men who all stood frozen in mid-task, watching them. "Yes!" he yelled.

The men let out a chorus of cheers.

Awkwardly, she smoothed her hand over the jumble of her hair. Somewhere during their embrace, her hat had vaulted from her head. She could see it, lying in the scrubby grass behind him.

"When did she return?" he asked.

"Just now, this afternoon. It was a very hurried visit. She's angry with me for showing Brody the note."

"Is she?" Lee couldn't have looked more proud if she'd

told him that Jasmine had come home with the crown jewels in her saddle bags.

"Yes, she's angry." Emma attempted to chastise him with a frown, but she knew it lacked sting.

He chuckled. "It looks like you and I are in the same predicament with her. Only I won't be in it with you much longer. I'm going to ride over there right now and apologize."

Regret panged through Emma. For him. For herself. She didn't want to tell him the rest yet, but clearly had to. "Lee, I'm afraid she's already gone."

His forehead furrowed. "Gone?"

"Yes." How she hated this. Loved bearing good news and making him happy. Detested bearing sad news and giving him grief. "They've already left for Nacogdoches."

"What's in Nacogdoches?"

"Brody's brother's wedding, evidently."

"I see." His blue eyes cooled by two shades.

Her heart ached for him.

"It's nothing that can't wait till she gets back," he said quietly.

She nodded. "There's something else."

He raised his brows and waited.

"Jasmine asked me to tell you that Brody's a Texas Ranger." She scrutinized his reaction, but could detect no change, save for a careful blanking of his expression. "She said to say that she's doing the best she can, but that she needs you to help her out a little. I haven't any idea what that means."

"It's all right, Emma. I do."

She wanted to ask him to share the meaning with her, to confide in her, but didn't have the nerve.

He seemed to stare right through her as he thrust his hands in his pockets. "Well, I'd best—" He glanced at his men who were milling around the sick animal. "I'd best get back."

"Of course." She didn't know what else to say, couldn't quite bring herself to let him go.

"I'll be seeing you." He was already turning, striding away.

"Sure."

After just a couple steps he came across her hat. He stopped and plucked it from the ground. Gently, he dusted it off and handed it to her.

Before she could thank him, he was gone. She couldn't move. She could only watch him walk toward his men, his gait smooth. She saw how they looked up at him when he joined them. Reverent and respectfully.

Her horse buried its nose in her shoulder and gave her a good-natured push. Automatically, she sunk a hand into her pocket and retrieved a sugar cube. Without looking, she slid the treat into her horse's mouth.

He munched contentedly.

Emma pushed her hair behind her ears and settled her hat on her head. Over the past few days of Jasmine's absence, she'd seen more of Lee than in the last three years combined. He'd ridden out to visit her several times so that he could check on whether Jasmine had returned. Each night she had made him dinner. They'd sat together at her table and talked about Jasmine and about all the memories Lee had hoarded of her over a lifetime.

She'd comforted him, listened avidly to his stories. After they'd eaten, she'd tried to divert his worry with games. They'd played every respectable card game she'd been able to think of. They'd had coffee by the gallon and thick slices of pie.

Emma watched him kneel down to examine the bull's injured leg. He handled the animal with hands both expert and kind.

Suddenly, she felt very, very old. She climbed into the saddle and still she couldn't make herself leave.

Except for her anxiety over Jasmine, these past days had

been glorious. Every time she was with Lee, even when she'd walked into her living room and seen his head bent over an old book, her hope had soared. Secretly, she'd begun planning the remainder of their lives together.

It was only at night, when he'd left for his own ranch and she'd lain in her bed alone, that reality had intruded. Her tears had blanketed her pillow as she'd remembered that Lee was an independent man, that he'd never expressed any affection for her, that he was too handsome and too wealthy and too set in his ways. That he was married. *Married*.

And what was she? A withered spinster.

She drank in the sight of him in one last gulp, then forced her vision away, turning her mount in the direction of home. Not for the first time, she wondered how one would go about dissolving a twenty-five year dead marriage. Hope wreathed through her as she turned her intellect to solving Lee's problem.

Her horse hadn't even reached a trot before she recalled that Lee hadn't made a move in all these years to end his marriage. What made her think he'd do so now? He'd given her no indication whatsoever that he was even considering it.

Hope shriveled.

She took in two deep breaths. How long? How long before this tug-of-war of hope pulled her soul apart piece by miserable piece?

Chapter 14

J asmine's vision kept fogging at the corners, obliterat-
ing the already black landscape into a void of darkness.
Her head would loll to the side, her grip on the reins would
slacken. And then her neck would catch her falling head,
snapping it back into place and jerking her eyelids open.

She'd survived the last few hours of their journey to
Nacogdoches in this fashion, always managing to look alert
and competent when Brody glanced back to check on her.
But this time when her eyes wrenched open, she found
herself looking directly into Brody's concerned face.

Instantly she came awake, straightening her spine, and
puckering her lips to exercise her facial muscles.

But her heroic performance came too late. She saw that
Brody was already searching the shadows of the surrounding countryside for a place to camp.

Jasmine sat atop Vengeance in a resigned trance, too
tired to move or talk or keep pretending that she wasn't
about to fall off her horse with exhaustion.

Minutes later, Brody selected a flat patch of land and
dismounted. Tom, too, directed his horse to their impromptu camp and slid off the saddle with a single lithe
movement.

They spoke little as they lit a fire and tended to their
horses. As soon as Vengeance had been cared for, Jasmine

lay out her pallet and collapsed onto it. She was still wearing her nightgown beneath the warmth of her father's coat. Thankfully, all she had to do in preparation for bed was pry off her boots and scoot between the blankets.

Through the dimming haze of her consciousness, she noticed Brody arranging his pallet next to hers. Silently, she studied him as he reclined onto the makeshift bed and stretched out his long frame. He propped his weight on his elbow and looked at her.

A sleepy smile played across her lips. Inexplicably, she was glad that he would sleep beside her. So glad. . . .

"Comfortable?" he whispered.

Before she could reply, a wayward sweep of wind tossed a thick curl across her eyes, stealing him from sight. Masculine fingers brushed her cheek, then carefully tucked the curl behind her ear.

"Yes," she answered.

He stared at her solemnly. She noticed the grazing of stubble across his jaw and cheeks. Beautiful cheeks. Eyes like splinters of mahogany. How could one man's eyes have so many moods and shades?

He pulled his saddle closer and settled back against it.

Jasmine let her lids sink close. Peacefulness shuddered through her. She hadn't felt this safe or contented or warm in . . . at the moment she couldn't remember how long.

Brody's spicy scent, woodsy and deeply male, twined through the air. Sighing, she breathed deeply of it and allowed her mind to tumble into sleep.

"Are we getting close?" Jasmine hated to pester Tom with the question again, but the hours kept crawling by, and her restlessness had grown so intense that she couldn't stop herself from asking.

Tom gave her a look of patient, unperturbable good humor. "Yes."

She maneuvered her horse alongside his. Brody rode a

good distance ahead of them, well beyond earshot. "Truly?"

"We've passed through Millard's Crossing. Shouldn't be long now."

"How long?"

"Maybe a couple of hours."

She yawned. A couple of hours seemed near to unbearable. They'd slept only four hours last night. This morning she'd barely had enough time to wash her face and change out of her nightgown before they'd begun the ride. The midday meal had come and gone recently—a hurried affair of bread and fruit. It had been their only stop, though she'd repeatedly longed for a chance to dismount and stretch her legs. Not only did her body want the exercise, but her brain pleaded for the diversion.

Still, she knew better than to complain. Her foray into criminality had cost them time. That's why they were rushing. Already it was Friday. Clay's wedding would take place tomorrow.

She wondered what Brody's brother would be like. How his bride would treat her. What manner of ranch house they owned. "What does McClintock ranch look like?" She glanced at Tom, who sat a horse as if he'd been born in the saddle. The leather seat and even the beast beneath him appeared to be mere extensions of the man.

"Well . . . let me think. It's been a long time since I've been to the McClintock place."

She frowned. "You don't accompany Brody home for visits?"

"He's never come home for a visit before."

Her brows drew together sharply above her nose. "He's never come home?"

"Not since I've been with him."

"But you've been with him for ten years—"

"Eleven."

"Eleven years."

"That's right."

Her brain whirred. "So you're telling me that this is the first time that Brody's returned home in eleven years."

His lips, lightly parched from the sun, straightened into a narrow line. He shifted his gaze to the silhouette of the tall cowboy who rode alone ahead of them. "Yes."

"He hasn't seen his brother in all this time?"

"Clay? Oh, sure. Clay's given his services to the Rangers on several occasions over the years. Whenever we needed good men and he could spare the time away from the ranch, he'd ride with us. Brody visited with him then."

"But never at home?"

"No."

Jasmine surveyed the strong, solitary line of Brody's back. A few inches of chestnut hair lay below his hat at the nape of his neck. That soft hair was the only vulnerable, human thing she recognized in him today. Everything else had been shuttered away, protected by an unyielding jaw and eyes that snapped warnings.

She didn't need Tom to tell her that Brody's memories were hounding him. She'd felt the dark edge of Brody's past nipping at her heels all day.

He'd left the ranch that was his birthright and hadn't set foot on it again for eleven years. What kind of tragedy would drive a man to such extremes? The answer struck her like a slap. "Did he love Elena that much?" she asked softly, emotion wringing her heart. The reins felt coarse in her hands. She gripped them. "Enough to leave his home and never come back?"

Tom squinted into the distance.

Jasmine waited tensely for him to answer.

"He loved her, all right," Tom said at last. "But I think he could have stood losing her . . . I think he would have stayed at the ranch, if she'd been the only one he lost."

"He lost more than her?"

A sadness that reached deeper than the healing hands of time pulled down his lips. "He did."

"Who?"

The nostalgic light in his eyes slipped away. "You know I like you, don't you, Jasmine?"

She tilted her head, befuddled by the question. "Sure."

"I'd do just about anything for you." He shrugged and smiled at his own folly. "I mean it. Just about anything. But that question. . . ."

"Yes?"

"Is for Brody to answer." He looked both apologetic and uncomfortable.

Reluctantly, she surrendered the question. Leaning over precariously far in her saddle, she gave his shoulder an affectionate pat. "In that case, I'll just have to think of another, more outrageous, way to exploit your affection for me." The sidelong glance she gave him held a wink. "Maybe, when we reach the ranch, you could make me a little of that peach cobbler of yours."

Two wooden crosses.

A day of baking, unforgiving heat.

Sweat rippled down his arms, making his grip on the shovel slippery. Clay worked beside him. Brody could hear the pant of his brother's breath, the occasional racking sob when the enormity of what had happened overwhelmed him.

But there were no tears for Brody. Only a twisting, wrenching sorrow that burrowed deeper with every lift of the shovel. And guilt. Guilt that burned his skin hotter than any Texas sun. It seared him to the very core of who he was. And who he had thought he had been.

All around them McClintock land rolled away in shallow, undulating plains of grass. He recognized the clusters of trees where he'd played as a boy, saw in the distance the house of whitewashed clapboards that rambled outward in one long wing. The familiar sound of insects droned through the still air—

Damn it. Brody wished he could stop remembering. Instead, he kept recalling that day with piercing clarity. The more he tried to focus on the present reality of the horse beneath him, the trail before him, and Jasmine riding behind him, the more he felt the shovel in his blistered hands, the more he saw the shattered sorrow in Clay's eyes.

He arched his back a little and resettled himself in the familiar curve of his saddle.

He had thought, after the war, that the memory of his home might have been tarnished by the cascades of blood he'd witnessed. But he'd been wrong. He remembered coming home that other time, how the familiarity of it had spoken to him in a sweet song of comfort.

Would it sing to him again? Or would its memory truly be tarnished this time, not by blood, but by bloodlessness? By a vengeance he'd sworn to claim but had not claimed?

He searched absently for the ring he always wore around his neck, finally locating its slender bulk through the cover of his shirt. It hung against his chest, soothing him, binding him with its graceful chain to a promise he couldn't escape. He pressed the band of silver into the heart of his palm, then flexed his hand, releasing it.

Desperately, he tried to push his mind to any other topic. Anything would be preferable to this cruel circle of memories that kept chasing one another round and round in his head. He'd tortured himself with each one in turn over every mile of this damned journey.

He'd not have returned to McClintock Ranch for any other reason. If Clay hadn't caught up with him in Austin three months ago and asked him to stand beside him at his wedding, he'd not have come back. Ever. But his brother had never requested anything else of him. Only this one favor. And Clay had asked it honorably, without probing questions or censure.

Brody had been unable to refuse.

He pulled the brim of his hat lower. He was coming home. Not alone, but with a wife who couldn't be trusted to sit through so much as the wedding ceremony without making a mad dash toward freedom.

Jasmine. Her face as it had been last night hovered in his mind. Pale and sleepy, the sloping angles of her cheekbones so perfect they mesmerized him. Lashes of ebony, nearly disguising the unending blue they sheltered.

Two wooden crosses interposed over the image. A day of unbearable heat. Remorse so deep and wide it had no end.

"This is it," Tom whispered to her.

Jasmine's anticipation swelled. She leaned forward in the saddle and eased Vengeance into a gallop. Only when she and Tom drew even with Brody did they halt.

The three of them sat in silence at the edge of a high ridge and surveyed the landscape spread before them. The earth fell in a wide bowl of green before rising again at the outer edges in a pattern of overlapping hills. The afternoon sun streamed onto the ranch, illuminating it with ethereal softness and whispering to Jasmine of new beginnings.

The beauty of it dared her to examine it more closely, to ride to the peaks of the distantmost hills and discover what lay on the other side. To walk through the closely knit throngs of trees and investigate their shady secrets. To live in the house a little and listen to its night noises.

She peeked at Brody, wondering if the land spoke to him as it did her. He sat on his mount staring at the scene before him without moving a muscle. No obvious happiness or sadness marked his handsome features.

Jasmine would have given much to know what he was thinking and feeling. But there were no words to voice the question. And none to answer it with.

As she watched, Brody's gaze riveted on a point in the foreground.

Straining to see over her horse's ears, Jasmine followed the direction of his gaze and discovered a house. A simple two-story with gaily painted green window trim and a riot of wildflowers out front.

"Whose house?" Brody asked.

Tom's saddle creaked as he shifted position. "Don't know."

Brody tugged off his gloves. "Clay must have built it for his wife. Or his wife's family."

"Probably," Tom answered.

"You want to have a look?"

The pause lengthened until Jasmine realized he'd posed the question to her. He was regarding her with serious eyes.

A bolt of sensual awareness rocked her. Molten heat swirled through her stomach and pooled near the juncture of her legs. She wanted to tell him that instead of having a look at the house, she would really prefer to continue gazing into his eyes and hugging this wondrous feeling into her.

With some struggle, she managed to dredge up an adventurous nod.

Brody's horse lunged forward and began descending the ridge at a fearsome pace. Jasmine urged Vengeance to follow. She suddenly needed to stay beside Brody, to assert her ownership of him. It wouldn't do for her to skulk up to his family on his coattails, coughing up mouthfuls dust.

Vengeance adopted her heightened impatience. He careened down the slippery path of rock and dirt. When they reached the bottom, he tore after Brody.

As the two-story house drew closer, Jasmine's emotions jumbled into a nauseated knot. She felt curiosity, sharp and demanding. Nervousness about meeting the family members who knew Brody best. Awkwardness over how to behave and what to say. Excitement at having reached their destination and being so close to the fulfillment of discovery. A thread of unease laced all the others together.

From this distance the little house appeared clean, but not as well cared for as it had looked from above. In some places, the clapboards were splintered. One window had a crack crawling up its surface, and the green paint on the trim was peeling and in need of another coat.

They stopped before the flower-covered front lawn.

Jasmine could tell from Brody's gentle frown that the state of the house bewildered him.

The moment that Brody arched his leg over the saddle, Jasmine mimicked his action. Their boots hit the dirt in the same instant.

A clopping chorus of hooves announced that Tom had cantered up behind them. "I'll tend to the horses," he offered, as he swung down.

Jasmine gratefully handed him the reins.

"You've got a smudge," Tom murmured, leaning close. He patted her right cheek and gave her a warm, confidential smile.

"Thanks," she whispered back, then noticed that Brody was already halfway to the house. She ran until she pulled even with him. Together they stopped before the green door. Jasmine narrowly resisted the urge to sidle against him. Should she lift his hand and drop it casually over her shoulders? Would that present the right picture of marital familiarity?

Brody knocked.

She smoothed her hands over the front of her wrinkled trousers. Her doubts about how to act and what to say intensified.

"This should be interesting," Brody said to her, his tone reassuring.

She shot him a hopeful smile.

The doorknob twisted and the door swung back. A dark-haired girl, no older than four, stood on the threshold. She wore a simple calico dress, the fabric of which matched the bows at the ends of her neatly plaited braids. The interest she aimed up at them quickly disintegrated into shyness when she realized that she didn't recognize them.

Her round-eyed gaze dropped from their faces and fastened on their kneecaps.

Brody cleared his throat. "May we speak with your—"

"Maddie!" The satiny voice drifted from the murky recesses of the hall. "Is there someone at the door?"

The little girl looked over her shoulder in the direction of the voice, but didn't answer.

"Maddie?"

Her gaze returned to their kneecaps.

The woman's voice drew closer. "Maddie, you know very well that you are to greet visitors and then come and fetch me." A slender hand slid onto the girl's shiny dark brown head as the woman appeared in the doorway. "It isn't polite to—". Her gaze transfixed on Brody.

Jasmine heard the sharp intake of Brody's breath. Though his face hardened into contours of marble, the depths of his eyes smoldered with feeling.

Recognition traveled between him and the woman, so powerful it vibrated through the air like a living thing.

Jasmine watched the woman's shock at seeing him give way to mild distress and then self-consciousness.

Sickness swirled through Jasmine. A feminine intuition more forceful than truth recognized her.

This woman was Brody's great love.

This was Elena.

Blonde tendrils had escaped her loose bun to curl around her earlobes and neck. Her eyes were enormous liquid pools of green. A slim nose crowned lips of tenderest pink.

Feeling her heart shrivel within her chest, Jasmine frantically searched the woman's face for imperfections. There were few. Only fine wrinkles beside her eyes and faint bags in the fragile skin below her lashes.

She wore a pale yellow blouse tucked into a well-worn gingham skirt. Her attire accented her daintiness and set off elegant, womanly curves.

No wonder Brody loved her. She was alive, horribly alive—and much too beautiful. Jasmine would never be able to compete with this woman. Whatever affection Brody harbored toward her had just been lost.

A young boy wedged into the space beyond the threshold. He looked to be ten or so, with light brown hair and quiet hazel eyes. He peered curiously at them.

His arrival appeared to wake the woman from her daze. "Would you take Maddie into the backyard for me?" she asked the boy. "Keep her occupied for a little while?" Her voice was melodic, as wispy as down.

Never in her life had Jasmine felt so ugly. In comparison to Elena, her medium height seemed gigantic, her body gangly. It was no consolation that she'd traded in her nightgown for a work shirt this morning. She glanced down and noticed that one side of the garment had come untucked. Her hair flopped over her face in its usual state of upheaval.

"Yes, Mother," the boy answered.

Gently, the woman scooted the tiny girl in his direction and the two children made their way down the hall holding hands, both aiming looks over their shoulders.

In a sick flash, Jasmine remembered the smudge on her cheek. She clamped a hand over her skin. Misery flooded through her.

With heavy pressure, she rubbed her palm over her entire cheek, not caring that her nails raked her flesh painfully. She was such a mess. What a fool she'd been, a damned idiot ever to have thought Brody might desire her.

The woman was staring at Brody again.

Jasmine dropped her hand. She didn't think she could bear their oppressive quiet for a moment longer. Her brain hurtled through several tacks of conversation. None were suitable.

Finally, the woman spoke. "Hello, Brody."

"Elena."

Jasmine chewed the inside of her cheek and tried to brace against the pain tearing into her.

"Who have you brought with you?" Elena asked politely. Her emerald gaze shifted to Jasmine.

"This is Jasmine," Brody answered. "My wife."

Just for an instant, Jasmine saw disappointment flicker in the depths of Elena's eyes.

"Pleased to meet you," Elena said.

Jasmine pulled her lips into what she hoped was a smile. "Likewise."

The woman's gaze returned to Brody. "Have you not spoken with Clay yet?"

"No."

"I'm so sorry. This must be quite a surprise. Perhaps you should come in, so that I can explain." She gestured toward a shadowy sitting room.

The porch boards creaked as Brody took an abrupt step backward. "Thank you, but we really should be heading up to the main house. Sorry for troubling you."

"You know it's no trouble," she said, giving him a meaningful look tinged with sadness.

He tipped his hat to her.

Elena stepped from the threshold onto the porch, anxiously twining her fingers together. "I'm glad to see you back, Brody."

The words were spoken with a sincerity that made Jasmine want to scream.

"Thank you," Brody replied, then turned on his heel and stalked toward the horses.

Elena watched his retreat with plaintive regret. Her attention didn't stray for a moment to the woman who stood next to her on the front porch, staring at her.

Jasmine watched the play of emotions crossing Elena's features.

The images were bitingly painful for her to see, so much so that she couldn't bring herself to look away. She considered making some dire threat to Elena. Then she contemplated launching herself at the shapely woman and attempting to rip her hair out.

"Jasmine." Tom's voice summoned her.

She pried her gaze from Elena. Tom stood just beyond the wildflowers, patiently holding her horse for her. Next to him, she saw Brody swing into the saddle and take off at a gallop.

Setting her lips, she crossed the front lawn. Tom held Vengeance while she mounted up. As soon as his fingers unclenched, releasing the bridle, Vengeance shot forward. Jasmine goaded her horse to fly across the vast expanse of spring grass.

Her brain mercifully released all other concerns, save the concern of catching Brody. He rode well ahead of her, his horse's tail tossing on the wind. In front of his charging figure, the white bulk of the main ranch house loomed.

Wind thundered against her face and whipped across her chest. She savored its sting. The earth rolled under her, unfurling acre after acre beneath the unrelenting rhythm of Vengeance's hooves.

Just as they were storming into the enclosure of ranch buildings, Brody slowed his pace enough so that Jasmine could reach his side. She didn't look at him, didn't want to be cut by his expression.

They tied the horses at the corral and walked side by side toward the house. Before they'd reached the porch, the front door swept open and a man emerged. Jasmine immediately pegged the stranger as Brody's brother. He had the same sandy brown hair and imposing height as Brody. However, his features were milder, not as chiseled. And his smile came much easier and held no shadows.

The man halted at the edge of the front step. His joyful

grin of welcome wavered when he saw his brother's face. "You've been to Elena's," he guessed.

They stopped in front of him. "Yes."

Looking chagrined, the man bypassed Brody's scowl and walked directly to Jasmine. "I'm Clay," he said, extending his hand.

Jasmine set her fingers in his. "I'm Jasmine, Brody's wife."

His lips stalled above her hand, which he'd been about to kiss. Gradually, he tilted his head up to observe her. "Did you say wife?"

"I did."

"By God!" He laughed with delight. His big hand squeezed her fingers. "You couldn't have surprised me more if you'd ridden up to meet me in your night clothes."

It was Jasmine's turn to smile. The sweet man had no idea how close he'd come to witnessing exactly that.

"Welcome to McClintock Ranch, Jasmine." Clay finished the gesture he'd intended by kissing the back of her hand. He beamed at her as if he'd never seen a woman who pleased him more.

"Thank you."

Clay pounded Brody on the back before encompassing his older brother in a hug.

Clay led them across the porch. "Come on in. You must be exhausted, Jasmine." He held the door open so that she could pass through first. Racks for coats and boots lined the narrow entry. Beyond that, the great room yawned. Arranged throughout the cavernous space were groupings of couches and wing-backed chairs, two rugs and a fireplace at each end. Hallways led away from the room in both directions.

Clay looped an arm around her shoulders and gave her an impromptu hug. "I'm so glad that you're here," he said. Then, to Brody, "I was beginning to get a little worried when you didn't show yesterday."

"Jasmine had us running late," Brody said.

Clay rubbed his hand affectionately against her upper arm. "So long as you made it." He guided them to the left and down the hallway. When they reached the door at the end of the corridor, he pushed it open. "I didn't know we'd have the pleasure of your company," Clay said to her. "It's just as well that you're married and can share a room, because all the other beds are taken."

Her steps faltered.

Clay motioned for her to enter.

Jasmine obediently padded in, then waited awkwardly for Brody to join her. He had to duck his head to enter through the low frame of the door.

"Take a little time to rest and unpack," Clay said. "I'll be in the office if you need me."

"I'll meet you there," Brody replied.

Clay nodded and disappeared, shutting the portal behind him.

Jasmine and Brody stood in the center of the room, both avoiding the other's eyes.

It's just as well that you're married and can share a room.

The bed dominated the space, looming larger and larger each second as the import of sleeping in it with Brody fully sunk in for Jasmine.

Pillows of pastel gingham and embroidered linen rested on a lavender and rose quilt. A loving hand had painted the walls white and hung gauzy lace curtains at the windows. A dresser of warm, honey colored wood held a bowl, a pitcher and a vase of hand picked flowers. The blushing femininity of the room surprised her.

"Whose bedroom is this?" she asked.

Stony silence answered her. Brody's lips curled in disgust.

"Don't you know whose bedroom this is?"

"It's mine," he growled, turning to peer out the window.

She couldn't help but smile at the absurdity of the most rugged man she knew dwelling in such girlish splendor. "How . . . pretty."

"It's been changed since I lived here."

"Of course." Walking deeper into the room, she pulled off her hat and set it on the dresser. She shook out her hair until it fell in waves around her shoulders. Following the dictates of habit, she ran her fingers through it. When the worst of the knots had been combed free, she unfastened her bandana.

Brody hadn't so much as taken a single step, but she knew without looking that he'd adjusted his position enough to watch her. His perusal felt warm on the back of her neck. Slowly, she faced him.

"I've got to go talk to my brother," he said.

"I understand."

"First, I'll carry in your pack and—"

"No." She swallowed. The desperate lightheartedness of moments before had solidified like a leaden ball in her stomach. "No, Tom and I can take care of that. Just go ahead and speak with him."

He jerked off his hat and slapped it once against his thigh. For a moment he hesitated. Then he strode out.

Jasmine stood looking at the vacant space he'd occupied. Her pulse thrummed across her temples. Quietly, she closed the door he'd left ajar, walked to the bed, and sat on its edge. Pain speared through the center of her as if she'd been gut shot. Crossing both arms over her abdomen, she leaned forward and softly rocked.

Elena.

She'd assumed the woman had died years ago. Hadn't Tom told her as much? She tried to recall the conversation she'd shared with him that day in the kitchen at Colin House. He'd said that Brody had lost Elena. Lost her. But evidently not to death.

She groaned and screwed shut her eyes. The hurt amazed her with its consuming, racking force.

Even when she'd thought Elena dead, she'd known the woman to be supreme in Brody's heart. But alive, with her melting eyes and golden hair, Elena was infinitely more powerful.

Just how precious was she to Brody? He'd pined for her for eleven years. He'd never wanted to marry, after her. How much would a man have to love a woman to live his life that way?

Enormously.

The pressure behind her temples grew fierce.

He must have loved her enormously.

Chapter 15

The masculine clutter of the office framed Clay with soothing shades of walnut and maple. This had been their father's domain once and Brody could still sense the man's presence.

"I'm sorry you had to discover Elena like that," Clay said as he walked out from behind his massive desk. "I really thought you'd ride directly here, to the main house."

Brody studied his brother. The face so like his own had not aged much over the years. Clay still looked youthful and relaxed, with the same cowlick curving the hair over his right eye.

With a flick of his fingers, Brody sent his hat slicing across the air. It coasted along the top of the cabinet before sliding to a stop. "I came by way of the ridge and couldn't help seeing her house. We assumed you'd built it for your fiancée or her family, so we stopped to introduce ourselves."

"You thought that was Jessica's place?" Clay propped his hip against the edge of his desk. "No, her family lives near town. They're real closely knit. I'm going to have trouble persuading her to live out here even after we're married." He smiled.

Inexplicably, that smile grated across Brody's nerves. "It

appears you didn't have any such trouble persuading Elena Morgan.''

Clay skirted the desk and lowered himself into the leather chair behind it. "Have a seat." He motioned toward the twin chairs.

"No thanks."

"You sure you want to know the story of how she came to live here?"

"No. But tell me anyway."

Beyond the hush of the office, Brody heard boots treading dully along a distant hallway. Sunlight traveled through the room's single window, shining upon a sheaf of papers, a dirty coffee mug, and a faintly dusty cigar box. The smell of brisket baking slid beneath the door and slowly invaded the space.

Clay ran blunt fingertips over the ledger in front of him. "First, it's not Elena Morgan anymore."

"What does that have to do—"

"You said Elena Morgan just now. It's been Elena Stodges for a decade."

Hearing her name over and over again was like rubbing salt into a mortal wound. It brought everything back. "Elena Stodges, then."

"She married Sam right after you left here. The next week, I think."

"Four days later."

Clay gave him a long, level look. "Right. Anyway, she married and moved into town. After that, I didn't see her again for some time. It must have been at least six months before I went to visit her."

"You went to visit her?"

Discomfort etched into the skin around Clay's eyes. "Before the war she was practically a part of our family. I'd always liked her."

Brody made himself nod.

"When I came to call I discovered that she was pregnant,

pretty far along. I could see in those big eyes of hers that she was terrified.''

"Terrified of what?"

"The future. You know what an idiot Sam is. Well, when he was a bachelor, he was lazy and a little reckless, but for the most part harmless. His good looks made up for a lot with the women, Elena included.''

Brody crossed his arms.

"But after Sam married her and found himself with a wife to support and a baby on the way, he started drinking more. His lack of responsibility wasn't so harmless any more.''

"He mistreated her?"

"Nothing obvious. But when I went to see her that first time, they were living with his parents. Her face was thinner than I'd ever seen it. It wasn't long before she was sobbing on my shoulder.''

"So you brought her here to live.''

"Not exactly.''

Brody clenched his teeth so hard that pain flecked sharply into his gums. "Then tell me how it was exactly.''

"She was sobbing because she said poor Sam was trying so hard, but that he just couldn't seem to bring in any money. She said she knew he was a good worker, that he just needed an employer to give him a fair chance.'' Clay gazed at his brother, his lips set in a sarcastic line which informed Brody just how many of Elena's assurances he'd believed. "You see my predicament.''

Brody needed a chair. He lowered into the nearest one, resting both wrists on the padded arms and curving his fingers around the ends. "So what did you do?"

"I felt protective of her, sorry for her. I couldn't just leave her there.'' He sighed. "So I hired him.''

"Jesus.''

Clay rushed onward, obviously trying to shed all the bad news in one breath. "The boys and I built them that house ten years ago. They've lived there ever since.''

"Jesus!"

Clay sighed. "Unfortunately, Sam has gotten worse over the years instead of better. He drinks too much and he cheats on her. I've been waiting for her to throw him out for a long time. She never does." He shrugged. "A couple of times I've lost my patience with Sam and thrown him out myself. Both times, Elena's begged me to take him back."

Brody remembered how he'd felt when he came home from the war to find Elena Morgan, the love of his life, just one week away from marriage to Sam Stodges.

She hadn't waited for him, as she'd promised. Hadn't loved him enough to wait. She'd lost faith that he'd return and chosen to give her love and her body to another man in marriage. With that single decision, she'd stabbed him more viciously than any opponent on the southern battlefields ever had.

Now he'd discovered that the happiness Elena had bargained him away for had been elusive. Sam had brought her only misery.

He supposed he should have been gratified.

Instead, he was horrified. Sickened.

Nothing good had come of Elena's choice all those years ago. Not for her. And certainly not for him and his family. "How many children does she have?" he asked, his voice thin.

"Four." Clay tapped a finger on the table for each one. "There's Sam, the oldest. And then David, Maddie, and the baby."

"Baby?"

"Just a few months old. Her name's Brooke."

Breath slid slowly, sorrowfully from Brody's lips.

"For what it's worth," Clay said, "I've been glad over the years, about the decision I made to bring her here. She's needed someone."

"How come you never told me?"

"What good would it have done?"

"I could have—"

"What? What could you have done? She's married."

Brody knew that Clay and Tom assumed he still loved Elena. He'd let them believe the fallacy, thinking it easier than facing their pity and their well-meaning attempts at matchmaking. The plain truth was that Elena had burned the love out of him.

Clay's expression warmed with teasing pleasure. "And now you are married, too."

"My marriage is not what you think."

"Isn't it? I saw the way you looked at your wife." He grinned and nodded in the direction of the front corral, where he'd met Jasmine. "She's incredibly beautiful."

Despite himself, Brody smiled. Fondness for his unconventional wife soothed away some of the crushing regret. "She does have nice eyes, doesn't she?"

"Hell yes! Nice everything. And a lovely personality, too."

Brody's laugh of disbelief rebounded off the walls. "You don't know her very well yet."

Beyond the closed doorway, outside in the corridor, Jasmine leaned her head against the crack between door and wall where she'd been eavesdropping. The entire conversation had carried fairly well through the single, long slit.

You don't know her very well yet.

Her emotions plummeted below their previous sagging depth. Saint Elena, the perfect woman. Elena, who'd struggled against all odds to raise her children, to be loyal to her husband, and to grow her wildflowers. She probably even did dishes.

The helpless frustration inside Jasmine surged, pushing a trio of tears past her lashes. She swatted them away.

Footfalls approached along the hallway, warning her that

she was about to be discovered. She didn't move. Didn't really care.

Tom rounded the corner and halted when he saw her. Matter of factly, he bent down, hooked his hands beneath her arms and hoisted her to her feet. Then he propelled her in the direction of her room.

A perfectly folded white handkerchief appeared in front of her. She took it and blotted the last of the wetness from her cheeks.

Tom. *Her savior.* How she loved this sweet-natured little cowboy who seemed to understand her soul. Fresh moisture filled her eyes, but she soaked it up with the fabric before it could fall.

He led her across the great room without even glancing at the people who now populated it, then steered her along the hallway. When they stopped at her doorway, he cocked his head and considered her, his gaze shrewd. "A lot of tears to shed over a husband you dislike so intensely."

He was right. She sniffed.

"Take a nap before dinner," he said. "I'll go see if I can rustle up some of that peach cobbler you like so much." He gave her arm a gentle pat and disappeared toward the kitchen.

Though peach cobbler sounded good, she doubted it could cure what ailed her.

She leaned against the wall. What did ail her? Ever since meeting Elena she'd felt utterly miserable, completely beaten.

Brody had done this to her. That much was sure. But how? How could her unwanted husband make her feel so badly? He was simply a pawn in her game. A distraction.

No.

It was past time to be honest with herself. Truthfulness was one of the few dignities she had left.

Brody could no longer be classified as a distraction. Somehow, along the way, he'd become much, much more.

With a jolt, she realized that she wanted him. Not for a lifetime of dominion. But for tonight and tomorrow night. For these few days away from home.

She wasn't romantic or foolish enough to think that there would be other men like Brody in her life. There wouldn't be. The fact that she desired him was in itself an anomaly, a small miracle. Never had she been attracted this way to another man and she knew instinctively that she never would be again. He was the only one. The only chance she would ever have at being married, at experiencing passion.

Deep inside, she ached to own him, to conquer him, to make him want her back. She needed to prove to him and to herself that she was as desirable as Elena. As worthy of his love.

It was weak of her to harbor such feelings, she knew. But so be it. She would succumb to the character flaw of wanting Brody, because she couldn't help but feel that she deserved to be loved. Just this once.

A chill of anticipation slithered between her shoulder blades. She could scarcely wrap her brain around the thought of it. Making love to Brody. It was a brash idea, wild and wholly unadvisable. But then, she specialized in just such ideas.

Adrenaline flowed in streaks through her body, renewing her.

Tonight she'd share Brody's bed. In more ways than one.

Jasmine bathed. She washed her hair and scrubbed herself all over, even between her toes. After patting herself dry, she carefully donned her chemise. The gown she chose was dove gray in color, the fabric of such fine quality that it shone with pearly opalescence. The neckline scooped low and tight before smoothing over her breasts to a ferociously snug waist. The skirt fell in wide sweeps, especially in back, where the cloth tucked three times before expanding into a small train.

The overall effect was classically elegant, Jasmine decided. A jarring departure from her normal attire. Once her hair had dried into curls, she struggled with her hair pins until she'd secured the front and sides. The excess fell in a cascade down her back.

She peered at the result in her hand mirror and wished for jewelry. Her father had given her a whole stable of beautiful pieces. But Brody hadn't had the foresight to pack her any. So she'd go without.

The dinner hour drew nearer and nearer, and though she sat on the edge of their bed and waited anxiously for Brody, he didn't return to their room to dress. She could only assume he was avoiding her.

When she heard the clatter of guests arriving, she took a deep breath and decided to leave the safety of the bedroom without him.

With jerky steps, she made her way down the hallway. The gown weighed unusually heavily on her body and the masses of fabric slowed her gait. Maybe she'd been wrong. Maybe she looked ridiculous like this. What if they were all dressed casually except for her? What if she tripped and fell face first in front of them? Then her dress would flip up in back and expose her bottom. Of all the hideous ideas she'd had in her life, dressing up for Brody was probably the worst.

She paused in the hallway, cursed her cowardice, and forced herself to take the last few steps into the great room. People milled throughout the space. Her gaze scanned over them, searching for but not spotting Brody. Disappointment birthed within her, deepening moment by moment. Worse than making a fool of herself, worse than anything, was the possibility that he might not show up tonight.

"Jasmine!" Clay, who was surrounded by a knot of guests, beckoned to her.

She followed his summons and he immediately introduced her to his fiancée, Jessica, and her parents, Mr. and

Mrs. Potter. Mercifully, they were all clothed in formal attire like her own.

"We've got ourselves a packed house," Clay commented.

"Indeed," Mrs. Potter said. "I didn't realize your family was this extensive, Clay."

He smiled. "Well, in addition to the relatives who traveled in, five of my Ranger friends have come for the wedding."

"Indeed." Mrs. Potter said. "Indeed."

Jessica leaned toward Jasmine. "I'm anxious to meet your husband." The petite brunette had the widest, most genuine smile Jasmine had ever seen. Her sparkling teeth lit up half her face.

"Brody should be here any moment," she replied. "Don't you think so, Clay?"

Clay nodded. "Any moment."

Jasmine found little comfort in his reassurance. She chewed her cheek and stared past Mr. Potter's shoulder toward the front door. Maybe Brody would enter from there. But then, maybe he'd come from one of the hallways. Or the back door—

"Jasmine?" Clay said hesitantly. "Mrs. Potter just asked you how you find the weather in Tyler this time of year."

She whipped her attention back to the group who were all looking at her, awaiting her answer. "Very much like here."

Mrs. Potter smiled vaguely. "Indeed."

"If you'll excuse me." She edged away.

Jasmine made a wide sweep of the room, managing to dodge eye contact with anyone who appeared eager to trap her in meaningless conversation.

He still hadn't come. Her spirits sank. He *had* to come. This was the night before his brother's wedding.

She stopped beside one of the fireplaces. Barely a second later, two McClintock uncles and a male cousin cornered her. Their bold, wandering gazes and their silly small talk reminded her of the treatment she'd received from several of her previous suitors. She answered when appropriate and idly wondered just how many of her father's suitors she'd spurned. Maybe fifteen?

The longer the gentlemen rambled, the thinner her patience grew. Continually, she searched the doorways for Brody. In the middle of a particularly dull tale courtesy of Brody's uncle, she glanced up. And saw him.

Her breath wedged in her throat.

Brody had bathed and dressed for the occasion. He wore beautifully fitted black trousers and a simple white shirt, opened at the neck. His hair was combed back from his face, still slightly damp from washing.

With effort, she tugged her attention to the portly uncle. She watched his lips move, but heard nothing save her own frantic thoughts of Brody. She wondered where he had bathed and changed. Doubted that she could look him in the eye because he was so impossibly handsome tonight. Tried to-gauge when he might be approaching. . . .

Brody felt as if he'd been poleaxed. Unblinking, unthinking, he stood in the doorway and forgot to move.

Jasmine was ravishing in her figure-hugging breeches and work shirts. But this, this was another dimension entirely.

Perfect. She looked so shockingly, obviously beautiful that he couldn't damn believe it. By God, that dress. Her hair. Even the way she held herself.

For long moments he simply watched her. It appeared that she was staring with rapt attention at his uncle's lips. He squinted. Why in the hell was she staring as his uncle's lips?

Clay raised his voice and invited all his guests into the dining room for supper.

Jasmine panicked for a moment, worrying that in the black hole of time she'd spent gaping at the uncle's mouth,

Brody had left her in favor of food. She was almost to the desperate point of looking up and seeking him out when his scent reached her. Fresh and spiced with a dash of pine.

Her heart sprinted.

A strong hand slid around her waist and cupped her side. Conversation in their small circle lurched to a halt.

"I see you've met my wife," Brody said to the men.

They answered with a chorus of affirmative answers and hushed compliments. Jasmine couldn't speak over the tornado of desire roaring through her.

"If you'll excuse us, I think it's time I escorted her in to dinner."

"Certainly."

"Of course."

"Sure, Brody."

He steered her to the dining room. "I can't tell you how glad I am that I packed that dress for you," he whispered.

She blushed at his words, mostly because of the velvety way his voice caressed her ear. "I'm relieved you like it. I haven't worn a dress since that awful thing I had on the night of our . . ."

The lines of his face turned harsh.

". . . Wedding," she finished lamely.

He pulled her chair out and seated her. The remaining guests crowded around the colossal dining room table.

Jasmine couldn't think of enough ways to call herself a fool. Stupid idiot girl didn't seem strong enough. She'd gotten flustered, said the first thing that popped into her head and successfully managed to repulse him.

Brody took the chair next to hers and Clay sat beside him, at the head of the table. During the first course, Clay regulated conversation between the guests and generally worked to make everyone feel welcome.

Brody was far more reserved. Though Jasmine waited patiently during the serving of the main course for him to forgive her and focus his attention on her, he never did.

She began to dabble in conversation with the good-looking young Ranger on her left, who introduced himself as Seth Olds.

It had been thoughtless of her to remind Brody of their wedding night. But as time wore on she didn't think it had been terrible enough to justify his ignoring her. The longer he went without speaking to her, the more involved she pretended to become in Seth and the more unbearably aware she really became of her stony-faced husband. Her futile preoccupation with trying to make Brody jealous all but obliterated her appetite.

Whenever she glanced up from a comment Seth had made, she'd find Brody watching her. He'd quickly look away. Twice she thought she heard his teeth grind after she offered Seth fake giggles. And the one time she'd unconsciously touched Seth's arm while making a point, Brody had actually grabbed her knee beneath the table and squeezed a warning.

By dessert, Jasmine wondered how things had gone so horribly wrong. She kept trying to appear calm and indifferent. But every time she heard Brody reply to a question someone else had asked him, her heartbeat stuttered and her ears strained to catch every syllable. When he passed her a bowl of cream, their fingers brushed and the contact caused chills to race up her arms, then zigzag down her spine.

Mercifully, the meal finally ended and the party retired to the great room. Following a tradition Jasmine detested, the men grouped in a throng at one end of the room and the women congregated at the other. That left Jasmine stranded with Jessica, Jessica's mother, somebody's second cousin, an elderly aunt, and the wife of one of the Rangers.

Throughout the polite, ambling conversation with the women, Jasmine kept her hearing primed toward the masculine topics of discussion, hoping desperately to catch an interesting tidbit. Occasionally, she gave in to over-whelming temptation and peeked at Brody.

One such peek revealed Brody talking with a short, older man in an ill-fitting black suit. She tried to recall from Clay's introductions just who the man was.

"Eavesdropping on their conversation?" Jessica whispered.

Jasmine glanced at her. "Was I that obvious?"

"To use my mother's word, *indeed*." She grinned. "Who were you staring at?"

The other ladies in their circle launched into a heated discussion about the best way to fry chicken.

Jasmine flicked her chin toward the men. "I was wondering who the man in the black suit is."

Jessica searched the group, her vision stopping on the person Jasmine had described. "Oh. I believe his name is Mr. Grayson. One of the Rangers is accompanying him on a search. In fact, the Ranger accompanying him is Seth Olds, the man standing beside your husband. I think you sat next to Seth at dinner."

"I did." Jasmine's attention gravitated to Brody. He sat in a deep armchair, one boot propped across the opposite knee. She noticed that he smiled at the appropriate times, but commented only when necessary. The color of his eyes had deepened from hazel to guarded brown.

Seth stood before him, admiration wreathing his expression. Mr. Grayson regarded Brody with almost hawkish interest.

"He's terribly handsome," Jessica said.

Jasmine roused from her reverie and focused on the young woman beside her, trying in vain to imagine what Jessica found handsome about a squat old man in a bad suit.

"Your husband," Jessica prompted with one of her dazzling smiles. "Clay always told me that Brody got the lion's share of the McClintock good looks. But I never believed him, because Clay is so handsome himself. That is, I never believed him until tonight, when I met your husband." She giggled.

Jasmine smiled, her pride in Brody purely feminine.

"How long have you been married?" Jessica asked.

"Two weeks."

"Is that all?"

It seemed like forever. "Yes."

Jessica scooted even closer. "You're practically still on your honeymoon!"

No, Jasmine thought. *But as of tonight we will be.* "That's right."

Another flash of shiny white teeth. "Then you know what I'm going through! I can hardly believe that all these people have come for our wedding. Imagine, tomorrow is the day!"

"I'm sure it will be wonderful," Jasmine said, hoping she sounded sincere, but worried that Jessica might launch into a discussion about weddings. If that happened, she doubted her capacity to feign interest.

The noise level dropped and the ladies around them slowly rose to their feet.

Jessica glanced at her mother. "It looks like it's time to return home." She stood and smoothed her dress into place. "I'll see you tomorrow at the wedding."

Jasmine rose to her feet. "You will." She reached out and gave the girl's hand an impromptu squeeze.

"Any advice for me?" Jessica asked.

"Ahh...." Jasmine snatched the first thought that occurred. "Just be sure to wear a becoming ..." she gestured toward Jessica's head, scouring her memory, "headdress."

"A veil?" Jessica asked, caught between bewilderment and more giggles.

"Yes. That. A veil."

"I will." Jessica squeezed her hand back, then turned to go.

As soon as the women had eased away, Jasmine checked on Brody. He was still caught in conversation with Seth and Mr. Grayson.

She simply couldn't stand to continue pretending to be aloof under the scrutiny of so many strangers any longer. Better to wait for him in the bedroom. There, she could concentrate on rescuing her planned seduction.

She lifted a handful of her skirts and hurried down the hall.

Chapter 16

O nce she'd reached the bedroom, Jasmine fumbled around in the dark, trying to feel her way to the lamp. Her shin banged smartly against the bed frame. "Damn!"

Her leg throbbing, she managed to teeter over to the dresser, locate the lamp, and light it. The flame danced to life, painting her surroundings in peachy light.

What would be provocative to Brody? She glanced down at herself. Hesitantly, she pushed one of the sleeves off her shoulder. Her bare skin looked flushed and felt overly sensitive to the touch, which was odd. Maybe she was coming down with something.

Picking up the mirror with shaky fingers, she released a couple of strategic pins and tried to arrange her hair in an alluringly mussed style.

After a few frustrating attempts, she gave up and set the mirror down. She had absolutely no experience at this. Attracting men had always been the furthest thing from her mind. More than that. It had been the opposite of what she'd wanted to accomplish. With the single exception of that night in the hut.

He had found her arousing then.

He hadn't known her then.

She swiveled toward the bed, confronting it. Maybe she

should try a tantalizing pose, as she had that night. She groaned. Maybe she should simply extinguish the light.

No, she amended. *No.* She could do this. She pressed damp palms down the sides of her waist. She'd try a tantalizing pose. It would work.

She stalked the bed as if it were a wild horse and she a cowboy intent on breaking it. Her eyes narrowed with gritty determination. Perhaps, if she draped herself over the side—

The door whooshed open. She swiveled.

Brody slammed the door behind him. In two strides he was upon her. He slid his tongue into her mouth as his hands pushed into her hair.

Scorching need ripped through her, throwing all thought to the wind.

Their tongues delved hard and searched deep. His breath rasped against her lips. She heard him moan. Dimly, she was aware of his hands running restlessly along her shoulders, her ribs. He traced kisses down to the hollow of her throat and she threw her head back, glorying in the sensation. How badly she had needed to feel those kisses on her flesh.

His fingers slid along the neckline of her gown, pulling down on the fabric that shielded her breasts. Instinctively, she pressed into his hands, wanting more.

Quick, like he'd draw his gun or change the direction of his horse, he grasped her shoulders and pressed her against the wall.

She tried to assimilate what was happening. Couldn't.

His breath came unevenly. "Were you trying to make me jealous?"

"What? I—"

"Don't. Don't play games that hurt me."

Her swollen lips parted. "I hurt you?"

He imprisoned her chin between thumb and forefinger. His lips took hers in a kiss so intensely, tenderly sweet that a sob rose in her throat. He didn't touch her anywhere else, except with his lips and tongue. The ache of the pain she'd caused him pulsed from him into her, communicated in a silent explanation more eloquent than words.

He broke the contact and leaned back just enough to gaze at her. "I don't want to see you, like that, with other men."

"I understand." Oh, heaven, he was so beautiful to her. Longing peaked inside her in a crescendo of feeling. She trembled.

He crushed her against him, claiming her with another fierce kiss.

She bore his passion, grasped at it, gave her own passion back to him. Sightlessly, she gripped his shoulders, then buried her fingers in his hair.

His free hand stroked along the swell of a breast before rounding over her buttocks and pressing her hips against the insistence of his arousal.

She sunk her nails into his scalp. And then, abruptly, he stepped away. All the warmth went with him, leaving her in a writhing hole of need.

He stared down at her with turbulent, dark eyes. "What are you doing to me?"

She was desolate without him. Desperate. Her breath came in thready gulps. "Nothing."

"Is this acquiescence of yours some sort of a trick?"

"No!"

"A manipulation, then."

"No." She craved him. He was so close, and his desire for her obvious in every line of his body. It would be easy to go to him. But she held back because she remembered too well. The last time she'd approached him with a timid, truthful kiss, he'd rejected her.

This time he would come to her. Begging.

Without taking her eyes off him, she reached for the back of her gown and began unfastening the row of buttons. "I want to be with you tonight," she said. "That's all."

She had no time to waste on modesty. They should be together. Her confidence in that truth goaded her onward. The remaining sleeve slipped off the ivory curve of her shoulder.

Brody's chest hitched. He couldn't take his eyes off her. One long, auburn curl slid over a bare shoulder and came to rest between her breasts. Her skin glistened with exertion.

He licked dry lips as she pulled the gown lower, nearly exposing a tightened nipple to him. His body burned, raging to take her. But the unholy challenge he saw in her eyes held him back. Her sparkling gaze beckoned to him, seduced him, and promised him hell if he lost himself in her spell.

Her lungs expanded rhythmically, flattening her breasts against the thin wall of fabric. The auburn curl that rested there shuddered.

Unable to stop himself, he jerked his shirt from his trousers and pulled apart the buttons. She gazed at his revealed chest and extended her hand halfway to him. He grasped her fingers and guided them the rest of the way, flattening them against his ribs.

Her lips parted on a gasp.

Christ, she made him crazy. He drew her fingers lower, over the muscle of his stomach, to the line of his trousers. He paused, his breath coming hard.

Her gaze flicked up to his. There was awe in her eyes, and smoke.

He stared at her as he dragged her hand lower and pressed it directly over the evidence of his desire for her.

For an instant she froze. Then caught her bottom lip in her teeth. Her fingers began to move. To probe the shape of him, to rub.

He wanted to throw back his head and scream. The sensation was so intense it broke his will. He captured her lips and tongue in another urgent kiss. She responded wildly, her hand-moving over him more hungrily.

He couldn't stop the groan that filled his throat, couldn't stop tasting her. He wanted her vitality. Wanted her beneath him. Needed her naked.

He jerked away and grabbed the top of her gown, his fingers shaking with the desire to free her breasts, to feel them.

Take her now and be lost. Or leave.

He hesitated. He knew his choices, and wanted the first with everything he was. Except for one tiny kernel of reason. That small bastion edged into his consciousness, reminding him that he could never surrender himself to a woman again. His love for Elena had ravaged him and destroyed his family.

Jasmine gazed at him, doubt clouding her expression. "Brody?"

"I can't."

"Of course you can. We—"

He stepped away from her.

She pressed her tender, rosy lips together and waited.

"Let me make the right decision for both of us," he said, "while I still have that capability."

Jasmine watched his jaw tighten, saw the entrancing play of muscles leaping up his cheeks. Before she could even decide whether to reach for him, he was through the doorway.

She listened to his fading footfalls.

"Damn!" She turned to the bed and pounded a fist into the mattress. "Damn. Damn. *Damn!*" Far too distressed to sit, she paced from one side of the room to the other and back again. Her body seethed with a restlessness unlike any she'd ever known. She couldn't think.

Her hands fisted. Unfisted. She strode harder and shook out her arms. Her brain was impossibly alert, yet muddled. Too many thoughts surged and ebbed. She couldn't catch any of them. Frustration flew past. Excitement. Hurt. Desire.

She continued to pace. Finally, the rhythm of her steps lulled her body and the worst of the storm blew by. Sanity drifted back in long, unwinding segments.

She sat down on the bed and immediately couldn't bear it. She jumped back up and resumed her pacing, but at a more moderate speed.

Despite what he'd said and despite the fact that he'd walked out on her, she knew that Brody McClintock had wanted her. There was no denying it. The evidence had been in his eyes, in his kisses, in the feel of him beneath her hand.

At first, she'd been stunned by the immediate success of her seduction. If only she'd had the time to arrange herself in a tantalizing pose, she'd have been naked in his arms, perched of the verge of womanhood by now.

Instead, she was achingly alone, with messy hair and tingly lips and a gaping dress.

He will come back. She consoled herself with that fact. He had no other choice but to sleep with her, seeing as all the other beds were taken. He could do nothing except return to the comfort of her bed and the welcoming embrace of her two arms. She examined her arms and long fingers. Her hands looked foreign to her, like sensual attachments belonging to another, more mature woman.

She slipped out of the gray gown and threw it over the edge of the dresser. Her stockings and chemise followed before she extinguished the lamp.

Feeling deliciously wicked, she slipped into bed without a stitch of clothing and delighted in the feel of the crisp sheets rubbing against the expanse of her bare skin.

She curled the quilt beneath her chin and huddled into a ball to wait. Her eyes gleamed like polished sapphires in the darkened chamber.

He'll be back.

*   *   *

He didn't come back.

At some point during the night, Jasmine finally drifted off to sleep, her frenzied mind giving up its quest to explain Brody's continued absence.

She woke to an insistent knocking.

Wedging open her puffy eyes, she stared at the door. Her thoughts immediately picked up where they'd left off the previous night. It must be Brody, finally come to accept her generous offer of love making. "Who is it?" she called, attempting to make her scratchy morning voice sound as attractive as possible.

"Tom."

Tom. Of course it was Tom.

"Jasmine?"

She was on the verge of telling him to come in when she remembered that she wasn't wearing anything.

"Is everything all right?" he called.

What should she do? Her gaze leapt around the room, finally settling on the dresser which held her nightgown. She'd just dash over there and throw it on.

"Jasmine?" He knocked twice more in quick succession.

Half leaping to the edge of the bed, she set her feet on the floor. The knob started to turn. She shot back under the covers like a lightning bolt.

Then heard the door wheel open. "Jasmine?"

"Yes," came her reply, muffled by sheets and quilt.

"I've been knocking for ages. What's the matter? Are you sick?"

The bumpy lump on the bed shifted, and a thatch of russet curls appeared. Next came a pair of glittering, light blue eyes. "Nope."

Tom immediately averted his gaze to the floor. "I'm sorry to disturb you," he muttered. He walked backward. "But breakfast is about to be cleared away and I didn't want you to miss it."

"I'll be right there. Thank you."

He nodded quickly.

She tried to ease his mortification. "You know how I hate to—"

The door shut behind him.

". . . miss my eggs," she finished, her voice petering to a stop.

Her lips trembled into a smile as she reemerged from the cocoon of warm blankets. Darling Tom.

She glanced at the window. Bright sunlight beamed through the panes. She could just see the canopy of a walnut tree beyond, its branches swaying lazily in the breeze.

It was going to be a perfect spring day. Ideal for an afternoon wedding.

Hope lightened her movements as she dressed. She even attempted to hum an off-key chorus. Brody hadn't returned to her last night. But it didn't matter. She'd laid the foundation. Tonight she'd catch him.

More sure than ever of her decision to make love to him, she tugged on her boots. Brody was the only husband she was ever going to have. The least she could expect from him was one measly night of lovemaking. Hell. He owed it to her.

Sweet smelling air swirled around the underside of Jasmine's hat, pinkening her nose and watering her eyes. She moved with Vengeance's gallop, rising and returning to the saddle, maneuvering the reins.

How she loved to ride.

It was especially wonderful this morning with so much unexplored countryside unfolding around her in every direction. As she progressed down the path that wound away from McClintock Ranch, she slowed Vengeance's pace to a mincing trot.

He tossed his head.

"Whoa, boy. We'll go again soon enough." She brought

him around in a circle, taking a quick survey of the land-scape. One particular hill, its graceful mound capped with a grove of trees, caught her attention. It had an idyllic, almost mystic beauty about it, framed as it was by a sun-kissed backdrop of rising plains.

She pointed Vengeance toward it. The horse needed no more invitation. They hurtled forward.

Brody hadn't been at breakfast. In fact, by the time she'd risen, only Tom had been available for table conversation. The remaining guests were either in the great room chatting, or out on various excursions around the property.

At first, she'd opted to stay indoors and wait for Brody's return. But the house had hemmed her in, stifling her more and more until she'd run for the corral. She knew of no better way to work off her tension than a hard ride.

She swept her hat from her head and let the wind brush out her hair. It combed through the heavy mass with twisting, streaking fingers. Jasmine tilted her face to the sun and let its rays gild her skin.

Vengeance bent into the hill's incline. She checked his speed and focused on the approaching summit. The grass was as smooth here as a billiard table. It bent and rose with the terrain, a seamless carpet. At the top, a cluster of trees clung to the earth, speckling the ground with shade.

She eased Vengeance to a walk, ducked under the lowest branches and was admitted to the inner circle.

An almost tangible stillness encompassed her. Silent and cool, the small glade seemed to wait with hushed breath and a lulled heart. Her intuition pricked.

She scanned the knot of vegetation to her right. Nothing. Just grass and trees, hopeful for a wind that never came. She looked to the left. What was it about this place that— her heart began to thud. The eeriness of the glade swished about her, cloaking her in a conspiracy of tranquility.

Directly to her left on a flat patch of land, two wooden crosses rose from the earth.

Vengeance fidgeted beneath her. She slipped from the saddle and led him aside.

Returning, she stood with her toes on the outer edge of the burial ground and stared at the simple, skillfully crafted wooden crosses. They were identical in shape and style.

The small hairs at the back of her neck rose and foreboding stitched down her spine. She felt like an intruder in an undisturbed, sacred place. Uninvited.

She glanced toward the ranch. Beyond the main house and its outbuildings, the prairie spread in lush expanses of earth and bluebonnets. In the extreme distance the buildings of Nacogdoches nestled between land and sky. It was lovely. But in this sheltered place she felt as removed from the scene as if it were a one dimensional painting she couldn't reenter.

Her attention returned to the graves. Her instinct to leave the owners of this hill in peace conflicted sharply with her curiosity.

She took a deep breath and gently knelt beside the crosses. A layer of leaves and dirt concealed the barely visible carvings. She used her teeth to tug free her right glove, then pressed fingers to the wood. A shiver traveled up her arm, reverberating pain and loss.

She brushed away a strip of nature's debris. *Bea.* She'd revealed only part of the name. In one fast sweep she cleared the rest. *Beatrice McClintock.* Below it read simply, *May 17, 1864.*

Blood howled in her ears, escalating, throbbing. She leaned toward the remaining cross and wiped it clean. *Ross McClintock. May 17, 1864.*

Jasmine sat back on her heels and peered at the markers. Were these Brody's parents? Why would they have died on the same day? She couldn't bring herself to reach for the crosses again, but nor could she look away.

A twig cracked behind her, shattering the veil of silence. Jasmine jerked around to see Brody standing with legs planted apart, one hand clasping his hat against his thigh.

"Brody."

His face, already grim, became haunted. "Who told you about this place?"

Disappointment knifed through her. She had wanted their next meeting to be a good one. Instead he was looking at her with bitterness, speaking to her in a tone laced with suspicion. She tried to tell herself that his mistrust didn't matter. But the pain of it burrowed deep. "No one told me about it. I was out on a ride and stumbled across it." She rose to her feet and stepped away from the plots.

His gaze followed her.

She looked him in the eye, squared her shoulders and hoped she didn't appear as guilty as she felt. He had no right to make her feel guilty. She had done nothing to be ashamed of.

Saints, but he looked dangerous this morning. Mean and unpredictable. Obviously, he'd not slept well the night before. His hair was rumpled, the same shirt he'd worn last night was wrinkled and falling open at the neck. The ever-changing hazel eyes were lined with red.

"Go back to the ranch, Jasmine," he said.

His words stung, but she squelched the hurt and set her lips with resolve. Clearly, these crosses, these people buried here, were important to him. If it would give her insight into the hidden motives of his heart, she would stay and fight for the truth. "Who were they?" she asked.

He stepped more fully into the tiny clearing. "It's none of your business."

"I disagree. I'm your wife, aren't I?"

Anger creased his brow. "Is that what you want now, to play my wife?"

"No. I wanted to stay home. You were the one who insisted that I come and play this damnable part." She scowled. "If you want me to be a believable wife, the least you can do is spare me the truth."

"The truth," he scoffed. "When have you ever dealt in truth?"

"I . . . I . . ." She halted, unable to defend herself. The fact that she had lied and tricked him into marriage was an indisputable fact between them. She chose her words carefully. "What I did the night I married you, I did out of desperation." She nudged up her chin. "Despite what you think of me, my Daddy raised me to be honest."

"Is that the same father that drove you to such desperation that you were forced to wed yourself to a stranger?"

She had a right to be angry with her father, but she'd be damned if she'd stand here and let Brody slight him. "Don't you dare," she hissed. "Don't you dare insult him."

"Then don't come up here and ask me for answers you have no right to know." He yanked his gaze away from her.

Her nails curled into her palms.

Leaves rustled softly overhead, gratified by the wind that had finally reached them. The softness of the sound opposed the deafening rage and anguish churning within her. She badly wanted to storm away from him, as she'd been so fond of doing throughout her childhood. Her pride fairly demanded it.

And yet something about him, the heartache in his eyes, bade her stay. A coarse rope of perseverance twined her feet to the spot. She would fight for him. "Who were they, Brody?"

He didn't look up. Veins snaked into the hand that clasped his hat. "Just go away."

"I asked you who—"

"And I asked you to go away!"

She sucked in air. "I want to know."

"It's none of your concern."

"I think it is."

"Then you're damn well mistaken," he growled.

"Please, I—"

"Leave me alone!"

"Tell me the what happened!"

Furious eyes pierced her. "You want to know what happened?" he spat.

"Yes."

He stalked to her, flinging a hand toward the graves. "These are my parents."

She stood speechless.

"Is that what you needed to hear?" he demanded. "Is that enough for you?"

Her lips opened, but no sound came out.

"Ask me how they died," he hissed.

"No . . . I—"

"Ask me!"

"Brody, I—"

He towered over her, a terrifying expression twisting his features. "I said ask me."

"How did they die?" she whispered.

Chaotic hazel eyes bored into blue. He waited, waited until she could see almost directly into the tortured depths of his soul. Waited until the bleakness there infected her own soul.

"I killed them."

Chapter 17

"**N**o," Jasmine breathed, feeling as if the air were being strangled out of her.

"Is that so hard to believe of me?"

She swallowed, trying to make sense of her riotous thoughts. Logic fled. Reason crumbled. But her heart's opinion rose from their ashes, quieting the tumult within. She'd seen too much integrity in Brody, too much honor and honesty to believe such a thing of him. "It's impossible," she said. "Impossible to believe that you killed your parents. I refuse to. And no one could persuade me otherwise."

"Not even me?"

"Not even you."

He cursed and turned to face the twin crosses.

Brody was a man of power, of secrets and of unknown ruthlessness. Sometimes, he frightened her. But she'd never accept that he'd killed his parents. The ravaged, guilt-ridden expression he wore confirmed it.

Quietly, she picked her way across the small stretch of earth to stand beside him. She laced her fingers together and held herself very still. A jumbled prayer for him formed in her mind. She petitioned God with it, feeling humble and unworthy.

The seconds stretched.

"Why?" he asked suddenly, his voice echoing in the surrounding hush.

"Why don't I believe you could be responsible for their deaths?" she asked, her instincts filling in the words he hadn't spoken.

He nodded.

"Because my heart tells me so."

Their gazes met. She could feel him measuring and weighing her expression, testing her statement for truth.

Chewing on the inside of her cheek, she asked, "Have I ruined your trust so completely that you doubt everything I say?"

"I don't know. Will you ever give me cause to believe you?"

"I just have."

He scanned her eyes. Then he turned and knelt before the crosses. Painstakingly, he wiped away the last of the dirt, finishing the job she had begun. His touch lingered noticeably against his mother's name before he straightened. Without a glance, he walked past her, toward his horse.

He was leaving?

She scurried after him, throwing her slight frame in front of him to stop his progress. "That's it?"

He halted, focusing his attention on donning his gloves. "That's it." He attempted to shoulder past her.

Again, she blocked his path. "I want to know what happened to them."

"Go ask Tom. He's your confidant."

"I want to hear it from you."

Annoyance flickered across his features as he again made to move by her. "For God's sake, Jasmine, we've got a wedding to attend."

She stopped him by thumping both palms against the wall of his chest. Her heels dug into the soft earth. With eyes glinting clearest blue she said, "Now."

He scowled at her.

She didn't budge.

His expression cleared, becoming neutral in the instant before a grin swept across his features. The cleft in his chin deepened.

His smile was so unexpected and so breathtakingly handsome, that her fingers curled into the fabric of his shirt.

"Is this the part where I'm supposed to beg for my life?" he asked.

"You could try. But I'd not be swayed."

He glanced at the fingers entwined in the cloth covering his chest. Then he gave her a look which demanded she release him and simultaneously dared her not to.

Self-conscious, now that her fierceness had trembled away on a wave of humor, Jasmine unclenched her fingers. Awkwardly, she patted the bunched cloth into some semblance of normalcy. "I can be a little . . . stubborn . . . when I set my mind to something."

"Really? I hadn't noticed." He whisked his gloved thumb over the hollow of her cheek. The casual caress jolted her to her toes. His touch had been rough in texture, yet softer than a sigh.

He leaned against the trunk of a nearby mesquite tree and crossed his arms. "I fought in the war."

Jasmine managed to shake off the drugging effects of his touch long enough to realize that in his own offhand, modest way Brody was relating his story to her. "You served the Confederacy, I presume?"

A fleeting smile, wry this time. "Well, I am a Texan, Jasmine."

She gestured impatiently. "Of course. Go on."

"Clay enlisted, too. He fought beside me. For three years I never let him out of my sight. There were several times, several battles, when I feared that he'd die, when I doubted my ability to get him through alive. Somehow we managed." He paused, memories engraving wrinkles into the skin around his eyes. His gaze rose above her, fastening on the cloudless sky. "I made my mother a promise when we left that I'd bring Clay home safely."

"I'm sure she was equally concerned about your safety."

"That was part of the promise. I had to bring him back."

"I see." She studied his face, its planes, shadows, and angles. How could it be that this one masculine face, just a compilation of features like any other, could attract her so strongly? The sadness she saw there now made her want to fall to her knees and sob for him. Her throat tightened.

"That promise to my mother is what brought me through the war," he said. "That, and one other thing. . . ."

She could read what was coming in his eyes. "Elena," she said dully.

He nodded, his lips thinning. "Elena. Before I left to fight, she promised me that she'd wait for me."

Beyond the clinging jealousy, Jasmine experienced a stab of fury. "Then why didn't she?"

"Because she lost faith that I'd come back. She fell in love with another man."

Jasmine couldn't decide whether she wanted to beat Brody over the head for continuing to love the woman, or whether she wanted to beat Elena's head. Brody's more so, she supposed. How could he stand there looking like the irresistible star of some romantic novel and tell her of his love for another woman? How *could* he, when she herself would have waited till her hair turned gray and her heart stopped beating for him to return to her? *If I were Elena, they'd have had to pluck your picture from my cold, dead fingers before they buried me.*

"When I came home," he said, "I went to her. She told me then that she was engaged to marry another in a week's time."

His words had become more deliberate, more carefully modulated. She could tell how intensely private these memories were to him.

"I didn't know what to do at that point," he said. "I couldn't bear to go home and face my mother's sad, understanding glances. Nor could I bear the sight of Elena any longer. So I rode. For three days . . . just rode." He uncrossed his arms, briefly massaged his temple and then let his hands drop to his sides.

"When I finally came back to the ranch, I found Clay on the front steps, sobbing. Our parents had been killed the day before by bandits. Jasmine, they murdered them for a handful of horses."

Horror racked through her, hollowing out her insides. She couldn't move.

"There was nothing I could do," he said. "Except dig graves and carve crosses." Moisture shone in his eyes, making the hazel depths look like pebbles washed by a flood of grief.

Tears sprang to her own eyes.

They gazed at each other, caught in a timeless moment of understanding. Then he blinked, once, and the moment broke. The moisture in his eyes vanished.

"You . . ." she sniffed. "You think you could have saved them had you been at home?"

"I know I could have. I saved my brother, didn't I? Countless times. Against far worse threats than horse thieves."

"Did Clay try to protect them?"

She saw his throat tighten. "That's the worst part. When I didn't come home that second night, my mother grew worried and sent Clay to look for me. If he hadn't been out searching for me, he'd have been there to fight alongside my father."

"Oh, Brody." She wanted to say a thousand things. Beautiful things that would ease his pain. But nothing beautiful came to mind. And the poor phrases that did come weren't adequate. "Were the bandits caught?"

"No."

She noted the defensive set of his jaw, the flex of his hands. A suspicion slithered into her thoughts and quickly solidified into a certainty. "It's why you joined the Rangers, isn't it? To apprehend them."

Abruptly, he looked away. This time when he attempted to walk by her, she let him. She swiveled to watch as he retrieved his horse's reins. "You've been looking for them all these years," she said.

He flipped the reins over the animal's neck.

"You told me once that you broke a vow by marrying me," she said.

He ignored her.

"You—you must have made that vow back then, after Elena." Her brain hummed. "Because you blamed what happened on your love of her."

He mounted his horse and sat in the saddle stiffly, presenting her with nothing but his profile.

A strand of Jasmine's hair lifted on the breeze. She captured it and pushed it aside. "You've never found your parents' killers," she said, her heart overflowing with sorrow.

His gaze snapped toward her. "I already told you. I am my parents' killer."

He looked at her with regret and frustration and confusion. Then he galloped down the slope of the hill.

The bride blushed.

Jasmine sat in the second pew of the little chapel and surveyed her soon to be sister-in-law as she paraded down the aisle. Jessica had even worn a veil, she noticed, and a very becoming one. Beneath its gauzy folds Jessica's smile shone with its usual brilliance. Her lips quivered a tiny bit as her father escorted her past Jasmine's seat up to the front of the airy, clapboard church. Sunlight filtered through the stained glass window behind the preacher, illuminating the image of Jesus on his cross with sparkling shades of emerald and ivory and palest pink.

The preacher greeted the congregation and placed Jessica's hand into Clay's. The groom's face glowed with pride and pleasure. His adoration of his bride was so blatant, that Jasmine felt mildly embarrassed to witness it.

The preacher launched into a prayer and all around her, heads bowed in reverence. Jasmine kept her head up and her eyes open. She stared at Brody, who stood beside his brother, tall and imposing. Clothed all in black, he looked more somber and more formal than she'd ever seen him.

Pride expanded within her. Mine, she thought. *My* husband.

The prayer concluded with an echoing amen and the couple began repeating vows. Jasmine continued to stare at Brody.

All day, she'd thought of little but the things he had told her in the glade. She wondered, not for the first time, how deeply his parents deaths had affected him. The answer came back the same as it had before. Losing his mother and father must have scarred him to his soul. She could understand now why he hadn't returned to the ranch in so many years. For Brody, his home was filled with demons. Demons he'd hoped to banish by taking the responsibility for his parents' fate onto his own shoulders and avenging their death. Demons that remained because he'd never found their killers.

She wished she knew how to comfort him. But she still hadn't a clue what he longed to hear. Throughout her years in Tyler, there had been many times when she'd tried to offer her compassion to friends. Each time she'd sensed that her attempts were clumsy and overly gruff.

Her attention skated down the length of Brody's long legs and up again to his profile. She loved the way his hair fell over his collar in back—

He glanced at her.

She cut her gaze to the couple who were now in the process of exchanging rings. Tilting her head slightly, she tried to look as if she'd been fully engrossed in the ceremony. She even yawned, hoping to add a convincing bit of boredom to her act.

Inside she felt anything but bored. Every cell of her face burned with sensitivity. Her lip muscles strained and her cheeks felt wooden.

She risked another peek at Brody. Once again, he was calmly regarding the bride and groom.

She sighed and happily settled into staring at him again. Her plan to seduce him hadn't wavered. In fact, her awareness of him was growing more intense by the minute.

She was glad he'd brought the burgundy gown for her to wear to the dance tonight. At the moment she had on a refined navy and white, but she'd carried the burgundy with her in her saddle bag. Surely. Dear God in heaven. Surely, the body-hugging burgundy gown would crumble the last of his resolve and she'd be making love to her husband come morning.

Faintly, she heard the preacher say, "I now pronounce you man and wife."

Brody sipped his glass of McBryan. The fiery liquid slid down his throat, warming his insides. With mounting frustration, he surveyed the milling crowd. Again.

She wasn't among them.

After the ceremony, the congregation had traveled to Jessica's family home on the outskirts of Nacogdoches. They'd shared a jovial supper, served off a vast outdoor table and serviced by a bevy of fluttering women who wore white aprons over their best dresses. By the time the guests had turned their attention to dessert, the sun was setting in a blaze of orange, abdicating its heavenly throne to the moon.

The table and chairs they'd used for the meal remained,

but now they .stood like skeletons on the darkened lawn, free of the people and food that had enlivened them. Everyone had moved into the barn, which was doubling as a dance hall for the occasion. Ribbons and flowers festooned the vast interior, lending it a celebratory atmosphere. The fiddler had recently launched into the second tune of the night and the caller standing next to him was beginning to hit his stride.

"All alone?" Clay strode up to Brody and thumped him on the shoulder.

"Seems so." Where in the hell was she?

Clay grinned and pulled Brody into a manly hug. "Your wife finally came to her senses and decided to abandon you, did she?"

Brody tried to pretend he found the question funny. But with Jasmine for a wife, abandonment was a very real possibility. "It looks that way."

"Well." Clay gestured toward the roomful of shiny faces. "There are plenty of local girls who'd be happy to take a turn with you until she returns."

"Not interested."

"No?"

Brody gave his brother an affectionate push. "No. Leave me in peace. This is your wedding, so go socialize. You've got a whole crowd of people to charm."

"Here's hoping they're less surly and more susceptible to my charm than you are." Clay bobbed his glass and took a deep swallow.

Brody squinted into the crowd. A glint of burgundy caught his eye.

"Brody? Are you paying attention to my insults at all?"

If the throng would just shift slightly. . . .

"Brody? I asked you if—"

"Excuse me." Absently, he handed Clay his drink and began walking toward the gown he could almost glimpse through the web of bodies.

My God. He stopped.

It was Jasmine. Wearing the gown he'd chosen for her from her own closet.

Fabric cupped her breasts so erotically that he hardened for her. His reaction would have angered him if he'd taken the time to think about it. But all he could consider was Jasmine. And the dress that molded to her waist and cradled her hips before swooping in a snug bell shape to the floor.

She looked ravishing. Like an exotic bird among a flock of pigeons.

His arousal almost pained him. How in the hell was he going to control himself around her?

She glanced up and spotted him. Her silvery eyes stopped his heart, even across the distance. Rose flushed the luminous hue of her cheeks and the burgundy gown deepened the rich auburn of her hair.

He nodded to her and forced his feet to move. The surrounding noise of fiddler, conversations and shrill laughter faded away. When he reached her, he bent his head to her ear. "Do you have any idea how beautiful you are?"

Her pale eyes widened in amazement "I've never been beautiful."

He detected no coyness in her words, nor sorrow. Just simple, unblemished opinion. "You're mistaken," he said. "I can't speak for the past, but for as long as I've known you, you've been beautiful."

She gaped at him.

Taking her hand, he led her to the nearest, quiet niche. "You changed clothes."

She graced him with a man-killing smile. "This dress is only suitable under moonlight."

He had to concede the point. "Did you get enough to eat at dinner?" he asked, feeling like the definition of a fool because it was the only question that came to mind.

"Plenty, thank you."

He hadn't any idea what else to say to her. He knew how

to ride for months at a stretch, could rope a calf with four kinds of throws, or track an outlaw across Texas. But this, chatting politely with a tough cowgirl turned exquisite woman, this escaped him. There were no familiar smudges on her creamy skin tonight. No work-scarred boots. No pink bandana. Just an elegant seductress, wearing a dress that inflamed his senses.

Next to her, he felt coarse.

"I wondered where you were during the meal," he lied. He hadn't had to wonder. He'd known exactly.

"Oh . . . I sat with Jessica's cousins."

"I see." Nothing! Nothing to say. Silence elongated as the current melody died with a dramatic flourish. "Would you care to dance?"

She regarded him with laughing skepticism. "Don't let the gown fool you. I'm not a very graceful dancer."

"Then you'll be in good company." He extended his arm. She laid her hand on it and he guided her onto the floor through a maze of chattering, panting couples.

He could smell her. The fall of auburn curls that tumbled down her back smelled of sunshine. The scent, bright and clear, wound through him, melding with his desire in a feverish rush.

On a strong up beat, the music resumed. The caller relayed his instructions to the dancers in a loud, lucid voice. The bodies around them lurched into motion and Brody and Jasmine followed suit.

The tempo, the evening air and simple pleasure invigorated Jasmine. She'd never felt so alive as she did at this moment, her pulse skipping in time to the pace of the fiddle.

Brody danced next to her with both skill and reserve. Somehow his serious regard of her was more sensual than any reckless smile could have been. It overwhelmed her to look at him for very long, so she stole glances.

Their hands met and then separated over and over again. At every parting, her anticipation spiked to an almost shivering need. And at every joining, silky delight rolled in her belly. Twice during the song, he held her with both hands and guided her in a circle. Once, his grip supported her waist.

When the dance came to an end her legs stopped, but her senses continued to spin in joyous circles.

Clay threaded his way over to them, pulling Jessica in tow. "Mind if I have a turn with your lovely wife?" he asked Brody, breaking the private world they'd created.

"One turn," Brody warned.

Clay and Jessica laughed good-naturedly, assuming Brody's response had been a jest.

Brody passed her hand to his brother, while Clay transferred his bride's hand to Brody.

Jasmine had time to sneak just one more look at her husband as he walked away. He caught her stare. Then the music began again and Clay pulled her into a fresh dance. Throughout the tune, Jasmine tried valiantly to pay attention to Clay. But her gaze kept returning to a spot over his shoulder where Brody danced among the blur of faces and color.

One dance turned into two when Tom asked for the honor of the next round. After that, a steady stream of cowboys and ranchers and Rangers asked for dances. She was so filled with elation that she accepted several offers in a row.

Not so of Brody, she knew. After his turn with Jessica, he'd retired to a vacant corner of the barn. So far she'd seen him turn down two particularly bold women. Instead of dancing, he'd been watching her like a hawk, his perusal flushing her with confidence.

Finally, when her feet began to throb from the newness of her shoes, Jasmine decided to take a rest. She thanked her partner, declined the offer of yet another dance and turned toward Brody. Unfortunately, she found herself on the opposite corner of the floor to where he was standing.

Between the movements of those around her, her gaze locked with Brody's. She saw him push away from the wall and walk toward her. Her heart picking up speed, she moved in his direction.

With a string of 'excuse me's she reached the perimeter of the dancing area, then made her way through the crush of guests. Twice, her skirts were stepped on by wayward boots and once she received a feminine elbow in the ribs. But she plowed on, anxious beyond reason to be by his side.

She was almost to him. She arched onto her tiptoes and peered over the meaty shoulder of a cowboy who was blocking her path.

Brody looked so gorgeous, winding his way toward her. Her lips curved into a smile. As soon as she got close, she'd say something flattering to him. He'd laugh and compliment her. Maybe he'd hold her hand.

She was on the verge of trying to squeeze past the cowboy when a wraith in a flowing green dress entered her field of vision. Jasmine didn't need to look closer to identify the softly curving figure.

Elena.

Dread rang in her ears as the woman intercepted Brody.

Immediately, Brody halted. He inclined his head and replied.

Jasmine could do nothing but stare. A conversation sparked between them, peppered with long, searching looks and shy smiles. At one point, Elena reached out and touched his forearm. The gesture skewered Jasmine's heart.

One by one, Elena's children found their mother, congregating in a halo around her. She introduced the oldest first. The tall, intelligent-looking boy Jasmine remembered from the other day shook hands with Brody and then casually tried to mimic Brody's stance. Elena motioned to the younger boy and then the little girl with the braids.

Jasmine's attention returned to the oldest boy. Something

about the blind admiration on his features tied her stomach into knots. The firm line of his jaw and the clean sweep of his brow reminded her of Brody. He looked like a miniature of him, standing just that way. Of the children present he was the only one with light brown hair, the others all had very dark hair, probably like their father.

Like their father. Ice banded around her throat—freezing her, choking her. How old was the boy? Ten? At least. How many years had it been since Brody had left Elena?

Eleven years.

What color had the boy's eyes been, she wondered frantically. Her mind produced a hazy picture of him when he'd come to the doorway and stood beside his mother. He'd observed them with curiosity, his face turning into the sunlight to study them, his gaze . . . hazel.

The sum of her thoughts amounted to an intuition which caused bile to rise up her throat.

The bulky cowboy who had served as her shield altered his position, leaving her standing alone, peering at Brody without the protection of secrecy.

Brody spotted her at once. Above Elena's head he shot her a look filled with unmistakable meaning. He wanted her to stay exactly where she was.

Stay? Hell, she couldn't leave fast enough. She spun toward the door and promptly collided into the body of the meaty cowboy. She teetered.

He wrapped a big hand around her elbow and righted her before she could fall. "Whoa, there."

Blankly, she stared into his face.

"Better watch where you're going in that pretty dress. Wouldn't want to tear it now, would you?"

"No."

"That's a girl." He held her a moment too long. Then he eased his grip by sliding the pads of his fingers over her skin. She could smell the strong stench of alcohol on his breath.

Fighting down a growing tide of revulsion, Jasmine attempted to brush past him. "Excuse me."

"Now, wait a minute," he said. "Aren't you Brody's wife?"

Against every instinct and desire, she stopped and looked up at him. "Yes."

"What's your name, honey?"

"Jasmine Jamison."

He cocked his head and seemed to wait—

"McClintock," she added.

The cowboy guffawed. "Pleased to meet you Mrs. Janice Jamison McClintock."

"Jasmine."

"Huh?"

"The name's Jasmine."

"Jasmine?"

She nodded curtly.

"I'm Sam Stodges."

His name sounded somewhat familiar, but she couldn't place it. She knew only that she couldn't bear to make small talk with him at this particular catastrophic moment in her life when she was dying inside.

"This here is Matthew Grayson," he said, gesturing to the short gentleman she'd seen Brody speaking to the night before at the ranch. He wore the same ill-fitting black suit.

"Pleased to meet you," he said.

She managed a nod.

Sam clapped his friend on the back. "Grayson here is traveling through with one of the Rangers. Ahh, which one was that, Matt?"

"Seth. Seth Olds."

"Right." He looked to Jasmine. "They're on a case."

She shifted restlessly and took a small step toward freedom. "How interesting. If you'll excuse—"

"Grayson's been telling me about the case for near to an hour," Sam said. He motioned between her and Grayson. "Maybe you can convince him to share his story with you. If he's as partial to a pretty smile as I am, we'll be here all evening."

Sam's leering grin disgusted her. Not because he was ugly. He had thick black hair and vestiges of good bone structure. However, his entire body had gone soft and he wore his belt too tight. His eyes glinted at her from beds of loose skin.

"And if I don't give you a smile?" she asked.

"What?" Sam replied, clearly confused.

Grayson studied her suspiciously.

"If I don't give you a smile, will you permit me to leave?" She knew she was being rude, but couldn't seem to gloss over her raw nerves with politeness. "I'm sorry, but I was just leaving. If you'll excuse me."

She saw anger tick in the depths of Sam's expression. He tried to cover it by laughing too loudly. "Sure! We wouldn't want to be keeping you up past your bedtime."

"Thank you." Her skirts swished as she turned. Careful to keep her spine straight and her steps modulated, she wove through the crowd.

Once she'd gauged herself beyond sight of both Brody and Sam, she increased her speed. By the time she rushed through the doorway and the cool night breeze hit her face, she'd reached a run. She pointed her steps toward the corral.

Change. She should change clothes.

Her gait slashed to a halt. She glanced at the house and mentally estimated how long it would take her to change into her pants and boots.

Too long.

She strode in the direction of the horses. She'd rather ruin her dress than risk being overtaken by Brody. Feeling oppressed, she tugged at the bodice of the gown. The constriction around her lungs refused to loosen. No relief.

Three old men sat on the front porch of the house, smoking and talking. She acknowledged them with a nod and proceeded to the edge of the corral.

She realized with a pang of dismay that she'd have to wade into the tight throng of horses. She hadn't owned Vengeance long enough to teach him the sound of her whistle. Her exhale wobbled with desperation as she unlatched the gate.

The men on the porch stopped chatting.

She slid into the enclosure, her eyes probing through the darkness for her horse. Her dress shoes sank into the soft, miry earth.

"Vengeance," she said, her voice thready. Helplessness shredded her composure. "Vengeance!" *Come to me.* Her splayed hands pressed sightlessly at manes and hind quarters. She trudged deeper into the pack.

A damp nose buried itself in her hair. Heated breath blew across the crown of her head. She swung around and found herself face to face with her horse.

"Bless you," she whispered.

She led him from the corral and secured his bridle. On the verge of hiking up her skirts and flinging herself into the saddle, she remembered her audience of three. Her chin high, she guided Vengeance past the old men.

They gawked at her. "Whatcha doin' there?" one asked.

"I'm bringing my friend's horse to her," Jasmine said, unwilling to tell them the truth. "She's not feeling well and needs to leave immediately."

"Who's sick?" asked one.

"What's troubling her?" croaked another.

"Women troubles," Jasmine responded, daring them to tread upon that mysterious, sacred ground.

None dared.

She pulled Vengeance behind the cover of the house, grabbed a handful of gown from the region of her knees and dragged it almost to her waist. Using her free hand and her legs, she levered herself into the saddle.

She steered Vengeance along a shadowy course until they burst free of the property. Her sense of direction guided her along the two streets that led into the open prairie. Then she pointed Vengeance toward McClintock Ranch, heedless of the wild pace she set.

The wind coursed over her bare legs, pricking the skin until it itched then numbed. Her formal shoes rode the stirrups, the heels clicking mournfully against wood.

Purposely, she forced her mind to drain and schooled her thoughts away from Brody. She assured herself that she was fine. Sane and driven. Clear headed.

If only it weren't for the tears.

They wouldn't stop. They slid from the corners of her eyes and spun into the deep mass of her hair.

Chapter 18

Jasmine let herself into Clay's empty ranch house. Not a single candle, nor a single human stirring welcomed her. Without flame to brighten its rooms or people to populate its halls, the house greeted her like a melancholy tomb.

Twice she stumbled as she shuffled along the corridor in the direction of her room. When she finally reached it, she felt her way to the dresser and lit the lamp.

Her arms dropped to her sides. Her gaze traveled worriedly around the small space. What was she to do now? She'd followed necessity and abandoned the wedding dance. She'd ridden back to the ranch alone with her pale legs naked to the elements. She'd cared for Vengeance, stabling him for the night.

All her impetus had been focused toward this moment. Now that she'd arrived in the quiet confines of her room, what on earth was she to do with herself? She *couldn't* be alone with her thoughts.

Frantic, she began opening dresser drawers. The first two contained her stash of clothing. She pulled everything out, folded each item with painstaking precision and then repacked it.

She should probably go. When Tom arrived home, she'd talk with him, see if he might be open to riding back to

Tyler with her. Not that she needed an escort. She could just leave another note and take off in a northerly direction. Yes.

No. What had gotten into her? She was thinking crazy. Brody had promised her he'd find her if she ran away again and he'd already proven his ability to do just that. Fleeing was an ignorant tactic, anyway, because it would clearly communicate her distress to Brody. Better to stay here and feign disinterest. In fact, it would have been best if she'd managed to stay at the dance and feign disinterest, but her instincts had gotten the better of her. She'd always needed to run when overwhelmed by emotion. Tonight had been no different.

She should be able to fake it from here on out. Nothing much had really happened, after all. She'd seen Brody talking to Elena. So he'd had a smitten expression on his face. That didn't mean . . . men got over such infatuations eventually, didn't they?

Occupy yourself. She fell to her knees on the floor, emptied her satchel and began refilling each and every compartment.

The image of Elena's son flitted through her thoughts.

As her fingers struggled with a buckle, she fought to banish the image. But it wouldn't go. A tall boy with hazel eyes, trying to imitate Brody. They looked so much alike. Brody himself had told her that he'd seen Elena when he came home from the war. It wasn't difficult to believe that they'd come together then. Elena had probably regretted her decision to marry another. God, of course she had. Brody was too desirable not to want. And so she'd taken comfort in his arms before carrying out her duty to her fiancé.

Misery tightened within her. She sat back on her heels and stared blindly at her perfectly organized satchel. The tightness coiled, threatening to suffocate her. A dry sob escaped her lips. Brody was the most courageous, desirable man she'd ever met. All purpose and strength. And he'd never love her. Nothing she could do about it.

He'd never love her.

She looked around the room, desperate for something, anything, to busy her hands.

From the front region of the house, she heard the door bang open. Brody had come after her—no. Why did she persist in tormenting herself? He'd not leave Clay's wedding dance for her. Especially not with Saint Elena there to fawn over him.

She pressed to her feet and walked from her room toward the entry. It didn't matter who the newcomer was. So long as they were reasonably polite and could divert her with even the most elementary conversation, they'd be satisfactory.

"Jasmine?"

She stopped so fast that her heels skidded.

Ominously heavy footfalls crossed the great room in her direction. "Jasmine!"

She clutched the wall. Her heartbeat doubled with alarm.

Brody.

The blackness solidified into a moving, walking shape.

She spun and dashed toward their room on quaking legs. Behind her, she heard his steps quicken to a run.

Jasmine reached their room first. She dashed inside, threw the door closed, and pushed her body weight against it. Her fingers grasped beneath the knob for a key. No key. Fingertips scrambled. No key!

Brody's gait halted on the other side of the door. His palms slapped the wood with a resounding crack.

She gasped. What in the hell was she doing? It had been pure survival instinct that had motivated her to run in here and slam the door on him. Now that she'd done it, she realized that the thin slab of wood posed no obstacle for him. It would only incense him further.

She should open the door and admit him.

She couldn't. Simply couldn't. Her breath panted from divided lips.

"What has gotten into you?" he demanded.

"Nothing."

"Nothing?" he yelled. "You left Clay's wedding, alone, without bothering to give me the courtesy of an explanation."

"Explanation?" she choked.

"Damn straight."

Her exhale hissed.

"Look, Jasmine, you're clearly angry about something. I have a right to know what it is."

"A right?"

His palms slapped the wood again. "Yes. A right. I left my brother's wedding, for Chrissake, and I want an explanation."

Ire trembled through her. "No!"

For an extended moment, neither moved nor spoke. Then the handle turned and pressure forced the door open a sliver. Her formal shoes slid across the hardwood floor, searching for a hold.

"I hate it when you shut me out," he gritted.

She wailed with frustration. Every muscle in her body strained to combat his strength.

Brody thrust the door all the way open with a shove, toppling her onto the floor. She landed with a severe jolt to her derrière. Burgundy skirts jumbled around her thighs.

He stood in the doorway looking exactly like what he was, a gunman spoiling for a fight. His hair was windblown and his boots muddied. His long coat fell nearly to his ankles.

She gaped up at him, her heart in her throat.

His brows drew together in confusion and his expression gentled. He knelt beside her and reached for the sodden rim of her skirt. With extreme care, he pulled it down the length of her legs, his fingers skimming the tender flesh inside her knee and along the top of her shin. "What happened to your gown?"

She didn't answer. Instead she bit her bottom lip, hard, hoping that small tide of pain would stem the more dangerous tide of longing. She didn't trust her traitorous heart to withstand the concern she saw in his gaze.

Slowly, he transferred his hold to her waist, then lifted her onto her feet. They stood just a fraction of distance apart. The air between their bodies hummed with expectation.

He lifted his right hand and stroked his fingers over the throbbing pulse in her neck before carefully cupping her jaw and cheek. His thumb rubbed away a stain she hadn't known she'd acquired.

"You rode home in your ballgown," he said.

She didn't need to answer. The evidence of her flight was before him—in her ruined dress and filthy shoes.

"God, Jasmine," he breathed. His hands coursed over her shoulders and the length of her arms, testing for scratches. "Why? What made you so angry?"

His question reminded her of the answer with graphic force. She flinched away from his touch and took two steps backward. Her spine came up firmly against the dresser. A drawer knob poked into her lower back.

The heat in his eyes cooled. "So tell me."

Jasmine swallowed, trying to gauge whether or not she had any voice. She prayed she had some slim capacity to speak because humiliation before him now was unthinkable. She collected her nerve. "Why bother?" she asked, her words scratchy but audible. "Why bother to chase me down and confront me, Brody? We both know this marriage is a joke." She frowned, angry at the unexpected rush of emotion she felt. "Just leave me alone."

He studied her with eyes too wise. "I'll give you your privacy, Jasmine. But first I need to know why I had to leave my brother's wedding and ride across half of Texas to catch you.''

She couldn't bring herself to say Elena's name out loud. Maybe if the woman wasn't so flawless and kind and beautiful, she could have.

"Elena," Brody said, saving her the effort. "You saw me talking with Elena and then you ran away."

When he said it like that, her actions sounded foolish, utterly cowardly. Her pride roused. The drawer handle gouged deeper.

"Am I not allowed to talk to her?" he asked.

"Damn it, Brody!" Tears pricked her eyes. "Do you think I'm so blind? So stupid that I couldn't see what was right before me?"

"What was before you? What in the hell are you talking about?"

"Her son!" she shouted. "The one that looks exactly like you and stands exactly like you. The one that is old enough to belong to you!"

Brody stared at her with a stricken expression that shattered her dreams.

In the tense quiet that followed, her accusation echoed around them. It seemed to swirl through the room, faster and faster, refusing to vanish into silence.

Brody broke the vicious song by moving. His hands rose to his face, rubbed his eyes and then slid down his features before dropping.

She gazed at him, fire and fight snapping from her. He'd broken her heart tonight. She wasn't going to allow him any more victories.

He started to step toward her.

She brandished her fists.

He stopped. And then, to her amazement, he smiled. Laugh lines grooved into the skin beside his eyes. He began to chuckle.

She scowled and clenched her fists tighter. "How dare you laugh at me you—you bastard!"

His amusement intensified. So did her fury. She stood there watching him laugh and sensed her control sliding away. A silent scream filled her lungs.

"Jasmine, you're wrong," he said.

"I don't think so," she growled.

His smile flashed again, then vanished. "Don't you suppose I'd know if Elena's eldest son were mine?"

"Maybe, if you weren't such an insensitive idiot."

His eyebrows flattened. "Watch that you don't insult me beyond forgiveness."

"Oh? And fathering a child with another man's wife is forgivable?"

"No," he said gravely. "And that's why I'd never do such a thing."

For the first time, her assurance began to waver. She released her fists. "But he looks exactly like you! Your hair, your eyes."

"What did he have?" Irritation chiseled into every line of him. "Brown hair?"

"Yes!"

"How unusual."

"But he had your eyes, too! And he looks just—"

"I never made love to Elena, Jasmine."

Her lips fell open. "Never?"

"No. If I had, I'd have married her. I'd die before I'd allow another man to raise my son."

"Oh." Her righteous indignation deflated.

He moved toward her, a predatory gleam sparking in his eyes.

She stiffened. Pressure beat beneath her temples. What had gotten into her? Had she lost all sense where this man was concerned? Of course he hadn't made love to Elena. He had too much honor.

He stopped so close that she could feel his breath slipping over her forehead.

Her skin pebbled in the instant before rough fingers slid into her hair. One by one he found the pins and pulled them from the tangle of wind-tossed curls.

Pleasure shivered all the way to the base of her spine. When her hair hung free of its bonds, he slid his hands into it, massaging her scalp, coaxing the tension from her body.

Her sigh shook.

Near her ear he whispered, "You were wrong, but God, you were passionate." His fingers stroked along the line of her jaw, then lifted her chin. "Would you be as passionate beneath me?"

"Yes."

His lips lowered to hers in a kiss both leisurely and burningly sensual.

She couldn't bear it. Need and love lashed her with silken whips. A soft groan eased from her throat as she deepened the kiss.

Instantly, his arms wound around her. His tongue mated with hers more deeply, stoking the fire that had been banked too long.

She was overwhelmingly grateful that he hadn't fathered Elena's child. Her hands streaked over his chest, pressing into his hard contours, pulling him closer.

Remorse over her tantrum fostered fresh desperation. She wanted to breathe him into her. Brand him as hers. Her hands slid beneath his jacket and pushed the garment over powerful shoulders. Heated air rushed between them. She yanked free the buttons of his shirt.

He cursed quietly, more a vow than an oath.

Her world tipped in a mural of hazy light and honey-colored wood. With one hand pillowing her head, he laid her on the floor. His lean body stretched out next to her.

She writhed and pulled free the last of his shirt's buttons. He shrugged out of the garment. Bare skin rippled and tensed under her gaze. She arched off the floor, greedily running her hands over the slabs of muscle.

The fever inside her raged higher. Her womanhood was melting. Vaguely, she felt his hands move along the closure at the back of her gown. The binding around her chest slackened.

He was kissing her again, so deeply.

Expensive burgundy fabric whispered down her arms. He lifted away from her just enough to watch as he pulled the dress lower. The gown coasted over her nipples, exposing her breasts.

His palm covered a creamy mound. "Tell me now if you don't want me," he said roughly.

Her gaze locked with his.

His eyes were overly bright. "I will leave you. But I can't stop . . . if we go further."

In answer, she covered his hand with both of hers, pressing down on the palm that clasped her breast.

He needed no more assurances. In one powerful pull, he stripped her body of the gown. She arched upward, a bow string quivering. He tugged off her chemise and slid her drawers down the shapely length of her legs.

Emotion twined through her. Love of him. Overpowering love. A feeling stronger than her passion for freedom or her need of wild places. This love transcended herself.

She gloried in her nakedness, took exquisite, shaking joy in his perusal of her.

"Beautiful," he whispered, the pads of his fingers skating up the inside of one thigh. He paused just below the vee at the juncture of her legs.

She was wet for him there.

Her hips lifted.

The reserve he'd shown her broke at the instinctual invitation. In a heady shower of sparks, he captured one nipple in his mouth as he slid a finger over the slick folds of her womanhood.

She cried out, the pleasure so intense that it jarred her to the core. He kissed her again. And she responded. But his fingers . . . God, his fingers. They explored her with such brazen intimacy. Circling and stroking. Delving to the center of her.

Sensation coursed through her in waves. Her hands pressed down the flat plane of his stomach. She found the flap of his pants and freed the buttons there. She tried to push the fabric over his lean hips and couldn't reach.

His hands were there, helping her. The thrust of his arousal arched free.

She lifted her hips again.

"Not yet, love." He covered her shiny forehead with kisses.

She groaned, restless. Mad with a yearning she didn't fully understand. "I want you. Now."

"It's too soon."

"Brody," she cried, her voice breaking. She lifted her knees and spread her legs for him. Her hands pressed down his spine and covered his tight buttocks.

His breath sucked inward.

"Now," she begged. "Please." She lifted moist lips to him.

His tongue plunged into her mouth.

She felt him shifting position, centering himself on top of her. He cupped a hand beneath her hips, tilting her up to meet him.

She gazed into his soul and opened herself even wider. The hard tip of him nudged against her swollen flesh.

"Brody," she sobbed.

"Jasmine."

"Now."

He drove into her. His sleek manhood filled her to capacity, all the way to the foundation of her being.

She stiffened as pain slashed deep inside.

He held still.

"I want . . . I don't know."

"Shhh," he murmured. "*I* know." He began to move, the motion of his hips controlled but sure.

Arousal licked at her, banishing the pain to insignificance. Brody was loving her. That truth was sweeter even than his touch.

He bent his head and sucked her breast. The sight of him taking her nipple into his mouth sent her careening over the edge of thought. She thrust upward, her hips moving hard against him, meeting his rhythm. The beat intensified, quickened.

Color climbed over Brody's cheeks, sweat gleamed across his chest. She stared at him through dimmed vision. She panted. The feelings mounted. So unbelievably good, she could do nothing but follow their demands.

He swept into her and out, faster. Deeply.

She throbbed. The sensations continued to grow, a tempest that blotted out all else. They raged higher. Stronger. Higher still, until in one shimmering second of bliss, her entire body bent upward. Muscles convulsed. And a raging wave of pleasure sang along her nerves.

He thrust into her again. She cried out. And again.

And then he spilled his own arousal into her, gifting her with the essence of himself.

She gasped, clinging to the seed that pulsed deep within her, reveling in the tender surges that racked her own body. They stayed suspended like that for long moments. Then, very slowly, he lowered himself, wrapped his arms around her, and rolled them both onto their sides. His bicep cushioned her head.

Their lips met in an unbroken string of kisses. The world glowed amber around Jasmine. A haze of adoration, comfort, and protection.

She didn't know how much time had passed when the muffled sound of voices penetrated the walls of their solitude. Brody must have heard the intruders before she did, because her muddled brain was still sorting through the possible sources of the noise when he walked naked to the gaping doorway. Quietly, he shut the door.

She gazed at him through half-closed eyes. Fulfillment drugged her.

He tossed back the quilt that covered the bed, then bent and lifted her from the floor. Cool, clean sheets caressed her hot skin as he laid her on the mattress.

Brody moved to the lamp, his strong hands cupping the glass.

"No," she said, her voice thick. She didn't want darkness. She wanted her heaven illuminated with gold.

He glanced at her.

"Please."

Without a word he abandoned the lamp and returned, slipping beneath the covers. He lay on his back, then pulled her directly on top of him. Her sated body nestled along the rock hard planes of his. Softly, he shifted her hair, smoothing the wavy strands over the curve of her neck.

In response, she kissed his collarbone and curled her fingers possessively around his ear.

He swept the quilt up over her, protecting her from chill. The beloved warmth of his arms enfolded her.

Jasmine closed her eyes on a velvet sigh.

And slept.

Brody stayed awake until every last guest had ceased his excited chatter and retired to bed. He stayed awake until the lamp exhausted itself, its last gasp of kerosene sputtering into darkness. And still he stayed awake, staring into the fathomless darkness.

What in the hell was he doing? Of all the places on earth where he could be tonight, he wanted to be in this place most of all. And yet lying here, with the lovely length of Jasmine's body spread on top of him, was the last place he ought to have found himself.

He'd successfully managed to resist her during the previous weeks of their marriage. Why had he fallen tonight?

Because tonight she'd touched him.

She'd threatened him with fisted hands, her hair tumbling around her shoulders. Her eyes has sparkled with unshed tears when she'd shouted her suspicions. Her lips had quivered, just a little, when he'd finally kissed her.

She had been magnificent. The fact that jealousy over him had aroused such a glorious show of temper had seduced him. Softened him. Made him want to love her until she cried out his name.

So he had.

Just remembering it made his body stir and thicken. He wanted her again. Already, the urge to turn her on her back and make love to her was a gnawing, anxious demand within him.

He gritted his teeth against it.

Even if he woke her now and claimed her over and over, there would still come a morning. And they'd still have to face what had transpired between them.

He flicked a look downward at the array of curls.

When he found out that she'd tricked him into marriage, he'd been set on hurting her. And God knows, he'd tried. At times he'd attempted to frighten her and threaten her and chain her. But none of his tactics had dented her spirit. She'd scurried back each time, full of ever increasing resolve.

He now realized that he'd deluded himself. No one could tame Jasmine. If anyone could have controlled her, it would have been the father she loved so dearly. But even her father had failed. Jasmine had sacrificed him to the cause of her one unfailing quest. The quest for freedom.

Moonlight doused Jasmine's cheek and forehead in platinum hues. As he watched, a cloud drifted over a portion of the moon, causing a shadow to skate across her skin, darkening the lashes that rested in crescents on her cheeks.

Jasmine would be for her entire life exactly as she had been the first night he'd met her. Unconquered. Independent. Vibrantly beautiful.

The fact that the law recognized him as her husband would never hold her. She was not his to own.

He'd seen the way she eyed the open countryside with unabashed yearning. He knew she seethed for freedom, that she'd never be content to live confined within the black and white boundaries of one ranch.

A doomed longing drew at his heart, so fiercely that he closed his eyes. When had his search for revenge against her bowed to a secret hope? He didn't know. The borders of his emotions were impossibly blurred. But at some indefinable point, he'd begun to hope that there might be a chance for them as husband and wife.

She moaned in sleep. Her head shifted and her small hand curved around his shoulder. He held her closer to him, comforting her with his embrace.

His mind offered up new strategies, new plans for winning her. But he set each idea away. They would never work. He'd spend his life chasing after her, running to save her from harm, scavenging for crumbs of her affection.

He couldn't live that way and call himself a man.

And neither could she change.

The tragedy that had resulted from loving Elena had nearly killed him. For eleven years he'd remained true to his vow to be alone and never to love.

And then Jasmine had ensnared him in her godforsaken scheme. Jasmine, who was more rare and more precious than anyone he'd ever met. The one woman since Elena who had been able to reach him. The one woman he might risk keeping, if he hadn't known for certain that loving her was a lost cause.

He couldn't afford to love any more lost causes.

From the moment she'd fallen asleep atop him he'd

known what he had to do. But his heart kept refusing to accept it.

He had to escort her back to Tyler. Then, somehow, he had to find it in him to release her from his promise to steal away her independence. Wild things weren't meant to be caged.

With an agonizing twist of remorse, he accepted it. His mind clicked to unfeeling darkness and he slid her warm, curving body off his. He'd been lying still for so long while he sheltered her that his muscles were dead and listless. Halfheartedly, he forced them to move.

Jasmine rolled onto the mound of bed covers. Her head fell to the side, exposing the graceful column of her neck. He resisted the almost shattering urge to bury his face there and breathe the unforgettable fragrance of her skin.

Why bother? We both know this marriage is a joke. Her words swam across his brain. *Just leave me alone.*

With hands that shook, he tucked the quilt gently around her. He'd do exactly that.

He'd leave her alone.

Chapter 19

Lee knocked on Emma's door and waited. He heard the rapping approach of her boots and wondered again if he was a fool for having come.

Emma swung back the door and for a moment simply gaped. The night shadows that clung to him made the warm light that flowed around her all the more foreign, and inviting.

"Lee." The elegant arches of her brows glided upward.

"I hope I'm not disturbing you."

"No." One slender hand smoothed over the pewter-colored bob of hair. "Not at all."

He stared at her. She stared back at him, her eyes misty in the muted light.

He felt like a damned idiot. No man in his right mind should go gallivanting around after supper, appearing on a woman's doorstep without any apparent reason. He was probably a godforsaken nuisance to her.

"Where are my manners?" she murmured, stepping aside. "Please, Lee, come in." She motioned toward the cozy interior of her home.

Momentarily, he considered making a hasty apology and bolting. But that would push him beyond the level of a nuisance to the depths of downright rude.

"Thank you." He stepped into the foyer. Just as he was

about to dodge into the yellow parlor, the room where they visited whenever he came calling, she walked past him down the hall.

"I'm just finishing up in the kitchen. Will you join me?"

"You're eating?" He took a step backward. "Sorry. I— I'd best be going so that you can finish—"

She moved to him with fearsome alacrity and gripped his elbow. "I finished dinner hours ago. I'm just putting the final touches on a pie. Please join me."

The delicate smile she bestowed on him charmed him to the core. After a long pause, he nodded and set his hat on the rack.

She escorted him down the hallway and into the kitchen. A long harvest table dominated the room. White chairs with thatched seats graced its sides. She pulled one out for him and he lowered his sizable bulk onto it, concerned that the patchwork of thatching wouldn't support him.

Emma moved to the butcher block. "My brother made those chairs. They're stronger than they look." Her teasing smirk informed him that she'd read his thoughts.

He chuckled. "Guess I'm just accustomed to my own furniture."

"Guess so."

He watched with curiosity as she placed a circle of dough over an open-faced apple pie. She pressed her thumb around the rim, creating a scalloped border.

He sensed that she was a little nervous around him tonight and wondered if that was why she was pretending to be so completely engrossed with her pie. Hell, he was jumpy, too. They could both use a respite to adjust.

Above Emma, copper pots gleamed from their hooks. Beside her, cooking utensils reared from three blue pottery vases like bunches of wooden blooms.

His attention returned to her hands. With expert efficiency, she sliced out the pattern of a vine and leaves from the remaining square of flattened dough. Then she arranged the decoration on the top of the pie, perforated it with fork holes, and slid it into the oven.

His mouth began to water. He couldn't tell if it was because of the dessert, or because of the woman who moved about the room with such unconscious grace.

He'd missed Emma these last days. Seeing her again made her absence all the more intensely felt.

After washing her hands, Emma untied her apron and hung it on its peg. "I assume you like apple pie?"

"You assume correctly."

Snagging an apple and a knife, she walked to the table and took the seat next to him. "Care for an appetizer?"

His cook had stuffed him full of vegetables, meat, and potatoes an hour ago, but nothing he'd eaten in weeks sounded as good to him as the small, shiny green apple cushioned in her palm. "Sure."

Her knife flashed, biting into the skin of the fruit. Juice welled at the line of incision. She extended a perfect wedge to him.

He didn't know whether to take it from her fingers or open his mouth. He noticed that her gaze was firmly fastened on his lips. Clear enough. He opened his mouth.

She set the apple between his teeth. He bit down hard, severing the fruit with a crack.

Emma shrieked with laughter, her fingers flying back. "I should have known better than to hand-feed the beast."

"Hell, yes, you should have." He chewed the apple and grinned at her. This was why he'd come. To sit across from her and talk with her, to borrow a little of her affection and intelligence and warmth. "I can't believe I was lucky enough to visit when you were making apple pie."

Not much of a coincidence, Emma thought. The pie was actually for the luncheon tomorrow at Reverend White's house. But what the heck? She could make another. A surprise visit from Lee was a far, far more treasured occasion than a gathering of the Christian Women.

When she'd opened the door just now to find him standing on her porch, for the first time in her life, she'd seriously considered succumbing to a good old-fashioned faint.

She smiled at him. "Yes, it happens that you've been lucky enough to visit on apple pie night. Is that why you came calling, to gobble my food?"

The flirtatious sparkle in his eyes dimmed. He swallowed his mouthful of apple. "No, actually."

Why had she asked him that? Damn it all, he didn't need to have a reason for coming. She set the apple and knife on the table's scarred surface and folded her hands into a knot, mentally preparing for a long discussion about Jasmine. "Of course that's not why you came. Have you had word from Jasmine?"

His dark blue gaze held hers unwaveringly. "I didn't come to talk about Jasmine either."

Her heart executed a queer dive. "No?"

"I don't know exactly why I came. Except that I . . . enjoyed those evenings we spent together. You know, when Jasmine had run away."

Her pulse pounded erratically. Never had she seen the supremely confident Lee Jamison look uncomfortable. But here he was, sitting in her kitchen at her table and turning an entirely gorgeous shade of ruddy red. "I enjoyed them, too."

"So, I thought I'd come over for a visit."

"I'm glad you did."

He shifted in his seat. "It sure is quiet around here."

"It is, isn't it?"

"Do you get lonely in this big house?"

Yes! she wanted to scream at him. She wanted to bend him over the table and kiss him insensible with affirmative answers. She managed a subdued, "Sometimes. What about you, at the Double J?"

"I was never lonely when Jasmine lived there. But since she's left . . ." He scratched his head. "Well. I guess I didn't realize before what a forceful presence she had."

Spontaneously, Emma reached across the table, placed her hand over his, and squeezed. In answer, Lee twined his tanned fingers with hers.

Elation spiraled through her, making her light-headed. She didn't dare breathe for fear that the movement of her lungs might somehow cause her fingers to twitch. "Houses have a way of changing when people leave," she said.

"Yes, they do. Did this house change much when your parents passed away?"

"It changed entirely."

"How so?"

She scrambled after some thread of reasonably interesting conversation. It was hard to think at all with the warm pressure of his hand encompassing hers. "After they were gone, this house that had always been theirs suddenly became mine. And yet everywhere I looked, I saw memories of them. My father built it himself. The whole of the first house was the parlor, and. . . ." She pursed her lips. "You know, the pie won't be ready for some time."

"Huh?"

"The pie." She pointed at the oven with her free hand. "While it's baking, I'll be happy to tell you all about the house, if you'll oblige me with a game of cards."

Nestled in a puzzled expression, his eyes shone with affection. "If that's what you want."

"It is."

He rose from his chair, then gallantly assisted her to her feet.

"The cards are just—just in the parlor," she stammered. They were standing in the center of her kitchen holding hands and neither of them was acknowledging that earthshaking fact.

Lee inclined his head and led her down the hall to the yellow parlor. When they reached the table, another moment of awkwardness assailed her. He'd stopped too far away for her to reach the drawer that held the cards, and yet she'd be damned before she'd relinquish their shared intimacy.

With a reassuring squeeze, Lee let go, taking the paralyzing decision away from her.

She bent to hide her blushing cheeks and plucked the cards from their drawer. Once they'd settled into opposite chairs, she began to deal.

"You want to play cards with me while you tell me about the house in order to distract me and win the game, don't you?" Lee's grin softened the masculine planes of his face.

"Actually," she said, "I thought I'd challenge you at cards to avert your mind from the crushing boredom of my story."

He laughed, a rich, deep sound that heated her insides more effectively than any liquor could have. "I wasn't bored," he said.

"Really? I was." She picked up her hand of cards and spread them coyly in front of her face.

His blue eyes rained pleasure over her.

"Your move, Jamison," she said. "And good luck. I won't need to distract you to win."

Lee swallowed the last bite of his second helping of apple pie. The few scraps of flaky crust that remained were quickly being overtaken by pools of sweet cream. "Delicious," he pronounced.

"Thank you." Emma could think of no better pastime than that of fielding compliments from Lee Jamison. She rested her chin on her joined hands and studied him. Contentment drifted through her like snow coasting toward earth. Along with that contentment came a swell of sleepiness. She yawned.

"Your yawn informs me that I've stayed past my welcome," Lee said.

"Oh no. Not at all. Why . . ." she looked around for something else to divert him with. All that looked back was a half-eaten pie. The Christian Women would have to settle for yesterday's banana loaf. "I only beat you at half the card games. Want to give me a chance to improve my average?" She smiled hopefully.

"I've created a monster," he grumbled. After rising to his feet, he raked his fingers through his tousled hair. "No, I'd better salvage what's left of my pride and get on home."

"Are you sure? I'd like—"

"To stay up all night entertaining me? What would the neighbors think?" He winked at her and started toward the door.

She followed him, every vestige of tiredness vanished.

He opened the door for himself and stepped onto the porch.

She halted on the threshold and tried to smooth the sharp longing she felt out of her expression.

"May I come back again?" he asked.

"Please do."

"I enjoyed seeing you."

"I enjoyed seeing *you*."

He tilted his head and donned his hat. "Has anyone told you lately how pretty you look in that color?"

She spared a peek at the lavender blouse she wore. "Not lately." *Never.*

"Well, they should have. It complements your hair and your eyes." He looked at her steadily for the space of two of her shallow breaths, then turned and was engulfed by darkness.

She waited until the hoofbeats of his horse disappeared into silence. Numbly, she closed the door and mounted the stairs. Near the top, her gait quickened. She dashed into her bedroom and leaned over the low vanity. A tall, rectangular mirror confronted her.

Balancing her upper body weight on shaking fingertips, she gazed fully into the glass. She didn't see her wrinkles staring back at her. Or her weariness. Or the sterling gray of her hair which telegraphed her age.

She saw only a woman—a beautiful woman whose eyes were flushed with excitement and whose skin shone with an inner luster. And she saw something else . . . deep in the contours of brows and lips.

Determination.

Come hell or high water, she, Emma Larkin, was going to win the heart of Lee Jamison.

Chapter 20

Brody knelt beside the bed, kissing her. He slid the supple line of her lower lip between his teeth and sucked on it gently.

"Oh Brody," Jasmine moaned. "Don't tease me. Just take me, please, hard and fast, like you want it."

He looked at her as if he'd never seen anything in the world more worthy of his love. His hands snaked into her hair. "Hard, like I want it?"

"Yes! God, yes."

Her heart pounded her ribs, so violently that it made a loud, insistent sound. Like the sound of knuckles rapping wood.

She gasped and tried to understand why her heart would beat so noisily. Brody's image wavered. Behind him, she could see the filmy reality of her room. The knocking came again. This time, Brody's wobbling face disappeared entirely.

She struggled to awaken her sleep-dulled brain, right up until the instant when she realized that she'd been in the middle of a wonderful dream. Immediately, she shut her eyes and tried to grab the dream back. Brody had been there, his expression adoring. She focused on that image, clung to it. Sleep had almost reclaimed her when the knocking resumed.

Ignore it, she told herself. Concentrate on returning to Brody.

The knock sounded again—four more times.

Grumpily, she cracked open her eyes. "Yes?" she croaked.

"Jasmine?"

"Uh-hmm."

"It's Tom."

"Come in."

It wasn't until the knob started turning that she glanced downward and was explicitly reminded of her nudity. Every memory of the past night rushed to her brain.

On a muffled squawk, she burrowed under the covers and kept going, only satisfied when she'd wedged her head against the tight sheets at the foot of the bed.

"Jasmine?"

"Yes?" How humiliating for him to walk in on her like this, not one, but two mornings in a row.

"What in the hell?"

A blast of cool air from the hallway swept over the bare bottoms of her feet. Mortified, she looked toward her legs and discovered that the line of the sheet ended at her ankles. Which meant her feet were poking out, nestled comfortably in the center of her pillow. "I—I like to sleep this way, sometimes." She curled and then broadly flexed her toes in an attempt to prove her point.

A foreboding silence followed. Her breath rebounded off the sheets and flushed her features.

"Jasmine Jamison McClintock. By God, you are the most confounding female."

She smiled and clicked her heels together. "Was there ever any doubt?"

Tom chuckled. Though Jasmine could see only the dark underbelly of the blankets, she could visualize the way his eyes would be gleaming and his wrinkles digging into his cheeks.

"Despite what you might think, I didn't wake you so that I could ogle your feet," he stated.

"No?"

"We're leaving in an hour. For home."

"Oh." She told herself to remain aloof, indifferent. Not, under any circumstances, to ask about Brody. "Is Brody, uhmmm, up this morning?"

"I'm certain he is, though I haven't seen him yet."

"Haven't seen him?" She tried to sound casual.

"No. But we always leave first thing in the morning when we travel. He'll be here in time."

"Oh."

"I'll see you at breakfast."

"Yep."

The door closed. She wheeled her body back into the correct position, her head reclaiming the pillow from her feet. After the stuffy air below, the fresh air pouring into her lungs tasted crisp and cool.

She was no expert on marital relations. But surely, on the night after the husband made love to the wife for the first time, he was reasonably expected to be around in the morning when she woke up?

Pressing her knotted hair away from her brow, she stared at the ceiling. Their coming together had been perfection. He couldn't have found any fault with it. Could he? Worry gnawed at her, slight at first, but quickly gaining strength. Maybe he hadn't found the same amount of pleasure in it that she had. Maybe she'd been too brazen. Maybe she'd been too inexperienced.

Her gaze raked over the painted boards above her. But why, if it had been so disappointing for him, had he held her like that afterward? He'd embraced her as if the world would stop turning if he let her go. He'd not have hugged her like that if he didn't care.

Her unease began to recede.

Brody had simply needed to get up early this morning

and he'd wanted to let her sleep. That was all. When she saw him, he'd smile his devastating smile at her and she'd feel silly for having been afraid.

She frowned, tossed away the covers and crossed to the dresser. As she tugged on her undergarments, her dream came back to her in tempting snatches.

His teasing kiss.

The burning admiration in his eyes.

Just take me, please, hard and fast like you want it.

She paused in her dressing. Her cheeks flamed.

Hard and fast like you want it? Oh God. How embarrassing.

Brody was conspicuously absent at breakfast.

All the temporary occupants of the ranch had risen early, wanting to get a head start on their various journeys. Everyone, except for Brody, sat around the long table, sharing a generous feast of sausage, eggs, and cornbread. Even Clay and Jessica were present. They sat at the head of the table, laughing happily at stories about their wedding and accepting thanks for their hospitality.

Jasmine ate silently.

She watched and listened to the people around her as if through an unaccustomed filter. Everything seemed new and exotic to her this morning.

She was a woman now. Fully. She'd been made love to last night, and that difference felt as obvious to her as if it had been engraved on her forehead.

At one point during the meal, she looked up and caught Jessica's eye. The girl gave her a secret smile that spoke volumes.

She nodded back, understanding entirely her friend's wide-eyed amazement. Jasmine's own sense of wonder lighted on the way the sun bronzed the lace curtains. The way the cool metal fork felt in her hand. And the way the butter ran from her cornbread onto her finger in a single, golden drip.

When they finished eating, she returned to her room and packed her things. Every time a voice sounded in the hall or footsteps approached, she froze. Each time it turned out to be someone other than Brody.

She kept scouring her mind, wondering where he could have gone. But no plausible reason for his absence occurred to her. With every passing minute she grew more nervous that something had gone wrong.

He didn't want her anymore.

She chewed the inside of her cheek and tried to steady her crackling nerves. Repeatedly, she told herself she was overreacting, but the growing tension roiling in her stomach didn't heed reason.

Damn him for not being here. Damn him. He had to show up at some point this morning, but his mysterious disappearance from their bed would make that inevitable meeting all the more uncomfortable and highly anticipated. Could nothing, nothing, be easy with Brody?

Before leaving the room, she stood in the doorway and surveyed the assembly of furniture and curtains and painted walls. Funny, how a simple, pretty little room could come to mean so much to her.

She slung her satchel over her shoulder, and walked through the house and out into the bright light of the spring morning. Her breath misted on the unexpectedly chilly breeze.

Tom already had their horses tethered to the outside rail.

"Morning again," she said.

"Morning again."

She didn't want Tom's perceptive gaze to uncover her insecurities, so she stepped behind Vengeance and busied herself readying him for the trip.

The porch door squealed open. She glanced up. Clay and Jessica emerged, followed closely by the Ranger named

Seth and Mr. Grayson, who were both dressed for traveling.

Where was Brody? For heaven's sake, they'd made love last night on the floor! Could he forget the blazingly intimate way they'd mated, with their skin a sheen of exertion, their breath intertwined, their hands probing and desperate?

Was he going to pretend it had never happened?

The uninvited burning behind her eyes angered her. She swallowed back the wall of sorrow. You can play his game, she told herself. If he is indifferent to you, you will be indifferent to him. You can pretend.

She tried to concentrate on tightening the cinch strap. While she worked, several of the guests left the ranch in a stream of murmured good-byes. Every time the porch door opened, she looked up. Otherwise, she was only partially listening.

Until she heard someone call Brody's name.

Her hands stilled on the satchel tie she'd been fastening.

"Glad we caught you, Brody, before we left," the voice said. "Sure was good to see you again."

"Good to see you, too."

Jasmine kept her back to the scene and gazed dumbly at the ties. Her heart took off at a wild sprint. She attempted to calm her body's reaction by force of will, but it wouldn't obey. A rebellious tremor shook her shoulders.

"Hey, Brody! Can you take it easy this season and give the rest of us a chance to look good?"

"See you soon, Brody."

"Brody, safe travels."

Her stomach solidified into rock. Each pump of blood through her limbs hurt. She'd just pretend that she hadn't noticed his arrival. *Act nonchalant.*

"Morning, Brody," Tom said, from right beside her.

She jumped. Her hands stumbled and she had to lunge to keep the satchel from falling.

"Morning," Brody answered, near the vicinity of her right ear.

She couldn't very well ignore him when he was this close. That would call undue attention to her. Wouldn't it? Yes. *Turn.*

She pooled every last bastion of strength and faced him. She'd meant to say something light, to show how comfortable she was with the situation, how casually at ease, as if shattering things like lovemaking happened to her every day. But when she turned and looked at him, words failed her.

He was gazing at her through eyes she'd come to love. Bright, hazel eyes that held nothing but solemn regard on this morning that meant so much to her. She noted that the wind had ruffled his hair and tinted his cheeks. He'd already donned his duster.

"Morning, Jasmine," he said.

No words. Nothing. She nodded.

He moved past her, making his way to his brother.

Just as she'd suspected, something was drastically wrong. No tenderness had warmed his expression when he'd looked at her.

Her heart plummeted. Up until this moment, she'd sustained some small hope that he might not regret what they'd done. That he'd still desire her. But the remoteness in his eyes had left her no room to doubt.

As she watched him approach Clay and Jessica, she noticed that his unreachable air had returned. His jaw had hardened, his shoulders jutted at a defensive angle, his strides radiated purpose and danger. That way he had of carrying himself, of holding himself apart—it was back.

Her fingertips dug into the leather of her satchel. At some point after she'd fallen asleep and before she'd awakened, she'd lost him.

Jessica called to her. Again, Jasmine wondered if she could get away with ignoring the situation. Again, she realized she couldn't. Placing one leaden foot in front of the other, she approached the small group.

"Thank you for coming," Jessica said to her.

"You're welcome."

"I hope you'll come back for a visit again soon."

Jasmine glanced apprehensively at Brody. "I'm sure Brody will. I don't know if I'll be making the trip with him."

Clay enfolded her in a strong hug. "Take good care of my brother, you hear?"

"Sure."

While Brody and Clay shared their last farewells, Jessica pulled Jasmine aside. "If you ask me," she whispered, "that husband of yours would never come to see us without you. He wouldn't let you out of his sight that long."

"Oh, he probably would."

"No," she scolded. "I see the way he looks at you."

Jasmine feigned a smile.

Jessica hugged her. "Good-bye."

"Bye."

Jasmine gratefully returned to Tom and the horses. Before she could begin to compose herself, Brody joined them. "Ready?" he asked.

"Ready," Tom replied.

Jasmine swung into the saddle.

"You boys ready?" Brody called.

Confused, she swiveled to see who he was talking to. His attention had landed on Seth and Grayson, who sat their mounts just a few yards away.

"We're ready," Seth answered.

Seth and Grayson were coming with them? She squinted at the two men, trying to figure out what was happening.

Brody and Tom saddled up and then all five of them headed away from the ranch house. Jasmine waited until she and Tom had fallen back from the others before asking, "Are Seth and Grayson riding with us?"

"Yes. Brody talked with them the other night. Seems they're heading to Tyler. He invited them to ride with us."

"No one told me."

"No?"

"No."

"I'm sorry, I thought Brody might have said something."

Her heartache throbbed. She was tempted to lay her forehead on Vengeance's mane and scream the worst of it away. The last thing her fragile relationship with Brody needed was an audience of strangers.

She noticed the little whitewashed cottage with the green shutters come into view. Her irritation at the presence of fellow travelers deepened into dread. "Where are we going?"

"To Elena's. Her husband Sam will also be riding with us."

Chapter 21

⟨◦⟩◦⟩◦⟩

J asmine watched the children pour out of the small white cottage, followed by Elena, who clasped a baby on her hip. They presented a gorgeous picture. The hair of the two older boys stood up in early morning tangles and spikes. The little girl wore her night dress, coupled with oversized pink slippers. And the baby was round cheeked and happy, a glossy smile on her miniature mouth.

Jasmine felt physically ill.

Elena, her dress neat and her hair gleaming, approached the assembled riders. "Good morning."

Jasmine wasn't able to dredge up a reply. Nor did she allow herself to look at Brody. She couldn't stand to see the evidence of his love for Elena on this particular morning.

The front door banged shut behind Sam as he strode into the yard, pulling his jacket on over his work shirt. "Morning," he called.

The men surrounding her returned his greeting.

Jasmine's gaze narrowed on the brawny cowboy who would be accompanying them. She recognized him as the man she'd spoken with at the dance. No wonder his name had sounded familiar.

She must have done something evil indeed to deserve this twist in their plans. The unwanted company of Sam,

Grayson, and Seth robbed her of any opportunity, no matter how slight, to niggle her way back under Brody's skin. Damn it to hell. Her fingers itched to hurl something. Something breakable. Something heavy. Perhaps herself, at the nearest tree limb. Maybe she could manage to impale her heart on it.

Sam lifted his horse's reins from the corral post and turned to his children.

They hesitated.

"Go on now," Elena urged. "Say good-bye to your father." She gave the eldest boy a subtle shove.

Jasmine watched the edges of Sam's lips thin.

The children approached him one by one and gave him stiff hugs. The little girl looked downright uncomfortable in his embrace. Elena and the baby approached him last. "Are you sure you don't want me to pack more food?" she asked.

"I'm sure," he replied, too firmly.

"All right. What about a coat or another blanket? You might need—"

"No."

She took a step nearer. "When will you be back?"

Sam glanced at Grayson, faintly embarrassed. "Don't know."

"Isn't there some indication you can give me?"

"No."

"Two weeks? Three?"

"Goddamnit!" Sam snarled, turning on her. "I'm not some child that needs answer to you! I go where I want and I'll be back when I'm back."

Elena's face paled.

Jasmine's vision sliced to Brody. His gloved hands gripped his saddle horn. One boot had already slipped from the stirrup. He was on the verge of dismounting and beating Sam senseless.

"Step back," Sam hissed at Elena.

Elena staggered back two steps. Sam stepped into the saddle and trotted past her without so much as a gesture or a tipping of his hat.

Jasmine had instinctively disliked Elena. But she really hated Sam. What an unforgivable idiot. She hoped that he'd dare talk to her like that over the course of their trip. It would give her an excuse to practice her aim.

"Let's head out," Sam said, when he'd joined them. From close up she could see that his eyes were bloodshot. Two brackets framed the edges of his mouth. No doubt he was paying this morning for his overindulgence last night.

Brody tugged his hat lower and pointed his horse toward home. But before setting into motion, Jasmine saw him catch Elena's eye and give her one long, courteous nod.

Elena smiled wanly in return.

Jasmine diverted her attention by untying her pink bandana. When she retied it, the knot cinched too tightly around her neck. She left it that way.

The throng of horses trotted forward. Though she didn't really want to, Jasmine felt compelled to take a backward glance.

She saw a beautiful, willowy blond woman. Three children standing protectively at her skirts. One child nestled in her arms. Wildflowers growing in a tumult around them.

She was certain that Brody would have given the heart from his chest to call that scene his own.

Her boot heels nudged into Vengeance's sides and she cantered forward. Grayson and Sam were already thick in conversation. As she passed, Sam bestowed a false smile on her, Grayson a look of wary interest.

She ignored them both.

Seth rode beside Brody at the head. When she pulled up beside them, the young Ranger observed her appreciatively. "You're looking lovely this morning, Mrs. McClintock."

She nodded, incapable of any other response. "Could you excuse us for a moment, Seth?"

"Certainly."

His horse fell off the pace, leaving her and Brody alone. He didn't acknowledge her presence in any way.

Mute frustration jangled inside her, demanding an outlet. She'd swallowed her emotions all morning. Now her bitterness and hurt had grown so intolerable that she couldn't hold them back any longer. Brody was going to have to face her whether he liked it or not. "Ignoring me this morning, I see," she said.

A muscle flecked near his ear.

"As I recall, you were slightly more attentive last night."

His gaze cut to her. Shaded eyes burned beneath the brim of his hat. "Watch yourself, Jasmine."

"Oh, so you do remember. I thought perhaps you'd forgotten."

"I remember," he gritted. "And I regret."

Her fingers spasmed as she fought to control the stab of pain his words caused her. She channeled her vision directly forward, on the approaching grove of trees. She noted the texture of the bark. Examined the exact color of the leaves. Memorized the shape of the branches. None of it made her forget that Brody regretted their lovemaking.

She wanted to lash back at him. Angry retorts clogged her mind. But on the verge of hurling them at him, she realized how petty they'd sound. How weak.

She needed to steer the conversation toward more impersonal irritations before she shamed herself. "Why are these men accompanying us?" she asked, her words curt, but even.

"Because they have business in Tyler."

"And you invited them along?"

"No. They asked me if they could come. And I said they could."

She pulled her father's oversized coat more snugly around her neck. "I've heard that Grayson is undergoing some sort of a search and that Seth is the Ranger assigned to him.''

"Right.''

"But what about Sam?''

Brody flicked his reins. "Sam is . . . unfortunate.''

"Very.''

His eyes narrowed. "It seems Grayson and Sam formed a friendship over these last days. Sam has no causes of his own, so he's committed himself to Grayson's cause.''

She grunted. "That doesn't explain why you allowed him to come.''

"You want to know why I allowed him to come?''

"Yes, I do.''

"So that Elena could have a few weeks' peace.''

She examined his face: the fierce chin with the cleft in the center, the lean cheeks, the tiny lines radiating from his eyes. "How chivalrous of you.''

Anger blazed from every inch of him as he leaned over and grabbed Vengeance's bridle. Both horses lunged to a halt. With a wave of his hand, Brody signaled to the others. The two of them waited, immobile, until the rest of their party had issued past. In the wake of their companions, the air seemed unnaturally calm.

Jasmine fidgeted. Clearly, he hadn't appreciated her sarcasm. She'd pushed him too far. Damn her hide! And damn her self-destructive tendency to jab her opponent one time too many. She found herself once again balancing on the cliff's edge, too far out to scurry back to safety.

"I want you to understand something,'' Brody said.

Her stomach quivered. Remorse and defiance. "What's that?''

"I'm releasing you.''

"What?''

"From the promise I made to you. I'm going to see you safely back to Tyler and then I'm going to give you your freedom.''

She held herself perfectly still. Inwardly, her emotions flew into turmoil.

Freedom. The keening cry of her spirit had become a sobbing curse. It was exactly what she'd always wanted. And precisely what she didn't want. She clutched the reins as tightly as she could. "You're . . . you're going to break your marriage vow to me?"

"No. I'll be married to you until the day I die, only I won't be around in the meantime."

The harsh honesty of his words hit her like a mallet between the eyes.

"What's the matter?" he asked. "Freedom is what you want, isn't it?" Brody measured Jasmine's reaction, desperately searching for some remnant of the love she'd shown him the night before. But he saw nothing in the beautiful lines of her face except blank control. No softening or sorrow.

"It is what you want?" he asked again, giving her another chance to prove him wrong.

"Of course it is."

Eyes like diamonds washed by river water stared at him with fragile hope. A hope that he figured must belong to the promise of independence he'd just given her. He peeled his gaze away. "Good. Then we're both happy."

"Ecstatic."

He forced his hand to release its hold on her horse. Then he rode like a demon to the front of the pack and beyond.

The frigid air lashed his skin. He'd done it. He'd released her. He should feel relieved. He had his life back, his job, and his sanity.

He clenched and unclenched his hands several times. He circled his shoulders. The attempts to bring a measure of warmth to his numb body were of no use. It wasn't the temperature that had frozen his soul.

* * *

The fire crackled. Amber sparks shot skyward, then circled toward the earth in golden sizzles.

One such spark spiraled onto the toe of Jasmine's boot, turning on contact into a gray, flaky rectangle. Moodily, she launched it back into the air, then watched it float earthward and mesh into the neutral brown of the surrounding dirt.

They'd just finished supper. Tom was still clearing the dishes and packing the remaining rations into his saddle bags. His work punctuated the night noises with dull clunks and rustling.

"Are you cold, Mrs. McClintock?"

Heaven, she hated it when Seth called her that. She tried to look at him and reply, only to realize that she'd inadvertently buried her head in her father's coat. Like a turtle, she stuck her head out the neckhole and turned to look at him. He sat cross-legged beside her, his eyes filled with concern.

"No, I'm fine," she said.

"I just thought . . . you had your head in there pretty far."

"I guess I did."

"And the wind's chilly."

"Yes."

He reached for the collar of her coat. "Maybe if I just turn this up—"

"My wife said she's warm enough," Brody warned.

Both Jasmine and Seth glanced at him. He sat across the fire, leaning his lower back against his saddle. His long legs were outstretched and crossed at the ankles, his upper body hunched slightly against the gale that blew at his back.

He'd been acting like a bear all day. Surly and mean. As it happened, his disposition suited Jasmine perfectly, because it exactly matched her own.

Mrs. McClintock. She wouldn't be worthy of the title for

much longer, she thought, as she gazed at Brody. One more day, in fact. Just one more day.

Throughout the long hours of the ride, she'd tried to sort through the helpless tangle of her emotions. But sadness clung to her like a thick veil, and every time she attempted to lift it and sift below for the underlying emotion, she could find nothing but more of the writhing, twisting veil. Sadness. Layer upon layer. Unending.

She understood little of her own heart, except for this. Her marriage to Brody had become a welcome bond. She'd tied herself to a makeshift husband. He'd dogged her, fought her, aborted her attempts at freedom, until somehow . . . sometime . . . she'd come to like being caged.

The sad truth of it was that her goal, her quest for freedom, had gotten lost. The ground she'd stood upon so firmly since childhood was now quaking, shifting, and she couldn't tell what topography her new priorities would take. Today she'd tried to regain her goals. She'd tried to rediscover her passion for independence in the mire of her depression. Instead, she'd discovered that her passion for Brody mattered more.

She stared into the flames and struggled to envision returning to Colin House and making a home for herself there. The loneliness of it stretched out into eternity like a colorless banner. Without Brody, what would be left to brighten her days? Shooting? Riding the lines of the ranch? How could those things compare to the glory of being with him? To the way his eyes sparkled when struck by sunshine? Or the way he smiled at her from beneath the dark brim of his hat? How would she ever counterfeit the bolt of joy she experienced at the mere brush of his fingers?

Her sigh whispered into the air, blending with the fragrant blackening smoke that twined in her direction.

She didn't want to be an outlaw anymore. It was an awful truth to admit to herself, because it heralded the death of a lifelong dream. But its harshness couldn't blemish its truth. She didn't want to be an outlaw.

The lure of banditry had been overshadowed by the lure of something even stronger. Justice. Brody's currency.

She envied the way he sat a horse, sure of the fairness of his cause. He looked people in the eye with honesty. His pursuits were noble, his motives honorable.

When she'd robbed the stagecoach, then sat beneath the vehicle, shivering in the shade and smelling gun smoke on the air, she hadn't felt honorable. The cries of the women. The stolen money. Endangering the life of her beloved horse. These had been the realities of her dream. And they'd shamed her.

She still longed for the adventure. But she'd no longer fight to obtain it if it meant stealing the livelihood of others. She wanted to earn for herself the gratitude she saw in people's eyes when they looked at Brody. She wanted to fight for a cause, as he did. She wanted to be worthy.

Her eyes stung in response to the acid smoke. She blinked and whipped the moisture away from her lids with her gloved finger. All around her, the men spoke in low tones. She made herself listen to them, needing relief from her thoughts.

"How did you discover that he might be in Tyler?" Sam asked.

"One of the boys he used to ride with told us," Grayson answered.

"We're going to get that son of a bitch. Mark my word." Sam's face glowed with feverish intent.

Jasmine supposed they were talking about the fugitive Grayson sought. She wondered if she should inform him just how fruitless his search would be. It was impossible to believe that Grayson's bandit could be living in her closely knit town of Tyler.

Matthew Grayson's thin gray hair lay slicked across the

crown of his head. His gaze moved quickly, settling on those around the fire.

Jasmine sensed the bitterness in him and wondered if it pricked like a hundred sharp razors, or grew through him silently, like a disease. She tried to imagine how deep her own grievance would have to be before she'd set off on a trek across the country to hunt the offender down.

"How did this man wrong you?" she asked.

The men glanced at her, clearly surprised by her first foray into their conversation all evening.

"He killed my sister," Grayson replied.

"Don't worry," Sam said to her, "I've promised Grayson here that I'm going to help him hunt this man down and see him killed for what he did."

She ignored Sam. "Why did he kill your sister?"

"Don't know," Grayson answered.

"How'd he do it?"

"Gave her over to Comanches to be tortured."

Sam shifted uncomfortably and made a tutting sound. He leaned behind Seth so that he could pat her on the back. "That's probably too much for this little lady to be hearing, Grayson. You'll be giving her nightmares."

She stiffened.

Sam's hand slid off her back. His flask, muted by the imprint of his fingertips, rose to his lips. He took a quick swallow while he assessed her in the manner she'd come to expect from him.

"I like nightmares," she replied.

The startling admission shocked him into silence for a few moments. Then he chuckled. "You don't mean that."

"Yes I do. The bloodier, the better."

His guffaws deepened. "Oh, Jasmine . . ."

The condescending tone of his voice was the last straw. She whisked her gun from its position at her hip. The silver and pearl blurred together as the weapon swung around her finger. She cocked it and aimed at Sam's forehead.

His eyebrows streaked back.

Behind him, Tom dropped the dish he'd been wiping. It clattered and spun on the hard dirt.

"No—no need for firearms between us," Grayson said, his voice frail.

She drew a tiny circle in the air with the barrel.

"Mrs. McClintock," Seth pleaded.

"Jasmine, maybe you ought to put the gun down," Tom said carefully.

She cut a look at Brody. Of them all, he was the only man fast enough to have done something about her maneuver. And the only one who hadn't moved a muscle. He smiled at her, amusement flickering in his eyes.

Jasmine laughed. Then she raised the gun and fired.

A tree limb at the far edge of their camp cracked and severed. It toppled to the ground, splintering into shards. She holstered the gun with a soundless whoosh. "We needed more kindling, didn't we, Tom?"

Gradually, like the sun peeking over the horizon, two deep dimples gouged Tom's cheeks. "I suppose."

Her wonderful Tom. She'd known he wouldn't rob her of the first stab of pleasure she'd experienced all day.

"Now." She hunkered forward, resting her elbows on her knees, and gazed at Sam. "If I say I like nightmares, then I like nightmares. Next time I make a statement you might want to believe me. Unless, of course, you're ready to challenge me to a gunfight. Because if you are, I'm willing."

Sam pulled his flask to his lips and gulped twice. The metal container shook slightly, spilling a little of the whiskey down the side of his lip and onto his chin. "I'm not going to be gunfighting with no woman," he muttered, as he lowered his drink.

"No?" she asked. "Then you better keep your mouth shut." She'd been wanting to do that all day. Look at Sam down the barrel of her gun.

She returned her attention to Grayson and their earlier topic. "How long ago was your sister killed?"

Grayson's feral gaze darted around the circle. Clearly he was looking to the others to decide whether he should reply to the madwoman. His attention settled on her three times before he finally answered. "My sister was killed over twenty years ago."

"Twenty years?" Brody asked sharply, rousing from his disinterest for the first time.

"Yes."

Brody looked to Seth. "Not an easy assignment."

"No," Seth answered. "But Mr. Grayson has made it this far by himself. I was assigned to him because the captain feels it's in the interest of the law to help him the rest of the way."

"I agree," Brody said. "But the man you seek could be dead by now, or living in any of a hundred cities under a new identity."

"True." The look Seth gave Brody held little optimism.

"What else do you know about the man you're looking for?" Brody asked Grayson.

"I know a few possible aliases. I have a picture."

Jasmine could feel Brody's attention lingering on her. The force of it was like a balm—tingling, soothing, heating.

"Hand the picture to Jasmine," he said. "She grew up in Tyler. She knows the people who live there."

Grayson hesitated for an awkward moment before deciding to trust her with his evidence. Twisting, he reached for his bag and dug inside. Once he'd recovered the photograph, he rose, walked around the circle, and delivered it directly into her palm.

Jasmine nestled the picture in her gloved hands and angled it toward the firelight. The photograph had browned with age and the edges were tattered, but she could clearly make out the young man who'd been captured on film.

Bearded and cocky, he glared into the camera with compelling eyes.

Eyes that were midnight blue in real life. Hair of mahogany brown that had long since been trimmed. A beard she'd shaved for him when they moved to Tyler.

Recognition hit her with shattering force.

One breath. Two.

Everyone was watching her.

She struggled to school her features into a mask of calm curiosity.

She grasped hard around her father's waist and watched the scenery flash by. They raced along a ridge and she leaned over, so that she could see the wink of the silvery river that snaked through the canyon. The wind lifted and twined through her hair, tugging the strands high. She laughed. Her father laughed, too, a song of pure, sweet joy.

In her memories of early childhood her father looked exactly like he did in this picture. Younger, tougher, more chiseled. This must have been taken . . . her mind raced too quickly, then lagged unbearably . . . around that time.

Her mother. God, could her mother be Grayson's sister? No.

Before her quaking fingers could rattle the photograph, she handed it back to the slight old man who stood hovering over her shoulder, waiting for her reaction.

Grayson couldn't be her own relative. Yes, he could. Oh, God. He was her mother's brother. Her own uncle. Come to hunt down her father.

He killed my sister. Gave her over to Comanches to be tortured. Twenty years ago.

Her stomach contracted violently. No. It was impossible. Her father had told her that her mother had run away. How had the facts gotten so horribly misunderstood?

"Well?" Brody asked.

The strain of appearing unaffected under the observation of so many caused muscles to tick beneath the skin of her face. She fought to smooth them, to control her outward expression. "I don't know him."

Grayson's narrow lips pursed in disappointment. "He'd be older now," he urged. "Maybe heavier, without facial hair."

"No." She wanted desperately to say more, to fabricate a convincing lie on her father's behalf. But she didn't trust herself to speak. Emotion gusted within her like a hurricane contained by paper and paste. Speaking again would be too great a risk.

She pulled her head into the coat's collar, hiding herself, except for the window of her eyes.

Grayson, his head bowed, began walking back to his position.

"Let me see it."

Her entire being stilled at Brody's words.

No! The denial shrieked through her head, her heart, her brain, all the more powerful because of its inability to find voice.

Grayson made his way around the camp.

She saw Brody extend his hand for the photograph

She wanted to scream. To run to Grayson and snatch the evidence from his hands and throw it in the fire. Her body ached with the effort of remaining motionless.

Grayson handed the photograph to Brody.

She could hear nothing, see nothing, except him. He studied the picture, his eyes narrowing in concentration.

Please, God, no. No. Don't let him recognize my father.

The seconds stretched. Her ligaments quivered.

Brody frowned and gave the picture back to Grayson. His gaze met Jasmine's. "I don't know him either."

Sound returned to her in a feverish rush of relief, along with feeling and movement and breath. She wondered briefly if there was any possibility that Brody had recognized her father and lied. Almost as quickly she rejected the idea. Brody was far too honorable. And even if he wasn't, he didn't care enough about her to lie for her. If he'd recognized her father, he'd have sacrificed him in a heartbeat.

Grayson took his seat by the fire. He moved gingerly, with limbs that appeared to work painfully. "If I don't find him in Tyler, I'll keep looking." He cradled the photograph in his hands and rocked slightly. "I'll just keep looking."

Jasmine gnawed the inside of her cheek. Grayson had said he'd gathered aliases. She had to find out what he knew before she could act to protect her father. "What . . ." She cleared her throat of the dry croak that plagued it. "What names do you have for him?"

Again, Grayson paused before answering, seeming to weigh the prudence of trusting them with his information. A strong look from Brody prodded him to speak. "Well . . . I've got a list that I compiled from his birth record, newspaper articles, and sheriffs' accounts."

She needed to hear what he was about to say, and yet never had she wanted to cover her ears more urgently. She tried to swallow.

"The names I know are, uh . . ."

Sweat beaded on her upper lip. She wiped it away.

"Holden Thompson—that's his birth name. Then Holden Smith and Holden Jenks. When he was with the gang it was mostly Buddy Neil. On occasion he's used John Myer and Hayden Simmons."

She forced down the worst of the tension. Though each name was familiar to her, no one in Tyler would know them. Even less would they associate them with her father, a man they knew only as Lee Jamison.

The photograph was the most damaging evidence. Whereas Brody had seen her father only once, many of the townspeople had known her father for all of the fourteen years they'd lived in Tyler. Sooner or later one of them would recognize the man in the fading picture.

"Which alias did he use when he was married to your

sister?'' she asked, hoping to confirm that he'd not forgotten to mention one of the aliases.

Grayson frowned. ''How'd you know he was married to my sister?''

Panic iced through her at the realization of her mistake. God, she'd given herself up. ''I—I'm sorry.'' She tried in vain to think of a way to repair the damage. Her brain blanked. They were all studying her. ''I simply assumed they were married.''

For a terrifying moment silence greeted her reply.

''You're right, Mrs. McClintock,'' Seth said. ''They were married.''

She glanced at him, grateful beyond words that he'd rescued her.

''So how was it that your sister came to be married to an outlaw?'' Tom asked. The dishes finished, he settled himself into the narrow opening between Jasmine and Seth.

Grayson's nose pinched. ''She met him in our hometown. At the time none of us knew of his profession. Still, we tried to talk sense into her, but she ran off with him anyway. Eloped. At first her letters came regularly. But after a time, they came less often. And then they stopped entirely.''

Jasmine couldn't believe that this man who spoke to her across the narrow distance of logs and smoke was her uncle, and the woman he spoke of her mother. She felt no remorse over the death of a woman she'd never known, a woman who had abandoned them. At the same time, she fervently wished that her mother had lived so that Grayson wouldn't have come on this quest for revenge which so gravely endangered her father's life.

''It wasn't until later,'' Grayson continued, ''when they found her body and brought us the news, that we realized she'd died. And later still when we discovered that her husband was a criminal.''

"Why didn't you chase the man down then?" Tom asked. "Why wait all these years?"

"Because my mother forbade me to go. There were only the two of us, Kathryn and I. When she lost Kathryn, she went mad with sorrow. She couldn't bear to see me go, too." He wrapped his ragged coat more closely around him. "My parents were never the same after her death. It ruined them. Ruined our family."

"What made you decide to launch a search now?" Tom asked.

"My mother died." His eyes were obsidian gems. Hard, sharp, endlessly cold. "My father passed almost five years ago. But my mother lived up until this October. On her deathbed I swore to her I'd find him and make him suffer the way he's made all of us suffer."

His words chilled Jasmine to the bone. Anguished by the ruthlessness in him, her gaze sought the one among them who was her rock.

Brody gazed back at her, his expression level and grave.

Was that the same expression he would give her when he found out that Grayson's outlaw was her father? Would his duty matter more than his compassion in that moment? Could she trust him with the truth?

Gradually, each of them sought their bed rolls and sleep. Jasmine huddled under her covers, but couldn't relax. Both times that she risked looking at Brody, she caught him staring back at her.

Not wanting to awaken his suspicion with her sleeplessness, she rolled over and faced the inky darkness of the surrounding trees. She tossed and shifted and tried to find comfort in her own meager body heat, to no avail. Her mind kept careening along the pathway of her worries. Over and over her brain conjured up the same terrifying image. She saw Brody raising his gun and shooting her father. The bullet lodged deep, pouring blood from Lee's heart before he staggered and fell. She ran to her daddy and dropped onto her knees beside him, her sobs racking her chest. Ever so carefully, she lifted his head into her hands. He couldn't speak. Neither could she. There was so much to say and no time left to say it. They looked at one another, overcome by guilt and love. She read the sadness in his eyes in the instant before they turned murky. Searing pain ripped through her at the realization of his death.

She curled into a ball and tried to warm herself by lifting the collar of her shirt and blowing onto her skin. It didn't help.

No matter the price, she *couldn't* lose her father. She'd failed him by marrying Brody, but in this she refused to fail.

First she needed to destroy the photograph. Then she needed to go to the Double J, long before the others, and confirm that her father had heeded her message to run. And somehow, between now and their arrival in Tyler, she had to make Brody love her.

Just a little.

Because maybe, if he loved her a little, he'd side with her. And if worse came to worst, he'd have mercy on her father.

Chapter 22

"**M**ore wine?"

Emma giggled. "I shouldn't."

"Of course you should." Lee emptied the bottle by refilling both their glasses.

"Thank you." She swallowed a portion of the deep red liquid. It seemed to curl inside her mouth and unwind in a silken stream down her throat. She gloried in the dry, rich flavor. "It's wonderful."

"It is good, isn't it?"

"Yes, very."

Lee considered her, eyes sparkling. "Have you drunk a lot of wine in your time, Miss Larkin?"

She laughed. "Actually, this is only the second time in my life. But already I'm developing a very real affection for it."

He grinned at her, a thoroughly male grin that set her nerves to singing.

They were picnicking. A wool plaid blanket rested beneath them, the remains of their lunch scattered across it. Emma had packed sandwiches, raw vegetables, cheese, and dessert. Lee had supplied the wine.

As far as the eye could see, nature reigned in springtime glory, undisturbed by the trivial fancies of man.

"Had I known you had such an ideal picnic spot just

waiting to be used, I'd have insisted upon a picnic years ago," Emma said.

Lee polished off the last of his wine, then reclined onto the blanket, resting his weight on one elbow. "Had I known that I'd enjoy it this much, you wouldn't have had to insist."

The matchless blue of his eyes held her in thrall. Pleasure warmed her body from the inside out. She felt deeply relaxed, mildly euphoric, and a little woozy. "Are you admitting that you didn't realize you'd enjoy my company, Lee Jamison? What exactly have you thought of me for all these years?"

"That you were a respectable, upstanding, formidable woman. A trustworthy neighbor. A good influence on Jasmine."

Her beautiful brows converged. "Respectable? Upstanding? Trustworthy?"

"What's wrong with those?"

"Nothing. They just don't make me sound terribly . . . exciting."

"Well, you asked me what I used to think. The exciting part I've just recently discovered."

Delight tingled through her. "I see."

Lee's jaw jutted outward in challenge. "What have you thought of me for all these years?"

That you were the most desirable man on the planet. That I'd sell my soul to the devil to have you.

She took another sip and tried to hide her guilty blush behind the rim of the glass. "To be honest, I felt like I knew you from the first moment I met you. I thought you were forceful, intelligent, and stubborn, with a kind streak everyone pretended not to know about."

"Kind streak." He snorted.

"Most definitely. It's the kind streak that makes all the other qualities so noble."

His scoffing smile disappeared. His gaze searched hers. "You think I'm noble?"

She wasn't sure why the reassurance would mean so much to him, but it very clearly did. "I do."

His free hand scooted across the blanket and captured her fingers. She barely had time to set aside her glass before he tugged her toward him. Emma landed on her side on the woolen blanket, just a whisper away from him. A thrill of arousal swirled low in her belly.

The face she'd dreamed of a thousand times, neared. Her vision caught hopelessly in the bottomless pools of his eyes. And then his lips touched hers. Feather soft.

The heavenly pressure increased. Tentatively, she responded. As she kissed him back, she remembered in a vivid crash what it was like to be caressed, held, wanted. It had been so long. Forever.

She parted her lips for him. His hand dug beneath her hair as he deepened the kiss.

Wanting was a thick weight inside her. She was kissing Lee. Her great love. *Oh, Lord.* Her mind struggled to comprehend the enormity of it.

She opened her eyes and peered close up at his closed eyelids. Lee. The heart that had loved him so long, thumped painfully in her chest.

His tongue probed, swirled, and then retreated. She shut off her vision and savored the string of soft, adoring kisses. Then, gently, he pulled back. His thumb stroked along the back of her neck once before sliding away.

They gazed at each other in wonder.

The shade shifted across his face, tipping his features with sunlight. "I didn't scare you did I?" he asked.

"No," she whispered, low and breathy.

He frowned slightly and levered up to sitting. Twice, he raked his fingers through his hair. "I don't know . . . I'm not sure what came over me."

Apprehension slithered across her joy. What was he talking about? Was he sorry?

"I hope you'll overlook—"

"Overlook!" She bolted up and laid a hand on his elbow, gaining his attention. "I will not overlook that kiss. And spare me any awkward apologies. You have my permission to kiss me in that manner at any time. Unequivocally."

He regarded her with such amazement that she laughed.

A pair of birds sailed from the tree which towered above them, then skated heavenward.

She decided she needed to lighten the mood and put him back at ease. "But before you take me up on my generous offer," she said, "I intend to teach you a thing or two about shooting." She reached for her rifle, scrambled to her feet, and ran from beneath the cover of branches.

Lee remained immobile.

"What's the matter?" she taunted. "Afraid of defeat? Worried the wine's impaired your aim?"

With a chuckle and a growl, he leapt to his feet and ran toward her. "You'll pay for that!"

She shrieked and lifted her skirts as she bounded across the field. The breeze twirled through her hair. Sunshine doused her. Never had she felt so fully alive, so deeply exhilarated.

A quick peek over her shoulder confirmed that Lee was almost upon her. Her heart kicked with anticipation. Her life's dreams were finally within reach.

She had to destroy the photograph. The necessity of it pressed in on Jasmine, suffocating her.

Throughout the morning, she'd studied Grayson, searching for opportunity and weakness. The way she figured it, there would only be one chance to find the photograph and dispose of it. When they broke for their midday meal, they'd rest the horses and let them drink. Grayson's horse, and thus his satchel, would be unattended for a brief margin of time.

She *had* to retrieve the photograph then, because tonight they'd unsaddle the horses before letting them drink and Grayson would use his satchel as a pillow, just as he had last night. Tomorrow they'd reach Tyler.

Near noon, Brody slowed the pace and started searching the terrain for a convenient resting place. Jasmine directed Vengeance past the other riders and reined in beside him. "Time for dinner?"

He nodded, sparing her the briefest glance.

"That grove looks like the best spot." She pointed to a dense stretch of trees beside the stream.

He frowned skeptically.

"It's warm today." For good measure, she lifted her collar a couple times to fan her chest. "I could use the shade."

What she really needed was cover. The more the better.

Brody's gaze lingered on the vee of her shirt, before snapping back to the path. "Fine."

"Thank you." She fell off the lead and followed him the rest of the way. Before any of the men had even pulled their horses to a complete stop, she dropped to the earth and led Vengeance toward the creek.

Purposefully, she guided him downstream from the clearing, hoping that the others would follow and bring their mounts to the deeply thicketed bank. They did.

She pretended to be engrossed in stroking Vengeance's neck while the men came, left their horses, and retreated to the clearing. Even after they'd gone, she waited and listened. Over the noise of swishing tails and lapping tongues, their conversation grew more distant.

She threaded soundlessly among the animals, stopping before the nondescript brown mare that belonged to Grayson. As she'd hoped, the bag containing the photograph had been left attached to the saddle.

One quick look toward camp. Nothing.

She reached for the first buckle. With extreme concentration, she unlatched the clasp and slid the strap from its bond.

She glanced up again. Nothing.

Her fingers went to work on the second buckle. Finally, it gave way. Barely breathing, she inched her palm into the bag's opening.

"Mrs. McClintock?" The weight of approaching footsteps broke twigs.

On a gasp, she flung the bag's flap back into place and jumped away.

Seth ducked under a low bough and came to a halt. "I don't want you attending to chores that I could be attending to, Mrs. McClintock."

Adrenaline coursed through her body in disconcerting fits and leaps. This was her only chance. "No, it's nothing." She needed a reason for remaining here alone that he'd believe. "I simply wanted to check on the horses," she said, struggling to make her voice sound normal.

"Well, allow me."

"No, really. I have a good eye for a horse who's favoring a leg. I thought I'd just look them over—"

"Not when I can relieve you. I insist. You must be hungry."

Her hands clamped together behind her back, so tightly that the blood squeezed from her knuckles. The small window of opportunity was closing. "You're right, I could use a meal. If you'll excuse me for a moment, I'll just freshen up."

"Oh. Freshen up."

"Yes. Here at the stream." She gestured impatiently toward the tumbling water, praying that her request for feminine privacy would send him away.

The seconds he spent observing her scratched past. "In that case, please excuse me."

"Of course."

Just as he turned to rejoin the group, Brody walked up behind him. "What's going on?" he asked, looking back and forth between them.

Her hope crashed into a myriad of shining pieces.

"Your wife was tending to the horses. Now she's freshening up." Seth scooted past Brody down the path.

Brody raised an eyebrow at her. "Freshening up?"

"Yes, and if you don't mind, I could use a little privacy."

He crossed his arms. "I do mind. First you need shade. Then you need to freshen. What are you up to?"

"Nothing."

"Whatever it is, you can forget it."

"Brody—"

"Forget it."

"I simply—"

"Come on back with me, where I can keep an eye on you."

Her breath rushed from her lungs in an angry torrent. She spun and presented him with her back, then knelt at the stream's edge and plunged her hands into the current. Even beneath the crystal waters, she could see her fingers trembling. That same shaking extended up her arms and down to the deepest regions of her heart.

In order to save her father, she *needed* that photograph.

She made an elaborate presentation of cleaning because she didn't know what else to do. Her brain spun, working to churn up new options.

None came.

She rose and turned. In Brody's hazel eyes she saw the glint of implacable resolve. With a sinking feeling she realized he would be as firm on this one, ridiculous point as he would be when he discovered her father was a criminal.

She'd failed. The photograph still existed and it seemed certain now that Brody would find out about her father's past. When he did, he'd side with fairness and justice. He'd stand against her and her daddy.

A sob of frustration lodged in her throat. With slow, regulated movements she dried her hands on her pants. Having no other choice, she walked past him.

One furtive glance at Grayson's bag was all she risked. As close, now, as she would come.

Defeat weighing her heels, she made her way through the trees ahead of Brody. The men sat in a disjointed semi-circle in the clearing, stretching their legs and eating. After a cursory glance at the surroundings, she chose a rough, moss-speckled log to sit on.

Tom served her a simple meal which she pushed list-lessly around her plate. She couldn't even consider food.

Several times during the repast, she looked up to find the stares of the men upon her. In turn, each of them eyed her. Tom with concern. Sam with wariness. Seth with kindness. Grayson with uncertainty. And Brody . . . Brody with a grave intensity that gave her chills.

Her exhale slid from between lips that felt dry and cold. Jasmine knelt over Brody's sleeping form in an almost si-lent chorus of creasing fabric and bending leather.

Nearby, the fire breathed peacefully, its powerful flames having faded to subtle crackles and orange-gold embers The light it shed fell lovingly on her husband.

Her gaze slid over the line of Brody's chin, past his nose and over the sweep of his brows. Longing tightened in her breast. He looked so beautiful.

Bone deep tiredness raked over her. Desolation. Tor-ment. These same emotions had wrung her all of last night and all of today, especially this afternoon and evening, after her catastrophic attempt to destroy the photograph. Now they overpowered the last of her control. Tears swelled at the corners of her eyes and trickled down her cheeks. She didn't fight to subdue them. Didn't lift a hand to wipe them away. She simply let them fall.

The men had been asleep for hours. She'd lain motionless on her pallet, wide awake, staring at the star-laden sky and trying to work up her courage.

At first when she'd thrown off her blanket and come to her feet, she'd approached Grayson, hoping by some miracle that the photograph would be unattended. But he slept just as she'd known he would, with his head resting on his satchel, his hand curved protectively around its edge.

So she'd come to Brody.

Because he'd decided to slacken the pace and spread the trip over two nights, Tyler lay just three or four hours from here. The men would rise early and be in town before noon.

But not her. She would do this one last thing. And then she'd be gone.

She licked her lips and tasted the saltiness of her own tears. By the time Brody discovered the identity of the man in Grayson's photograph, she'd be home. She prayed that her father had taken her warning to heart and already fled. But if he hadn't, she needed to ensure that he'd still have time to escape.

She let a fingertip hover just above Brody's brow and the lashes that rested on tanned cheeks. When he discovered the identity of her father, he would know what she had done. And he would hate her for her deception.

Maybe. . . . She swallowed hard. Maybe he wouldn't hate her completely. If she could make him understand how she felt about him tonight, maybe he'd take pity on her when the time came. Perhaps he'd let her father disappear.

Sadness pounded her so hard she had to bite her lip to stave off the pain of it. Brody had already chosen to rid himself of her when they reached Tyler. He still would. The only hope she had left was protecting her daddy.

"Brody," she whispered, so downy soft that his name barely brushed the air.

He didn't respond. Wind gusted past her, lonely and dark.

She leaned close to his ear. "Brody."

His eyes sprung open. He sat up and reached for his gun in one dangerously swift movement.

Jasmine jumped away, stifling a surprised yelp.

No evidence of weariness remained in his expression. He stared at her with sharp concern. "What's the matter?"

Her pulse pumped erratically. She tried to smile. "Nothing."

"You're crying."

"I never cry."

He swiped his thumb over her cheekbone, then held his hand up to her. The firelight illuminated the gleaming strand of moisture that slipped along his skin and vanished into the cuff at his wrist.

From across the circle, blankets rustled and dirt crunched. She glanced at the sleeping bodies. Tom's form shifted and resettled.

Brody's callused fingertip pressed against her chin, gently nudging her face back to his. He frowned as he scoured her expression.

Beneath the layers of her clothing, she shivered, her skin prickling with heightened sensitivity. She pooled what was left of her nerve. If he could touch her, she could touch him.

She reached for his face. Air gasped from her lips as the tender pads of her fingertips met his stubbly cheek. A sensation more elemental than lightning tremored up her veins. Her hand, pale against the dark of his skin, glided over his jaw and down his neck and came to rest on the broad plane of his shoulder.

Confusion sparked in his eyes.

She refused to let her confidence falter. Instead, she followed the dictates of her body and heart. She closed her eyes, leaned forward, and lightly touched her lips to his.

Smooth and warm. Unmoving.

She deepened the pressure of the kiss.

His body stiffened.

He doesn't want me, she thought wildly. The hurt sank deep. He's rejected me this way before. I can't do this if he doesn't want me. Tears burned again at her eyes. Very softly, she licked along the line of his lips and kissed the edge of his mouth.

Nothing.

A silent cry spiraled through her. Her throat convulsed. She began to pull away.

On a groan, he turned his lips to hers. His tongue plunged into her mouth, claiming her with such unrestrained hunger that her senses blurred. His arms banded around her, crushing her to his chest.

Her legs bent. The hard earth met and supported her back. His tongue baited hers, demanded response. And she gave it to him.

He does want me. If nothing else, he cannot deny me that. Relief poured over her bruised and battered emotions. And then desire overtook all else and she could no longer think. Within the tumult of sensual feeling, nothing existed but the two of them and the blaze they'd created.

She grasped at him with all her might, hearing only the harsh sweep of his breath, feeling only the power of his hands as they tangled into her hair.

The kiss broke. Her eyelids swept open. The firelight intervened between them, revealing his cheekbone to her, his ear. He was checking their slumbering audience.

She, too, looked furtively at the men. Her heartbeat alone seemed loud enough to wake them. But none stirred.

Brody's gaze swung back to her. The fierce need she read in his eyes made her heady, drunk for him.

He lifted the length of his body on top of hers. Hard arousal ground against her abdomen. His hips thrust with a rhythm so carnal she wanted to tear her clothes off. To scream.

The men were so near.

She arched into him, her nails raking down his back.

He molded the swell of her breasts through the covering of her shirt. Then he lowered his head and she kissed him as if he were the source of her air and breath and very life.

In the next instant, his heat, his lifeblood pulled away from her. And she knew that she would die if he rejected her now.

He lifted her into his arms and stood. Carried her forward.

She gulped for air, groped for sanity.

He strode deep into the covering of trees with her in his arms. Looked down at her. Bent his head again to kiss her.

She leaned up and took his tongue greedily into her mouth. Her feet lowered. Her body slid down the length of his until she stood. But did not stand. Could not have stood were it not for his hands, his beloved hands, which supported her.

Her spine rested flush against the trunk of a tree.

"God, I need you," he breathed.

She felt the words in the violent ache of her body. "I need you, too."

Night air snaked around her waist as he yanked free her shirt. "I can't stop," he warned.

"I don't want you to."

"We shouldn't."

"We must." Impatience hurtled her forward. She pushed aside the barrier of his coat and ran her palm down the front of his stomach to cup his manhood.

He threw his head back and his hands stilled. She heard the ragged intake of breath. Felt the tensing of his muscles. She stroked him once. Then again, with more force.

A groan ripped from him. He pressed on her shoulders. She released him as she came up against the tree.

He gripped the waistline of her pants, parted the flap with a jerk and pushed them to her thighs. He slid his finger into her glistening center.

She reared at the invasion, her body contracting with erotic pleasure.

He eased from her, tugged her pants down to her ankles, pulled off one of her boots, and freed that foot. Then he ripped open his own trousers.

His hand slipped beneath her buttocks, which were naked under the layers of her shirt and coat. He lifted her higher against the bark. Her legs parted, raised. She hooked her feet behind his waist and pulled him to her.

The tip of his arousal pressed against her. He took her lips in an urgent kiss. Lifted his head. Gazed at her with eyes that burned black in the darkness.

"I love you," she whispered.

He thrust deeply into her.

She cried out.

He filled her. Completed her.

Powerfully, he began to move. So strong. Stroking her on the inside, both demanding and tender. Her body started to climb as it had climbed the time before. The sensations shot higher and higher.

He drove her forward, not letting her grasp at consciousness.

She tasted his lips. Drank his breath. Heard him groan.

Dazedly, she tried to prolong it. To calm the storm and hold onto it just a little longer . . . Her body broke under the torrent of feelings, each too exquisite to restrain. She wept his name as she throbbed around him. And he answered her, shuddering under the force of his ecstasy, surrendering himself to her in a pulsing stream.

I love you.

That's what she'd said to him.

Brody lay on his side by the fire, Jasmine clasped firmly

within his arms. The pressure of her rounded bottom against his thighs was a hellish kind of heaven.

After making love, they'd held each other for long moments, stirring only when the cold licked at them. Then they'd readjusted their clothing and returned to the comfort of the campfire. There had been no words between them. Except those three.

I love you.

Three words that changed his life.

Since hearing them, he'd been trying to restrain his hope. Over and over he'd told himself they didn't mean anything, that they'd been spoken in the heat of passion. But he remembered the look in her eyes when she'd said them. He could still see the glittering fervor there, the desperate honesty. And that look dared him to believe that her feelings for him might be strong enough to temper her need of freedom.

God, she was lovely. Even in sleep, with her magnificent eyes shuttered, she was incredibly lovely. Painfully so. He pulled the blanket higher, tucking it around her chin.

He was glad she slept. Since Grayson had shown her that godforsaken picture of her father, she'd barely gotten any rest or eaten anything. All day today, dark rings had marred the skin beneath her eyes, giving her a haggard appearance that scared the hell out of him.

He could only guess how devastating it had been for her to discover that the men she traveled with were intent on hunting down and arresting her father. Hell, it devastated him, too. The last thing on earth he'd wanted when he'd asked to see the photograph of Grayson's outlaw was to recognize Jasmine's father in the fading image.

But he had. And in that second, when all his training and all his ideals had demanded that he reveal the identity of the bandit, he'd realized that he cared about Jasmine more. More than the law, or justice.

So he'd held his tongue. And with his silence he'd

bought her time. He owed her that much. Time to adjust to the reality of her father's situation, to think, and to entrust him with her knowledge. Over every moment since he'd seen the photograph, Brody had been praying that Jasmine would find it in her heart to confide in him. She hadn't so far, but after what had passed between them tonight, he knew she would in the morning.

Try as he might, Brody couldn't fault Lee Jamison. Whatever bad he'd done, he'd managed to raise one hell of a daughter. Knowing about Lee's past explained a lot about his child. Her fearless personality. Her desperation for independence. Her attempt to join a gang of bandits. They all made sense to him now. And for her sake, he was willing to do whatever he could to help her father.

A strand of her hair lifted and floated on the wind. He captured it and smoothed it behind her ear.

As soon as she confided in him, he'd discuss the identity of the man in the photograph with Grayson and the others. Then he'd move heaven and earth to ensure a settlement, or a truce, or the most lenient punishment available for Lee.

Resting his head on his saddle, he closed his eyes. The smell of the outdoors spiced with Jasmine's unique scent twined about him. Above and below his sorrow over Jasmine's predicament, he felt . . . God, it had been so long since he'd been blessed by this emotion he barely recognized it.

Contentment. That's what it was. Contentment, coasting over him like warm rain. He wanted to trap it in his fist and never let it go.

Jasmine edged closer to him. From the depths of her dreams, she released a satisfied sigh.

The edges of his lips tilted into a smile. Her sigh perfectly captured his state of mind.

Tomorrow, after they'd settled her worry over her father, he'd ask her how she really felt about him as her husband, what she really wanted.

She'd said she loved him.

And God help him, he was ready to believe she did. For the first time in eleven years, the future seemed full of potential and promise.

Chapter 23

$\sim\!\!\!\curvearrowright\!\!\curvearrowleft\!\!\sim$

S he'd run from him. Brody read Jasmine's note one last time before crushing it in his fist.

"Did she say in the note where she went?" Seth asked.

"Says she went to her friend Emma's for a visit," Brody said, knowing that wasn't where she'd gone. She'd vanished from his bed to warn her father. By now the two of them were probably streaking across the prairie on a mad dash for the Mexican border. His mouth dried. Christ. He'd deluded himself into believing that she loved him. And she'd answered his belief by running.

Worried grooves snaked across Seth's hairline. "Would you like for me to go after her?"

"No."

"You think she knows her way to Emma's house from here?"

Tom, who stood alongside them, chuckled. "Of course she does. She was raised in these parts."

"But . . . maybe I should ride after her and see." Seth glanced back and forth between them. "We rose at dawn. She must have left when it was still dark. Would she know her way home in the dark?"

Brody considered killing the younger man. It wouldn't be difficult—a simple matter of unsheathing the knife he wore beside his boot and thrusting it into the region of

Seth's heart. It seemed fair punishment for his over-protective treatment of Jasmine. Treatment that was Brody's alone to give by law and by right.

"She doesn't need anyone riding after her and interrupting her visit with her lady friend," Tom said.

"I won't interrupt," Seth answered. "I'll just track the horse as far as—"

"No."

At Brody's roughly spoken word both Sam and Grayson looked up from their chores. Curiosity plain on their faces, they approached and stood next to Seth.

In the ensuing silence, Brody knelt beside the remains of the fire and stared at the dead, gray ashes. Did Jasmine really trust him so little? He still didn't want to accept it, even with the evidence staring him in the face.

"Where do we go next, Brody?"

"Yeah, where to?"

". . . Even though your wife's left, Brody, you'll still help me find the man I'm hunting, won't you?"

Sam's and Grayson's voices swam through his head. He pressed his fingers against his temples, trying to shut them out.

"Where do you think a murderer might hide?"

"Who do you reckon we should question first, Brody?"

"We'll just keep looking until we find somebody who knows him. We'll track him down."

Brody dropped his hands from his face. "*I* know him." His words emerged as little more than a dry rasp.

"Maybe we should start asking around on Broadway. Someone there might know—"

Brody's chin cut toward them. "I said that I know him!"

All four men stared at him incredulously.

He pushed to his feet and looked Grayson directly in the eye. "The man you're looking for is Lee Jamison, Jasmine's father." It gave him no pleasure to make the declaration. He hadn't wanted it to be like this.

After a moment of tense quiet, Sam chuckled. "Well, I'll be damned," he sneered, his words slurred by the whiskey he'd had for breakfast.

"You're telling us that Mrs. McClintock is the fugitive's daughter?" Seth asked, clearly stunned.

"Yes."

"Well, pardon me for pointing out the obvious," Sam said, "but in that case, it would seem that both you and she are accomplices of his."

Brody held his jaw so rigid, it ached. "If that were true, why would I be telling you now?"

"All I'm saying is that *it would seem* you were both withholding information from the law the other night when you told us you didn't recognize the man in the photograph. Now it's too late." Sam shook his head with disgust. "She's ridden off to warn him that we're coming."

Grayson looked to Seth, anxiety sharpening his expression. "Do you think that's what's happened?"

"We . . . we can't ignore the possibility."

Sam fouled the air with a string of expletives. "If I see that girl again, why, I'll—"

Tom sprang into action. He rounded on Sam with his fists at the ready. "Don't you *dare* threaten her."

"I don't think," Brody said through thin lips, "that Sam would be so stupid as to threaten my wife."

Sam gazed at him with unfiltered hatred. "No, I'm not threatening her. I'm just pointing out, real friendly like, that because of her, Jamison will be on the run by the time we reach Tyler."

The pallid skin on Grayson's forehead creased as he nodded his agreement. Both he and Sam glared at Brody.

Brody had absolutely nothing to say to them. They were right.

Tom, still grimacing at Sam, released his fists, and pulled his shirt back into place.

"Let's all just think for a minute," Seth said. "Lee Jamison is the man we're after. For the time being we need to focus on how we're going to bring him in.''

"It would have been a lot easier to bring him in," Sam snarled, "if McClintock here had told us the murderer's identity when he discovered it."

"That's true," Seth said. "But I'm certain he didn't expect Jasmine to run this morning. He probably thought he had more time."

Brody just stood there, gritting his teeth. He'd be damned before he'd make excuses for himself, or explain. Why should he? They could all see the explanation for themselves, clear as day. His wife had betrayed him.

It was a truth that burned like acid. The harder he tried to overcome it and think logically, the more his thoughts tangled.

"Well, I for one don't care who Jamison's related to," Sam muttered. "I'm still going to shoot the murdering son of a bitch."

Brody took one swift step toward him. "What did you just say?"

Sam thrust up his chin, but didn't have the guts to answer.

"You'd best watch yourself," Brody said, his voice low. "The law still stands. And it still protects Lee Jamison as innocent until proven guilty." He scowled at Sam until the man's facial muscles started to fleck. Still, he scowled. Finally, Sam's gaze withered away.

"Brody, do you know where Lee Jamison lives?" Seth asked.

"Yes."

"Will you take us there?"

He gave a curt nod. He'd take them there, for all the good it would do. Lee and Jasmine would already be gone when they arrived at the Double J. The certainty was like a writhing snake in his gut. She'd left him to flee with the father she loved so much.

"You heard him," Seth said to the others, motioning toward their horses and the remaining items yet to be packed up. "Let's get going."

Grudgingly, Sam and Grayson turned away. Brody knelt again beside the fire. The ashes weren't any more alive now than they had been the last time he'd looked.

Jasmine didn't trust him with the truth. It was all he could think. Over and over again. She'd lied to him about her father because she hadn't trusted him enough. His chin hardened into a granite ridge.

Powerlessness choked him. He wanted to lash out at her. To make her see how deeply she'd wounded him. He could understand her need to protect her father. But he couldn't accept her refusal to share that burden with him. Not when she'd made love to him last night with such blinding honesty, then looked into his eyes and said she loved him.

She didn't love him. He'd been a fool to ever hope she might.

His eyes narrowed against the breeze blowing across his features. He'd never been a man to lie. But since he'd met Jasmine, he'd made himself a liar by breaking his vow to remain alone, by breaking his vow to keep her trapped and by saying he didn't recognize Lee's photograph.

If he was to have an ounce of self respect left, he had to keep his last promise to Jasmine. He had to set her free.

As far as his heart and his future were concerned, she was exactly what he'd always known her to be. She was a lost cause.

Angrily, he shoved dirt over the remains of the fire, burying the evidence that it had ever existed.

Their lovemaking last night hadn't been a beginning.

It had been a good-bye.

Jasmine reined in before the Double J and allowed herself a few moments to savor the sight of her home. How well she knew the contour of the landscape. The shape of the rails that composed the corral. The kitchen garden. The porch. The smells. Even the windows that beamed down at her like an assortment of shiny eyes seemed to recognize her.

This was her home. And at the same time . . . it was no longer her home. This beloved place where she'd grown up had changed in her absence, she realized. She would never fully belong to this ranch and these hills again.

She sniffed to control the swarm of feeling that hovered around her like a cloud of bees, always waiting lately, to swoop down and attack her.

She arched her leg over Vengeance's back and dropped to the earth. A slight residual soreness remained from their lovemaking of the past night. She cherished the reminder that her body bore, treasured the gentle pain. Even now she could see Brody's eyes—dark and hungry. His touch—sliding over her breasts, massaging. The feel of him stroking deep inside her.

With a groan, she looped Vengeance's reins over the corral post and headed toward the house. A voice from the deepest regions of her heart wondered if she'd ever love that way again.

No, came the answer. Only Brody. She knew it with a certainty that delved beyond intuition. There had never been anyone before him who had stirred her. And none would come after him. That truth weighted her every thought and every step. She couldn't run from it. Couldn't escape the pain of it.

She stopped before the front door, remembering when they'd settled here. When her father had bought this land and built this house. He loved Tyler and the quiet, respectable life he'd created for them here. With little more than a stash of stolen gold and a dream, he had fashioned this place. The Double J meant the world to him.

She let her eyes sink closed. For his sake, she fervently wanted him to be gone. But for her own sake, she wanted him to be here so that she could see him again and feel his arms around her.

Gathering her resolve, she pushed open the door. Beyond the threshold, the house lay still. She recognized the companionable quiet of the rooms and the scent of lemon furniture polish that hung in the air. She licked her lips. "Daddy?"

Her father. Heaven, how she'd missed him.

She set her hat onto its peg and walked down the hall. The living room was vacant. She quickened her pace and peeked into the dining room. It, too, was empty.

Panic shot through her. Suddenly, she needed badly to see him face to face. "Daddy?"

Her boot heels pounded an echoing rhythm through the deserted rooms. She leaned into the kitchen.

No one.

"Daddy!"

"Jasmine?" came the muffled reply.

She swiveled, relief and dread coinciding within her. His voice had come from the direction of the office. She ran to the little room at the back of the house and flung open the door.

Her father stood directly in front of her.

The skin across her neck and shoulders pebbled. Love of him welled in her chest, spilling down her arms and stomach, overtaking her completely.

He was staring at her with an expression of astonishment, mixed with hope and a little uncertainty. His dark hair had been combed away from his face. Ruddy color painted his cheeks. He looked healthy and vibrant and . . . wonderful. A feminine hand entered her line of vision as it reached out to pull his vacant chair out of the way.

Jasmine's gaze cut to the woman, who sat on the edge of her seat, smiling at them.

"Hello, Emma," Jasmine said, deeply surprised to discover her friend in her father's office.

"Welcome home," Emma said, joy sparkling in her eyes.

Jasmine nodded and returned her gaze to the man who towered before her, every angle of his face, every line of his body so familiar to her that she wanted to weep. "Hello, Daddy."

He tried to smile, but his lips wobbled, so he simply held open his arms.

She took two steps and fell into his embrace. Her face snuggled into its usual place just below his shoulder. The sturdy texture of his dark blue shirt and the scratchy fabric of his vest assured her that some things in life really were constant.

She was tempted to surrender herself and her troubles to his broad shoulders. At any other time in her life, she would have. But this time his own troubles overshadowed her heartbreak.

She loosened her hold on him. He dropped a kiss on her head and squeezed her tight before releasing her. As she moved away, his big hands captured her shoulders. "Thank God you're back, Jasmine."

She bit her bottom lip and nodded.

"I'm sorry," he said, "for everything."

"I'm sorry, too, Daddy."

"Have you forgiven me?"

"Yes. Have you forgiven me?"

"Yes."

"Then it's forgotten."

He nodded, tightened his hold on her shoulders and then let her go.

Her gaze traveled to Emma. Something had changed. When she'd left, her father had thought of Emma as Miss Larkin, an acquaintance, a kindly neighbor. He'd never have allowed the Miss Larkin of old to witness a scene as personal as the one that had just passed between them. But there Emma sat. And her father seemed perfectly comfortable with her presence.

Both Emma and Lee watched her expectantly, clearly waiting for her to explain her sudden appearance. She stuffed her hands into her pockets and tried to squelch her growing unease. She wished she had a way with words, or knew how to break this to him gently. She didn't. "I'd like to have come for a happier reason," she said.

Lee's forehead wrinkled.

"Daddy, I need to talk to you."

"You know you can tell me anything."

She glanced at Emma. "Could you excuse us for a little while, Em?"

"Of course." Emma rose and tried to slide past Lee on her way to the door.

He caught her elbow, stopping her. "You can stay, Emma."

Jasmine stared at the pair, amazed. The adoration passing between them was almost palpable. In Emma's eyes she saw mirrored the exact same desire that she herself felt for Brody. "Oh," she murmured, not knowing quite what else to say. "Oh."

They both smiled at her.

Jasmine loved Emma and would gladly have trusted her friend with her life. But she didn't want to share her father's secret with her unless she was certain it was what he wanted. "Daddy," she said carefully, "this is the one subject on earth I'd hesitate to speak of in front of Emma. Are you certain that you want me to?"

His eyes registered understanding. He paled.

Emma lifted her chin and looked directly at him. "I'll go, Lee."

"No." He sighed raggedly, his big chest heaving. "It's best you know."

Regret flowed heavily through Jasmine, pinning her feet to the floor. She hated what she must tell them. Somehow during these last weeks they had discovered each other. And after all their endless years alone, she couldn't help but think that they both deserved the promise of happiness she was witnessing between them. After she told them her news, nothing could ever be the same for them again.

"Are you sure, Daddy?" She gave him one last chance to change his mind, to spare Emma the truth if he chose.

He nodded at her.

"I sent that message, about Brody, to you through Emma. Didn't you get it?"

"I did."

She tried, and failed, to understand. "But I was attempting to tell you to run. To get out of Tyler."

"I know."

He'd known and refused to run. The realization penetrated, bringing with it a harrowing stab of fear. She needed to make him see what he was up against. "Do you recognize the name Matthew Grayson?"

She could almost visualize his mind running down the tunnels of his memory.

"I do."

"He's on his way here, Daddy, to track you down."

His eyes narrowed, and she could tell that he was trying to assimilate what she was telling him.

"I met him last weekend in Nacogdoches. He's been coming after you for months. When he entered Texas, he enlisted the help of a Ranger. And in turn, that Ranger asked for Brody's assistance. I've been traveling with them for the past two days. They're on their way here right now to find you."

"How long do I have?" he asked quietly.

"An hour. Two. That's all I could manage without raising suspicion."

He pinched the bridge of his nose. "Do they know my name?"

"No, but they have a picture. It's only a matter of time before someone in town recognizes you."

He swore under his breath. "McClintock didn't recognize me?"

She shook her head.

A thick silence fell over the threesome. Each passing second took on new meaning.

Emma stood beside Lee, looking stricken. Her elegant features had leached of color, causing milky white cheekbones to stand out starkly beneath gray eyes. "Are you a wanted man?" she asked Lee, her voice little more than a whisper.

His ravaged gaze met hers. "Yes."

She blinked twice, but didn't crumble. "How can that be? You've lived here for so long. Did—did you commit this crime in the years before you came here?"

Lee nodded.

"What did you—" Her voice broke. "What did you do?"

"My gang and I robbed banks." He didn't attempt to rationalize or embellish the truth. "It's not something I'm proud of. I moved here because I wanted to leave that life behind."

"And you have. Lee, you've been here for fourteen years."

"Based on what Jasmine's just told me, fourteen years wasn't long enough."

Emma's fear and confusion appeared to sink away, leaving a solemn, determined woman in their wake. "Who is this man who is coming after you?"

"Do you remember me telling you about my wife Kathryn?"

She nodded.

"Matthew is Kathryn's brother."

"But why would he be tracking you?"

Both Lee and Emma looked to Jasmine for the answer.

"Kathryn is dead," she said.

Her father's expression slackened. She could tell that the truth deeply shocked him.

"It must have happened just after she left us, Daddy, when she was traveling home."

"How?"

"Comanches."

"Jesus."

Jasmine locked her arms tightly across her chest and waited for the information to register. "Grayson blames you for her death. He's come to avenge her."

He looked at her as if she'd spoken in a language he didn't understand. "What of the robberies I committed?"

She shook her head. "As I understand it, they want you on the charge of murder alone. You need to leave, Daddy. Right away."

When her statement met with silence, she rushed on. "We don't have much time. Let's take what money you've saved and go. Now."

He thrust both hands through his hair. "You mean to come with me?"

"Of course."

"What about McClintock?"

It took a concerted effort to keep from flinching at the mention of Brody's name. "He doesn't want me."

With a low growl, Lee swung away from the women and walked to the room's single window. He planted his hands on the back of his hips and peered at the view. Beyond the pane of glass, Double J land spread into the distance, a peaceful vista of springtime hues.

Lee's chest rose and fell with one deep breath. Then two. Three.

Jasmine looked worriedly at Emma.

Emma acknowledged her glance with an anguished nod. Tears welled along the older woman's lashes, but did not fall. She stood ramrod straight, dreadfully composed.

"No," Lee said at last, still facing the view.

"Daddy?" Jasmine whispered.

"No." He turned toward them. "My answer is the same now as it was when you sent me that message, Jasmine. I won't run." He lifted a hand toward the view beyond the window. "This is my home. The only home I've ever had."

Tears spilled over Emma's cheeks in soundless streams.

Fear clawed at Jasmine. Her world tilted and spun from her control. She had to grasp at it somehow, master it again. She needed to fix this. "Daddy." She struggled to control her shaking voice. "Please reconsider."

"I won't."

"But you don't know Brody! You haven't seen how much Grayson hates you. I have." She strode across the small space and pressed her palms against his chest. "They'll jail you, or worse."

In the tumbling chaos, her father's midnight blue eyes were an anchor. Calm and certain.

"They might," he answered. "But it's time I faced up to my past. The night I decided to leave the gang, something changed inside me. More than I wanted the money, I wanted to give you a better life. A life of respect and safety." He smiled sadly. "I guess I wanted to give myself those things, too. So I brought you to Tyler and we both got a second chance. Over these years I've become the man I wanted to be when I was a kid. Fourteen years ago I would have fled. But not anymore. I'm not the same man."

She pounded her fists helplessly against him. "Daddy, I'll go with you. Just the two of us, like always. We can leave right away and—"

"Jasmine." He communicated all his love for her in that one softly spoken word.

Her fists stilled.

"You know I would do anything in the world for you," he said. "Except this."

She tried again to fight him, to pull away.

He captured her wrists in gentle hands and waited for her to still.

She struggled wildly, not really wanting for him to release her. Wanting only to be freed from this terrible situation which threatened all of them, but her father most. Her precious father.

When she ran out of breath and hope, she quieted.

"I love this place we've built, you and I," he murmured, looking deep into her eyes. "I'll not leave it to run from a crime I didn't commit. If you'll just think for a moment, you'll see that I'm right."

Terror racked her body, crippling her. "I'm afraid they'll try you and hang you. Nothing is right, if you must give your life for it."

"You're wrong. There are things worth dying for."

"No!"

"Honor is one."

The storm within her silenced. *Brody.* He had taught her that, shown her by example, just how worthy honor could be. Her breath came in little spurts. The sound of it whooshing in and out of her lungs filled her head.

All along she'd blamed her father for stealing her life of adventure away from her. It had been easier to resent him than to face the truth. She had no choice but to face it now. Her father had been right to aspire to a life of integrity. She'd been wrong. All this time.

"I've never had any honor," he said. "Until now. I need to do this. I need to take a stand, no matter the risks." He angled up her face, pressed a kiss to her forehead, and let her go.

Jasmine took a step back, feeling shaky and unsure. She looked at Emma. Her friend's tears were drying in tracks on her pearly skin. Fierce love blazed from her eyes.

Her father would stay and confront Grayson's accusations. The inevitability of it rang through the room like a gong. His decision set Jasmine's own course. "I'm going to send one of the cowboys into town to fetch Reverend White and some of the others,'' she said.

"Why?'' Lee asked.

"So we've got witnesses. I don't trust Grayson.'' She pursed her lips. "Then, when Brody and the others get here, I'm going to stand with you.''

"Jasmine—''

"I'm *going* to stand with you.''

"As am I,'' Emma said, straightening her shoulders. "As am I.''

Chapter 24

Carts, wagons, and carriages flooded the road that led to the Double J. The people who jostled and bumped within the contraptions favored Brody with solemn stares as he passed. He read worry in the faces of the women, resentment in the countenances of the men.

It appeared that someone had caught wind of Lee Jamison's upcoming arrest and spread the news through the whole damn town. Jasmine was the only one who knew, so she must have been the someone who'd tipped them off. Still, Brody couldn't imagine what motive she'd had for summoning them, unless she'd hoped the residents of Tyler would slow him down.

Brody shot a look over his shoulder at his small band of men. Tom and Seth, Grayson and Sam. With every mile closer to the ranch, Grayson had retreated more deeply into his coat, away from the glares of the townsfolk. His head had nearly vanished below his low-slung hat.

Sam had reacted in the opposite way. The longer they rode, the more he swigged his flask of whiskey and the more belligerent and challenging he became. He had absolutely no business being involved in Grayson's fight. And yet he'd adopted the cause as if avenging Grayson's sister had been his life's ambition. All his hatred and discontentment were channeled toward this one scapegoat quest.

Brody shifted the reins in his gloved hand and urged his mount to quicken the pace, distancing himself from the others. The ominous pall that had descended on him after discovering Jasmine's absence clung to him like a death shroud. Moment by moment, his disposition deteriorated.

His gaze raked across the horizon. Charcoal tipped clouds seethed against a hazy gray sky, blotting out the sun.

He rounded the last bend before Jasmine's home and pulled his horse up short. One by one, his companions came to a standstill beside him.

"Who are all these people?" Grayson hissed.

"These people are the town of Tyler," Tom answered.

The entire front lawn of the Double J milled with townfolk. They'd parked their wagons everywhere, without pattern or planning.

"Hell," Seth whispered. "Brody?"

"Hm?"

"Do you think there'll be trouble?"

He thought this whole damn thing was trouble. "Not if Lee Jamison's already fled."

"Right." Seth frowned.

"He better not have fled," Sam warned.

Brody didn't trust himself to respond to Sam in any way except a fist against the jaw, so he set his horse forward. At the edge of the crowd he dismounted, deciding that it would be better to leave the horses here rather than risk trampling anyone. Without waiting for the others, he strode through the mob of bodies.

The people gawked at him. As always, they stepped out of his path, clearing a wide swath for him to walk through.

This must be some goddammned great showdown for them, he thought bitterly. The deceived husband come to arrest his wife's father. Angrily, he tugged his glove from his right hand. He needed his gun fingers ready, just in case.

He came to a halt a few yards before the porch. Grayson and the rest of their party congregated around him. Brody met each man's gaze in turn. "If by any chance he's here, let's keep our wits about us," he said.

Sam scowled at him. Grayson's Adam's apple bobbed nervously.

Brody looked to the front door. Before he could start toward it, the knob twisted.

Across the assembled audience, conversations cut to silence. Mothers shushed children. Whispers that had been hidden behind hands ceased.

The door swung open and Lee Jamison filled its opening. Beneath his gait, the porchboards cried into a gloomy afternoon that had turned too still. Lee halted on the porch's edge.

Surprise flared hard within Brody. Lee hadn't run.

His brain, long accustomed to confronting unexpected situations, tried to deduce why the man would have remained here, knowing what he would face. Surely Jasmine had come to him, warned him.

Movement from behind Lee caught his eye. A pink bandana.

His heart wrenched so painfully he couldn't breathe.

Jasmine walked from the house and stood beside her father. Her hair hung in a wild tumble across her shoulders. She wore a defiant expression and her trademark snug-fitting britches. The same scuffed boots as always encased her feet. His attention halted on the gun belt which lay in a deadly circle around her waist.

How in the hell was he going to get her out of this unscathed?

Her face looked pale to him, but calm. He watched as her light blue eyes panned the throng of people, then settled on him.

He held her stare, his pulse thudding. He hoped she knew that he could do nothing less than his duty. In a flash of honesty, he realized that a small part of him had actually hoped they'd fled. It would have ensured their freedom and safety. Instead, he stood here, facing off against them—against Jasmine—cast as the enforcer of the law. It was a role he found himself despising.

He noticed the sadness in Jasmine's eyes and the gentle entreaty. He tore his gaze away. She'd hate him forever for arresting her father.

Coldly, he stifled the emotion that threatened to dilute his responsibility. This was his job. This was justice.

He glanced at the second woman who had come to stand at Lee's other elbow. Emma. She, too, wore her guns.

Brody's fingers waited at his sides as he mentally rehearsed drawing his weapon. Aiming. Firing.

Lee cleared his throat and turned his full attention to Brody. "What am I being accused of?"

The mass of spectators hunched forward. In the distance came the sound of wagon wheels crunching rock as even more people arrived.

"Of murder," Brody replied.

"Is that the only accusation against me?"

Sam stepped forward, his expression furious. "No! There are others. Robbery, assault, probably raping, too."

Lee scowled at Sam. "Who are you?"

"Sam Stodges."

"Do you have proof of those accusations, Sam Stodges?"

Sam's face mottled red. He muttered something incoherent and looked to Grayson.

Clearly uncomfortable before so large a gallery of spectators, Grayson barely managed to meet Lee's intimidating gaze. His bony shoulders straightened. "The—" He swallowed thickly. "The only charge we bring against you today is the killing of my sister, Kathryn Grayson."

His words traveled far. The crowd bristled upon hearing them.

"And who are you?" Lee asked.

"Matthew Grayson, Kathryn's brother."

Lee considered the withered man standing before him for a long moment. "I didn't kill your sister, Mr. Grayson. She left me."

"No." Grayson shook his head vehemently. "You gave her over to Comanches to be tortured. Her body was found beaten, scalped."

"She was my wife," Lee said, weariness settling into the wrinkles beside his eyes. "The mother of my child. Do you really think that I'd have had her tortured and killed?"

"Yes I do," Grayson insisted. "She was your responsibility."

Lee paused before taking a single step closer to the edge of the porch. "What are you saying? That a husband must watch his wife every minute of the day? Every minute of the night? Kathryn fled."

Brody glanced at Jasmine. She stared directly at him, her lips hard and cold.

"When I discovered she'd gone," Lee continued, "I looked for her for two days. But I didn't find her."

"Are we to believe this story?" Grayson asked, his voice shrill. "Why would she have ridden off alone? How was she to get home?"

"She took enough gold to see her home and I was glad of it. On the second day of looking, I came across a settler who'd seen her. He told me that he'd sent his son with her, to escort her to the train station. All these years I assumed she'd made it."

"What . . ." Grayson sputtered, his expression aghast. "If—if you knew she was going home, why didn't you follow her? Not once," he gestured angrily, "not once did you show your face on our property. Not once did you bring her child to see her."

"No."

"Because you killed her."

"You're wrong." Lee's nostrils flared. "I didn't come

to claim her because there was no love left between us. She wanted her freedom. I let her have it.''

Brody saw the sheen of sweat glowing on Grayson's skin. Grayson was a man racked by sorrow, maddened by pain and bitterness. Brody knew Grayson wouldn't be swayed from his own gruesome version of the story. Yet if Lee spoke truthfully, and Brody suspected he did, then fate alone had ended Kathryn's life. Cruel, random fate.

Chills slithered over his shoulders and arms. The same unjust fate that had taken the life of his parents.

He stared more deeply at Grayson. This time he saw himself. His own sorrow and pain. His own bitterness. He, too, had been unable to let go of the past. To live. He had clung to his old vows, and, like Grayson, had chased the murderers to the ends of the state and beyond. Except he'd never found them. He'd never had his revenge.

"You killed her," Grayson said, more softly now, but with the same blind conviction.

"I'm sorry she died," Lee said. "And I'm truly sorry for your loss. But I didn't kill her. Kathryn's death wasn't my fault.''

"He's proved himself!" The shout came from the region behind Brody and to the right.

All eyes swung to the man who'd cried out. He stood on the bed of his wagon, his boots planted apart. "Lee'd have run if he was guilty. Instead he stayed and faced the charges. He's proved his honor by doing so!"

Calls of agreement peppered the air.

Jasmine stared at the crowd of faces she knew so well. Her chin wobbled, but only for an instant. She'd never expected so many to come. It was a testament to her father that they had.

From the corner of the porch, movement caught her eye. Reverend White strutted forward, his hands braced beneath his suspenders. From under bushy eyebrows he leveled a frowning glare on Grayson. "I don't know you, Sir. But I do know Lee Jamison, have known him for years. Like these good people, I believe his account of what happened. If he says your sister ran away, then she ran away."

Grayson, who couldn't meet the reverend's gaze, grimaced at the ground near his feet.

"We here in Tyler, all of us, came to escape something. I don't know what Lee came to escape, but I do know better than to ask. Lee's redemption is between him and God."

The reverend's lips compressed into a harsh line. "I sure hope there's a place left in this world where a man can find a new start. If there's not, Mr. Grayson, then God help us all." The reverend didn't retreat or move forward. He simply held his ground, his hands moving smoothly along the insides of his suspenders.

"What say you, Grayson?"

Brody. Jasmine's senses leapt in recognition of his voice. She looked toward him, greedily savoring the picture he presented. His eyes burned like coals, making the angle of his cheekbones and jaw seem more severe than they were. The collar of his jacket stood up around his neck, almost meeting the low brim of his hat. From several feet away, she could sense his piercing concentration.

She licked her lips. He'd never understand this. Never accept the position she'd taken beside her father.

Her gaze returned to Grayson, who looked anxiously at Brody and then briefly at the reverend before fastening his attention on her father.

"I offer you half of everything I own as payment for any disservice I did your sister," Lee said to him.

The crowd murmured.

Jasmine tensed. Half of her father's holdings was a fortune. He'd sweated and toiled over every acre, painstakingly raising his herd.

"Will you accept my apology and my offer?" Lee asked.

"Yes," Grayson answered. Bony shoulders clothed in a dusty black suit hunched. "I suppose I have little choice but to accept it."

A chorus of relieved sighs wove through the throng, along with a smattering of applause.

Jasmine's instincts sharpened. This wasn't right. Grayson's hatred of her father ran too deep for such a swift relenting.

"Thank you," Lee said simply.

"There are other ways to be punished, as I well know," Grayson murmured. "Often death is too easy."

"Too easy?" Sam barked. "What?" His hand latched onto Grayson's arm and he spun the man around to face him.

Jasmine watched Sam's expression twist with scorn, and knew the moment when his fury overflowed its bounds. "You would let him off?" he yelled. "For such a cheap bargain?"

"Now, Sam—"

"No! This isn't right. The bastard killed your sister, Goddamnit! He's a murderer. He should hang!"

"But I—"

Sam shoved Grayson aside, knocking him to the ground.

"Sam, this isn't your injustice to right," Brody warned.

The false bravery of too much whiskey spurred Sam forward. His eyes shining with rabid passion for Grayson's cause, he raised his gun from under the flap of his coat and pointed it at Brody.

Terror racked through Jasmine in one violent throb, stilling her blood in her veins. *Oh, Lord, don't let him be hurt. Lord, don't let him—*

"Put the gun down," Brody said. His face revealed no fear, only controlled rage.

She couldn't move. Her lungs convulsed. *Brody.*

Sam swore viciously, then swung the gun. It cut through the air, its sights coming to rest on her chest.

"No!" Brody yelled.

The gun jerked again. This time Sam aimed its lethal eye on her father. He clicked back the hammer.

Pure instinct surged through Jasmine, guiding her muscles along the paths of an old ritual. Her hand flashed up to grip her gun. She hauled it from its resting place.

Simultaneously, she heard the rush of two other weapons streaking from their holsters. She aimed from the hip.

A gun blast ripped through the prairie. Deafening her. Freezing time for a horrifying moment. Her deadened gaze jerked around the circle. Brody. Her father. Emma. Sam.

Sam. A perfect red hole burrowed into his forehead. As she watched, the wound oozed blood, spilling a scarlet stream down his dazed face. His knees gave way. He crumpled to the earth beside Grayson's cowering form.

Her attention shot around the circle once more. Brody. His gun was at his hip, as was hers. Her father. Standing mute with shock. Emma. Her gun extended in an expert grip, her features lethally calm. A fine wreath of gun smoke spun on the breeze above her weapon and then vanished.

Emma had killed him.

Seth sprang into action first. He knelt over Sam. The dying man's arms and legs shuddered, tensed. Shivered. And then fell still.

Jasmine looked at the crowd. No one spoke or moved. The women had covered their mouths. Little girls buried their heads in their skirts. Men stared, grim-faced. They understood that this was how the law worked in the West. Kill or be killed.

Jasmine felt her knees quiver. She sheathed her gun. Near to her, she heard Brody sheath his, too. He stood immobile, his hands hanging at his sides, staring at the dead man. At Sam.

"Emma," her father breathed.

Emma handed her gun to Lee. Her friend's complexion was as white as a sheet. But the expression in her silvery eyes held more intensity than any sea storm. "I'd do it again to save you," she said.

Lee pulled her into his embrace, cradling her head snugly against the bulk of his shoulder.

Jasmine's lips tugged into a tremulous smile. Pride in Emma washed through her. Her beautiful, brave friend. A delicate woman with a core of purified steel and an aim more sure and swift than any man in two counties.

"Go back to your homes." Seth had risen. He cupped his hands around his lips. "It's over. Go back to your homes."

Obediently, the massive gathering ground out of its stupor and began to move. People turned away, mounted their horses, and ascended into their wagons. Once again, the grating of wheels on rock droned through the fields.

Seth hauled Grayson to his feet. Grayson barely managed to stand, his legs were shaking so badly. He averted his face from Sam's dead body, then ran toward the side of the house with a haste that told Jasmine he was about to retch.

Seth turned to Brody. "Sam's dead," he said softly. He'd just proclaimed what every man, woman, and child who had watched the exchange already knew. And yet hearing him say the words brought a finality to it for Jasmine.

"Take him into town," Brody said. "Tom will help you to secure a casket and a wagon."

Seth nodded, then knelt again and began preparing the body for transport.

Brody looked up at her. Their eyes met in a clash of sparks. Slowly, his gaze never wavering, he approached her. He stepped up onto the porch and halted just inches away.

Hope fought within her breast, wrestling against all the doubts and surviving by sheer force of will. Every part of her pined for him. For his forgiveness. His love.

"I have to go," he said.

Her optimism burst, showering her with a pain that felt like the stabbing of a hundred tiny daggers. "Go?"

"I have to take Sam's body back to Elena. I have to try and explain this to her."

The pain she saw in his eyes made her want to claw him with her nails, slap him, anything, to make it go away. "But—but what of Seth?" she asked. "This is his case. Shouldn't he be the one to take the body back to her?"

"Seth barely knows her. I can't let Elena hear of her husband's death from a stranger."

"Can't you?"

"No. It wouldn't be right."

A sob pushed up her throat. She stifled it by covering her mouth with her fingers and looking away.

The final implication of Sam's death struck home with devastating force. Elena's husband was dead, which meant that the great love of Brody's life was now free.

That realization hurt so badly that for a fleeting moment she thought she might die. For a much longer space of time, she wished she would.

One last risk, she thought madly. For Brody. She'd slash her pride and risk just one more plea. She met his gaze. "Don't go."

"Jasmine—"

She lifted her hands to his shoulders, curled her fingers into the thick fabric of his coat. "Please don't go."

A subtle war flickered across his features. She watched the play of emotions and prayed that he would care about her enough to stay.

When the uncertainty on his face cleared, she knew that the choice he'd reached would determine her whole life, her fate.

Please care about me enough to stay.

"I have to go," he said. "But I'll come back, if you want me to."

Of course. Brody, ever the honorable one. He was willing to return and sacrifice himself on the altar of their marriage vows. He would martyr himself for them, live in misery because of them, always pining for another. She bit her bottom lip. Maybe he could do that. But she couldn't watch it happen.

"I'll come back," he said again. "Can you understand why I have to go—"

"I understand perfectly." Her fingers released him in one short spasm. She took two steps back. "Will you at least give me my freedom then, as you promised?"

He looked ashen. "Do you want your freedom, Jasmine?"

She'd used up the last of her pleas. No more risks. She looked past the devastated hazel eyes, directly into his adulterous heart. "Yes. I want my freedom."

His big body braced, as if against the lash of a whip.

"Leave," she hissed.

His breath caught on a painful inhale. "What can I say to convince you to let me come back?"

"Nothing."

"Do you hate me so much?"

Oh, God, she didn't think she could take much more. How could he ask such a thing of her? She'd told him she loved him last night. And she'd continue to love him—always. Enough to give him the wife he deserved. "Just leave," she said, unable to manage any more eloquent words.

He pulled the brim of his hat lower. Donned his gloves. Looked at her one last time.

Frantically, she memorized the lines of his face, the color of his eyes, the way it felt to be the center of his attention. She grasped at the seconds, knowing he was leaving her, trying to drink in—

He turned too quickly, stealing his beloved face from view.

She wanted to yell out, but couldn't. He strode across

the yard, his forceful strides eating the distance.

His name formed on her tongue, waited on her lips, begged to be screamed. *Brody*.

He walked farther.

Her thoughts careened wildly. *Call to him. Hold your tongue and your pride. Don't let him go. Turn your back.* She stood speechless while the conflicting voices raged.

He was almost to his horse.

Look back. Look back, she thought, *and I'll call to you. Run to you.*

He mounted his horse with a single controlled movement. The beast reared beneath him, catching his owner's turbulent emotions. Then the animal lunged into a hectic sprint.

"Brody," she whispered.

He disappeared from her sight, engulfed in the dip and curve of Double J land.

She gasped at the sharp, searing edge of pain.

It was over.

He'd never looked back.

Chapter 25

❧

Brody braced a hand against his hotel room's window frame. His gaze scoured over the early morning activity on Tyler's main street. When he didn't see Jasmine, he peered toward the sweep of open fields that led to the Double J.

"Brody," Tom said from behind him.

"Yeah?"

"We've waited two days."

Brody squinted hard into the distance, trying to will her into reality. A woman riding ferocious fast on a horse two sizes too big for her.

"I hate to say it," Tom said, "but Sam's body isn't going to keep. We need to be getting him back to Elena."

Brody's fingers tightened on the wooden frame. "I know." Tom had wanted to leave Tyler that first day, the day Sam had been shot. But Brody hadn't been able to leave. Instead, they'd checked into the Blue Horeshoe and had been given rooms above the saloon.

"So we'll ride today?" Tom asked.

Brody let his head drop forward. He couldn't explain to Tom how he'd come to love his unorthodox wife. Hell, he couldn't even explain it to himself. That he loved Jasmine so much he ached with it, physically hurt because of it, was an unexplainable kind of truth.

Every thought he'd had over the last two days had belonged to Jasmine. Her swagger and her smile. Her challenging glances. Her heartfelt laughter. The ire that turned her eyes to glinting silver. That absurd pink bandana. The smudges across her skin and everything else about her.

Over the hours he'd spent here waiting for her, he'd realized for good that Jasmine was the only woman in the world for him. No other had her depth of courage and spirit. Her rebellious heart. Her unexpected tenderness.

Leaving Tyler meant giving up on her. Maybe tomorrow he could do it. But not today. She might come today. "We'll wait. If she doesn't come by tomorrow, we'll leave then."

He heard Tom's boots scuff at the floor. "Brody...."

"One more day, Tom."

He sighed heavily. "You going to wait at the window 'til tomorrow morning?"

Brody gritted his teeth and nodded.

"I'm not hungry." Jasmine pushed away the plate of food laden with her breakfast.

Lee thoughtfully observed her as he finished chewing a mouthful of bacon. After he'd swallowed, he set aside his fork and steepled his hands. "This is the second morning in a row that I've sat across from you and watched you refuse food. Just how long do you plan to go without eating?"

They sat in the dining room while morning light streaked its way across the horizon beyond the room's solitary window.

"I've been eating," she said defensively.

"A little soup? Some bread? Water? Is that supposed to ease my mind?"

She frowned at him. "I'm not doing this to upset you, Daddy. I just don't have any appetite. The sight of that," she nodded at her heaping plate, "makes me nauseous."

Lee stared at her for a long moment, then slid his own plate out of reach and scooted his chair around the corner of the table until he sat next to her. His brows lowered over serious eyes. "What's the matter, Jasmine?"

She fidgeted. The last two days had been awful. Should she come right out and tell her father that living with him again had been sheer torment? No. It wasn't his fault. He'd been wonderful. "I guess I'm just having trouble readjusting to everything."

"You weren't gone that long, sweetheart."

"I know. But a lot has changed."

Dark blue eyes fastened on her. Shrewdly intelligent. Warm. "I've tried to give you your privacy, a little space."

"I know."

"But now you've got me worried."

"Oh, Daddy, don't be. It's nothing—"

"Hell, yes, it's something," he bellowed.

She'd roused his temper. The man hated to be contradicted.

"When my daughter doesn't eat for three days, it's something."

His words frayed along her already strained nerves, prodding her frustration. "Fine." She reached for her food. "I'll eat this whole damn—"

His hand shot out, covering hers before she could grip the hated plate. Jasmine waited, heartache seething in her breast. She prayed that her father would simply let her go so she could escape.

"Look at me," he said gently.

Her gaze had never felt so heavy. With effort, she hauled it to his face.

"This . . ." He scrunched his lips and clearly groped for the right term. "This sadness of yours. It wouldn't have to do with a certain Texas Ranger, now, would it?"

Her fathomless misery ebbed slightly. Somehow, it helped to hear him spoken of. "It would."

"I can't see why." He sandwiched her hand between both of his. "It seems to me that in this game of yours, you emerged the victor. You won."

"Did I?"

"Yes. I know why you married McClintock. I know that you did it only to escape the ultimatum I gave to you." He squeezed her hand. "I'm sorry that I pressured you. I honestly didn't expect you to take such a drastic measure."

She nodded at him, giving him her forgiveness in her eyes.

"But the fact is, sweetheart, that you never wanted McClintock. Remember? You wanted your freedom. And you got it."

She hated the word "freedom." Her blind quest for it had almost cost her the love of her father. And had, in the end, cost her something far more valuable than her original dream. Brody. He'd handed her her independence, only for her to discover that she'd never wanted anything less. Never loathed a gift so much.

"Damn it to hell," her father whispered.

Too late, she tried to mask her crestfallen expression.

"You love him," he stated.

No lies left. She was actually relieved. No matter how unutterable her anguish had been, trying to hide it had made it even worse. "I'm afraid I do."

"Oh, Jasmine."

"I know, I know." A line creased the skin between her brows. "Stupid."

To her amazement, he chuckled. "Not stupid, sweetheart. Human."

She plunked her forehead onto the mound of their joined hands. "Then I hate my humanity."

"Of course you do. You've been invincible far too long." He sighed. "Listen to me. Look up at me."

Gradually, she raised her face.

"If you want him, I'll go and get him for you. It's his

responsibility as your husband to be with you, to support you for the rest of your life.''

"Like you supported Kathryn?" Her ironic smile took the sting out of her words. "No. As you well know, when one party wants to leave, it's best to let them go.''

"To hell with that!" His eyes glowed with purpose. "You're my daughter. If you love him, I'll bring him back to you.''

"No, Daddy. He's gone. That's it. He's just . . . gone and I'm not going to torment him any more.''

"He might come back.''

"No. It's over.''

Her father waited. The eggs sat cooling. The coffee ceased steaming. "Anybody ever told you that you're stubborn?" he asked.

"No," she said, schooling her face into the epitome of innocence. "Never.''

"Well, you are.'' He peeled one of his hands away from hers and stroked his thumb across her chin. "You've got a little smudge,'' he said, rubbing carefully, "right there.''

Unexpectedly, the tender gesture caused tears to burn her throat.

"It's all better now.'' He gave her a worried look, then promptly enveloped her in one of his bone-breaking hugs. "It's all better now, sweetheart. It's going to be all better.''

Jasmine wished she could believe him. But in her heart, she knew this was one hurt that was never going to get better.

Covertly, Emma fingered back a tiny corner of her lace curtain and peeked out the window. Her heart jolted.

Lee.

She let the curtain fall closed and covered her racing heart with both her hands, to steady it with outward pressure. But her heart defied her, pounding even more erratically.

All day she'd been as jumpy and as flustered as a virgin on her wedding night. . . . She smiled at the analogy that had sprung to mind. If only she should be so lucky!

Ever since she'd left the Double J late on the evening of the shooting, her concentration had been skittish. She hadn't seen Lee since. Not for two whole days. And the waiting had played havoc with her mind.

Now he was here. Riding up to her house.

She stepped away from the window and stood on the edge of her yellow rug in her yellow parlor. Accept what he has to say to you, she told herself. If it's bad, take it with grace and bravery. Don't show him how deeply he's hurt you.

Her teeth trapped her bottom lip. She didn't know if she could manage it. He was the world to her. How could she act unaffected when her very earth, her sky, her home, and her hope were crumbling around her?

His steps rang across the porch.

She pulled in a deep breath and fed it to her lungs, hoping it would bring her some sense of calm. It didn't. Only more tension. More dread.

He knocked.

He must be ending things with her. Otherwise he'd have just let himself in. Wouldn't he? He'd never let himself in before, but if he wanted her he probably would have. Yes, he'd have barged in and taken her in his arms. He didn't want her. Oh God.

She moved toward the door. Stopped. Shouldn't appear too eager, she reminded herself. Her self-imposed stalling lasted all of five seconds. Unable to bear the suspense, she plunged toward the door and swung it back.

"Oh! Lee." She feigned surprise, painfully aware of what a terrible actress she made.

"Emma." A slow grin spread across his lips.

Her stomach dropped. "Come in."

"Thank you." He doffed his hat and set it on the hallway peg.

"Where—where is Jasmine?" she asked. As soon as the words were uttered, she wished she could squish them back in. They made it sound as if she were disappointed he'd come alone.

"Jasmine?" he asked.

"I just . . . assumed the two of you had been spending a lot of—of time together the last few days. And that she might have accompanied you."

Eyes, like the blue of the ocean's deepest currents, studied her, disturbingly observant. "You're right. Jasmine and I have been spending a lot of time together lately. But what I've got to say to you is private."

Her mouth went completely dry. Not a drop of moisture.

In a sudden flash, she realized that they were still standing in the restricted space of the hall.

Awkwardly, she led him into the parlor and motioned him toward a chair. Her entire body was a mass of writhing nerves and she didn't feel like sitting. But she couldn't very well stand there gawking at him, so she lowered her disjointed body onto the edge of the sofa.

He remained standing. For a moment she considered leaping back to her feet, but then decided that would only make matters worse.

An innocuous subject. That's what she needed. "Have you heard from Matthew Grayson yet?"

He appeared mildly surprised at the swift change of subject. "Ah, no. I'm told that he's staying at the Horseshoe. James Bledsoe says that he's gone all day and that he keeps to himself."

"What is he waiting for? Wouldn't you have expected him to come and claim his acreage and money before now?"

"Yes, frankly. But then, I don't pretend to understand the man."

Her brain grasped for more conversation. She needed time. "Do you think he will stay in Tyler? Or do you think he'll allow you to buy your property back from him?"

He gazed down at her with a quizzical expression. "Emma, I didn't come here to talk about Matthew Grayson."

She forced a swallow down her parched throat. "Can I get you something to drink?"

"No."

"Food, then. It's almost dinnertime and you're probably starving—"

"Emma." Worry grooved around his eyes.

She held herself very still, bracing for the fatal blow. *Accept what he has to say to you. If it's bad, take it with grace and bravery. Don't show him how deeply he's hurt you.*

"I can see that my presence makes your nervous," he said, "that you don't want to talk about . . . us. But I have to say this to you."

She nodded. Everything in life she cared about came to a screeching halt, on hold until he'd said his piece.

"Emma, we . . ." He started to gesture, but his hands froze halfway and he let them fall. "There has been something," he cleared his throat, "going on between us over these last weeks. And. . . ."

She couldn't speak. Could only wait.

"And, well, it's been good."

Had he said "good"?

"It's meant a lot to me," he continued. The floor creaked beneath his boots. "A lot. I didn't realize how much I'd been missing in my life. Until you."

A wild, circling, tumbling joy fisted around her heart, took her body by the throat and shook her. "Lee, I—"

"Let me finish," he said. His face was grim now, intensely focused. "I understand that this might not be something you want to hear, Emma, but I'm not a man who has ever held back words for fear of offending.''

He glanced at her face, then spun on his heel and stalked to the window. His palm slapped soundly against his thigh. ''Damn it. I'm no good at this.'' He glared out at the scenery.

Emma's ecstasy stumbled. He had to finish. He *had* to.

Lee turned. Slowly he approached her, displaying the same legendary determination that he used to break a horse or drive his herd. Directly before her, he halted. ''I'm just going to say it, Emma.'' He frowned. ''I'm just going to say it.''

He knelt before her on one knee.

Shock gripped her, along with anticipation so brash, so piquant, that she trembled under its force.

He picked up her hands, kissed the tops of them, cradled them in his strong hold. ''I've fallen in love with you,'' he said sternly. ''And I want to marry you, if you'll have me.''

He'd just delivered her most precious hope to her in a tone too dour for a funeral. Oh, Lord, how she loved this man, loved him with every fiber, every ounce of herself.

''Will you have me?'' he asked.

Tears sprang to her eyes, wavering his image. ''Yes,'' she squeaked.

''Yes?'' he asked.

''Yes!'' She flung herself at him with such force that he toppled backward. They landed in a tangle, Emma gazing down at him with adoration.

Lee laughed and nudged aside the strands of hair that had fallen over her face.

''I love you,'' she said. A tear dripped off her chin and onto his cheek.

''I love you, too,'' he answered. ''I thought maybe you didn't want me—''

''Oh, I could kill you, Lee Jamison.'' She socked his shoulder. ''I've wanted you for fourteen years, you big fool.''

Amazement glazed his eyes. "Fourteen years?"

"That's right."

"And I'm the fool?"

She gasped and laughed and cried all at once. "Yes. You're the fool."

He planted his hands on either side of her face and guided her lips to his. He kissed her sweetly, reverently.

Emma's senses muddled. It was too exquisite, this overload of emotion and sensation. Their lips met again and again.

Finally, she leaned back so that she could look into his gorgeous face. "What will Jasmine think?" she asked.

"Who do you suppose talked me into coming over here and making an absolute ass of myself?"

"Jasmine. Really?"

"Really."

She ran her fingertips lovingly over his cheek and chin. "In that case, I can't wait to tell her."

"Neither can I. Maybe the news will cheer her up."

"Has she been down?"

"Yes. Pretty down."

Sympathy entered the ranks of Emma's myriad emotions. Her gaze searched his. "Will she recover?"

"I don't know." He hugged her to him, pressing her head against the bulk of his shoulder. "I just don't know."

Chapter 26

The sunlight hit his face like an insult. Brody tugged the brim of his hat even lower, trying to escape it. He'd have preferred this day to dawn as bleak as he felt. Instead, cheerful white clouds dotted the sky and a spring breeze whisked across the saloon's porch.

Brody walked to his horse and swung into the saddle. Tom already sat on the seat of the wagon they'd secured to transport Sam's body.

Brody's gaze passed over the outline of the coffin and lifted to the passersby milling along the street. Holding his breath behind a jaw that felt like rusted metal, he searched the faces for her one last time.

Again, she was nowhere among them.

His exhale burned his lungs. God, he was being such a coward. He had to face the fact that Jasmine wasn't going to change her mind.

He flicked the reins and his mount moved forward. Beside him, he heard the wagon wheels rumble into motion and knew the sound heralded the end of his vigil and the end of his marriage. Jasmine had always been a lost cause. But damn it to hell if she hadn't been the sweetest lost cause in a life of lost causes. Losing her tied his gut in knots.

Just as his horse was walking past the end of the saloon's

porch, Brody caught sight of Grayson exiting the building's swinging doors. Their gazes locked momentarily, before Grayson lowered his head and walked in the opposite direction.

Brody urged his mount into a trot. Seeing Grayson this morning was just the most recent in a long list of things that reminded him of Jasmine. Everywhere he looked in Tyler, he saw a memory of her.

He wondered where she was this morning. What she was thinking, how she was feeling. If her dream of freedom had made her happy.

He closed his eyes.

Will you at least give me my freedom, Brody, as you promised?

Do you want your freedom, Jasmine?

Yes. I want my freedom. Leave.

He tried to shut the words from his mind, but they refused to go. *I want my freedom. Leave.*

So he was leaving. He couldn't go back again, now or ever, to see if her dream had purchased her contentment. He'd promised her freedom. And she'd forced him to make good on that promise.

He listened, but no woman's voice called out for him to come back. No horse's galloping hooves sped to catch up with him. The only sound that reached his ears was the mournful whine of Sam's death cart, reminding him how much he'd lost.

"Do you want to stop and eat?" Tom asked.

"Only if you're hungry," Brody said. The dinner hour had come and gone some time ago and the day was dragging deep into afternoon.

"No. I'm fine, got some food right here in the pack." Tom patted the bag next to him on the seat. "Just thought a meal might do you good."

"No. Thank you." It was the first conversation they'd

shared since leaving Tyler hours before. Obviously, Tom had sensed Brody didn't want to talk. Tom had been right.

"Did you see Grayson come out of the saloon, as we were leaving town this morning?" Tom asked.

Brody nodded.

"I've seen him a few other times over the last couple days. Guess he's sticking around to claim his half of Lee's land."

"Guess so."

For a long moment, nothing but the sound of earth passing beneath them interrupted their thoughts. God, Brody was growing sick of traveling. For eleven years, and for the war years before that, he'd roamed ceaselessly. He'd ridden over almost every rise and fall of the great state of Texas. More times than he cared to remember, he'd come within inches of losing his life. On countless nights, he'd sat around a campfire drinking bitter coffee and trying to warm his bones. He'd slept with his head on his saddle until his neck ached.

Until now, he'd never contemplated any other life. But over these last days, he'd had ample time to consider his existence and he'd realized that it no longer pleased him. He was tired.

Tom used his wrist to push his hat back on his forehead. "I wasn't really expecting Grayson to accept Lee's offer and then let him go like that. Kind of surprised me when he did."

It had surprised Brody, too. But he'd been relieved enough for Jasmine's sake that he hadn't delved into the issue. Afterward, he'd purposely avoided thinking of the confrontation, because he hadn't wanted to relive the moment when Sam pointed his gun at Jasmine. But this time, he didn't resist it. He let the memory come, allowed his brain to travel over each word and gesture like a train over a well-oiled track.

They'd stood before the porch at the Double J. He and

Grayson and the others against Jasmine and her father. Grayson had been making his accusations, defending his sister. Brody had listened to him and watched him and been struck by Grayson's startling reflection of his own darkest heart. In those seconds he'd known that Grayson's fate would be his own if he didn't change the course of his life.

His parents' murder had been a stone in his stomach all these years. A bitter agony that never eased.

Now he wondered what kind of pride had ever made him think he *could* avenge his parents. It had been a dangerous, fate-challenging kind of pride. A pride fed by guilt and protected by rage.

No such pride remained in him now.

He wouldn't find the killers. They were gone. Like smoke. His beloved justice extended far and long, but it didn't cover everything. Some crimes and cruelties would go unpunished. The senseless violence that had killed his parents was one such crime.

The best he could hope for was that Reverend White had been right when he'd said there was a place of redemption for each man. A place where a man could release the past and be forgiven.

He hooked a finger around the silver chain at the base of his throat and pulled. The necklace slid from beneath his collar. He cushioned the charm, his mother's plain silver wedding ring, in the coarse leather of his gloved palm. His fingers closed over it, squeezing hard. *I love you both. Forgive me.*

A sense of calm came over him by degrees, allowing the memory of that afternoon at the Double J to return, clacking along its rails, taking him irrevocably forward.

Whether it had been because of the pressure from the bystanders, or his own fragmented sense of vindication, Grayson had accepted the deal Lee offered him. *There are other ways to be punished, as I well know. Often death is too easy.*

Brody frowned as he tried to examine exactly how and when the situation had spun from his control.

Sam had stepped forward, his expression nasty. *You would let him off? For such a cheap bargain? The bastard killed your sister! He should hang!*

Brody had tried to reason with him, but Sam wouldn't accept reason. He'd aimed his gun at Jasmine. Brody recalled too vividly the way his heart had turned to rock, the way his scream had twisted from the deepest reaches of his soul. Then Sam had leveled the weapon at Lee. After that, he'd. . . .

Worry pricked at him. Trying to squelch his growing discomfort, Brody revolved the memory of those final seconds again in his mind, examining each instant. Grayson's words had rung across the hushed prairie. *There are other ways to be punished, as I well know. Often death is too easy.*

What had Grayson meant by "as I well know"? How had Grayson been punished? He'd been punished by the murder of his sister, by losing the closest person to him.

Brody's blood began to rush in his ears, a harrowing messenger.

What would Grayson consider to be a more fitting punishment than death, in Lee's case? The same punishment he believed he'd received at Lee's hand. The murder of someone close to him.

Who was closest to Lee?

Jasmine.

Brody began to shake. An inner turmoil of revelation and fear and love coursed over him. "Tom."

His friend looked up, worry immediately piercing his expression.

"I've got to go back." Brody was already turning his horse.

"Back? To Tyler?"

"Yes. Jasmine's in trouble."

"From who? Grayson?"

"Yes." His horse pranced forward, as eager as he to be gone.

Tom pulled the wagon to a halt and stood on the buckboard. "What do you want me to do?"

"Take Sam's body to Elena. I need to know I can trust you to do that."

"You can."

Brody held his friend's eye, believing beyond a shadow of a doubt that he could indeed depend on Tom.

"I'll meet back up with you afterward," Tom said. "Now, go! Protect that wife of yours for us."

Brody nodded. The tips of his reins whistled through the air and landed on the animal's hindquarters.

The resulting burst of speed appeased him little. He was too far away. He'd been riding since morning. It would take him till sunset to reach her. His stomach muscles tightened, rebelling against his helplessness. Already it might be too late.

That chilling suspicion forced a howl from his lips.

It couldn't be too late. Christ.

This is how he'd lost his parents. By his absence.

Now Jasmine was in danger. And again, he was too far away to help. He couldn't stand to lose someone he loved this way a second time.

The old demons reared up, blotting out rational thought. His horse charged into the afternoon wind, its great muscles heaving. Brody bent low over its back, driving the beast forward with a madness borne of purest terror.

Grayson's gaze fastened onto the slim, auburn-haired woman. He watched her emerge from the house and walk alone to the corral, carrying a bridle.

A heady dose of adrenaline pumped through his body. The magnitude of the moment was not lost on him. This was it. The opportunity he'd been waiting for half his life.

Ride, he urged her silently. *Ride*.

She swung free the latch on the gate and let herself into the horse's enclosure.

Grayson hunched lower into his cramped position, loathing the little compartment of mashed grass and shrubbery that had been his post ever since the day they'd killed Sam. He'd been lying in wait here, watching them, following the girl everywhere she went.

Sweat beaded on his upper lip. He licked it away.

The stupid bitch hadn't once left the company of her father. For all her supposed independence, she hadn't been further than a hundred yards from Lee's sight in three days.

Until now.

Skinny fingers dashed at the moisture that had formed along his brow. He'd almost given up hope for today, been on the verge of retiring to the hotel.

He laughed, a sharp sound instantly aborted. Good thing he'd stayed.

Under his intent scrutiny, Mrs. Jasmine Jamison McClintock guided her horse from the pen and pulled herself onto the bare back of her sorrel mare. She directed the horse in a tight circle, then pointed her toward the fields where sunset splashed its colors.

Grayson pushed to his feet, cursed the cramps that plagued his legs, then crept to where his horse waited. He continually flicked glances at her, keeping his prey firmly within his sights.

To hell with Lee Jamison's tainted land and money. Tonight, at long last, he would earn a far better reward. His just revenge.

Chapter 27

The first bullet zinged past Jasmine's shoulder.

She gasped and instinctively pulled back on Diamond's reins. Hard and fast, she twisted in the saddle. Her gaze scoured the tranquil scene. Nothing. Could she have mistaken that sound? The bang of a gun firing, the whiz of a bullet cutting air?

No. She'd fired too many guns, heard the call of too many bullets.

Jasmine flicked the reins. "Run, girl!"

Diamond burst into a full gallop.

Jasmine had been trying to ease her mind with one of her shortcuts to nowhere when she'd heard the shot. She was a long way from home, farther from town or any other ranch.

Another shot fired, missing high and to the right.

Who in the hell was shooting at her? She spared another furtive glance over her shoulder. This time she caught the outline of a man and horse streaking through the line of trees that ran beside her.

She veered to the side, taking Diamond away from the trees that sheltered her attacker. "Let's see you," she hissed, peeking behind her as she leaned over Diamond's straining neck.

She'd been riding Diamond lightly, not wanting to ag-

361

gravate her freshly-healed strain. But she couldn't afford that now. She whispered words of encouragement to her horse as they sprinted hell-for-leather toward the open prairie and the setting sun.

She slid her hand toward her gun belt and freed her six-shooter from its holster. She tossed a look behind her, ready to return fire, if need be.

The man emerged from the line of trees, slapping a whip against the hindquarters of his animal.

She squinted. Too far to recognize the face beneath the hat. But the black clothing . . .

Grayson.

Her jaw clenched. Her father had given him half their ranch, but apparently that hadn't been good enough for him. Her temper flashed to the surface, whiting out all fear. Grayson had threatened her father with his misbegotten notions of truth. And his search for revenge had ultimately cost her Brody's love.

Let him come, she thought, her fury spilling over.

With Diamond's leg the way it was, she couldn't depend on outrunning Grayson. Better to draw him out.

She scanned the setting, then pointed Diamond toward the closely spaced trees that enclosed the prairie on the far side.

A third gunshot split the air. Too far, she knew. He was too far away for his bullets to reach her.

When Diamond barreled beneath the canopy of shade, Jasmine brought her to a lunging halt. She spotted a tree with a low-hanging branch and positioned Diamond beside it. In seconds, she'd holstered her gun and jumped to the ground.

Diamond tossed her head anxiously.

"Stay, girl," Jasmine said, quieting the horse with one soft stroke. Then she pushed up her sleeves and climbed the tree, hand over fist. Her breath billowed her lungs and anticipation coursed along her veins, speeding her heart rate, numbing her limbs. *Fight me, Grayson,* she thought. *Just try and fight me. I'm spoiling for it.*

She could hear him coming now. Almost to the trees. She perched on a branch two branches above the lowest, shielding herself from view.

Grayson entered the grove at a dead run. When he spotted her riderless horse, his face creased with surprise. He sawed back on his reins and looked around the clearing. Silence answered him.

He trotted his sweating horse over to Diamond. Just as Jasmine had hoped, he was searching for her on the ground, assuming she'd been unseated by the low limb. He inched a little closer to her position. Then closer still.

Jasmine sprang from her hiding place. She dropped on top of him with tremendous force, knocking him from the saddle as she fell. Grayson wheezed with pain when they hit the ground. His body had shielded hers from the hard earth. The gun he'd been holding skittered from his hand and came to a stop at the base of a tree.

Jasmine slugged him on the chin, then untangled her limbs and leapt to her feet. She stared down at him as he struggled for the breath that had been knocked from his lungs.

She slid her six-shooter from its holster. Wiped the perspiration from her brow with her forearm. And advanced on him.

Grayson reached for his second gun.

She kicked his wrist just as he cleared it, which sent the weapon flying into the brush.

He glanced up at her, fear in his beady eyes.

She cocked her weapon and pointed it at his heart. "What did you come after me for?"

"Revenge." He snarled like a wounded animal.

"What was that?"

"I said revenge."

She smiled at him, a taunting smile that assuaged little

of the gaping heartache within her. "Some revenge. You should have taken my father's land while you had the chance. You'll never see an acre of it now."

"I don't want his land," he bit out, his head sagging under the enormity of his defeat.

"Do you want your life?" Jasmine asked.

His head snapped up. Thin lips pinched together.

She walked slowly to where his gun lay at the base of the tree. "I'm in one hell of a bad mood, Grayson, and I'd love nothing better than to shoot a hole through your heart. So I'm going to give you two choices." She came to a stop, the toe of her boot resting next to his weapon. "Either I take you home and tie you up until the sheriff comes and gets you, or you draw on me like a man and take your chances."

She kicked the gun and sent it spiraling across the dirt to his fingertips.

He licked his lips. Looked at the gun, then up at her. "I'll . . . I'll let you take me to the sheriff." He presented his palms to her in a gesture of surrender. "I won't give you any more trouble. I swear."

"That's what I thought." She stashed her six-shooter and approached him.

Faster than she'd ever thought him capable of moving, he threw himself toward his gun and came up with the barrel pointed at her chest.

Her hand streaked to her gun.

"I wouldn't, if I were you," he said. Hatred poured unchecked from the obsidian depths of his eyes.

"You swore to me."

"You can't take a criminal at his word. You, of all people, should know that."

She scowled. "I don't know anything of the kind." She'd made an unforgivable mistake by trusting his word. But her own word meant a lot these days. And she'd come to expect the same standard of others.

"Take your hand up!" Grayson demanded.

She lifted her fingers. He was sweating. She could see it dripping down his temples, pooling on his upper lip. His calm was slipping fast. Dangerously fast.

God, she hadn't told anyone about this ride. She was all alone out here and she'd bungled her initial chance at disarming him. Fear's bony fingers scratched at her heart. *No.* She forced the fear back. If Brody were here, he wouldn't be afraid. He wouldn't want her to be afraid, either.

The point of Grayson's gun wobbled. He rose unsteadily to his feet and brought his free hand up to bolster his grip on the weapon. "Now, turn around!"

Jasmine gnawed her lip.

"I said, turn around!"

Her fingers curled into fists. She'd be goddamned before she'd let this sonofabitch shoot her in the back. If he wanted to kill her, he'd have to do it to her face.

He was quaking with rage now. "I *said*, turn—"

The distant thunder of horse's hooves rolled across the air.

Jasmine waited for Grayson to look toward the origin of the noise and give her an opportunity. He didn't. He cut only the briefest glances toward the coming threat, without faltering his aim.

On one such glance, his eyes widened. "Don't move!" he screamed, looking back to her.

"I'm not. I'm not going to move."

The thrashing of hooves against earth grew more deafening. She couldn't imagine who had come. Out of the corner of her eye, she watched, waiting for the rider to top the rise.

When he did, her heart lurched. Then soared, puckering her skin with goosebumps.

Looking like an avenger of Satan, Brody charged across the open prairie, every line of his body mean and unforgiving. His duster billowed out behind him as he bent over his horse, goading the animal to fly.

A chill raced along her skin. Her emotions rose from the depths and tugged her past elation. Brody had come for her. She could hardly damn believe it! He'd cared enough to come.

Grayson released a frightened whimper. He moved his sights from her onto Brody, then back to her.

Jasmine inched her fingers over the handle of her gun.

"Get your hands up!" he yelled, blinking furiously to clear his eyes of the perspiration running into them.

She raised her hands.

The powerful hoofbeats of Brody's horse pounded to a stop. Jasmine chanced a look at him and for a split second their gazes met. She read a crazed kind of desperation in his eyes that terrified her.

He dismounted in a single harsh motion. "Get your gun off my wife," he growled.

Grayson whipped his six-shooter through the air and pointed it at Brody. Brody stalked toward him anyway, his duster swirling about his ankles. "Run, Jasmine."

Alarm leapt up her throat. "No!" she yelled. "Grayson, it's me you want to kill. Don't hurt him."

Grayson swung the gun toward her. "I'll kill her if you come any closer!"

Brody stopped immediately.

"I will!" Grayson's voice screeched with panic. "I'll kill her!"

"If you so much as *bruise* her," Brody said, his tone pitched lethally low, "I'll shoot you in the stomach in the next instant. Then I'll watch you die slow."

"I—"

"Lower the gun."

Grayson's nose pinched in and out with the pant of his breath.

Jasmine waited, holding herself perfectly still, silently beseeching Brody not to endanger himself.

"You've got no other choice," Brody said, advancing on Grayson in two slow steps. "Give me the gun."

Grayson wailed, swiveled toward Brody, and cocked his weapon. Jasmine whipped free her six-shooter as Brody lunged. He shoved Grayson's arm to the side just as his gun blasted.

The bullet shot into the treetops, coaxing a family of birds to squawk in fright and scatter to the heavens.

Glaring into Grayson's face, Brody squeezed the older man's wrist until the gun fell from lax fingers onto the ground. Brody kicked it to her. She stashed it in the waistband of her trousers.

"Please," Grayson begged. "Please, don't shoot me."

Brody snarled, drew back his fist and slammed it into Grayson's jaw. Grayson grunted at the impact, which sent him spinning to the earth. He landed in a pathetic heap, motionless.

Brody rolled him onto his back, crouched over him, and drew his fist back again.

Jasmine hurried to Brody and caught his wrist before he could deal Grayson another blow. He looked up at her.

"It's all right," she said. "You knocked him out."

"He almost shot you, Jasmine."

"I know."

"He . . . almost shot you."

"I know. You can arrest him when he wakes up." She tested a smile on him. Lord, he was easy on the eyes. His hazel gaze glimmered up at her from beneath his hat, full of feelings she couldn't read. Her mouth grew dry. This was the same man who had left her three days ago to return to the woman he loved.

And that woman wasn't her.

She released his wrist and backed away.

Never for a second freeing her from the weight of his scrutiny, Brody rose and matched her retreat step for step with his approach. " 'It's me you want to kill'?" he asked. "Is that what you said to Grayson?" His expression turned black. " 'It's me you want to kill'?"

"You were strolling up to him like a madman!"

"So you told Grayson to kill you?" He jerked off his hat and smashed it against his thigh. "I'll kill you myself if you *ever* risk your neck for me like that again."

In a flash, she yanked her six-shooter into the air. "Stop."

He did.

"You no longer have the right to tell me what to do, Brody. I'll damn well risk myself for you if I want to."

His eyebrows lifted.

She continued to glare at him, eyes narrowed.

After a moment his lips twitched into a smile.

"I wouldn't smile if I were you," she warned.

Brody stared down the cold silver barrel and tried to squelch his grin. His wife was magnificent. Insane. But incredibly magnificent. Relief over her safety washed through him in a crashing tide, sapping his strength.

Jasmine, however, looked anything but relieved. He recognized the sheen of passion in her eyes and realized how deeply angry she was. If he succeeded at nothing the rest of his life, he needed to succeed at this. At making her understand.

Very deliberately, he brought his hands to his waist. His fingers sought and found the buckle on his gun belt. He released it slowly and let the leather slide through his fingers. The belt dropped to the grass with a dull thud. "Shoot me if you want, Jasmine. It would be better than living without you."

He watched her lovely forehead furrow. "Just what in all hell were you thinking when you insisted on returning to Elena?"

She stood before him with her messy hair, her bandana, and Grayson's six-shooter stuck in her man's trousers. She created such a wild picture already that the added element of her apparent jealousy sent him over the edge. He grinned again.

The gun fired. A bullet whined past his ear.

The birds that had just returned from their earlier escape squawked again, this time indignantly.

"I asked you a question," she said.

She was spitting mad, but if she'd meant to shoot him, he knew implicitly that she'd have succeeded. "Jasmine, just settle down a little and I'll tell you."

"I'll settle down when you answer my question." She cocked the weapon. "I've got five bullets left."

He needed to remember to take that damned gun away from her. "I didn't return to Elena. I waited at the Blue Horseshoe for you until this morning. Tom and I weren't even halfway to her place when I figured out what Grayson was up to and circled back."

"So, what? You're going to return to her, now that Grayson's been taken care of?"

"No."

"But you want to go back."

"No."

She advanced on him. The fire in her eyes roared so hot it snapped white sparks. "You expect me to believe that you don't love her anymore?"

The air between them grew very quiet. Fiercely serious. Nothing but the link of their eyes existed. "Yes," he said. "It's the truth and it's what I expect you to believe."

"And what if I don't?"

"Then I'll stay as long as it takes to convince you. Even if you never believe me, I'll stay, because I swear to you, Jasmine, I'm not leaving you again."

Her tongue darted out to lick her lips. The gun swayed

a little. "Damn you, Brody. Do you have any idea how much you hurt me?"

"I—"

"Any idea?"

He couldn't find words. Love of her swirled through him, consuming everything.

She took two more steps forward. "If you ever hurt me like that again, do you know what I'll do to you?"

"Jasmine—"

"I'll shoot you through your cheating heart, that's what I'll do. Then I'll carve it from your chest and I'll knife it to pieces, and. . . ."

He reached out and pulled her to him, crushing her against his chest. The hard cylinder of her gun wedged against his manhood. Delicately, he pointed the barrel in a safer direction.

"I'll feed a bite to Diamond," she said, her voice muffled against the fabric of his coat. "And a bite to Vengeance, and my father would probably like some. But the rest of your heart will be mine. I'll eat it myself, piece by piece."

She was the most breathtaking, bloodthirsty woman in the world. He placed his hands on both sides of her face and tilted it up to him, until he could look straight into the majesty of her eyes. "It would be a shame to kill this heart, or to share it with anyone else." He took a breath. "Because my heart belongs only to you."

Air seeped from between her parted lips.

He slid his palm down her neck, bringing it to rest over the pale skin of her chest. "I thought your heart belonged to freedom."

She shivered.

"Was I wrong?" he asked.

"Yes," she whispered. "You were wrong."

He couldn't contain the joy welling within him. "I love you, Jasmine. God, you're beautiful."

"I love you, too. And God. You're beautiful, too."

He leaned down to take her lips in a kiss, just as footsteps pattered across the clearing accompanied by a banchee howl.

Jasmine turned to see a revived Grayson hurtling toward them, still bent on attacking. Brody moved to shield her, but Jasmine pushed her way in front of him.

"I'll take care of this." She shoved a chunk of hair out of the way and waited for Grayson to draw close enough. The second he did, she punched him in the stomach. He doubled over, huffing and puffing. Jasmine set her boot on his backside and sent him face first into the dirt. Then she planted her knee in the center of his back. "Rope, please."

Seconds later, Brody handed her the coil of rope from his saddle.

"D-Don't hurt me," Grayson pleaded. "I won't try anything again."

"Oh yeah?" Jasmine asked. "You swear?"

He groaned and she stuffed a chunk of his shirt into his mouth.

Deftly, she bound his wrists to his feet. No sooner had she risen, then she noticed Grayson staring up at them. "Excuse me just one more second, Brody."

"Take as long as you need."

"I just have to . . ." She freed the bandana from her neck and secured it over Grayson's bulging eyes. "Fix this."

When her prisoner made a few guttural sounds of protest, Jasmine shot Brody a grin of wicked glee.

Before she could catch her wits, Brody swung her into his arms and strode into the tall wildflowers of the open prairie. She gazed up at him, awed. His hold was snug around her. A perfect fit. "How is it that you found me?" she murmured.

He glanced at her, love in his eyes. "I'd almost reached the Double J when I heard the gunshots."

"Hm. I thought of you, you know, before you arrived. I thought about how you're never scared."

He snorted. "My heart was in my throat the whole time Grayson was pointing that gun at you. I'd never been so scared in my life."

"Really?"

"Really."

"Oh." She could barely contain the warm pleasure that rushed all through her.

"Enough about Grayson." He set her feet gently on the grass.

They were deep enough into the treeless expanse that she could now see the glorious bonfire of the fading sunset, a violet canopy above them.

"Where were we?" he asked, his eyes glittering with delight.

"Here." She lifted her lips.

He cradled her head with both hands and plundered her mouth so sweetly that her insides turned over and curled at the edges.

He pulled just a hairsbreadth away, then drew her down onto her knees and carefully laid her back onto the cushion of wildflowers. He peeled his duster off and tossed it aside. Rolled up his shirt sleeves.

She giggled.

He stretched out on top of her, positioning an elbow on either side of her face. "I realized on my way here that I'd forgotten something on our wedding night."

"Your shirt?"

He laughed. "More like *your* shirt." His crooked grin made her heart flip.

He lowered his head and tasted her with leisurely hunger, taking the time to tease and savor. His fingers stroked down the side of her throat.

She gloried in the melting inside herself. It was yearning

and pleasure at once, a promise so delicious that she knew coherent thought would flee in moments and she'd be screaming at him to hurry. "What?" she asked against his lips. "What did you forget on our wedding night?"

He pulled his necklace out from under his collar and lifted it over his head. Once he'd freed the clasp, the silver ring slid down the length of the chain and plopped into his hand.

He gazed at her. His dimples appeared. "You might have forgotten your shirt on our wedding night—"

"I did not!"

"—but I forgot to give you a wedding ring."

Wonder circled through Jasmine.

He picked up her left hand, flicked a piece of grass from her knuckle and slid the silver band onto her third finger. "It belonged to my mother once."

"Oh, Brody."

"With this ring I thee wed," he whispered.

"Thank you," she whispered back, barely able to push the words through the wad of emotion in her chest. She gazed into his magical hazel eyes and was transfixed by the sheer beauty of the man. "How very much I love you, Brody."

"Almost as much as I love you." He slipped the silver necklace over her head. "But that's not the only reason I laid you down in this field."

"No?"

"I've been wondering what's beneath these clothes, besides Grayson's gun." His hand coasted up the inside of her leg, leaving a path of burning nerves in its wake.

"Have you?" she asked.

"Yes." He kissed her more insistently than before, communicating his need so vividly that her body writhed in answer.

"Just how wild does the jasmine grow in these parts?" he asked, his voice a husky murmur.

"Wild enough, my love." Her fingertips dug into his back. "Wild enough to make love to you in a prairie of flowers."

"Just as I'd hoped." He raised his head and gave her a smile that stole her breath. "Jasmine, you're everything I'd hoped."

*Celebrate the Millennium
with another irresistible
romance from the pen of
Susan Elizabeth Phillips!*

The beautiful young widow of the President
of the United States is on the run, crossing
America on a journey to find herself. She
plans to travel alone, and she's chosen the
perfect disguise. Well, almost perfect...and
not exactly alone...

FIRST LADY
by Susan Elizabeth Phillips

Coming from Avon Books February 2000

Dear Reader,

You loved *How to Marry a Marquis* by Julia Quinn, and you're going to simply adore *The Duke and I*, her latest delightful, sensuous Avon Romantic Treasure. Simon Basset, the Duke of Hastings, must marry and produce an heir, even though he has vowed never to marry. But he made that vow before he met Daphne Bridgerton, the eldest daughter of eight children. And when Daphne is compromised, society dictates that she must marry her reluctant duke—but that's only the beginning!

Sue Civil-Brown is so well known for her delightful, playful contemporary love stories, and *Catching Kelly* is no exception. Kelly Burke left home at 18 and has never looked back. After all, she's much too sensible for that crowd of harmless, but frustrating, eccentrics. Then she gets word that a sexy interloper has taken her place in the family, so she hurries home—never expecting that he'd take his place in her heart!

Next, it's off to Scotland in Lois Greiman's *Highland Hawk*, a tie-in to her successful *Highland Brides* series. Lovely Catriona is on a mission—one that brings her directly in conflict with Haydan MacGowan, captain of the king's guard. This seductive Scotsman knows Catriona is up to something—and he's determined to use every bit of his wiles to learn what that is!

Maureen McKade's western romances are simply delicious, and with *Mail-Order Bride*, she creates one of her most memorable stories yet! Kate Murphy arrives in Colorado expecting to marry one man...but she ends up wed to another. "Trev" Trevelyan needs a mother to his children, and a wife in his bed. But can Kate find love with this improper stranger?

Enjoy!

Lucia Macro
Lucia Macro
Senior Editor